COUNTDOWN

COUNTDOWN

Frank G. Slaughter

DOUBLEDAY & COMPANY, INC., GARDEN CITY, NEW YORK

All of the characters in this book are fictitious,
and any resemblance to actual persons, living or
dead, is purely coincidental.

COUNTDOWN

CHAPTER I

The familiar black shape of a Florida September thunderstorm was taking form out to sea, when Dr. Michael Barnes swung his car off the somewhat rutted state road he had been following southward along the west bank of the Indian River and took the UP ramp to the new causeway leading to the Pegasus space complex. He had purposely not followed Interstate 95, whose four-laned geometric pattern knifed through the piney woods several miles inland from the densely populated area served by US 1, which, winding along the west bank of the lovely Indian River, was Main Street for a series of small cities.

This was the land of his birth and his boyhood, and he drove slowly in the warm morning sunlight, savoring the memory of familiar scenes: the golden promise of oranges ripening upon the trees; the mottled richness of mangoes that grew in profusion here, a full hundred miles north of where they were most prolific in South Florida; the lush beauty of semitropical flowering shrubs; the soft murmur of the wind through palm fronds, and the lap of water against the pilings of a bridge.

The projecting hump of Cape Canaveral—renamed Cape Kennedy —gave Brevard County an air-conditioned climate and allowed even tropical fruits and flowers to grow in profusion. A few dozen miles to the north or inland to the west, similar vegetation was cut down by frost early in the season but in September the chill hand had not reached far south yet. Other hands, equally destructive to natural beauty, had, however; in the journey along the coast from Daytona and New Symrna Mike had seen ample evidence of man's inroads upon the bounty of nature.

The phenomenal growth of the county in which lay America's pioneer rocket launching center had long since changed the face of the area. Both the cottage and the orange grove on the river where Mike had lived as a boy were gone now, replaced by a huge mobile home park that was a phantasmagoria of garish clashing colors. The giant water oak in whose branches he'd built his first tree house, and from it surveyed the expanse of water to the east like a Columbus-in-reverse seeing in his imagination the coasts of Europe, had yielded long ago to the inexorable march of progress. And, in the shallows where he'd splashed happily as a boy, a row of signs now warned: "NO SWIM-MING—POLLUTED."

Saddened by the absence of so many things he remembered even as recently as eight years ago, when he'd left the Cape for California, Mike eased his car into a pull-out the builders of the causeway had provided just beyond the highest elevation of the overpass. From it, those approaching Spaceport City, itself only a few years old, could safely stop to observe the marvels man had wrought in what had been simply the handiwork of God—and be tempted to buy.

Mike had often rowed a boat or guided a small kicker through the maze of tidal creeks that had cut the salt marsh into a thousand different patterns of mud and swaying oaks, but he could see little that was familiar any more. The beep-beep of Russian Sputniks had brought huge dredges, great towering draglines, and pile drivers to form sea walls and remove all traces, except the water itself, of a salt marsh where snowy-white cranes had stalked and fed.

Even the grayish black coots that had dived for small fish were gone now; there was no place for them in the network of narrow waterways. Man-made arteries barely wide enough for a boat to maneuver in, they allowed access to the Inland Waterway and the broader reaches of the Indian and Banana rivers, as well as letting the more venturesome reach the ocean itself by way of inlets at New Smyrna to the north and Sebastian to the south.

The view that met Mike's eyes from the top of the overpass was more like a real estate salesman's dream than reality. Stretching away to the north and east, the newly claimed land was packed with houses. Concrete block walls painted white gave off a glare in the bright sun—stucco was too expensive to maintain any more. Shingled roofs had replaced the tiles of an earlier Mediterranean period that were much too expensive now for such a mass construction project. The inevitable kidney-shaped swimming pool lay behind almost every house, sandwiched between the patio and the small dock where a boat was tied, leaving only a brief border of lawn around them.

Mike suspected that he could have taken an accurate economic census of Spaceport City merely by observing the watercraft tied up at the docks. The inboard cruisers of yesterday had largely given way to high-sided outboards, sometimes nearly as tall as they were long and often with sport-fishing outriggers extending from their sterns like the antennae of an insect built for going backward. Only here and there did a sleek inboard yacht identify the owner as belonging to the upper echelon of the vast industrial complex of the Cape.

The men who actually plotted the course the astronauts followed to the stars, Mike Barnes knew from personal experience, were rarely paid well enough to afford such expensive items as inboard yachts. Those who manufactured the hardware, usually on government contracts negotiated without competitive bidding, were the new economic elite, while the scientists whose vision and knowledge had made all of this possible were relegated to the status of mere technicians.

The houses were eye-fatiguingly identical in their landscaping: always an orange and a grapefruit tree, occasionally a mango, here and there a kumquat, hedges of the hibiscus strain called "Turk's Cap" because of its tiny red blossom, oleanders in profusion and conventional hibiscus of every hue—plus the inevitable palms.

Only here and there had an oak been left standing on a higher slice of earth; most of them had been cut down and their stumps buried beneath the newly pumped up land which, a few millenniums ago had been sea bottom. There, as any native knew, they would eventually form a fertile source of food for the termites that would one day destroy everything made of wood in these houses.

Seeking to reconstruct what had been here even so recently as eight years ago, Mike found that he could recapture only a string of fading images: rickety fisherman's piers; a tarpaper-walled shack on the island where the old wino had lived with his exciting tales of the days when rum runners had landed cargoes from the Bahamas on the nearby beach; hordes of fiddler crabs scuttling across the muddy bottom at low tide, each carrying his absurdly gargantuan claw before him like a concert violinist guarding a Stradivarius; the occasional glimpse of a skate—a manta-in-miniature—cruising along in search of food, its spiked tail capable of delivering a painful wound to an unwary wader; and, of course, huge blue crabs scuttling across the mud flats at the approach of an intruder, their eyes on short stalks swiveling constantly like a radarscope, scanning the terrain for any sign of danger. These had been the delights of boyhood but they could hardly be expected to endure in what had been until recently the fastest growing county in the United States, a once sleepy string of towns and beach cottages galvanized overnight into the sort of mushroom architectural nightmare that had become a hallmark of progress in America.

You Can't Go Home Again, Thomas Wolfe had once written and, if it had been true of Asheville nearly half a century ago, how much more true was it of this section of Florida in the Space Age, where man, having conquered the moon, was now seeking new frontiers? When no one could escape the reality of time's passage, Mike knew he had no reason to expect the scenes of his boyhood to remain the same. For he was himself not the same man who had fled from this place eight years ago, driven by a strange series of events whose denouement had at last brought him back again.

Turning back to the car, Mike paused momentarily to study a huge billboard featuring a bikini-clad blonde sunbathing by the pool behind her house. A sleek outboard cruiser anchored at the nearby landing proved that this was a dream to which any man could aspire.

Across the bottom of the giant poster, huge letters proclaimed:

"SPACEPORT CITY"

Below them a sub-legend said: "Perfect Homes for Discriminating People," while still smaller letters in the lower right hand corner of the billboard identified the developer of this sunlit paradise as, "Spaceport Development Corporation, a Unit of Taggar Aircraft."

Standing with his hand upon the open door of the car, Mike was able to see, jutting above the range of dunes to the east, the upper halves of a row of high-rise buildings marking the portion of ocean front not occupied by the gantry cranes of the rocket launch complex. Silhouetted in the afternoon sky against the background of the north-moving rainstorm, they seemed alien here in an area where, until the coming of the rockets, even two-storied houses had been a rarity, as if some magician's wand had created a whole new city where before had been only mud flats, suspending buildings in mid-air between the realities of ocean and sky toward which every activity here was eventually oriented.

Some of the new buildings were not yet finished, mute evidence of the burgeoning growth of the newest space project that might one day loft men to Mars and perhaps beyond—named Pegasus after the mythical winged horse of the Greeks and also a much earlier rocket, which, its batteries and motors long since spent, was doomed to cruise silently through space, presumably forever.

ii.

The car radio had been playing softly but, lost in memories, Mike had hardly been conscious of it. Now the voice of an announcer broke into the plaintive story in song of a housewife's experience with a PTA, riveting his attention upon the words of the speaker instead of the memories of the past:

"We take you now to the launch complex at the Cape during the final moments of the countdown for ignition of America's newest defensive weapon, the Super-Regulus missile, with which the Navy's atomic killer submarines are to be equipped soon, doubling their defensive capability.

"Here is Cape Launch Control. . . ."

Feeling the old tension start to grip him as the countdown was taken up in the familiar monotone, Mike needed all his strength to resist the urge to turn off the radio.

"T minus twenty-five seconds and counting. . . . Twenty . . . Nineteen . . ."

Noticing a service station a few hundred yards along the causeway, he shoved the car in "Drive" and moved rapidly down the slope, bringing it to a screeching halt between the rows of gas pumps.

"Fourteen . . . Thirteen . . ."

Fighting for control against the surge of anxiety that rose within him, he didn't notice a girl in a white convertible waiting in the next line of pumps lean forward to study him with a frown.

"Twelve . . . Eleven . . ." He had switched off the motor automatically and with it the radio, but the one in the white convertible was still playing, so he could not escape the drone of the countdown.

"Eight . . . Seven . . ."

"Fill her up, mister?" An attendant appeared at the open window.

"Y—yes." Mike Barnes controlled his voice enough to answer.

"Six . . . Five . . ."

Memories he had almost succeeded in excluding from consciousness during the eight years since he'd left the Cape came flooding back now, setting his heart to pounding and causing sweat to pop out on his forehead and in the palms of his trembling hands.

"Four . . ."

Knowing he must face the reality represented by the impending launch, or lose control entirely, he searched the distant skyline of the Cape with his eyes, looking for a gantry against which a rocket was silhouetted and expecting momentarily to see the burst of smoke and flame identifying the point where the missile was being fired.

"T minus Three . . . Two . . . One . . ."

His muscles tensed into a rigidity almost as great as the convulsion that had seized him so long ago, alone in a spacecraft hurtling through an almost airless void.

"Zero . . . !"

When the gush of flame appeared, however, it was not from any of the gantry towers he could see. When it seemed to burst from the earth itself instead, he realized what the name of the rocket itself should have told him, had the countdown not thrown him into near panic—that a missile designed for launch from submarines beneath the sea must naturally begin its test flight in an underground silo.

The rocket itself was still invisible when a circular pattern of smoke appeared like a ring from a giant's pipe, above the silo, splitting apart a moment later as a silvery, cigar-shaped object, breathtakingly beautiful in the noonday sunlight, began to rise from its hidden berth. As if reluctant to leave the snug harbor beneath the surface of the earth, it climbed with agonizing slowness at the start. Then, as it cleared the silo, the almost pristine pattern of the initial smoke ring was blurred by the cloud gushing out behind it and the rocket began to gain speed.

When finally the roar of exhaust struck Mike's ears with hammer blows of sound, its sheer force even here miles from the launch location startled him. With it came the memory of those tense moments at the beginning of his own flight, when the G-pressure of acceleration had started to build up, causing a momentary near-loss of consciousness, as blood was driven from his brain toward the protecting pool of the great arteries and veins inside his torso.

Suddenly conscious that the cramped space inside his car was hardly larger than had been the cabin of the Hermes spacecraft he had ridden so triumphantly into the sky on just such a morning as this some eight years before—and so nearly lost his life before the day was finished—Mike jerked open the door of the car and ran to the bank of drink machines set between the entrances to the grease bays of the service station. Fumbling in his pocket for a coin, he didn't see the girl in the white convertible get out of her own car in the next lane and move toward him.

His shaking fingers almost dropped the bottle after he had removed it from the slot at the bottom of the machine, and he was forced to make a second try before the opener caught the serrated edge of the top and pulled it off. The liquid foamed over the mouth of the bottle as the carbonation inside was released, but he thrust it into his mouth nevertheless, shuddering as the cold liquid poured down his throat and dribbled from his chin.

"Are you all right, sir?" He hadn't known the girl was there until she appeared at his elbow.

"Of course I'm all right!"

Ashamed that anyone else had witnessed this public exhibition of terror over which he had no control, he spoke more sharply than he had intended. The girl gasped at the shock of his words and a flush of anger stained her cheeks before she moved quickly toward her own car. Realizing how brusque his terror had made him sound, Mike took a step toward the convertible to apologize. But she started the car before he could reach it and he had only a glimpse of dark red hair and a firmly averted, though nevertheless lovely, sun-tanned profile, before she whirled out of the station and into the traffic pattern on the causeway.

"Them rockets can really shake you the first time you hear one go off this close." The attendant's voice was sympathetic as he took Mike's credit card and began to fill in the cost of the gasoline. "The morning news broadcast said that thing can spray five or six hydrogen warheads hundreds of miles apart—that is if they ever get one of 'em to go off right."

Mike's pulse was beginning to steady now, although his throat was still tight from spasm. He drank the rest of the bottle slowly, feeling its coldness begin to settle the queasy sensation in his stomach that always went with one of these spells of anxiety.

"Too bad we didn't spray the Russians with a few of them bombs soon's we learned to make 'em." The attendant handed Mike the charge ticket to sign. "If we'd have let the Communists know just what would happen if they start makin' trouble, like Khrushchev tried to do in Cuba back a while ago, they'd certainly think twice about tryin' anything else the way they're always doin' nowadays."

Mike's fingers were fairly steady as he scribbled his signature on the ticket and put his credit card back into his wallet. "Do you know who the girl was that drove out just now?" he asked.

"That's Jan Cooper, pretty ain't she? Sings in the lounge of the Astronaut Inn weekends." The attendant tore out the copy and was handing it to Mike, but paused and looked at the slip of paper a second time.

"Dr. Michael Barnes—seems like that's a familiar name. You practice around here, Doctor?"

"I was at the Cape for a while about eight years ago."

"Weren't you one of the first astronauts?"

"Not the first seven."

"Flew in the Gemini program then?"

"No. Hermes."

"I remember now! You're the one that almost drowned. Come back to fly again?"

"Not any more," said Mike. "I've been doing research on space problems at the Anderson Center in California."

"From what I hear they've got problems at Pegasus, too." The attendant nodded toward a sprawl of new structures on the skyline. Like the row of gantry towers in the older section of the launch complex, these, too, were spaced apart, separated from each other by acres of dune land and palmettos so, in case of a disaster on firing, the destruction other than to the pad involved would be minimal.

"Why do you say that?" Mike asked.

"We service a lot of cars for workers over there and you hear things all the time."

Another car pulled into the station and Mike had no opportunity to question the man further, as he would have liked. Placing the empty bottle in a rack, he went to a telephone booth at the edge of the service station lot and opened the directory hanging there from a chain. When he found the number he sought, he dropped in a dime and dialed it.

"Astronaut Inn," a voice said, "good morning."

"Reservations, please."

"This is the desk."

"This is Dr. Michael Barnes. Can you give me a nice room fronting on the ocean?"

"One was just vacated this morning, Doctor. It will be ready in about an hour."

"Hold it for me. I'll be over after a while."

It wasn't simply the girl in the convertible and the need to apologize for his boorishness that had made Mike suddenly decide to stay at the older Astronaut Inn, instead of the more modern Spaceport Hilton in the newer section of the beach. Rather it was the realization, an aftermath of the anxiety caused by the rocket launch, that he could not escape the old memories here at the Cape, where they'd happened, or the pain they had brought, and the conviction that it was better to face up to them in a familiar environment where, hopefully, the psychic energy they had just proved they still possessed, could be neutralized.

Going to his car, he turned on the switch, activating the radio again in time to hear the voice of the Cape announcer say:

"An apparent failure of guidance has just been reported for the missile launched moments ago—"

"Here we go again," the service station attendant said and Mike instinctively turned his eyes to the south in the direction where he knew the Atlantic Missile Tracking Range stretched for thousands of miles.

He had no trouble identifying the exhaust of the rocket, a tiny glowing spot fading rapidly in the bright noonday sunlight.

"The Range Safety Officer is just pressing the destruct switch to destroy the rocket," the broadcast continued, and while Mike watched, the dot of brightness marking the missile's exhaust was momentarily intensified, then disappeared, indicating that destruction of the missile was complete. Knowing so well how many hours of human effort, to say nothing of dollars, were required to launch even a small rocket, Mike could imagine how the men responsible for it were feeling now.

"Sure am glad I decided not to go deep sea fishing this morning," said the service station attendant. "About now that thing is spraying hot metal all over Sebastian Inlet."

The name was familiar to Mike from the past, a narrow inlet between the ocean and the tidal river system, some fifty or sixty miles to the south.

While he waited for traffic to be halted by the signal at the corner, so he could drive out upon the causeway from the service station, a familiar voice came on the radio, replacing that of the Launch Control announcer.

"This is Richard P. Hudnall in New York with the noon CBS news. At Cape Kennedy just moments ago, still another of the Super-Regulus missiles designed to be fired from our atomic killer submarines went out of control after launch and had to be destroyed. This is the fourth such failure in the Super-Regulus program and just ten days ago, the Mars Orbiter under preparation for more than a year suffered the same fate.

"Before the day is out several senators who have been calling for a thorough restudy of America's space program will no doubt be demanding to know what effect these failures will have on the highly complex Pegasus program, successor to Apollo. The first launch in this series is scheduled less than a month from now."

At least one senator, Mike was sure, would have something pungent to say in Congress about the unprecedented string of failures in America's space program. He'd already said some of it ten days ago, when the telephone had rung long past midnight in Mike's apartment in Mountain City, California.

CHAPTER II

"This is Lars Todt."

"Who else would yank me out of bed at five o'clock in the morning?" Mike had recognized the harsh voice in the phone immediately, although it had been eight years since he had last heard it, during his own grilling by the House Space Committee. The two had been undergraduates at Harvard College together but Lars had gone on to law school in Cambridge, and thence into politics, while Mike had chosen Baltimore and the Johns Hopkins Medical School.

"Sorry, Mike. I forgot about the time difference."

"How are things, now that you're a senator?"

"Fine. They put me on the Space Oversight Committee."

"That's the first sensible thing I've known Washington to do in a long time."

"It didn't just happen." Lars chuckled. "When I threatened to conduct my own investigation of the Federal Space Authority, the Majority Leader decided I might know something about the subject—having been a minority member of the House Space Committee before I became a senator."

"As well as an expert on twisting arms," Mike reminded his friend. "I haven't forgotten how you made me admit during the hearing that we really wouldn't be ready to send men on interplanetary missions for another twenty years—and darn near ended my career."

"I didn't make you say anything you hadn't already said—in writing."

"Until then I'd had the good sense to put my reports through official channels, where they were promptly buried because NASA didn't want word to get out. But you made me say it on national TV and look where I am now—the forgotten man."

"Things had to wait until I got into the Senate and my party got control, Mike. Now I'm ready to start exploding some of those myths FSA's been conjuring up about the lack of danger in what they're doing before we fry another bunch of astronauts—or leave some circling up there forever. You still believe the same things, don't you?"

"Of course—but who would listen after your esteemed colleague on the committee publicly labeled me 'Space Chicken'?"

"At least you're the only chicken who ever flew in orbit," Lars Todt's voice had boomed over the telephone.

"And lost his wings in the bargain—plus other things."

"I was sorry to hear about your marriage breaking up, Mike, but I'm sure that didn't happen just because Israel Pond gave you a going over."

"I guess the hearing finally proved I wasn't the hero Shirley hoped I would be."

"When can you come to Washington?"

"Another committee hearing?"

"A committee of two this time—you and I. There've been enough failures at the Cape lately to make me worry about Pegasus and I've about convinced Jim Green that you're the man to find out what's going wrong."

General James Green of the Air Force was head of the newly organized Federal Space Agency, whose field of authority now encompassed all the activities formerly falling within NASA, plus any other governmental matters relating to space. A career officer from the McNamara whiz kid days, Green was a coming figure in the Administration, now girding itself for a test at the polls.

In the almost eight years since he'd left the Cape under a cloud following his session before the House committee, Mike had longed for the day when he could prove his innocence of the charges made against him then by Representative Israel Pond. Lars, he recognized, was giving him the chance he had been waiting for. Yet he couldn't help feeling somewhat reluctant to return to the place where he'd known so much disappointment, even though it was his boyhood home, and this might well be his last opportunity for vindication.

"I wouldn't mind looking things over at the Cape," he said.

"Bring your car so you can stay; time is short for Pegasus. Anderson will get a teletype from Jim Green's office as soon as Washington goes to work, detailing you on a special assignment to the Cape, but stop by Washington on the way so I can brief you a little."

Driving down Pennsylvania Avenue a week later, Mike had been carried back to another day, when he'd ridden along this same route after his swift flight around the earth to receive the plaudits—and a medal—from a young President. Shirley had been happy, and afterward, while they'd made the usual tour of welcoming celebrations in various cities before coming back to Florida, it had seemed that they might still make a go of it.

But when NASA had announced its plan to put men on the moon

within a decade and he'd dared to warn publicly against some of the dangers that might well turn an Apollo spacecraft into a mausoleum in space, orbiting silently forever as a monument to man's impetuosity and desire for political gain, reaction had been immediate, angry and explosive, with a summons to appear before the House Space Committee headed by Representative Israel Pond, in whose district were located almost as many NASA installations as in the rest of the country, with more planned when the Apollo moon race really gained full momentum.

The savage attack upon Mike by Chairman Pond, who saw any cutback in appropriations for the space program as a blow to the economy of his district, had been rich grist for the news media. The TV cameras particularly had enjoyed a field day when Israel Pond dubbed Mike a "Space Chicken" and after that nobody had really listened to him—except Lars Todt.

Even Israel Pond hadn't been powerful enough to fire an expert in space medicine whose opinions were shared by many scientists all over the country, however, so Mike had been shifted to a position at the Anderson Research Center in the mountains of California. And there, doing important work, he'd been content—until the telephone had rung.

"Mike!" Lars Todt had been as lean and tense with pent-up energy as when he and Mike had rowed together on a Harvard crew. "It was good of you to come."

"Did I have any choice?"

"Of course. I'm not Israel Pond."

"How is God's gift to the space program taking his demotion, now that he belongs to the minority party."

"About as you would expect. Israel is still on several important committees, though, and our majority in Congress isn't large enough for us to ignore anyone, so the Administration has had to play along with him a little."

"You seem to be in the driver's seat, Lars."

"I'm making progress," said the senator, "but I didn't drag you across the country to talk politics. What do you think of the Pegasus project?"

"Putting a space station in orbit and keeping it there should be simple enough after Apollo. The Air Force's MOL program was just such a venture, until Apollo ate up all the money and it had to be cancelled, and that dated back to '65 or before. The way I see it the Pegasus space station is something of an anti-climax."

"But still important?"

"Damned important."

"In what ways?"

"The Apollo flights were too short to learn much about how men fare during long periods in space, and so were the Gemini programs. It's true that weightlessness hasn't turned out to be as much of a handicap as we expected, but a lot still needs to be learned about the effects of long exposure to conditions peculiar to deep space—things like decalcification of bones, variations in blood chemistry, and the like."

"Are they necessarily dangerous to life?"

"Possibly."

"How?"

"During prolonged inaction such as the confined area of a spacecraft tends to cause, calcium is absorbed from the bones and carried in the blood for eventual elimination by the kidneys," Mike explained. "At the same time, changes in the hydrogen-ion concentration of the blood make the calcium less soluble, so there's an increased likelihood of kidney stone formation. Can you imagine a worse place to have kidney colic than in a spaceship on the way to Mars?"

"Hardly. Anything else?"

"The Gemini and Apollo missions showed that blood volume decreases from seven to fifteen percent during missions lasting several days or more. Astronauts who have been in space, or a space-equivalent test situation, sometimes show an unusual response to sharp changes in position, such as tilting, immediately afterward. A few even exhibit a vasodepressor reaction, with pallor, nausea, dimming of vision, sweating, air hunger, and loss of consciousness, due to an acute fall in blood pressure and a very slow pulse rate."

"Sounds ominous."

"It could be. Imagine how effective a man would be during reentry after a long space flight, when the G-force on him starts to build up rapidly and he experiences a sudden change in position causing a blackout. The Gemini and Apollo EVA periods, brief as they were, showed that men tire very easily, too, while working in a weightless environment. When we start building space stations in orbit, men will almost certainly have to get outside to hook the components together and we need to know in advance just how much they can do in any given time."

"What about the effects of radiation in space on man?" Lars asked.

"The Van Allen belts appear to be only a minor hazard because we know where they are and trajectories can be planned to avoid the most intense areas of radiation," said Mike. "But radiation from bursts of protons produced by solar flares is another matter; the Russians may even have had to bring down one of their Soyuz astronauts some years ago because of it."

"Then even the small space station to be lofted by the Pegasus program could be decisive for further exploration of space?"

"It might even be more important for exploring the earth," said Mike.

"Come again."

"ERTS—Earth Resources Technology Satellites—can survey the earth's water supply, measure farm crops, and identify promising areas for farming, mining, and petroleum exploration. The field is almost unexplored, so Pegasus could be the most important laboratory in history. But first we have to devise a method of ferrying men and materials back and forth between earth and the station. In a period of very high sunspot activity, the laboratory might even have to be evacuated temporarily until the radiation subsided in intensity—and on pretty short notice, too."

"I can see that I picked the right man for the job," said Lars Todt. "This Administration has a lot riding on the first Pegasus Orbiting Laboratory, Mike."

"If it fails, FSA can always pick up the pieces and start over again, the way NASA had to do after the Apollo fire."

"A lot of people are screaming already about costs and a backset right now would be a major political handicap for the Administration. With elections coming up, our party can't afford it."

"I'm a scientist, Lars, not a politician or a vote-getter."

"I'm not asking you to be anything except a scientist, but right now, you're a possible answer to our prayers. You know closed space ecology inside out, with enough savvy about boosters to know your way around there, too, so you should be able to spot any technical failures that might endanger Pegasus. Even more important, with your knowledge of the type of people who gravitate into space work and their problems, you may be able to tell us whether a possible source of disaster exists in the teams we've got down there now."

"You *have* been keeping up with me," said Mike. "My article on the Lockheed Syndrome only appeared a month ago."

"I do *my* homework, too," said Lars briskly. "How about going to the Cape as a private gumshoe for Jim Green and myself?"

Mike frowned. "Have you forgotten that Taggar Aircraft is the prime contractor on Pegasus and I'm the only astronaut who ever flew a Taggar ship that failed? Inject me into the picture now and a lot of people are going to be after my scalp—especially Israel Pond."

"Ralph Petty is chairman of House Space now; between us we can cover you, if Israel starts acting up to protect his vested interest in Taggar Aircraft."

"What sort of position did you have in mind for me at the Cape?"

"We could make you medical director, of course! You certainly have all the qualifications for the position. But I'm afraid that might limit you somewhat in your activities and, besides, it would mean booting out Ivan Saltman."

"I'll have no part of that," said Mike. "Saltman's highly regarded—in aerospace medical circles."

"Jim Green and I agree that for the moment you need to be in a position where you can look at practically everything that's going on at Pegasus. We both think you should be a roving consultant, something like a minister-without-portfolio."

"Neither fish nor fowl—and therefore without authority?"

"You'll be representing us personally and reporting to us directly. We'll furnish the authority when you need it."

"You're putting me in the position of a bastard at a family reunion, but if that's the best you can do, I suppose we'll have to let it go at that."

"I'm counting on your know-how in the rocket field to separate fact from rumor," said Lars Todt. "Besides you're the only man with unimpeachable credentials as a scientist who's also flown a Taggar spacecraft—"

"And nearly died doing it! Don't forget that!"

"Ergo, if there are bugs in this new one, you'll find them—and incidentally vindicate yourself in the process."

Lars' last words had been the clincher, so there'd been no point in Mike doing anything except heading for Florida. Now, however, with his pulse still hammering from the near panic he'd experienced during the rocket countdown and launch, he was far from sure he'd made the right decision—or that Lars had given him all the facts.

For if even a service station attendant miles from the Pegasus assembly and launch complex knew the project was in trouble, his job at the Cape might well be considerably more important than Lars' briefing had led him to believe.

CHAPTER III

The towering mass of the Saturn-Apollo Vertical Assembly Building broke the rolling contour of the higher ridge of sand dunes hiding the ocean, as Mike turned toward the beach and the Astronaut Inn. The center for the Pegasus program occupied a newer section of the broad hump of Cape Kennedy adjoining Spaceport City, with its maze of homes, waterways, and beachfront hotels. Which raised the question of why a new assembly and launch complex had been built on a relatively isolated section of the government reservation when extensive facilities, such as those used for Apollo, already existed.

Like many East Coast communities in Florida, both the new complex and the real estate development it had obviously spawned were separated from the mainland by tidal rivers and islands. Scanning the terrain as he drove along and remembering how it had been when he'd left the Cape, Mike was sure much of the land upon which both stood had been pumped from the salt marshes that had formerly claimed a great deal of this region.

At a roadside fruit stand, he had stopped to buy a half dozen ripe mangoes. Although confined for the most part to Florida's southern tip, the lush, mottled-yellow fruit grew abundantly here upon Merritt Island, its climate tempered by the land mass of the Cape to the east and the nearby north-flowing current of the Gulf Stream. The juicy yellow flesh of the mango was a warmly remembered part of his boyhood here on what had been a sleepy mosquito infested island, until the headlong attack upon the space frontier by the United States had made it almost overnight the boundary line between earth and the rest of the universe.

The thunderhead he'd seen from the causeway had moved northward by the time he drove across another bridge, this time a drawspan to allow passage of yachts from the canals of Spaceport City to the Inland Waterway. On the strip of dune land whose eastern boundary was the ocean itself, he found himself in the bustling beach community that was both resort and home for many of the thousands of workers at the old Cape installation, as well as the new sprawl of Pegasus. High-rise, opulent-looking hotel structures studded the seaward side of the beach boulevard, while row on row of apartment houses lined the streets leading westward toward the tidal flats separating the ocean front section of Spaceport City from the remainder.

Compared to many of the newer plushy hotels, the Astronaut Inn was already beginning to look a little seedy, although dating no farther back than the beginning of the space program. As Mike pulled his car to a halt beneath the marquee covering part of the brief half circle of driveway before the motel, he saw between the building and the street, a tall sign announcing:

"THE TGIF HOUR, 5–7. All drinks 65¢."

Below it a second line ran:

"Songs by Jan Cooper in the Lounge for the Cocktail Hour and Dinner."

"Glad to have you with us, Doctor," said the clerk at the desk. "Will you be here long?"

"Perhaps a week or two."

"I played hooky from junior high to see you blast off. Spaceport City wasn't even built then, was it?"

"I'm afraid not."

"It's quite a showplace; be sure and look it over while you're here. Free tours leave twice a day; the bus stops here at the hotel." The clerk handed a room key to the bellboy. "Just call if you need anything."

Mike's room was on the corner of the building. Large and comfortable, it had windows both upon the ocean and the court inside, where young people were frolicking in the swimming pool. The air conditioner that doubled as a heat pump during the occasional cold spells of winter was purring softly and the room was comfortably cool.

"Anything else, sir?" the bellboy asked, after placing Mike's bag on the rack and checking the bath and the thermostat.

"Can you tell me what TGIF on that sign outside means?"

"That's the weekend slogan here in Spaceport City—Thank God It's Friday," the boy said with a smirk. "Everybody sort of cuts loose on Friday afternoon to start the weekend off—if you know what I mean."

ii.

It was almost five o'clock and Mike had finished dressing after a swim in the surf, when the telephone rang in his room.

"Dr. Barnes?" a feminine voice asked.

"Yes."

"My name is Yvonne Lang; I'm a feature writer on the Spaceport *Call.* Could I talk to you for a few minutes?"

"I'm here on vacation."

"You're still news, Doctor."

"After nearly ten years?"

"The originator of the 'Lockheed Syndrome' is legitimate prey for feature writers in any aerospace center, Doctor."

"All right," he said resignedly. "When?"

"Ten minutes—I use a tape recorder and work fast."

She was just two minutes under the ten, a tall and rather striking brunette, with the brisk and assured manner of the professional woman newshawk. She appeared to be in her middle thirties and her handshake was as businesslike as the way she set up a small tape recorder.

"How did you know I was here?" Mike asked.

"A friend works at the dog track in Orlando and occasionally gives me tips on the races. I pass them along to people who are in a position to do me favors."

"Like motel desk clerks?"

"You guessed it. When the Associated Press picked up your article, I was intrigued by it, so I got a copy of the medical journal it was in from the Bioastronautic Research Laboratory."

"Are you an aerospace wife?" He'd already noticed the wedding ring on her finger.

"Was! I shed my mate several years ago. Or rather he shed me—for a younger woman."

"I'm sorry."

"He saved me the trouble and this way I got a better settlement," Yvonne Lang said briskly. "My ex is a systems analyst with FSA. The only trouble was he started analyzing the wrong systems—other women."

"That could cause trouble."

"It happens fairly often here, and not just among aerospace people. Doctors and dentists are subject to the same disease—lawyers, too."

"I only called it the 'Lockheed Syndrome' because the study I made concerned the families of men working at a large Lockheed plant in California," said Mike. "Elsewhere it could be called the General Dynamics Syndrome—"

"Or Taggar?"

"I wouldn't know about that," he parried, recognizing an attempt to trap him in a quote that would make headlines here. "I haven't been back in quite a while."

"Do you still claim this is only a vacation?"

"I grew up here. Why do you doubt it?"

"You leave the Cape after being crucified for something I'd bet wasn't your fault. You make a name for yourself in fields like bio-astronautic research and psychiatric-oriented sociology, and you're pretty well known as an observer of the modern scene. So why would you come back here, where a lot of grown-up boys are busy shooting off firecrackers."

"Maybe because I like mangoes—and Merritt Island," Mike said with a smile.

"We have a common interest in both but let's get back to the 'Lock-heed Syndrome.' What makes it so different from any other sort of loneliness that attacks the wives of successful husbands?"

"Nothing, really—except that the engineer personality seems to be more definitely identifiable. The husband is a success in his profession but succeeding keeps him so busy the wife starts feeling that she's left behind—"

"She doesn't just *feel* left behind, Doctor; a lot of time she *is* left behind. Lonely women who don't know him well tend to put a professional husband on a pedestal. From there it's only a small step to wondering what it would be like to be made love to by a god—and finding out."

"Which makes her just as guilty."

"Not quite. Here at the Cape husbands have mistresses wives can't fight—slide rules, computers, even rockets. How can any woman compete for a man's affection and attention with a machine that keeps him on his toes all the time just to stay ahead of it?"

"You have a point there."

Yvonne Lang picked up the microphone of her tape recorder and pointed it toward Mike. "Tell me more about this 'engineer personality' you identified in your article."

"The concept isn't mine; it was described by a New York psycho-analyst in a published article quite a while ago. Don't get the idea that the occupation shapes the man either; people with particular personality traits seem to gravitate into certain fields. The rocket man is usually precise and meticulous, making almost a fetish of attention to detail and accuracy."

"The very qualities that make him a good engineer."

"I told you it's the man who seeks the job. Engineers are very in-telligent as a class but for the most part their intelligence is used only

narrowly. Instead of developing a broad outlook, they tend to special-
ize in ever-shrinking fields of interest."

Yvonne Lang's recorder whirred softly, as Mike continued: "People
who seek perfection, like most engineers, set impossible standards for
themselves. Then instinctively fearing that they will fail to measure
up, they develop rather brittle shells for their own protection. Thus
the engineer type finds himself less and less able to give to others, lest
they discover his Achilles' heel."

"If he could only understand that those who love him are trying to
shield him from the pain of failure." Yvonne Lang appeared to be
talking to herself. "Instead he turns to others, with less intelligence."

"Probably because he can dominate them more easily," Mike
observed.

"I wondered when you'd get around to blaming the women,"
Yvonne Lang said, a little tartly.

"Are they without blame?"

"Of course not; I went the route, so who knows it any better than
I do? At first you keep busy with all the things a woman can occupy
herself with when she doesn't want to stop and think out what's happening to her—keeping house, raising children, PTA, church, and the
like. But the children grow up and new machines are always being
built to keep house a lot better than you can ever do, in a tenth of the
time. Now that we have wash and wear clothes, the energy you once
spent on an ironing board can now be put into woman-type recrea-
tions; luncheons, bridge-playing, community activities—and, of course,
drinking."

"That's a major symptom," he conceded.

"It leads to the next one, when a woman begins to wonder what it
would be like to sleep again with a man whose gonads haven't been
sidetracked, while his mind tries to keep up with a computer or stay
ahead of a hotshot young engineer who's bucking for his job. Once
you start wondering that, it's a pretty short step to finding out via the
divorce court—or TGIF."

"I noticed it on the marquee outside; the bellboy intimated that it's
something racy."

"Probably no more than the weekend activities of any town where
the average age of the population is twenty-six and the income level
high. It's more concentrated here because so many people with the
same basic interests live close together. In a lot of ways TGIF makes
sense, too."

"How do you figure that?"

"When I was a girl growing up on a Pennsylvania farm, mother would ladle out a good dose every Friday night of Fletcher's Castoria, syrup of figs, epsom salts, or castor oil, her theory being that a good cleaning out once a week never hurt anybody. Maybe TGIF is just that, an emotional catharsis."

"Has it solved any of the problems?"

"You're the doctor! Why not stay here a while and find out?" Yvonne Lang stubbed out the cigarette she had been smoking and gave him a sharply appraising look. "Could that possibly be why you're here?"

"I told you, I'm on a vacation."

"I won't give you away—if you promise me an exclusive, when you're ready to talk about Spaceport City and the Taggar Syndrome. Is it a deal?"

"You're the one who's jumping to conclusions," said Mike. "But if I discover anything specific down here, and if I decide to hold a press conference during my vacation, I'll call you first."

"Fair enough." Yvonne Lang took a card from her pocket, scribbled a telephone number and address on it and handed it to him.

"The number printed on the card is the paper's; the other's my home address and personal telephone number," she said. "I live just a block off the causeway in Spaceport City, so you won't have any trouble finding me. Mine is the only house in the block with a white picket fence in front."

"I'll try not to bother you there."

"My pleasure." She gathered up her tape recorder and note pad. "Hope I haven't kept you from anything."

"I was just going to have a drink and dinner at the motel."

"The drinks here are the best in town—Al's an old-timer who takes pride in his work. But there are several good restaurants farther south on the ocean with better food."

"Thanks for the tip. By the way, a friend of mine once owned a small newspaper down here; his name was Art McCord."

"Art's my boss. He's editor and publisher of the Spaceport *Call*."

"Tell him I'll call him later."

"I'll do that. Good night, Dr. Barnes."

"When will your feature appear?"

"Sunday, I imagine. More engineer types will be reading the paper then—and cussing you."

CHAPTER IV

It was past six when, wearing slacks, a sport shirt, and summer jacket, Mike entered the cocktail lounge of the Astronaut Inn. It opened through a wide double doorway to the dining room beyond and he recognized at once the girl in the short white evening dress playing the piano in a niche between them.

Her bronze skin and dark auburn hair were in sharp contrast to the white dress, just as they had been to the white convertible she'd been driving that morning. She was singing a lullaby from another era and her face was mobile with feeling, as Mike made his way to the end of the curving bar nearest the singer and took an empty stool.

"Bourbon and ginger," he told the bartender.

While waiting for the drink, he scanned the lounge idly. Two men at a table in the corner were discussing something animatedly over their drinks. At another table, two couples were laughing over cocktails, obviously not their first, for their faces were flushed, their eyes bright. The rest of the lounge was half filled by men and women in about equal amount, most of them, oddly enough, drinking singly.

"Here you are, sir." The bartender was a middle-aged man with a squashed nose and cauliflower ears of a former prize fighter. "Excuse me, sir. Aren't you Mike Barnes, the doctor-astronaut?"

"I'm only a doctor now," said Mike.

"It took a lot of guts to fly rockets in the days when you and others were here. I remember seeing you at the old Merritt Inn, before Spaceport City was built. Back here on an assignment, sir?"

"Just a vacation."

"In the old days there was plenty of excitement at the Cape." The bartender's tone was wistful. "Now, with a rocket going off nearly every day for something or other, you sometimes get the idea the whole thing's being run by them computers instead of by men."

A customer called for a drink, so Mike devoted his attention to his own—and the girl at the piano. She had changed the rhythm now and was playing a modern tune expertly, watching the keys idly but displaying a skill that indicated no real need for such close attention. At the end of the melody, she looked up from the keys and, seeing his eyes upon her, started to smile, then looked away quickly while a flush, obviously of annoyance, stained her cheeks. Realizing that she had recognized him, he stepped down from the stool and crossed the few yards to the piano.

"Would you remember anything as old as 'Stardust'?" he asked.

"Of course." Her tone was frosty.

"And accept my apology for this morning?"

She didn't answer but turned her attention to the keys, so he moved back to the bar while the piano broke into the opening bars of the Hoagy Carmichael melody. After a moment, her husky contralto took up the words:

"Sometimes I wonder why I spend the lonely night . . ."

When the song was ended, she left the piano and took the stool next to him.

"I was an airline stewardess for a couple of years and they taught us to recognize anxiety," she said. "The sound of a rocket launch can startle you when you're not expecting it."

He let it go at that, grateful that she had spared him a more detailed explanation.

"How about a drink in payment for the effort of memory you needed to find the words of 'Stardust'?" he asked.

"What are you having?"

"Bourbon and ginger—but they tell me that's not a very sophisticated drink."

"I'm not a very sophisticated person. I'll have the same as this gentleman, Al."

"This gentleman is Dr. Michael Barnes, Jan," said the bartender when he brought her the drink. "The doctor-astronaut."

"The almost drowned astronaut." Mike still couldn't keep a tingle of bitterness out of his voice.

"I'm not so young that I can't remember some of the details, Doctor," she said.

There was a stir at the entrance to the lounge as a stocky man, whose red hair was sprinkled with gray, entered, to be greeted with welcoming cries from the four at the table. As the newcomer moved over to shake hands with them, Mike felt the pulse start to throb in his temple.

Hal Brennan was the most famous—and flamboyant—of the astronauts who had circled the earth in the Hermes program of which

Mike had been a part. In that earlier day, the two men had been close, but all that had ended abruptly when Hal Brennan's testimony that Mike couldn't possibly have found it necessary to blow the hatch of the spaceship in which he had circled the earth, allowing it to fill and sink, had given Congressman Israel Pond the excuse to label him a coward publicly during the committee hearing.

ii.

Hal Brennan moved through the lounge like a conquering hero, greeting friends boisterously. When he saw Mike and Jan Cooper at the bar, he came over to them immediately, a pleased smile on his somewhat rugged features.

"Jan!" He kissed her on the cheek. "And Mike Barnes!" Hal held out his hand and Mike had no choice but to accept it.

"Glad to see you, Hal," he said without enthusiasm.

"After all these years." Hal Brennan put his arm across Mike's shoulder. "Where have you been keeping yourself, fellow?"

"I'm doing research for FSA—at Anderson. In closed space ecology."

"Of course! I remember reading a paper of yours not long ago. We'll be needing all the dope we can get on that when Pegasus lifts off, so I may be calling on you. Be here long?"

"I don't know yet."

Hal Brennan chuckled. "You didn't waste any time finding the prettiest girl in these parts anyway."

"This is a business drink, Hal," Jan Cooper said coolly. "Dr. Barnes requested a number and I made him pay for it."

"You still get off around ten or so, don't you, Jan?" Brennan asked.

"Yes." Her tone was wary.

"There's a TGIF party at the Stein house a little later; it should be in full blast by then. Why don't you bring Mike? Some of the people he remembers from the early days here will be there."

"Maybe the doctor doesn't like to have his dates arranged for him—"

"I like this one," Mike said promptly.

"See you later then." Hal Brennan moved toward the door, stopping to speak to several people before disappearing into the lobby.

"You don't have to be kind to the visiting stranger, Miss Cooper," said Mike when the astronaut was gone.

"Maybe I like visiting strangers," she said. "But if you aren't here when I quit for the night at ten-thirty, I'll know you had time to resent being manipulated by Hal Brennan. Some people do."

A waitress brought her a request slip and she glanced at it. "When

Irish Eyes Are Smiling," she read and slipped from the stool. "I'd better go polish my brogue."

The menu in the dining room of the Astronaut Inn didn't look very promising, when Mike examined it at the bar, and feeling the need for a change, he went outside to his car. Driving slowly along A1A southward toward the air force base, he searched for an ocean front restaurant called Sea View, which he remembered. When he finally found it, the Florida lobster—actually a large type of crayfish found on the keys—was delicious. And the lime pie, for which the establishment had been famous long before rockets had begun to roar up from what was then Cape Canaveral, was everything he remembered.

He ate leisurely, basking in the pleasure of hearing again the rush of long rollers breaking upon the sandy beach outside and expending what force was left against the newer revetment of piled up stones made necessary when a severe hurricane had attacked the beach itself. When the meal was finished, he lingered over excellent brandy and let pleasant memories of the past, driven into the background temporarily by the appearance of Hal Brennan, flow through his mind again.

Recalling the delicious flavor of mango slices dipped in brandy and remembering that he had a bag of them back in his room, he purchased a bottle at the desk as he was paying his bill and took it out to the car with him.

It was about nine-thirty when he got back to the motel. Jan Cooper's white convertible was in the front parking lot, so he knew she was still at work. Going to his room, he changed into a lightweight suit, white shirt, and bright tie as being more in keeping for a party with the short white evening dress she was wearing.

When he went into the lounge a little before ten-thirty, it was almost empty. Jan looked a little tired, but smiled at him as he sat at the bar waiting for her to finish. When finally she left the piano, he suggested a drink but she shook her head and took his arm instead, steering him toward the door.

"Let's take my convertible," she said. "I always need fresh salt air after cudgeling my brain for the lyrics to old songs. Would you believe I even had to sing 'Silver Threads Among the Gold' tonight?"

"I bet that threw you."

"It's part of my job. The Astronaut Inn is sort of old hat now; lately they've even had to start advertising those 'two-nights-and-three-days-of-fun-filled-vacation' packages to fill the place. The real swingers of Spaceport City prefer the newer spots along the beach."

"Hal Brennan used to be quite a swinger. I'm surprised that he'd even visit the Astronaut Inn, if it's as antiquated as you say."

"Hal usually makes the rounds of the old places on weekends, so people who remember him from the pre-Apollo days can see that he's a big shot at the Cape. It's part of his personal public relations program."

"You don't like Hal much, do you?"

"I can take him or leave him, but don't mind me, Doctor. I'm always a little morose when I'm tired."

"We don't have to go to that party—"

"It might do me good to see how the real swingers live again. Make me happier with my own lot."

"Just so I'll be prepared," he said as she drove out of the parking lot into the stream of traffic on the beach boulevard, "what's a TGIF party?"

"Practically everybody connected with FSA—which means nearly half the people up and down the coast for maybe fifty miles and another thirty or forty inland to Orlando—quit work around four-thirty Friday afternoon," she explained. " 'Thank God It's Friday' became sort of a byword among the rocket people and now it's spread to the rest of the population. From Friday afternoon until the wee hours of Sunday morning, the joints around here are really jumping."

"You'd hardly think it to look at the Astronaut Inn bar."

"The real excitement is at private parties or small hole-in-the-wall bars on both sides of A1A and US 1 for miles north and south of here. Any place where it's too dark for a husband to see his wife if he starts looking for her—which most of them don't."

"Then a TGIF party must be—"

"You've guessed it, Doctor—no husbands and wives allowed together. A half dozen or so gatherings are always going on Friday and Saturday nights, so neither partner need lack for recreation as long as they don't come together."

"Sounds cozy."

"You don't know how cozy it can be. TGIF takes the place of the wife-swapping key parties you'll find in a lot of towns where there isn't a space installation."

Taking the causeway inland from the ocean front, they crossed a drawbridge and turned into a road leading westward toward one of the tidal rivers that washed the shores of the narrow strip of beach land. At the end of a road several blocks away from the causeway, they crossed a narrow waterway on a short bridge. A large one-story house sprawled across a man-made island that was perhaps one acre in extent, replete with waving palm trees and recessed blacklight floods giving it the appearance of a fairyland.

"Before we go inside, I should warn you that I can only stay a little while," said Jan. "That doesn't mean you have to leave when I do, though; somebody here is bound to be going toward the Astronaut Inn later."

"From the sound of that combo blasting away on the hi-fi, about a half hour of this is about all my ears will take. Just say the word when you're ready to go."

iii.

The circular drive before the rambling Mediterranean-style villa was filled with cars and Jan was forced to park just beyond the bridge leading to the island. She was wearing high heels and when she took Mike's arm, as they walked up the graveled driveway to the house, the closeness of her body to his and the faint fragrance of her perfume were immensely pleasant.

Hal Brennan welcomed them with a hug for Jan and a firm handshake for Mike. "Some people are in the pool," he said. "Take a swim if you like; Jan knows where the suits are. The bar is over near the Florida room."

Through the open Florida room, Mike could see a large kidney-shaped pool with lights recessed into the walls below the surface, giving it the appearance of a giant fish bowl. A few people were splashing in the warm night air, but most of the twenty-five or thirty guests were on the large patio surrounding the pool with glasses in their hands. The din of conversation, along with the throbbing beat of the hi-fi system, turned the scene into a bedlam of noise.

"Do you want to swim?" Jan asked.

Mike shook his head. "I had a dip in the surf just before dinner. What would you like from the bar?"

"Brandy usually lifts my spirits." She moved with him to the bar where he poured two snifters and handed one to her.

"Do you want me to introduce you around?" she asked. "A lot of rather famous people in your field are here."

"I'd rather just talk to you," he told her. "I've been living for several years in a small mountain community and, if this TGIF culture is as advanced as you say it is, I'll have to accustom myself to it gradually." He held up his glass to the light revealing the rich golden hue of a really fine brandy. "The only thing I can see to get excited about so far is the quality of the liquor."

"These are considered to be the best bashes on the Cape, you really shouldn't make a final judgment on such short exposure. Let's go outside."

As they moved through the crowd on the patio, Jan stopped to introduce him to some of the people there. The few he already knew
from the old days at the Cape greeted him warmly once again. Most,
however, were new.

"With palms and the tiles on the roof, this could be Cannes," he
said, as they paused at one end of the pool, where perhaps a dozen
people were splashing in the water. "Except, of course, that there
aren't any topless starlets around."

"Give it time."

Across the pool Mike saw a tall man with graying temples and wavy
hair talking to a willowy blonde in a red dress. "Isn't that Professor
Abram McCandless?" he asked.

"Yes. You know him?"

"He taught computer techniques at Harvard when they were still
a curiosity, but I didn't know he was with FSA."

"Professor McCandless was at Redstone, until the Apollo planning
project there was phased out," she said. "Like a lot of the Redstone
personnel, he came here a couple of years ago. The scuttlebutt is that
he and his wife are breaking up and he's going to marry the blonde
he's with."

"How do you learn so much about what goes on here?"

"Fundamentally this is a small town, Doctor. I teach in the music
department of the county school system and take private pupils after
school and on Saturdays. You'd be surprised what these kids tell you."

They had been moving slowly around the pool, stopping to speak
to people Jan knew or Mike remembered. When they reached the spot
where McCandless was standing, Mike paused to greet him.

"Glad to see you again, Doctor." The computer expert's handshake
was something less than warm. "I thought you were still in California."

"I've been at Anderson. I'm just here on a vacation."

"I read your article on what you called the 'Lockheed Syndrome' in
Space Science. Of course, sociology isn't exactly my field but it seems
to me that some of your conclusions wouldn't stand up to a rigid
examination."

"The article was based on a study of only one community, and I
didn't claim any wider application," said Mike. "But even though I've
only been at the Cape a few hours, I can see definite similarities to
the situation here."

"We must discuss your paper some time, Barnes." The astrophysicist's tone was frosty. "Drop by my office if you have a chance. It's in
the Pegasus Computer Laboratory."

"I'll make it a point to," Mike promised.

"What in the world was that all about?" Jan asked, as they moved away.

"The article he mentioned was on the so-called aerospace syndrome —at a rocket hardware plant in California. One of the points I made was that a lot of men in high places in the rocket business divorce their wives when they're in their fifties and marry much younger women. I guess McCandless took it as a personal affront."

"Mrs. McCandless is a fine person; their son Jason is at the new university near Orlando," said Jan. "If you ask me somebody ought to knock some sense into that distinguished gray head."

"These breakups are always rougher on the children than anyone else," said Mike. "Usually the husband is pretty well fixed and the court requires him to make a settlement that takes care of the wife. The time he really gets clipped is when the second wife leaves him. I saw a lot of that in the study I made."

"You know, I could almost believe Dr. McCandless was afraid of you just now," she said.

"Seeing me probably reminded him of my article and brought on an acute attack of conscience."

"Did you ever stop to think that knowing where the body's buried, so to speak, could be dangerous for you?"

He gave her a startled look. "How could I know anything about people in Spaceport City? I just got here this afternoon?"

"But already two men are afraid of you."

"McCandless, maybe. Who else?"

"Hal Brennan."

"Hal isn't afraid of the devil himself."

"Maybe I used the wrong word; *wary* might express it better. When Hal saw you tonight for the first time, there was the same look in his eyes I saw in those of Dr. McCandless just now."

"Maybe you have ESP," he said with a laugh.

"Just a woman's intuition and capacity for observation. Why would Hal be wary of you?"

"He might feel guilty."

"About what?"

"When my spacecraft made an emergency landing in the ocean, I had to blow the hatch to keep from being suffocated and the ship filled and sank, almost drowning me. Hal testified before Representative Israel Pond's Space Committee in Congress that it couldn't possibly have been necessary for me to blow that hatch to save my life."

"Was it?"

"Absolutely. But I'm sure Hal was firmly convinced at the time that his testimony was true."

"Something could have happened since then to make him realize you were telling the truth at the hearing."

"I believe you do have ESP," said Mike. "Why don't we work our way out of here and go some place where we can hear ourselves talk?"

"I can't stay up too late," she warned. "My private classes start at nine on Saturday morning."

"I saw a Dobbs House on the way over here. If we leave now, you'll have time for a cup of coffee and a piece of pie."

"That will be nice."

"I've decided what this culture should be called," Mike said as they were moving slowly through the crowded patio toward the house. "It's hyper-thyroid."

"My medical knowledge is rather limited. Perhaps you'd better explain."

"The thyroid gland is something of a governor for the rest of the body; the thyroxin it produces controls the rate of metabolism. Too much of it—as in certain types of goiter—causes everything in the body to operate at a greater speed than normal. If overproduction of the hormone keeps up too long, parts of the body, particularly the heart, begin to wear out."

"I'd say another hormone is more often involved here, but a lot of things do wear out fast—especially marriages."

"Those are symptoms, not causes."

"What's the diagnosis then, Doctor?"

"My guess would be boredom—and disappointment."

"Why disappointment? These people represent the most successful group in Spaceport City."

"In the old days, when spaceships and rockets were a novelty, the whole program was seized with a sense of pioneering and adventure that was immensely exciting. But with Apollo, it became little more than a vast factory for fitting together pieces of hardware into giant machines and hurling them into space."

"The astronaut I go with finds it very exciting." It was the first time she had mentioned another man and Mike felt a sense of disappointment that she was already spoken for. But then, he told himself, he couldn't really have expected anything else with someone so obviously desirable.

"The flyers are a class to themselves and the Lockheed Syndrome doesn't apply to them," he assured her. "When an operation gets too big in its purely mechanical functions, an individual worker begins to feel that he's an ever smaller cog in the machine, no matter how high a position he may have. Pretty soon he starts losing his identity and has to make up for it in other ways—ergo, the TGIF culture."

"You know you're not what I would have expected you to be at all," she said.

"Why do you say that?"

"The astronauts I know are drivers, intensely competitive men with an enormous desire to see—and conquer."

"In the old days they had to have that spirit to submit themselves to the tight quarters of what we used to call 'space capsules.'"

"You did just that—and you're still not like them at all."

"Maybe the difference is that even then I was seeking mainly to learn, not just to make the name of Mike Barnes famous—which could also be the reason I failed."

Just as they reached the open doors of the Florida room and were leaving the patio, a hush stilled the buzz of conversation outside, and looking back, Mike saw that a woman in a bright red dress had appeared upon the high diving board some ten feet above the surface of the water. She teetered there while a blare of music with a savage throbbing beat burst from loudspeakers at each end of the pool. Then, as someone on the patio adjusted one of the spotlights by the pool to silhouette her in its beam, she began to perform a rather inept striptease.

Something about the woman had seemed familiar to Mike when she first stepped out on the board, but he hadn't been able to see her clearly until the glare of the spotlight was centered upon her.

It was Shirley—his ex-wife.

CHAPTER V

Mike didn't realize he had shouted a warning, until he saw Jan give him a quick look of surprise and remembered speaking Shirley's name, but the burst of applause as the light centered upon the performer drowned out any protest he would have made. As the music continued its beat, Shirley loosened the zipper at her back and, still teetering dangerously on the board, managed to open it and let her dress fall to the waist. The clapping of the crowd was rhythmic now, in cadence with the beat of the music, as were her movements when she pulled the dress down and stepped out of it, revealing that she wore only a low strapless bra and bikini-type, almost transparent, briefs.

"Atta girl, Shirley!" Mike recognized Hal Brennan's voice. As Shirley reached back to unhook the brassiere one hand couldn't quite manage it and, when she put the other behind her back to reach the hooks, the movement threw her off balance. As the bra fell from her body, she took a step forward to regain her equilibrium but, drunk as she obviously was, didn't manage it and tumbled headfirst into the water.

As if this were an awaited signal, bedlam seized the group on the patio around the pool. Some were pushed into the water fully clothed, to screams of drunken laughter. Others began to strip but most managed only half nudity before they, too, were dunked in the pool.

The crash of broken glass when someone dropped a drink upon the tile around the rim of the pool added to the pandemonium compounded from the wail of the music, the high-pitched screams of women, and shouts of laughter from the men.

Knowing that Shirley was an expert swimmer and diver, Mike was turning away from the pool in disgust when Jan said, "She hasn't come up yet, Mike! Something must be wrong!"

Peeling off his coat, he surveyed the surface of the pool with a quick glance but saw no sign of Shirley's bright blond head among the swimmers. He rather doubted that the pool could be more than the minimum depth of eight feet, but even that should have been adequate for an experienced diver like Shirley—unless she was too drunk to realize the danger.

"Call Hal," he told Jan and pushed his way to the edge of the pool through the press of shouting people around it. None seemed to have noticed that Shirley had not appeared on the surface and, when a second quick glance still showed no sign of her, he dived straight down, aiming at a point directly beneath the end of the board from which she had fallen.

Miraculously, as he shot to the bottom, he didn't hit any of the bodies that half filled the pool now. Fortunately, too, the lights recessed into the side walls beneath the water made the depths as clear as they would have been with the sun shining, so he was able to see her at once lying at the bottom of the pool. Nor was there any doubt about what had happened; plummeting into the water, Shirley must have struck her head on the concrete bottom hard enough to knock her out at least momentarily, though the way her hands were already beginning to move slightly in the reflex motion of swimming, told him she was probably not far from conscious.

Seizing her beneath the armpits and lifting her into an upright position, he set his feet upon the floor of the pool, then jackknifed his legs and shot upward, carrying them both to the surface in a single lunge. A dozen hands pulled Shirley from the pool and laid her out on the tile beside it as, seizing the rim with his hands, Mike lifted himself out with a single bound.

"Get back! He's a doctor!" Jan urged the others as, ignoring the babble of voices around him, Mike straddled Shirley's body and, putting his hands about her waist, lifted it with her head downward to allow any water that might have entered her lungs to drain out.

She coughed and retched, so he didn't use artificial respiration but lifted her in his arms and carried her to a reclining sun couch beside the pool. Certain that she would not suffer any ill effects from whatever small amount of water might have gotten into her lungs, he was turning to leave when Shirley opened her eyes and stared at him with an expression of utter astonishment that told him Hal Brennan hadn't warned her he might be coming to the party. Then the sudden hot light of anger burned in her eyes and she pushed herself up to a sitting position.

"God damn you, Mike Barnes!" she screamed. "Why do you always have to ruin everything?"

"Get her dress off the board," Mike snapped at Hal Brennan, who had appeared beside the couch now, an amused look on his face. "Jan and I will take her home."

"You dumb bastard!" Shirley's voice was shrill with venom. "I live here, understand? Here!"

Without answering, Mike turned through the open doorway of the Florida room, ignoring the fact that his clothes were streaming water all over the expensive rug as he passed through the house. He was starting down the driveway toward Jan's car when he heard her call and looked back to see her stumbling along in her high heels, carrying his jacket and a plastic raincoat she had seized as she was leaving.

"Sit on this raincoat," she said. "It will keep the car from getting drenched."

Spreading the coat out on the seat, he got in while she slid under the wheel from the other side of the car and turned the switch to start the motor.

"I didn't know, Mike," she apologized. "I'd never have taken you there, if I had."

"I don't blame you," he told her. "Hal didn't tell me Shirley would be there."

His teeth had begun to chatter from the chilling effect of the ocean breeze and his wet clothes before they crossed the drawbridge to the beach section and by the time they reached the motel, he was shaking all over in a hard chill.

"Your key?" Jan asked as they climbed the stairway to the landing that gave access to his room.

"In my jacket pocket," he mumbled, and she fished it out, opening the door and shoving him inside.

"Get into the bathroom and peel off those wet clothes," she directed. "You'd better take a hot shower, too; there's one of those heat lamps in the ceiling to warm you up." Her eyes fell upon the brandy bottle and the mangoes on a plate beside it. "I'll have some brandy for you when you get out. Got a robe?"

"In the c-c-closet." Still shivering, he opened the door of the bathroom and reached in to turn on the heat lamp and the shower. Peeling off his wet clothes and kicking them under the washbasin, he stepped into the shower and let the heat of the water soak into his body while the room filled with steam.

When he came out, his white silk dressing gown was hanging from a hook on the inside of the bathroom door. Taking a large towel from the rack, he rubbed his body briskly and, by the time he'd pulled on the robe, could feel a perceptible warmth stirring within him.

When he came out of the bathroom Jan was slicing mangoes on the plastic plate that had been under the ice container and dropping them into two glasses of brandy.

"I turned off the air conditioner so your teeth wouldn't start chattering again," she said. "You were positively blue when we got here."

"I guess the chill was as much from surprise and shock as anything else," he admitted.

"It must have been a shock," Jan agreed. "Shirley kept her second husband's name—Stein—after he died, so it never occurred to me that she was your ex."

"You're not to blame; this was just the sort of thing Hal would set up just to see what would happen. How long has this affair between him and Shirley been going on?"

"Six months or so; there were others before him. Wouldn't it be better if you didn't talk about it?"

"I can think of a more pleasant subject—you."

"I'm pretty unremarkable." Her smile was wry as she handed him a glass of brandy and mango slices. "I'm a Florida native, like you—from over near Tampa. We came to the air force base—"

"We?"

"My husband was a jet pilot in the Air Force, flying observer missions for the rocket launches—until his jet flamed out over a town south of here. He could have ejected and let the plane crash into the town but he stayed with it and guided it out to sea."

"I'm sorry, Jan."

"That was five years ago and I guess I'm pretty well over it now. Bob and I were childhood sweethearts; he went to the University of Florida while I made a try at being an airline stewardess to get money enough for college. When I left the airline, I majored in music at Rollins and graduated about the time Bob got his wings. He was going to Harvard Law School after he finished his period of active duty, but that didn't work out. Now I teach music in the county's public schools and entertain guests at the inn weekends, singing old songs most people have forgotten, so you can see I'm a pretty dull person, just as I warned you."

"Nobody who loves mangoes and brandy could possibly be dull."

"Skoal, fellow mango lover." She raised her glass. "Where did you learn about them?"

"Right here on Merritt Island; we had a grove of our own. By the way, what did you use to peel these with?"

"In the TGIF culture, women sometimes have to protect themselves— if they choose to." From her bag she took a small knife and pressed the button on the handle, sending a long narrow blade plunging from it. "This switchblade serves me pretty well."

"Don't tell me you carry a tear gas pencil in there, too."

"Why not? I'm a resourceful person." She took the small pencil from her handbag and laid it on the coffee table beside the knife.

They sat for a while in silence, enjoying the fruit and the brandy, until the plate and their glasses were empty. When he put his arm around her and kissed her, she didn't resist and her lips were warmly responsive, tasting a little of both fruit and brandy and unbelievably pleasant.

"You didn't reach for your weapons," he reminded her.

"A fellow mango lover can do no wrong," she said with a smile as she stood up.

"Please don't go," he said quickly.

"I wasn't planning to," she said. "Please turn out the lights, Mike. It's been so long since I've undressed before a man that I'm a little self-conscious."

ii.

The moment he saw Asa Childs at a table in the corner of the tavern, Dave Landers knew it had been a mistake to let Muriel talk him into stopping here for a drink on the way home from the dog track at Orlando. Winning both a quiniela and a perfecta in one night called for a celebration but when Dave saw Asa crowded into a booth with three others, he realized what kind of a place they'd gotten into.

"Why don't we go somewhere else, hon?" he asked.

"What's wrong with this place?" Muriel demanded. "I like it."

"There aren't many women." Actually he'd seen only two besides Muriel—and he couldn't be real sure of them.

"So what? As big as you are, nobody's going to try to take you away from me."

That, Dave could have told her, was the most unlikely of any number of things that could happen in a place like this.

"Besides, everybody seems to be having a good time," Muriel added. "This is the gayest place I've been in for a long time."

"That's just what it is—gay," he said. "The women are either 'fruit flies' or—"

"What in the world is a 'fruit fly'?"

"Women who hang around with homosexual men."

"You mean—" Her eyes widened and she looked around her with frank interest.

"Don't stare, Muriel!" Dave spoke under his breath. "And don't let on you know."

"You mean those handsome men are really—?"

"For God's sake, let's get out of here."

"That beautiful girl over there with the fine-looking man couldn't possibly be—"

"Shut up, damn it!"

"Oh, all right, if you're such a fraidy cat. But you don't win a quiniela and a perfecta in the same night and just go home to bed."

"I'll take you to the bar of the Spaceport Hilton," he promised. "And shut up about what we won—or we won't get home with it."

"You can't tell me all these nice-looking men—"

"These nice-looking men may roll us on the way to the car," he told her, still *sotto voce*. "And rape me into the bargain."

Muriel's eyes popped open at that, but after the first shock of the word, she giggled.

"Like that fellow on 'Laugh-In' used to say, that should be 'Ve-er-r-r-y In-ter-esting.'"

"Damn it, Muriel—"

"All right, I'm coming.

"You know I think they're sorta sweet, Dave," she added outside. "I saw that distinguished-looking man back there in the booth kiss that beautiful girl he was with and it was real touching. You haven't kissed me like that in a long time—you know sort of wistful like. All you do is—"

"I'll kiss you any way you want to be kissed. Just let us get the hell out of here."

"You still going to take me to the Spaceport Hilton?"

"We're on the way," he assured her. "By the way," he added when they were outside in the car, "that distinguished-looking man was Asa Childs, head metallurgical technician at Taggar Aircraft. And what you called a girl is his current love interest—named Albert."

"You mean they live together?"

"Just like man and wife; I hear Asa even hires a maid to look after the apartment."

"That's better than you do," said Muriel indignantly. "You mean she-he doesn't have to worry about cleaning and washing dishes?"

"So I hear."

"I'm going to strike for better working conditions. And just think, she-he doesn't even have to take that damned pill either."

iii.

The nightmare began, as always, with a tightening of Mike's throat muscles in the pre-convulsive spasm, threatening to choke off his breathing and setting his heart hammering with the frantic speed of intense anxiety. As always in those agonizing moments, when he felt himself drowning in the black void while the spacecraft plunged deeper into the vast sea of atmosphere separating it from the earth and safety, he fought against the tightening of muscles driven into contraction by a chemical factor he could not control.

Worst of all was the feeling of utter terror, the sense of helplessness, and the almost overpowering urge to seize the release handle inside the spacecraft, known familiarly—like the launch escape rocket control— as the "Chicken Switch." The effect, familiar from at least a dozen dry runs, would be instantaneous as explosive bolts blew the hatch and freed him from the atmosphere inside the confined spacecraft that was threatening to smother him. But even in that moment of pure panic, he'd known that with the hatch door open, he would die almost instantly in the virtual cauldron of flame surrounding the ship, as it raced through the ever thickening atmosphere toward the earth—and had managed to resist.

"Mike! Mike!" A voice penetrated at last into his nightmare and he awoke to the reality of Jan Cooper's arms holding him, while his body quivered in the spasm of convulsion so vividly remembered that his mind had still been able to re-create it in the dream, although the real threat to his life no longer existed.

He clung to her, taking solace from the warmth of her body, the softness of her breasts against his face, the even rise and fall of her breathing as she cradled him in her arms. Finally, when the terror of the nightmare had begun to fade with the realization that he was not in the spaceship breathing the poisonous atmosphere, which had almost destroyed him so long ago, his trembling subsided to the point where he was able to speak.

"Sedative tablets," he gasped. "In my shaving kit—a brown bottle."

Neon light filtered through the ground glass jalousies of the door, relieving the darkness of the room. As she moved toward the bath, Jan's naked body was as slim and lovely in his eyes as he'd felt it in his arms earlier, when the urgent demands of their shared need had brought them together in the ecstasy of explosive relief.

The graceful turn of her head as she opened the bathroom door, the slender column of her neck, the high proud breasts, the sweet curve of her waist, the slight fullness of her hips, and the graceful length of the thighs which had clasped him so tightly—all were like a lovely statue viewed by moonlight, a moving and living statue with the power to stir his senses again as the terror of the nightmare began to fade.

She was back in a moment with a glass of water and one of the powerful sedative tablets he always carried with him to wash away the terror of that moment, when death had been closer at hand even

than the quick release hatch of the space capsule he'd ridden so
triumphantly into the skies only hours before.

He swallowed the tablet and followed it with a gulp of brandy she
poured for him. The shyness that had made her ask him to put out the
light earlier seemed to have evaporated, for she sat upon the bed beside
him oblivious to her nakedness.

"Better now?" she asked.

"Much better. It's an old nightmare—"

"Don't talk about it," she urged. "You'll relax quicker if you don't."

"But I want you to understand—"

"There'll be other times. We'll talk about it then—if you like."

His hand moved to the curving satiny surface of her back. When he
pressed her gently toward him, she did not resist but, pulling back the
sheet, slipped into the bed beside him once again, nestling her warm
fragrant body against his.

Her mouth was soft and receptive, when he found it with his own,
and they lay there close together, letting awakening desire guide them
until finally her body opened to his and the urgency of shared passion
gripped them both once again.

This time their love making was relaxed and utterly satisfying. And
when release finally came, he drifted off to sleep with his head cushioned
against the softness of her breasts.

iv.

He should have talked Muriel out of going on to the bar of the Spaceport Hilton, after they'd left the tavern where he'd seen Asa Childs,
Dave Landers told himself, as he waited in the line of cars before the
main gate of the space center for the guards to check him in. But then
who could have anticipated a call at 6 A.M., telling him to come to work
Saturday morning?

He'd tried to talk Jed Tucker, the Taggar Aircraft metalcraft foreman, out of it, but hadn't gotten anywhere.

"I know it's Saturday morning," Jed had said over the phone. "But
the chief engineer wants both the cabin pop-off valve and the main
oxygen control replaced on the ship today. He called me a half hour
ago and told me to get my best metal craftsman on the job this morning,
and you're it."

"Why in hell would Craven want it in such a hurry?" Dave had protested.

"Search me, but you know how he is. When he wants something
done, he wants it done now. And Paul Taggar backs him up every
time."

"Jesus, Jed, I'm sick."

"No sick leave allowed for hangovers, Dave; you ought to know that. Make yourself some coffee and get over here; we've got an all day job here with those valves."

"Craven let it go 'til hardly two weeks before the launch. Why does he have to be in such a hurry now?"

"The scuttlebutt is that Paul Taggar is afraid an inspector from Washington will find something wrong with those valves and scrub the shot until they're replaced. So he orders Craven and Craven orders me and—"

"I know, I'm next in line," said Dave Landers resignedly. "The trouble is there's nobody I can buck it down to."

"That's what you get for being the best man I've got," said Jed Tucker. "Just think of the overtime you'll be drawing and maybe that'll make you feel better."

It hadn't, of course, not with the kind of hangover Dave had. Nothing could make him feel better except hair of the dog, and the hairier the better. Except this would be the time he'd forgotten to bring home a fifth or two.

Still, even as bad as he felt now, he wasn't really sorry he'd taken Muriel to the Spaceport Hilton. Looking after three kids kept her pretty much tied down and she'd been happier last night than he'd seen her in a long time, just with knowing he'd finally won enough to get her the mink stole she wanted. What the hell women wanted with furs where frost was a rarity, Dave could never see. But three of the girls in the bowling group Muriel belonged to had them and that was enough to make her want a stole, too.

Well, she had the money now, even if he did have the granddaddy of all headaches and a mouth that tasted like an old sock at the end of a fishing trip. Winning that quiniela and the perfecta had been a lot of fun, though, and Muriel had been more like her old self than she'd been for years. The trouble was they hadn't gotten home until they'd helped close the bar at 2 A.M. And then he'd spent another hour satisfying a mother of three who'd suddenly decided she was Cleopatra or something.

One thing he could say; if Cleo had been anything like Muriel was last night, no wonder Julius Caesar had stayed so long in Egypt the way they'd shown him doing in that movie on the "Late Late Show." Or maybe Caesar just hadn't had the strength to leave—which was the way Dave himself felt right now.

"Hiya, Dave!" The guard at the gate checked his pass. "Hear you hit the big ones last night."

"I did all right, Joe. How'd you know?"

"Asa Childs is up ahead; they've got the laboratory working this morning, too. Says he saw you and Muriel in a tavern outside Orlando." The guard smirked. "Didn't know you went in for the gay life."

At the metal fabrication shop, Dave shoved his time card into the slot on the clock and noted that he was five minutes early. The guard's mentioning Asa Childs had given him an idea and, sticking the card into his own rack, he headed for the laboratory.

Although primarily a center for tension estimations on metal going into the rockets and X-ray examinations for defects in the metal itself, the laboratory also used a lot of alcohol and Asa could usually be counted on to provide his friends with a shot of dog hair for a hangover. Of course, he'd probably borrow five bucks from you two days later and forget to pay you back, but that was just something you had to put up with for the privilege of being on his preferred list.

"Dave, boy!" Asa greeted him cordially. "Saw you last night at the Astro Bar."

"Muriel and I stopped in for a drink on the way home from the track. How 'bout a little snort for a friend, Asa? The hangover I've got this morning, they should preserve in the Smithsonian."

"Bad, eh?"

"That's the understatement of the year."

Asa reached for a bottle marked "Alcohol, 95%," but didn't take it.

"Heard you struck gold last night."

"Not much. A few hundred."

Asa's fingers were on the bottle, but he hadn't lifted it yet. "My luck's been lousy lately."

"Too bad." Dave was sweating and the pit of his stomach felt like Mammoth Cave as he reached for his wallet.

"How about lending me a fin?"

"Sure." Dave relaxed as Asa's hand closed about the bottle and lifted it from the shelf. Muriel would raise hell when he came up ten dollars short. She kept the books in the family and guarded the bank account.

"Grab you a Coke from the machine outside and drink half of it," said the technician briskly as Dave laid a ten dollar bill on the counter top. "I'll pour you a nip that'll set you up in no time."

By the time Dave Landers came back into the laboratory, Asa had measured some of the clear liquid into a glass beaker.

"Shake that up, Dave," he said as he poured it into the half empty Coke bottle. "It's pure 95—with a kick like a mule."

Even through the Coke, Dave could taste the raw shock of the alcohol, and the warmth spreading through his middle was like a flame, burning away the sick feeling of the hangover and starting to ease the throbbing in his head almost before he put down the bottle.

"Thanks, Asa," he said. "You're a real friend."

"I get that way myself sometimes," said the technician. "Always glad to help a friend in a time of need."

At the door of the fabricating shop, Dave met Jed Tucker; the foreman was carrying a clip board and wearing a harried expression.

"You're two minutes late," he said testily. "Just because you hit a double last night doesn't mean you can come walking in here whenever you please, Dave."

"Hell, Jed; what's two minutes?" Dave was feeling no pain now. "You're just sore because you weren't doing much winning yourself last night."

"Dropped fifty bucks and my wife screamin' her head off for a dishwasher," said the foreman. "Get your stuff and grab a ride over to the VAB. Craven wants those new valves in before quitting time."

"He'll have 'em and maybe sooner. But I still don't see why he's in such a rush."

"Don't blame the chief engineer for this one; I saw Paul Taggar's initials on the work sheet. Better get the hell over there quick but don't breathe toward the welding torch for a while or you'll set the whole damn place afire with that breath of yours."

CHAPTER VI

The room was bright with daylight when Mike awoke and the small travel clock he'd placed on the desk showed almost ten o'clock. The fragrance of Jan Cooper's presence was still in the room, the print of her body upon the sheets and the pillow beside him. When he threw the covers back and sat up, he found a note propped upon the small bedside stand against the telephone:

> Mike,
>   You were sleeping so peacefully, I didn't have the heart to wake you. Like I told you last night, I give private piano lessons on Saturday but I'll be playing in the lounge again tonight—and I'm in Spaceport City telephone book.
>   Chalk up another first at the Cape—the first girl to be seduced by mangoes and brandy.
>
> Love,
Jan.

When he found himself whistling in the shower, Mike wasn't surprised; it had been a long time since he'd felt so good. Even the recurrence of the nightmare—which he hadn't experienced for almost a year before returning to Florida—couldn't dampen the pleasure he felt at the prospect of seeing Jan Cooper again.

He was having a leisurely breakfast in the motel restaurant when he saw Shirley crossing the room toward his table. He could see no evidence of any aftereffects from last night and she was quite as beautiful as she had been when they were divorced nearly eight years ago.

"They rang your room from the desk but no one answered and the clerk said he thought he saw you going into the restaurant," she explained.

"Won't you join me?"

"Only for a cup of coffee. It's good to see you again, Mike." She took a cigarette from a case in her bag and lit it.

"You didn't seem so happy last night."

"I was loaded—and you were the last person I expected to see here."

"That goes double."

"Jake Stein—my second husband—died two years ago and I came back to the Cape to live. There's a lure to this place that never quite gets out of your skin—especially now."

"Why now?"

"Hal says when they had to speed up the rockets so they could head for the moon, everything here at the Cape had to speed up too. I like action and this is where you'll find it."

"That's an interesting theory."

"Maybe he's right; I don't know. I didn't come here to discuss the Cape—or the world—Mike, I want to apologize for what happened last night. Hal likes for parties to really swing and this one was slow getting off the pad."

"Then you really weren't knocked out."

"Oh, I was conked all right—temporarily; here's the medical proof." When she picked up his fingers and put them to her temple, he could feel a swelling just above the hairline. "Hearing your voice calling my name, while I was trying to keep from falling off that diving board, shook me up and I cracked my noggin hard on the bottom of the pool. But I was coming out of it by the time you grappled me underwater and saved my life so heroically."

"We were about to leave when you started your act," he told her. "I wouldn't have gone into the pool, if Jan hadn't noticed that you were still under the water. You must have stayed under longer than you realized."

"Or else she wanted to see whether you still cared enough for me to take the plunge."

"That's absurd!"

"Maybe yes, maybe no. Jan had a pretty torrid affair with an older man about a year after her husband's plane crashed, so there's plenty of fire under that sun tan, even if it's been banked for quite a while. And you're still a pretty handsome guy—in a conservative sort of way."

Remembering last night, Mike felt himself blush and looked away —but not quickly enough for Shirley to miss it.

"So you made out with her on your first date. Maybe you *have* learned something about women these past eight years."

Shirley's mention of Jan reminded Mike of her remark last night that Hal Brennan was wary of him. "Did Hal send you here this morning?" he asked bluntly.

"What makes you think that?" she asked, but the guarded look in her eyes told him he'd hit upon the truth.

"Hal never does anything without a purpose; even his inviting me to the bash last night was deliberate and your coming here this morning must be part of the same scheme."

"Really, Mike—"

"What does Hal want to know, Shirley?"

"You—you're not being assigned here again, are you?"

"I don't know yet."

"Why did Lars Todt call you to Washington?"

The fact that Hal Brennan already knew of his visit to the Capitol didn't surprise Mike, for the grapevine within FSA was highly organized, with a direct line between the Cape and Washington. But if Hal was so concerned about his being here, maybe something was really wrong with Pegasus, something he needed to discover, in time to warn Lars and General Green before the lift-off date, now less than three weeks away.

"Hal thinks you may have come back to cause trouble," Shirley's voice broke into his thoughts.

"What kind of trouble could I cause?"

"I don't know. But you did almost wreck the Hermes project years ago, when your spacecraft sank."

"I was only trying to find out what went wrong, so other people wouldn't have the same experience. Has Hal found out what really happened to the Hermes I rode in?"

"I really don't know, Mike. You know how he is."

"I know he's a gambler willing to take chances to win, but he has no right to gamble with the lives of the men who'll be in that ship when it lifts off the pad. Tell him that for me, please."

ii.

By ten-thirty, Dave Landers was having the sweats again. During the early part of the morning, he'd felt exhilarated by the jolt of the alcohol Asa Childs had given him in the Coke. Now the effect was wearing off, and the continued hangover from what he'd had last night, plus the pick-me-up this morning, was beginning to get him down. His stomach felt hollow and two cups of coffee during the morning break had only increased the outpouring of acid into his stomach. He wanted desperately to belch, but was afraid the sick-sour taste on top of the nausea he felt might be more than he could handle and he'd have to vomit, calling the attention of the supervisor, who'd been watching him pretty closely all morning anyway.

His hands were shaking a little as he followed the curved pattern of the slot into which the new cabin-exhaust valve of the spaceship had been fitted. He was working at the top of the rocket assembly with only the emergency escape tower above him, and the height didn't help either. Every time he looked down at the beehive of activity inside the giant VAB, he felt his head swim. Sweat pouring down off his forehead beneath the face shield tended to obstruct his vision, too, until sometimes he could barely see the joining point of the new metal to the old. Once while he was using a torch, his hand slipped and the flame struck the polished metal surface around the valve, blackening it and forcing him to rub it off quickly before the supervisor could notice.

He wasn't going to make the mistake of coming to work again after a night at the dog track, he promised himself, particularly one that had practically lasted until time to go to work that morning. His resentment mounted when he remembered that after keeping him awake the rest of the night, Muriel hadn't even bothered to get up when he'd left that morning. Women had the best of everything, he thought bitterly, for perhaps the dozenth time that morning; maybe Asa Childs had the right idea after all. But even Asa was always having a row with his current "queen," so the gay life wasn't without its difficulties.

Christ almighty! Wouldn't lunch time ever come? Dave was sure he'd fall in his tracks in another few moments and the damn job would never get finished, which meant he'd have to work on after knocking-off time and maybe be a couple of hours late getting the drinks he so badly needed.

The clanging of the noonday bell startled Dave and he quickly slipped off the welding mask and put it down. Jumping on the elevator that had carried him almost to the roof of the VAB, he pushed the control button sending it down and ignoring the angry shouts of workmen isolated at lower levels.

Streams of men were pouring out of the VAB toward the cafeteria Taggar Aircraft had installed to shorten the time the workmen spent at their meals. Dave Landers didn't waste much time in the line choosing food; it would only serve to dilute the effect of the two cans of beer he'd picked up at the beverage end of the long serving counter. A couple of rolls and butter, a ground meat patty, and some mashed potatoes were all he needed besides beer.

At a table near the wall, he opened a can of beer with shaking fingers and, without bothering to pour it into a glass, drank it down in shuddering gasps. Only when the can was empty, did he turn his attention to food.

"Mind if I join you, Dave?" He looked up to see an electrician named Ted Chandler standing by the table with his tray.

"Not at all, Ted. Pull up a chair."

"Hear you hit two big ones last night." Chandler poured his own beer.

"Middlin'. Enough to finish paying for Muriel's mink stole."

"Never could see what a woman needs mink for in Florida. But all of 'em want it, even though half the time they go around the house damn near naked."

Dave Landers grinned; the beer was already calming the queasy feeling in his stomach. "That why you gave up home electric repair calls? Couldn't stand the sight of bare woman flesh?"

"Me, I loved it! You'd be surprised how easy it is to make out in a town like this. But the little woman was keeping my books and when I kept going back to the same places so often on repair calls she got suspicious."

"Don't tell me you charged for that, too?"

"I was performing a service, wasn't I? And those babes really needed it. The way some of 'em acted, they must have been married to monks."

"High-salaried monks anyway."

"What good does that do 'em? The husband works like a Trojan all day making Paul Taggar rich, and when he comes home he's too pooped to do anything except fall in bed—and sleep. My problem was that by the time I took care of the repairs and the wife, too, I was as worn out when I got home as the other husbands were. My wife started smelling a rat when I'd come off service calls reeking of Chanel No. 5, so I had to choose between an eight-to-four job or a divorce. One thing though, nothing makes a wife more lovin' than knowin' there's a lot of free stuff around."

"Some folks have all the luck," said Dave Landers. "The only thing I got to repair before I joined this outfit was boilers and there ain't no bonuses in that kind of work like you were getting."

"What you doin' workin' on Saturday anyway?" Chandler asked.

"Rush job ordered by the chief engineer."

"Dollar says he'll be by before four o'clock to check up on you," said Chandler. "Since FSA stepped up work on this bird, the engineers have been wound up tight."

"Craven's the tightest of 'em all."

"He's a real son of a bitch all right," Chandler agreed.

"If he's on your back, why don't you talk to the shop steward of your union? You electricians have the strongest group at the Cape."

"Trouble is I don't have a legitimate beef," Ted Chandler admitted. "Sometime this morning I mislaid a pair of needle-nose pliers and if I don't find 'em before tool check-in time, all hell's going to break loose."

He opened his second can of beer. "The fuss they make over one pair of pliers, you'd think they were made out of gold."

"Why the stink?"

"Craven claims that if you drop a pin into the inside of a big rocket, it could cause a short circuit."

"Could be he's right."

"All that happens is it blows a fuse and one circuit goes out. The way they build what they call redundant circuits into these things, there's always another one to take over."

Outside a bell jangled and Ted Chandler stood up. "Back to the salt mines. I'll probably have to spend the rest of the day hunting for them damn pliers."

"And I've got a job to finish." Dave was feeling considerably better now and decided he'd better check the work on the installation he'd made during the last several hours, when he hadn't been seeing too well, just in case Craven or that nosy metallurgist in charge of the laboratory where Asa Childs worked decided to check on the job.

iii.

With Washington closed up tight weekends, Mike decided nothing would be gained by trying to communicate with Lars Todt about the situation at the Cape. He had no real facts to go on, except his suspicions about Hal Brennan. And, if he mentioned them to Lars, he knew the senator was enough of a realist to remember the ill-feeling that had existed between him and Hal ever since the House committee hearing —at least on Mike's part. Trying to get any information out of Hal himself would also be a waste of time, too, so he decided to survey the situation for himself as one of the thousands of tourists who swarmed through the Cape complex each day on guided tours.

Driving across to the mainland on the causeway that gave access to Spaceport City, he made his way to the Kennedy Space Center on Merritt Island, separated by a lazy tidal stream from the out-thrust dunes that kept the ocean from engulfing the beach area. It was just noon but the parking lot adjoining the Visitor Center was already filled and the rows of school buses lined up at one side testified to the absorbing interest of America's youth in the activities going on here at the country's major rocket center.

Inside the airy bright building, people were moving about like bees in a hive. The largest stream was directed toward the buses that departed every few minutes on guided tours of the sprawling complex itself. Another went toward the two small theaters to watch the motion pictures that ran continually, describing space flight and its problems. Still another line was headed for the lunch counter that was doing a thriving business.

Mike bought his tour ticket like any other tourist and, while waiting for his bus to be called, got a hamburger and a Coke and went outside in the sunlight. The motion pictures and the exhibits were old stuff to him; some of them had even been taken of his old Hermes flight, when the conquest of space was still a novelty.

When his bus number was called, he went to the loading ramp and boarded it, taking a seat near the front. The conveyances used for the tours were regular Greyhound buses; every few minutes a new one drove away, while another moved in beside the adjoining platform to unload passengers who had completed the tour of some two and a half hours. The driver, a red-haired fellow with an engaging grin, began his spiel as soon as they pulled out into the main access road but Mike paid little attention to the lecture with its stale jokes. He was more interested in noting familiar spots and the memories they brought.

The whole space complex had expanded enormously in the some eight years since he'd left the Cape, he saw at once. Only a little of what he remembered remained, and even that had obviously been preserved mainly because it was good public relations for FSA to show the throngs of tourists passing through the area every day some of the spots familiar to them from TV descriptions by Walter Cronkite, Huntley and Brinkley, and others during those early exciting flights into the unknown world of space.

Complex Fourteen, from which John Glenn's Friendship Seven had been launched skyward for the first American orbital flight, had been kept intact. So had the spacecraft itself—looking like a toy compared to the mighty Apollo—with its heat shield seared and blackened from the intense fires of reentry.

Complex Nineteen, site of the long since finished Gemini program, was nearby, but the operating center for the first Mission Control, where the Mercury and Hermes projects had been monitored, had long since been deactivated Mike had heard in favor of the much more complicated Manned Spacecraft Center at Houston. To his surprise, however, as they swung around the squat building near the sea during the course of the tour, he saw that the old center was being considerably enlarged.

"Why are they rebuilding Mission Control?" he asked the driver.

"All I know is they say it will be used for monitoring the Pegasus flight, mister, along with a new blockhouse near the launch pad. You can see a mock-up of the old center a little farther on."

When the passengers debarked to tour the replica of the original

Mission Control, from which the voice of Colonel Artemus McCord had announced to a breathless world the events of the Hermes flights and Mike's own emergency reentry, he could imagine himself back in the cramped space of the old ship during the exciting moments of lift-off and insertion into orbit.

Deliberately shutting from his mind all memory of the end of that flight with its power still to stir the old feelings of anxiety and fear, Mike devoted himself instead to the words of a lecturer inside the building, as he described how the path of the manned satellites had been traced around the world on a giant map covering one wall, with telemetry details and the voices of the astronauts themselves being reported from the vast network of tracking stations.

When they left Mission Control Mike saw that the industrial complex had expanded many times since his departure. One of the largest centers belonged to Taggar Aircraft, prime contractor for Pegasus, as it had been for Hermes. In addition, a new plant where Taggar supervised the final details of Pegasus, was pointed out in another part of the launch area by the driver, although the tour did not visit it.

One thing that hadn't changed very much was the compact Bioastronautics Facility where Mike had worked while preparing for his own flight. From it he had walked one brisk December morning, snugly warm in his silver-hued space suit, to the bus which had carried him to the launch pad. At the gantry beside the giant Titan rocket, an elevator had lifted him to the waiting Hermes spacecraft which had so nearly become his coffin.

He wasn't able to account for a new structure near the road that gave access to the sprawling complex of buildings connected with Pegasus. Eight-sided in shape, it was about two stories high.

"What's the octagonal building?" he asked the driver.

"That's the new centrifuge-simulator, sir. It's used to accustom astronauts in the Pegasus program to the G-pressure of takeoff and reentry."

"But there's one at Goddard, and another at Houston—plus the old Navy centrifuge at Johnsville, Pennsylvania, and several others."

"I only say what I've been told to say, mister," said the driver, and adjusted the microphone he wore so he could address the other passengers.

"We will not be able to show you the launch pad for Pegasus, the newest of man's ventures into space," he announced, and a murmur of disappointment went up from the passengers.

"Is it off limits?" Mike asked.

"They're working overtime there, sir, getting ready for the launch."

"Then it's usually part of the tour?"

"The Pegasus complex is off our route," said the driver, and Mike didn't question him further. He did, however, add this bit of information to the other odd facts he'd learned about America's newest space venture in the brief time he'd been at the Cape.

Nearing the end of the tour, the bus drew to a halt in the shadow of the giant Vehicle Assembly Building. Built originally for the Apollo program, it was one of the largest man-made structures in the world, said the guidebook he'd purchased at the Visitor Center, capable of containing the Pentagon, with almost enough space left over for the Chicago Merchandise Mart. More than five hundred feet tall, rivaling the Washington Monument in height, the VAB was large enough to allow assembly of several Apollo-Saturn vehicles like those which had hurled men toward the moon. Now, the driver stated, it was being used to assemble Pegasus, the first of America's orbiting space stations.

Filing out of the bus before the VAB, the queue of passengers entered the great structure along with the occupants of several other sightseeing vehicles drawn up on the vast concrete apron before it. Only a small portion of the building, one bay of the several it contained, was shown to them, just enough for them to be awed by its tremendous height. So great was this, according to the inevitable lecture, that the name of Taggar Aircraft, barely readable in a sign spread across the bottom of a huge movable crane suspended from the ceiling, was as large as the bus in which they had come there.

Mike looked around him during the lecture but could see nothing related to Pegasus. When he saw a workman come through a door and leave it open, he obeyed a sudden impulse and slipped into the passageway thus revealed. Lined with cables and pipes, it was perhaps fifty feet long and gave access at the other end to another bay of the VAB, a great open space in which a giant shining cylinder towered skyward almost to the ceiling of the building.

No one had to tell him this was Pegasus: its shape was familiar from newspaper sketches he'd seen, as was the giant transporter upon which it stood. Capable of moving eighteen million pounds, the latter had been built to move the Apollo moon rockets to the launching point and was now fulfilling the same purpose for Pegasus.

Swarms of workmen were busy around the base of the giant space vehicle and a few were on scaffolds suspended from cranes moving on tracks across the building near the roof. One man, resembling a midget at that height, seemed to be working on the spacecraft itself. Every kind of power tool imaginable appeared to be in use and the din was ear splitting. Mike was able to see little more of the giant structure than that, however, before a uniformed guard tapped him on the arm.

"Your badge, sir," he said. "You're supposed to wear it exposed at all times."

"I don't have one," Mike confessed, somewhat startled to note that the guard was actually a member of the Air Police.

"Who let you in here?" the soldier demanded.

"I'm a tourist." Intrigued by the mystery of the presence of air force guards in an area which had heretofore been entirely under civilian direction, Mike decided not to reveal his actual status as yet.

"Tourists aren't allowed here," the guard said.

"A door was open and I came in," Mike explained. "Sounds like your security is pretty lax here, Corporal, though I don't see why there's any need for it at all."

"Come with me," the soldier ordered.

"Am I under arrest?"

"We'll see about that later." The air policeman guided him to an office on the ground floor of the building where a sergeant was lounging behind a desk. He straightened up when the two came in.

"I found this guy snooping around the assembly area without a pass," said the first guard. "Claims he's a tourist that drifted in here by mistake."

"Of course I'm a tourist." Fumbling in his shirt pocket, Mike produced the other half of a ticket he'd purchased for the sightseeing trip. "I just happened to step through an open door and this fellow grabbed me like I was a Russian spy or something."

"Got any identification?" the sergeant asked.

"Sure." Opening his wallet, Mike produced his California driver's license, but purposely did not reveal his FSA pass.

"Dr. Michael Barnes, Mountain City, California." The sergeant handed back the license; obviously the name meant nothing to him.

"Looks like he's just a tourist, Al," he said. "Show him out."

"My bus will probably be gone by the time I get out there again," Mike objected.

"They run 'em every five minutes or so, Doc."

"But every seat is always filled."

"Take him to the guard post outside, Al," the sergeant said resignedly. "And tell somebody to drive him back to the Visitor Center in a jeep."

The soldier driving the jeep took the most direct route to the Visitor Center, cutting through the section devoted to the Pegasus project, which suited Mike fine. Parked beside a sprawling building with a Taggar Aircraft sign over its main doorway was a huge truck; Mike had passed a number of them on the way east, hauling the components of various rockets from the factories to the point of launch, where the final assembly was carried out. On the truck was a familiar-looking object and, as the jeep circled the road before the Taggar plant, Mike leaned forward to study it.

"Isn't that a Hermes spacecraft?" he asked the soldier driving the jeep.

The man glanced at the truck. "They call it Hermes II, but it's part of the Pegasus rocket. The first Hermes flight was several years ago."

Mike could have told him far more about those earlier flights than the guard was likely to know, but he was much more interested in the appearance of the spacecraft. As far as he could see on the outside, the original shape had not been changed materially for Hermes II, except in size, from the first Hermes ships.

"Is that thing going to ride on top of Pegasus?" he asked, pretending ignorance.

"That's what they say." The jeep driver made a right turn into the main road from the artery leading to the Pegasus complex, shutting away the view of the spacecraft.

Mike asked no more questions, but they were in his mind just the same. Although the sketches he'd seen of a proposed space station showed a metal cylinder some twenty-five or thirty feet in size, the giant craft inside the Vehicle Assembly Building was at least three times that long and, he was sure, half again as large in diameter. But even more troubling was the fact that, unless Taggar Aircraft had remedied in Hermes II the defects which had almost brought about Mike's own death in Hermes I, several astronauts might well end up less than a month from now in an orbiting coffin.

He needed more information about Pegasus but knew better by now than to try to learn it from Hal Brennan. Remembering, however, Yvonne Lang's saying the afternoon before that Art McCord was editor and publisher of the Spaceport *Call*, he decided to consult Art.

CHAPTER VII

The headquarters of the Spaceport *Call* was located on one of the man-made islands of the new city. Four stories high and beautifully land-scaped, the building represented a considerably larger investment than Art McCord had possessed when Mike had known him. Beside it towered the broadcast antenna of a radio and TV station whose studios, according to the directory inside the building, occupied the two top floors, while the newspaper used the lower ones.

"Mike! How in the hell are you?" Art McCord came out of his chair like an uncoiling spring to pump the visitor's hand enthusiastically. A lieutenant colonel in the public relations division of the Air Force, he'd been the voice of the Hermes series, the man whose nasal twang, broadcasting the progress of the astronauts to a waiting world, had been as much a part of those early flights as the roar of the boosters at lift-off.

But Art, too, had been a casualty of the tremendous preparations for the leap into outer space represented by Apollo, though just how Mike didn't know. The last he'd heard, until he'd asked Yvonne Lang about him yesterday, was that Art had retired from the Air Force and was running a small newspaper in the Cape area.

"I'm fine, Art. And you?"

"I get along. This gives me the excuse I've been needing to have my first drink of the day." The newspaperman pointed to a chair beside the desk and reached into the drawer for a couple of glasses. "Still like your bourbon neat?"

"As always." Mike looked around the room, which was furnished with quiet opulence. "Looks like you're in the chips these days."

"Yankee money, Mike. Yankee money." Art smacked his lips over the bourbon and leaned back in his chair. "After I left NASA at their request—"

"I never heard what really happened there."

"I made the mistake of speaking my mind when the Apollo project was first launched. Did you know I have a degree in sociology from FSU?"

"You managed to hide that in the old days."

"Along with a lot of other things. But when I saw all that money being poured into a race, so a few flyboys could build sand castles on the surface of the moon, and remembered how many starving Negro, Puerto Rican, and Mexican babies it would feed, I blew my top during an interview. It made the wire services but in the Kennedy days criticizing Apollo was the same thing as treason, so I got the shaft."

"I remember very well how it felt."

"Actually it was the best thing that ever happened to me. I bought a tri-weekly newspaper here and settled down to a newspaperman's dream—which usually turns out to be a nightmare."

"Obviously it didn't in your case."

"I can thank NASA and FSA for that, too. The population explosion that hit Brevard County with Apollo launched me into the big time and it's kept right on going with Pegasus. An area that grew three hundred and seventy percent in a few years obviously needed its own daily and even before they got the Pegasus contract Taggar Newspapers decided my sheet was it. I came out of the deal with a nice block of Taggar stock to keep me in my old age and the title of Editor and Publisher."

"Working on Saturdays? You never had to do that in the old days."

"The big bass are biting like mad in the upper St. Johns west of here. I'm taking a few days off with several fellows to do some fishing, but I still have to get my editorials written ahead of time."

"Needling the space program?"

"After forty you don't bite the hand that's feeding you, Mike. Taggar alone employs more people than were in all of Brevard County in the old Hermes days."

"How did Hal Brennan get to be head of Pegasus?"

"My guess is that Israel Pond arranged that. Hal and Israel came from the same neck of the woods and they're the same brand of bastard." The newspaperman gave Mike an appraising look. "Is this more than a casual visit to see an old friend?"

"I'm always happy to see any old friend who can drink Jack Daniels," said Mike. "But what I really need is some information."

"If I have it, you're welcome to it."

"It's still not fair to ask without telling you why—in confidence."

"Hell, Mike. You can trust me."

Mike gave Art McCord a quick rundown on the call from Lars Todt, the interview in Washington, the episode at Shirley's home and his conversation with her that morning at breakfast, leaving out only his meeting with Jan Cooper.

"You left the party too early," Art told him. "The real fun starts *after* Shirley does her strip act."

"Then you've been to one of them?"

"The widow Stein is noted—or perhaps I should say notorious—for her parties. I'm sort of a native now though, and us natives don't socialize much with the TGIF crowd. God knows we have plenty of fornication on the mainland among our leading citizens just like every other God-fearing American town. But Hal's brought it to a high art here in Spaceport City with that gang he runs with."

"I still don't understand why he invited me."

"Were you alone?"

"No. I took Jan Cooper."

"Fine girl, Jan. My guess is that Hal wanted you to know Shirley belongs to him now."

"He's welcome to her."

"They deserve each other—if you don't mind my speaking the truth about the broad who's your ex. On second thought, though, it may go a bit deeper than that. Hal must have guessed that you're here for some special purpose. After the shellacking Israel Pond gave you, it would take that to bring a dedicated guy like you back to—"

"The scene of the crime?"

"We both know there wasn't any crime, Mike. That hatch blew itself."

"No, Art. I pulled the chicken lever—but only to keep myself alive."

"Nobody could blame you for that."

"A lot of people did. And I couldn't answer back at the time, because I wasn't sure just what had happened myself."

"Are you now?"

"It was oxygen poisoning."

"Didn't know there was such a thing."

"I've been working on it at Anderson. Too high a concentration of oxygen makes the arteries contract; you can see them in pictures we took of the eye grounds of volunteers before and after exposure to oxygen under pressure. The arteries of the brain are constricted more than the rest of the body, but the effect is general as well."

"But people breathe pure oxygen all the time these days—for heart attacks, pneumonia, and a lot of things."

"Not under pressure, except as a form of treatment for diseases like emphysema. If you breathe hundred percent oxygen in a hyperbaric chamber at a pressure of several atmospheres, more and more of it is forced into solution in the plasma—that's the fluid part of the blood— as the pressure rises. The increase in tissue O_2 causes artery spasm;

if the pressure rises high enough, convulsions and even blindness can result."

"How could that have happened in your spacecraft?"

"I suspected from the beginning that two valves had stopped functioning properly at the same time. One was the main control of the tank that fed oxygen into the spacecraft; the other was a pressure valve designed to let out any excess—"

"What we used to call the 'pop-off.'"

Mike nodded. "Ordinarily both of them are watched by telemetry on the ground and, since I was pretty busy about that time, I didn't pay much attention to them. Besides, the symptoms of oxygen poisoning are insidious and I didn't realize what was happening until things got so bad that I had to make an emergency reentry."

"I'll never forget that last twenty minutes. We sweated you down with drops of blood, believe me."

"I know," said Mike. "I only stayed in the space program after Israel Pond gave me that going over so I could prove experimentally what really happened."

"Does that mean you've got proof that Taggar Aircraft built a defective capsule?" There was an odd intensity in Art McCord's voice.

"Jan Cooper put it a little bit differently last night. She said I know where the body's buried and she thinks Hal's wary of me for that reason."

"Hal's got a lot riding on this first Pegasus flight and as usual with him, there's more under the table than can be seen on top of it."

"What's he up to now?"

"Didn't you know he's planning to run for governor of Florida next year."

"I've been in California, remember?"

"Space is one of Florida's largest industries along with tourism and Hal combines them both. If he can bring off something as big as Pegasus, it will add to the glamor he's already got, making him practically impossible to beat in the voting booths."

"And Shirley's counting on going to Tallahassee with him. It all begins to add up."

"She may wind up holding the bag there," said Art. "TGIF isn't just for rocket people; it always attracts a few bored females from the jet set—usually young and eager ones with lots of money. Don't be surprised to read pretty soon after Pegasus takes off that Hal's dropped Shirley for the heiress to an Argentine corned beef fortune."

"And you still advertise Spaceport City as 'the perfect place for discriminating people'?"

"Some discriminate one way and some another." Art grinned. "One thing you can say for this place, though; hardly anybody gets bored —except between weekends." Then his face sobered. "I wish you hadn't come back, Mike."

"Why?"

"This isn't the same league you were playing in, when we were getting the Mercury and Hermes rockets off the ground ten years ago. Billions of dollars are riding on this Pegasus shot and, with luck, the project will keep humming for the next fifteen or twenty years—first with the space station, then with Mars shots, and maybe later with other planets. Everything's going fine and suddenly you turn up, the only man who almost died on a space flight because of a mechanical failure."

"The bastard at the family reunion."

"It's nothing to joke about, Mike. Take my advice and go right back to California before somebody hangs something worse than 'space chicken' on you."

"I've been through the temperature of reentry—and survived, don't forget that."

"But not without a heat shield, Mike."

ii.

The nearest bar to the section of the government reservation devoted to the Pegasus project was just off the ramp leading to the causeway. As Dave Landers pulled his car into the parking lot a few minutes after the day shift went off, another car parked beside him and Ted Chandler, the electrician he'd been talking to during the lunch break, got out. The two walked into the tavern together and took seats at the long bar, which was rapidly filling up, not only with men but with women from the vast feminine army employed in the manifold activities of the Cape.

Mini-skirted secretaries from FSA administration headquarters; waitresses from the several cafeterias and coffee shops on the reservation; trimly uniformed hostesses employed by Coastal Airlines, which had the housekeeping concession for the vast sprawl of the Pegasus rocket complex—all these and many more poured into the tavern to continue the rite of TGIF which had been somewhat interrupted by Saturday's work schedule.

The taverns just outside the reservation were happy hunting grounds for male and female alike, married or single. Temporary liaisons formed over the first drinks might extend to a dinner date, a pot or a Speed party at one of the apartment houses favored by swingers, or a week-

end in one of the dozens of motels along the course of US 1 up and
down the banks of the Indian River, many of them marked by the
plaintively familiar sign, "Five-Dollar Double," since the big motel
chains had started siphoning off the cream of the tourist trade.

"Don't usually see you in here, Dave," said Ted Chandler. "Muriel
away or something?"

"I had to have a drink to get me home." Dave emptied the glass the
bartender set before him and ordered another. "God what a day I've
had!"

"Finish the job?"

"Barely made it by closing but that bastard Craven will probably
make me do it over again Monday. Just because he's chief engineer, he
thinks he's Jesus Christ or something."

"I was sure my tail was going to be in a vise at closing time over
that tool check Craven's put in."

"Ever find the pair of needle-nose you lost?"

"Nah! The damn thing's probably somewhere in the middle of that
booster by now. I was sweatin' blood when it came to the check-out
but the guy ahead of me managed to slip me a pair after they cleared
him, so I made it."

"That was close all right."

"At least I put one over on Craven—and that doesn't happen very
often."

iii.

When Mike came into the motel dining room about seven that evening, the hostess seated him so he could easily see the piano and Jan.
She was wearing a pale green dress with a ribbon of the same color
about her dark auburn hair. Looking up between numbers, she saw
him and smiled, filling him with a warm glow of pleasure.

A small pad of blank slips marked "Requests for Jan Cooper" lay
upon the table. While he waited for the waitress to bring him a split of
sparkling burgundy, he wrote: "Harper Valley PTA" on a slip and on
the other side, "See you later?"

The waitress took the slip with his order for dinner and the song
came while he was enjoying the wine. He ate leisurely, taking his
time about finishing the bottle. Over an hour had passed since he'd
come in but, although Jan had taken one break for about ten minutes,
she didn't join him, by which he judged that, while it was all right
for her to have a drink with a customer at the bar during the TGIF
hour, coming to the table during the dinner hour was frowned
upon by the management.

On the way to the desk to sign his check, he stopped by the piano.

She was finishing a number and looked up with a smile as she played the final bars.

"Did you like the way I did your request?" she asked.

"Loved it. Will I see you later tonight?"

"Sorry." She touched the keys in the introduction to another song. "Jerry McGrath is leaving for Houston early tomorrow morning for some tests and I promised to see him."

He remembered her saying last night that she was seeing an astronaut and felt a spasm of jealousy for the man he didn't even know.

"How about tomorrow?" he asked.

"Call me. I'm in the book."

"Say ten o'clock in the morning?"

She nodded and turned back to the keys, as he continued on to the desk and charged the meal on his credit card. It was barely nine o'clock but, without Jan, he felt no particular desire to go anywhere so returned to his room and was watching TV morosely, when the telephone rang. It was Hal Brennan.

"Doing anything, Mike?" the ex-astronaut asked.

"No. Why?"

"Shirley tells me you're interested in Pegasus, so why don't you run over to the house? A few people are here watching TV and playing games, but they'll be leaving soon. We can have a long talk about the project."

"Sounds like a good idea," said Mike. "I started to call you earlier tonight; there are some things I'd like to know."

"We'll thrash everything out where we won't be interrupted," Hal Brennan promised. "I'm sorry about last night. When I told Jan the party would be at the Stein place, I thought you knew Shirley had married Jake Stein after your divorce."

"That's all right. I guess I made an ass of myself."

"Nothing of the sort. And thanks for pulling Shirley out of the pool; I didn't even know she was in trouble. I'm only ten minutes away from the inn; they'll order you a taxi at the motel and the driver will know the way."

"I have my own car."

"Take Spaceport Road off the causeway then and turn right on Brennan Drive; I live at the end."

"If you're having a brawl like last night—"

"This is a small party. We're playing a parlor game called 'Countdown.' Remember the directions?"

"Yes."

"I'll be looking for you then. After these people leave we'll have a good talk over beer and pretzels like old times."

CHAPTER VIII

Located on an island like many of the more expensive estates in Spaceport City, Hal Brennan's home was a large rambling villa with what looked like a guest cottage beside the small dock on the waterway connected to the main house by a covered walkway. Hal met him at the door and handed him a full glass.

"We're drinking stingers," he said. "A game is starting right now, so you can learn by watching. Here's your number and card."

Mike felt something drop into his jacket pocket but had no time to determine what it was for Hal pushed him on toward the library, where Shirley came to the door. The room was dimly lit but he could see that perhaps a dozen people were gathered before a very large television screen built into the end wall of the room. Some were sprawled in chairs and sofas, others were sitting on the floor. The screen itself was blank as Shirley took him in hand and led him to a sofa.

She didn't introduce him but, judging from what he'd already learned about the TGIF culture of Spaceport City, he was sure no two people there would have the same last names. The stinger was strong —as stingers should be—the conversation loud and punctuated by guffaws from the men and squeals from the women.

Mike was about halfway through the glass when Hal Brennan announced from his position by the door: "Launch two, ladies and gentlemen! The pool is ten dollars."

There was a scramble to toss ten dollar bills into a basket in the center of the room. Shirley put hers in and came back to sit close beside Mike.

"You can sit this one out while you learn the game," she said. "It's lots of fun."

"Time!" Hal called and everybody except Mike, who hadn't tossed in a bill, started writing on a small filing card like the one Hal had shoved into his pocket when he came into the house. As each finished writing, he or she announced the figure on the card but beyond that nobody made a move to explain the game and, content to enjoy his drink, Mike didn't ask.

"*Faites vos jeux, messieurs et m'selles.*" Hal intoned like a Monte Carlo croupier. "Play is about to begin."

When the large screen at the end of the room was suddenly illuminated Mike realized that is wasn't an ordinary television screen at all, as he had thought. Neither was the picture, which showed a man and woman on a couch in an otherwise unfurnished room.

Both were nude and they were making love.

Mike was so startled, he couldn't believe his own eyes. To the others, however, this was obviously a familiar experience for they began to cheer the participants on, as if they were all watching a football game.

"Exciting isn't it." Shirley's voice had taken on the throaty growl of passion he remembered from long ago and Mike felt his hackles rise and his pulse quicken in spite of himself. Without being conscious of his action, so caught was his attention by the picture on the screen, he finished the stinger in a gulp and put the empty glass on the coffee table before the love seat.

"Only Hal could have thought up a game like Countdown." Shirley moved closer and reached up to pull the arm Mike had thrown across the seat down about her. When she pressed his hand against her breast, he felt no urge to remove it, for a fever, compounded of the stinger he'd drunk so quickly and the scene he was witnessing, seemed to be taking control of his brain.

At first Mike couldn't figure where the picture on the screen was coming from, then he noted an odd haziness about it and decided that what they were seeing must have been photographed by infrared light with a camera sensitive to that relatively invisible section of the spectrum.

"Is it a film?" he asked.

"Hell no—this is as live as you can get," said Shirley.

"But—"

"Hal's got the guest house by the pool wired for closed circuit TV and lit with infrared. When you're in there, it seems to be dark, but for the camera it's almost as light as day."

"Then they don't know—"

"They know all right. That's what makes it exciting."

"Where does the Countdown come in—and the bets?"

"Wait and see." Shirley was breathing rapidly with the excitement of the frantic activity on the screen, which strangely enough seemed to have become much brighter during the few minutes since Mike had finished the glass Hal had given him.

"Countdown!" Hal Brennan called, as the activity on the screen seemed to be approaching a climax.

He began to count, and those in the room chanted the numbers along with him, until the activity ended suddenly and Hal shouted, "Blast-off!"

"I won! I won!" A woman cried excitedly. "Twenty-five! See. It's here on the card."

As the screen grew dark, the lights came on and she held up a card on which she had written the number "25."

"Exciting, wasn't it?" Shirley's eyes were glowing and the air of sexual tension in the room had increased perceptibly—even for Mike. "I wonder who's next?"

"You mean this is organized?"

"Only the first half dozen countdowns or so. After that it's everybody for themselves."

"But how?"

"You get a tag with a number on it when you arrive; Hal must have given you one." From where it was tucked into the low neckline of her dress, she took out a round white disk with the figure "Five" printed on it in red. "When your number's called, you go to the guest house while the room is dark."

"Ingenious." Mike recognized his own voice, though it too had changed.

"Some lucky male here tonight has No. 5, too," she added.

Just then the screen was illuminated again and Mike blinked, for the lights in the room seemed far brighter than they had been before, a reaction due, he supposed, to the darkness of the preceding scene.

At the call of "Launch Three," ten dollar bills began to rain once again into the basket in the center of the room. The lights were suddenly doused and when they came up again, a few moments later, Mike saw that two of those who had been in the room had left.

"It's George and Vannie this time," Shirley told him. "Better bet on a short countdown; George is pretty drunk. Too bad you came so late, darling, but when you catch up, you'll have some real fun."

Suddenly Mike realized what she was saying. Obviously the drink Hal Brennan had handed him when he came in had been doped with whatever the others were using to achieve the sort of synthetic gaiety that would fit the game they were playing. Just what the drug was: marijuana; methamphetamine, often the main ingredient of a concoction called "Speed"; perhaps even hashish or LSD, he couldn't be sure. But from the rapid effect it was having upon his own senses, heightening them to a frightening degree already, he would bet on one of the powerful amphetamines, dissolved in the stinger he'd drunk so quickly.

The way his body had begun to feel as if it were floating, plus the brightness of the lights, left no doubt that he must get away fast or not at all. And, when the lights in the room were doused again for the countdown, he made his way—not without some difficulty—to his car and slid beneath the wheel. As he started the motor, his heightened vision from the drug allowed him to detect the red glow of the infrared light in the guest house where another countdown was in progress, but he wanted no part of it. The important thing now was to get back to his room at the Astronaut Inn before all the drug was absorbed into his circulation and he would no longer be able to control his actions.

The next fifteen minutes seemed an eternity. Driving as slowly as he could without clogging the Saturday night traffic, fighting to keep control when part of his mind urged him to drive aimlessly anywhere he wished, Mike followed back streets toward the hotel, avoiding the light as much as possible. Traffic signals gave him the most trouble; often the red and green merged until he couldn't tell which was which and was forced to move only with the traffic.

He still hadn't reached the street on which the motel stood, when he realized he would never be able to make it. And remembering that Yvonne Lang had told him she lived in Spaceport City, he fished the card she had given him the afternoon before from his pocket and studied it in the illumination from a street lamp.

The figures and letters swam before his eyes in a daze and only by shaking his head sharply was he able to focus them momentarily and read: "425 Poinsett Drive."

Swinging away from the causeway with the bright lights that threatened to turn his vision into a fiery haze, he entered the residential part of Spaceport City again and found that he could see much better here, where it was relatively dark. He was even able to read the street signs at the crossings fairly easily, so much had his vision been heightened by the drug. But he was still troubled by a sensation of floating away from the steering wheel and had to clutch it tightly as his car crawled along.

Four twenty-five Poinsett was a small cottage banked with yellow hibiscus and surrounded by a picket fence. Lights showed in the window, and pulling the car to a stop, he got out and staggered toward the door, but collapsed upon the porch against it, as blackness seized him at last.

ii.

From the elevation of the pulpit, the Reverend Daniel Sears looked down upon his congregation and a familiar sense of exaltation and power flooded through him. The sea of faces lifted expectantly and silently to him were the new Israel. And, like the Prophet Ezekiel of old, he was called to warn them before they were destroyed.

The air conditioning system back of the chancel poured freshly cooled zephyrs through metal ducts to all parts of the church. The white painted walls reflected the sunlight streaming through the south windows, filling the house of God with His glory and crowning the Reverend Daniel Sears with a golden halo. Indeed, he felt like God Himself, as he stood there, resplendent in a robe of white satin with gold embroidery at neck and wrists, while the muted coughs, the shuffling feet, died to a whisper.

Before him upon the table below the pulpit was the offering to the Lord but most of all he knew, to himself. Silver, greenbacks, and chaste white envelopes filled the collection plates to overflowing for the Church of Prophecy were a loyal flock; farmers, grove owners, workmen, even good union men from the shops at the Cape, all white and firmly convinced that the Lord had never intended for the Sons of Cain to work with the tools of a trade but only with the hoe, the shovel, and the plow. Fond of their God-given right to join together for their own protection, the parishioners flocked to the Church of Prophecy each Sunday—except when special work offered overtime pay —to hear their shepherd bring the word of God to his flock.

Daniel Sears himself was eminently qualified in the eyes of his congregation to speak it, too. Six feet two, his face ruddy, his hair blond and wavy, his eyes blue, he could have been a god himself—in an Italian silk suit beneath the satin robe.

No one asked whether God might possibly have selected a humbler being to preach the gospel brought to earth by His Son. The Reverend Daniel Sears rarely preached from the New Testament—and then only to cite the redemptive blood of a Christ sent to earth as a substitute for the sacrificial lamb of the Old Testament. Not for Daniel Sears was the gentle doctrine of loving one another, of laying one's life down for a friend. The Old Testament prophets were his heroes; their obscure fulminations his gospel.

Instinctively realizing that his lack of a college degree left him unfitted intellectually to debate theology with the occasional member of the congregation who might have been capable of it, he chose instead the teachings of his counterparts in olden times. Men of the people, the prophets of old had been simple and largely silent until the hand of the Lord had come upon them and they began to shout forth the catalogue of wrongs committed by an Israel that had drifted away from the course God had set for it by parting the waters of the Red Sea for their passage and then sending that same flood sweeping in shortly afterward to swallow up the pursuing Egyptians.

When Daniel Sears shouted the Word of God from his pulpit, denouncing the whoredoms of the new Israel while he clutched a Bible in a fist browned from sunny afternoons on the golf course, what feminine heart could but flutter at the guilty thought of whoredom with the Reverend Daniel Sears himself, a man who came to your bed in the daytime, fresh, strong, and smelling of lemon, not sweaty and tired after a hard day's work, or half drunk from Firday or Saturday night binges.

Daniel Sears was as indefatigable in his pastoral counseling, too, as he was in expounding the murky sermons of the old prophets of Israel from his pulpit on Sunday. To the dying, he brought the assurance of a brighter land in the sky to which they would shortly ascend, propelled by the rockets of faith, joy, and anticipation. To the old, he brought assurance that, even though the world had seemingly passed them by and their offspring no longer appeared to want them, a welcoming God waited in the sky to accept them with open arms, a God who did not change, he assured them, any more than did the simple credo of redemption through confession and faith.

To the young wife, Daniel Sears brought a glimpse—and often more —of that bright glow of happiness she'd somehow lost in the physical reality of marriage. He brought, too, the promise of what love could be in the hands of an experienced lover, an ecstasy which somehow thereafter became a part of her religion but, like most religious beliefs, required the miracle of being regularly born again—more often than not in the arms of the handsome preacher.

As much as he loved the sermons he thundered from the pulpit on Sunday, Daniel Sears loved his pastoral duties more. He loved the men who, because they were interested first of all in their own pleasure, so often left their wives unfulfilled. He loved the children who went gaily off to school in the bright Florida sunlight each morning, leaving the young mother at home alone when he came to call. He loved the young girls who, when puberty stirred a strange disturbing warmth within their bodies and filled them with desires that were both scary and exciting, were disappointed by the uncertain fumblings of inept boys in the back seats of the cars and thereafter eagerly receptive to the skilled caresses of one who showed them what love could really be. Most of all, he loved the young housewives who, suntanned and bikini clad—in a climate where summers were muggy and the pool always inviting the garment was almost a feminine uniform at home—greeted him so warmly on his pastoral visits.

Looking out across the congregation now, he could count dozens of nubile young women sitting sedately with their husbands, their eyes lifted up to drink in his words, even as their bodies had received a considerably more tangible token of his presence. And as he mentally selected those whom pastoral duties required that he visit during the coming week, the memory of other such visits filled him with new zeal.

Opening his Bible, Daniel Sears held it out before him like a weapon, largely because he was beginning to have trouble reading at ordinary distances without the glasses no god should wear.

"The Prophet Ezekiel," he read, "says; *'And I looked, and, behold, a whirlwind came out of the north, a great cloud, and a fire infolding itself, and a brightness was about it, and out of the midst thereof as the color of amber, out of the midst of the fire. Also out of the midst thereof came the likeness of four living creatures. And this was their appearance; they had the likeness of a man. . . .'"*

He paused to let the significance of what he had read become apparent to these people who had so often witnessed the cloud and the fire to the north, and heard on television and radio the voices of the men who were in the midst of the fire.

"*'And when they went,'"* he resumed reading, "*'I heard the noise of their wings, like the noise of great waters, as the voice of the Almighty, the voice of speech, as the noise of an host. . . . And there was a voice from the firmament that was over their heads, when they stood and had let down their wings. . . . As the appearance of the bow that is in the cloud in the day of rain, so was the appearance of the brightness round about. This was the appearance of the likeness of the glory of the Lord. And when I saw it, I fell upon my face, and I heard a voice of one that spake. . . .*

"*'And he said unto me, Son of man, I send thee to the children of Israel, to a rebellious nation that hath rebelled against me; they and their fathers have transgressed against me, even unto this very day. For they are impudent children and stiffhearted. I do send thee unto them; and thou shalt say unto them, Thus saith the Lord God. And they, whether they will hear, or whether they will forbear (for they are a rebellious house) yet shall know that there hath been a prophet among them.'"*

He read again the words, *"Yet shall know that there hath been a prophet among them,"* pausing while the process of association with his own shining person took place in their minds.

"*'And thou, Son of Man,'"* he continued, "*'be not afraid of them, neither be afraid of their words, though briers and thorns be with thee, and thou dost dwell among scorpions; be not afraid of their words, nor be dismayed at their looks, though they be a rebellious house. And thou shalt speak my words unto them, whether they will hear or whether they will forbear; for they are most rebellious.'"*

Slowly, impressively, Daniel Sears closed the Bible but continued to hold it in his right hand like a sword.

"Dearly beloved." Seeing a warm light start to glow in a dozen pairs of feminine eyes, he knew each of their possessors understood that he was speaking especially to her. It was a familiar experience but one that always filled him with the final sense of power he needed to launch himself into his sermon.

"Dearly beloved." He rolled the phrase upon his tongue as he recalled how many lips had become soft and eager beneath his own at those same words, spoken under somewhat different circumstances. "You have heard the words of the Prophet Ezekiel but, though they were spoken in an ancient time to a rebellious people who had gone whoring after false gods, they could just as well have been spoken from this pulpit on this very day. Listen while I read them again:

"'And I looked, and, behold, a whirlwind came out of the north, a great cloud, and a fire infolding itself, and a brightness was about it, and out of the midst thereof as the color of amber, out of the midst of the fire. Also out of the midst thereof came the likeness of four living creatures. And this was their appearance; they had the likeness of a man.'*

"Could not the great cloud and the fire infolding itself be, in fact, the exhaust of the great machines which, in his impudent blasphemy, man is even now manufacturing to carry him on journeys into the firmament, perhaps even to the very gates of heaven itself? I say to you that it can and that it is.

"Think upon it beloved: how clearly do the words of Ezekiel describe the spaceships in which man now seeks to travel beyond the moon even to the planet Mars and to Venus—to God's own stars. Stars which, if God had asked us to know them, He would have brought down to earth for us to see and to touch.

"Our God is a loving God; He forgave us when we sent men to the moon, for scientists tell us the moon is but a chunk of earth, torn out by God on the day of its creation. The Holy Book itself tells us that in the beginning, God created heaven and earth, so the moon is but a part of the earth given us through the infinite mercy of the Heavenly Father to illuminate the night that we might not go in complete darkness."

His pause for effect was somewhat diluted when a toothless old man in the front row mumbled, "Amen," but Daniel Sears regained his stride and continued, his voice rising now:

"We can count it an evidence of God's love that He did not destroy a rebellious people when they dared journey to the moon, although the evidence of His displeasure was there for all who have eyes to see, when three men were consumed by the fires of heaven. How can we expect Him to stand by then, if we seek to unlock other secrets of His firmament, secrets which only God Himself has a right to know?

"Could the 'whirlwind from the north' be anything save the whirlwind of sound that assails our ears until it threatens to destroy our hearing? Or the fire that infolds itself other than the flame which lights up the sky when man seeks to harness the power that only God can dispense, so he may hurl himself beyond the boundaries set by God Himself?

"I say to you beloved that we are already beginning to reap the whirlwind. As surely as the wrath of God against a rebellious people was foretold by Ezekiel, the flame of which he spoke can destroy those who dare to question the Providence of God by invading the skies, of which the psalmist says:

> The heavens declare the glory of God;
> And the firmament sheweth his handiwork . . .
> His going forth is from the end of the heaven
> And his circuit unto the ends of it:
> And there is nothing hid from the heat thereof.

"Beware the wrath of God, my children." Daniel Sears' eyes moved swiftly over the congregation, as he thrust forth his Bible like a rod to deter them physically from sin. The glaze of verbal hypnosis in many an eye told him he had them in the palm of his hand but it was the young woman sitting in the front pew who arrested his gaze.

About thirty, she was a bit on the plump side, which he liked. And though not beautiful, she was vitally alive, which was far to be preferred. Her modestly short dress revealed a really remarkable pair of legs and, even as he intoned the sonorous phrases of the psalm, he racked his brain for her name.

Her husband was an important engineer with Taggar Aircraft, that much he remembered. And from the faraway look in the man's eyes as he sat beside his wife in the front row, he was probably even then working out some intricate problem in engineering rather than listening to the sermon.

Bits and pieces of memory began to form a pattern in Daniel Sears' mind while he continued to repeat the words of the psalm. They had come to the Cape about three months ago, and lived in the more expensive section of Spaceport City. All of which was good; he'd been wanting members among the affluent families of the island and beach communities, and this might be the entree he needed, especially with one so absorbed.

Sandra—Daniel Sears remembered suddenly—Sandra and Thomas Craven. He must pay them a pastoral call this very week, he decided, preferably in the morning, when the engineer-husband wasn't likely to be home. And the matter settled, he once more devoted his full attention to the sermon:

"Beware lest thou forget the Lord thy God and not keep His commandments and His judgments and His statutes," he thundered. "Lest when thou hath eaten and are full and hath builded goodly houses and dwelt therein; and when thy herds and thy flocks multiply and thy silver and thy gold is multiplied and all thou hast is multiplied; then thine heart be lifted up and thou forget the Lord thy God. . . .

"And thou say in thine heart, 'My power and the might of mine hand hath gotten me this wealth.' And it shall be, if thou do at all forget the Lord thy God and serve other gods to worship them, I testify against you this day that thou shalt surely perish. As the nations which the Lord destroyed before your face, so shall you perish because you would not be obedient unto the voice of the Lord your God."

Pausing he raised his hands and intoned the benediction, leaving them all a little stunned with the promised threat of God's wrath. While the choir sang the final amen, he strode down the central aisle of the church to the vestibule, like a king preparing to greet his subjects.

CHAPTER IX

A shaft of sunlight shining through a window and striking his face finally wakened Mike Barnes. Of what had happened since he'd stumbled up on the porch of Yvonne Lang's small cottage, he had little memory, except occasional mental images of a crouching, fear-ridden creature, riding a flaming chariot to a horrible waiting death.

He also recalled being violently ill and having been supported by a woman, while he drank glass after glass of ice water, losing much of it again and drinking more. And finally he had a definite memory of swallowing some foaming liquid, which she gave him before he fell back once again into oblivion.

Now, he found himself in a woman's room, judging by the draperies, the dressing table, and the jars upon it. The bed was three-quarter size but was mussed only in the center where he lay.

"Decided to live?" He raised himself high enough upon his elbows to see Yvonne Lang, wearing white Capri pants and a blouse, standing in the door. But the movement set up such a throbbing agony in his head that he fell back on the bed while the room whirled about him, instinctively clutching at the covers to keep from falling off the bed.

"Take these." Yvonne Lang's arm supported him as she handed him two yellow tablets and a glass of water.

"What is it?"

"Percodan. My doctor prescribes it for migraine."

He swallowed the tablets and the rest of the water, then lay back upon the pillow. Percodan, he knew, was a powerful pain killer and probably just what he needed, considering the throbbing in his head.

"How about some coffee?" she asked. "I doubt if you can handle anything else."

"If it isn't any trouble."

"A handsome man flops on my doorstep—out cold. I stay up half the night while he has nightmares and upchucks all over the place. Now he asks me if it's any trouble."

"I'm sorry."

"Think nothing about it, chum; I seem to have a habit of picking up strays. You certainly work fast though. From the way you were loaded when you got here you must have jumped into Spaceport City night life with both feet. Good thing the cop who helped me put you to bed was friendly."

"A policeman?"

"Apparently he was following you to make sure you didn't bust up somebody and yourself into the bargain. The Spaceport City police are used to giving celebrities that sort of protection. But how did you manage to get so loaded?"

"Would you believe I only had a stinger?"

She brought the coffee and poured a steaming cup for him. "I wouldn't believe it if anybody else told me, but strangely enough I do when you say it."

"Thanks."

"Care to tell me what happened—off the record of course?"

"I was at somebody's house. They were playing a game—"

"You were IT from the looks of things when you got here."

"I left before they could start another count—"

"Say no more, friend," Yvonne Lang interposed quickly. "The less I know about that, the better off I am."

"I'd better go."

"Get some more coffee into you first," she advised. "Or you'll pass out again before you get to the motel."

He drank two more cups and felt his head begin to settle as well as his stomach.

"Any idea what it was in the drink?" Yvonne Lang asked.

"My guess would be methamphetamine—what the kids call 'Speed.'"

"It certainly had you in high gear for a while; you rode that nightmare until early this morning. Then I finally got some Alka-Seltzer into you."

"I owe you a lot."

"Think nothing about it; after all you gave me a good story Friday afternoon. Read it in the Spaceport *Call* when you get back to the motel; my guess is it may be picked up by the wire services and my name might even get into the big time."

"I hope it does. I must be leaving now."

"I can't let you be seen coming out of here looking like a bum; or the neighbors will think I'm losing my touch. There's shaving cream and a razor in the bathroom."

"You look almost human again," she complimented him when he came out. "Sure you feel like driving to the motel?"

"I'll make it—thanks again."

"Any time, friend Mike. Just give me a little warning next time; I'm not always here alone. And bring your own pajamas, I never could see anything romantic about male underwear."

ii.

You really had to hand it to the pentecostal preachers, Tom Craven had been thinking while the Reverend Daniel Sears was working himself into the sermon. Their stuff was always predictable, so you didn't have to listen closely to know what had been said—or what was coming next.

Sandra loved it, though. The shouting and the thundering were part of her South Carolina small-town heritage and, even though it all made about as much sense as the ravings of a schizophrenic he'd once studied in psychology lab at MIT—when the sudden rush into the humanities had seized the technical schools—Tom was grateful to people like the Reverend Daniel Sears, nevertheless.

He'd taken Sandra to a pentecostal sect outdoors rally and all-day preaching, while she was still a college student in South Carolina and he was working on a project at the Atomic Energy Commission plant on the Savannah River southeast of Augusta, Georgia. They'd had sort of an understanding up to then, but he'd never been able to get to first base with her until the night of the pentecostal revival, when he'd discovered the effect this sort of preaching had on her. She'd gotten so steamed up—"turned on" would be the phrase now—that on the way home they'd had to cool off in a country lake *au naturel*—with equally natural consequences.

John Steinbeck had written a scene like that in the *Grapes of Wrath*, he'd remembered while Daniel Sears thundered on. In his and Sandra's case, however, it had all worked out fine. She wasn't the most intelligent girl in the world but who wanted a contest of wits at home after a day spent keeping yourself from being replaced by a computer.

Nobody could want a better wife than Sandra either and, even though he'd had to neglect her since Taggar Aircraft had put such a priority tag on getting that big metal cylinder of the space station into orbit, he was sure she'd been happy in Spaceport City—especially now that she'd found a Church of Prophecy.

With Sandra's problem solved Tom's mind inevitably went to the thing that was troubling him most, the question of how to use the metal tanks forming the second stage of Pegasus as a reservoir for fuel and still be able somehow to use the shell of the stage itself to form a laboratory sufficiently large for men to move about in and perform various types of work, as well as study the strange world through which they would be hurtling in orbit all the while.

He'd been pondering the question for a week without any inkling of a solution. But now, as he listened to the sermon with half an ear, something from the perorations of the Prophet Ezekiel about a great wheel in the sky brought to mind again the words of a Negro spiritual he'd heard long ago:

> "Ezekiel saw the wheel,
> Way up in the middle of the air,
> A wheel in a wheel,
> Way up in the middle of the sky."

"A wheel in a wheel!" The words rang so loudly in his brain that he looked around quickly to see whether he'd actually spoken them aloud. But Sandra's eyes were still glued to the handsome face of the preacher and those on either side of them seemed to be in a similar state of rapt contemplation, so he was sure the words had not actually been spoken.

They were the answer though; no doubt about it. Too bad it had come too late to be available for the first Pegasus launch, but it would be ideal for the second section that would be orbited later and attached to the first, doubling the size of the space laboratory.

Actually, the whole thing was so simple, he wondered why he hadn't thought of it before. In the massive second stage of Pegasus, the fuel components were separated by a metal bulkhead somewhat similar to the ones used in the earlier Mercury flights. The bulkhead was rigid, however, precluding its removal in orbit but now, the whole problem of making the second stage function both as a propulsive unit for the rocket and as the outer wall of the laboratory, once its fuel was spent had suddenly solved itself. Like the wheel in a wheel of Ezekiel, two tanks holding the fuels whose combustion together created the propulsive force of the second stage could be encased in an outer shell, with a plastic insulation bulkhead effectively separating them to absorb the shock of launch and prevent them from rupturing into each other and causing the sort of giant explosion that was a constant nightmare to the rocket men.

Once the fuel inside the two tanks was used up, the huge metal outer shell would first be locked into rendezvous with the rest of the Pegasus units already in orbit. And then explosive charges could expel the two inner tanks from the outer one very much like Tom himself, as a boy, had shot spitballs out of a gun made from a section of pith elder shrub.

Actually, his racing brain decided, there was no real reason why the two inner tanks couldn't also be put to use, even after they were expelled from the larger cylinder. It should be a relatively simple matter to attach a tether to them; then after they were blown out of the main compartment, they could be drawn alongside later by an astronaut working outside in a space suit during extra-vehicular activity—popularly called EVA.

Bolted into place then, windows could be cut from the inside into the auxiliary tanks and they could be used as additional rooms for the space vehicle, perhaps to store such things as the harvest of meteroids to be snared by a giant net device even then being manufactured in California.

A sharp nudge in the ribs from Sandra's elbow reminded Tom that the Reverend Daniel Sears had finished his sermon and they were to stand for the benediction.

"Wasn't he wonderful?" she asked as they moved up the aisle toward the door.

"If you like your prophecies loud—yes."

"Maybe there's something in what he was saying, Tom. You know there's been a lot of trouble at the Cape and Pegasus *is* eventually going farther out than anything else has ever been."

"That argument was used against human progress as far back as the Stone Age, hon," he said. "It's all right for preachers, particularly this kind, but an educated man can blast those arguments to smithereens in a few minutes."

"Mr. and Mrs. Craven!" The Reverend Daniel Sears greeted them warmly. "Nice to see you again."

"We enjoyed your sermon so much, Reverend," said Sandra.

"Some of these people you're preaching to work over on the Cape, Reverend," said Tom. "Did you ever stop to think that, if the Lord wants us to stop all our work over there, a lot of them are going to be out of jobs."

"The Lord will provide, Mr. Craven," the preacher said piously. "The Lord will provide."

"Yeah," Tom Craven said *sotto voce*, as they moved out into the churchyard. "Sorghum, grits, and sowbelly, instead of roast beef and light bread. But a lot of people aren't going to like going back to that diet again—or pellagra either."

"Shshh!" said Sandra. "Do you want them to hear you?"

"Maybe they ought to listen, but for most of them, what the curly haired Reverend was saying went in one ear and out the other anyway. Something really important is where do we go for dinner?"

"How about the Space Club?"

"Fine. We can have a drink there before dinner. Then I've got to run over to the plant for about an hour—"

"Oh, Tom, do you have to?"

"'Fraid so."

"But you practically live there."

"You can blame the preacher for my having to go today; he helped me solve a problem that's going to win me another promotion and couple of thousand extra a year in salary, but I've got to get a sketch of the idea down on a drawing board before it leaves me. Tell you what—why don't you stay on at the club after dinner for a while and have a swim. I'll come by about four and we'll take in a movie or something."

"Okay. If you promise not to be late."

"This shouldn't take me more than an hour and a half or so at most."

"The last time you left me at the club, I had to catch a ride home with the Thompsons and you didn't get in 'til midnight." Her tone was peevish again, as it was much of the time lately. "What you're really married to is that rocket you're building. Sometimes I really hate it."

iii.

Mike had gone back to sleep, after reaching the motel safely, when the telephone rang.

"Are you all right?" It was Jan.

"Yes. What time is it?"

"Nearly noon. When you didn't call me at ten, as you promised, I got worried."

"I forgot to set the clock when I went to bed last night and overslept." It seemed to be the simplest explanation. "What shall we do with the afternoon?"

"There's no school tomorrow because of a teachers' meeting, but I'm taking some music students to Orlando for competition early Monday morning, so I can't stay out late."

"We'd better get started early then."

"I have to run over some selections with my students early this afternoon but I can pick you up afterwards if you like. We could take some steaks and broil them in the waterfront park north of Spaceport Beach."

"Sounds wonderful to me."

"I can probably get away around four-thirty. They've got grills up there and we can have a swim before dinner."

"What can I bring?"

"We'll stop at a Seven-Eleven on the way to the beach and pick up a six-pack. I'll bring the cooler and you can get a bag of ice there. Shall we say about four-thirty."

"That will be fine."

"Better wear your swim trunks under your slacks," she said. "Dressing facilities at the park are pretty primitive."

In the motel restaurant, Mike had ham and eggs and a pot of steaming coffee, which quickly cleared away the vestiges of last night's drug effects. As he was leaving, he picked up a copy of the Sunday edition of the Spaceport *Call* from a rack beside the entrance to the restaurant.

Yvonne Lang's feature was on the front page of the second section, devoted to local news, with the headline:

"EX-ASTRONAUT DESCRIBES ENGINEER PERSONALITY."

She had faithfully set down what he had told her, adding a sharp word picture of Mike himself and leaving a question as to his reason for coming to Spaceport City. To his surprise, however, two columns bracketing the feature about him were devoted to comments on his opinions. One was an interview with Paul Taggar, identified as president of Taggar Aircraft, with the headline:

"NO AEROSPACE SYNDROME HERE—TAGGAR."

The interview described Spaceport City as an ideal community, peopled, it seemed, by right-living, churchgoing folk, whose idea of an exciting evening was a Rotary Club fish fry.

On the other side of Yvonne's feature was a second headline:

"BARNES THEORY HOGWASH, SAYS SCIENTIST."

The latter was a brief diatribe against Mike himself by Dr. Abram McCandless.

Mike was still reading the paper, when his telephone rang. It was Yvonne Lang.

"Seen the paper?" she asked.

"Yes."

"I just wanted you to know it wasn't my idea to have Paul Taggar and McCandless attack you from both flanks. The city room took care of that after I turned in my copy. When I called Art this morning to raise hell about it, he told me the orders came from the top."

"Paul Taggar?"

"Yes. Art's a straight shooter, except when he's issued instructions from higher up; then he doesn't have any choice. Hope it didn't upset you."

"Not at all. The Army calls what they did 'protecting your flank.' Have you seen that chick McCandless is hooked up with?"

"Who could miss her, particularly in profile? I hear she's already putting horns on the old boy with a service station operator, though. The word around town is that McCandless is fit to be tied."

"Thanks again for looking after me last night."

"I could have looked after you a lot better, if you'd been conscious," she told him. "Worse luck for me."

"And for me, too, I'm sure."

"Thanks for the gallantry. Drop by sometime."

As Mike was transferring the contents of his jacket pocket into the slacks he was planning to wear over swim trunks that afternoon, he noticed the small white disk Hal Brennan had dropped into his pocket along with the card last night.

The number printed on it was five—and its significance hit him like a blow in the midriff.

If he'd allowed himself to become excited enough by what he'd seen on the closed circuit screen, plus the drug and the stinger, to visit the guest house when the lights went down for what Shirley had called the fifth inning, he knew now that he would have found her in the red-tinted semi-darkness of the room. And remembering even after eight years how that could be quickened his pulse. Most intriguing of all, however, was the question of the motive behind Hal's attempt to involve him again with Shirley.

Could it be, as Art McCord had intimated, that Hal Brennan wished to get rid of her by involving him? Or was there a deeper purpose which, knowing Hal, he was more prepared to accept?

CHAPTER X

It was four o'clock but, with Daylight Saving Time, still bright and warm, when there was a knock on the door. Mike opened it to find Jan outside wearing a skirt buttoned over her swim suit and an open shirt, revealing a trim blue maillot. When he drew her to him, she didn't resist and her lips were soft and alive beneath his own.

"There." She pushed herself away after a moment but her cheeks were flushed and her breathing quicker. "Don't get the wrong idea, just because you caught me the other night with my defenses down."

"I was pretty defenseless myself."

"Judging from the anxiety you showed the other morning at the station when the missile was launched and again in the nightmare, you must have gone through a real ordeal during your flight."

"Let's forget about all that. Have I told you how lovely you are? And what a beautiful tan you have."

"It took a lot of suntan oil and a bikini to get it."

"Why didn't you wear one today?"

"You already know what I look like by moonlight and they say that's the most flattering of all to the female form. Besides, you're not exactly made of stone and neither am I. Shall we go?"

"Why did you really come back here, Mike?" she asked some twenty minutes later, when they had parked the car on a level strip of land near the beach and carried the picnic ice chest to a spot near one of the grates for building cooking fires just above the water's edge.

"Maybe to relive old times." He spread a blanket out in a clear spot on the sand.

"Even though they bring you pain?"

"So you know the truth about the 'Space Chicken'?"

"You said enough during your nightmare to arouse my curiosity, so yesterday I stopped at the local library and read the newspaper accounts of what happened to you eight years ago. I don't believe you were chicken, Mike."

"Hal Brennan does; he testified to it at the hearing."

"I think Hal knows better, too; that's why he's wary of you." It was the second time she'd mentioned Hal's reaction to him and, remembering last night, he was beginning to think she might be right.

"Does it disturb you to talk about it?" she asked.

"A little."

"Then don't."

"I want you of all people to know what really happened. The newspapers didn't say I was almost unconscious from oxygen poisoning, when the spacecraft landed. Or that I had been fighting convulsions and blackouts all the way down."

"Why didn't you claim that in your defense at the hearing?"

"I tried to but I wasn't real sure of it myself then. Besides, you don't get a chance to explain much to a congressional committee with a man like Israel Pond as chairman. And, of course, the spacecraft had sunk so I had no proof that the oxygen control valves didn't operate properly."

"Did you come back hoping to find some proof?"

"After eight years that's almost too much to hope for, I'm afraid." He told her about Lars Todt and the senator's questions about the Pegasus program, adding what he discovered himself since coming to the Cape. He didn't mention his visit to Hal Brennan's house and the game being played there, however. Or his nightmare journey to Yvonne Lang's cottage.

"Jerry McGrath will be command pilot of the first Pegasus flight," she said.

"The astronaut you're engaged to?"

"It isn't exactly an engagement, more of an understanding. Both of us are free to see other people."

"If I were your fiancé, I doubt if I could be so generous."

"I set the conditions, Mike. I was married once before and I'm not about to go rushing into it again."

"That puts us even at the start. Why don't we take a swim?"

The surf was alive with heads, and far out where the breakers rushing shoreward started to topple over, a group of young people with surfboards were riding the crests. When Jan unbuttoned her skirt and stepped out of it, he saw that she was as sweetly curved as he remembered from the moonlight glimpse in his motel room two nights before. She was a strong swimmer, too, and he had to stretch himself to keep up with her.

"I missed this most of all while I was away," he said as they paused upon a sand bar halfway between the breaker line and the shallows. The water just touched their shoulders and lifted them whenever a wave swept past to break upon the sand.

"I don't get to swim much," said Jan. "We're trying to build a youth orchestra and that means practice late in the afternoons. Then I have private pupils on the side, plus my work at the inn."

"Why not let up a little?"

"In the TGIF society, women who aren't busy usually find ways to occupy themselves. It's easy to become promiscuous when the opportunities are so many."

"Is that why you're half engaged—as protection for your independence?"

"Partly, I suppose. Jerry's an air force major; this will be his first space flight."

A large wave swept past them just then and, as they were lifted from their feet, she floated into his arms. The onrushing breaker hid them from the shore and he held her close to kiss her, disturbingly conscious of the touch of her body against his own. But when his hands crept up to cup her breasts, she dived through his arms and came up racing for the shore with an effortless crawl. He followed, but was panting when he waded across the narrow beach to where she was already drying her hair with a towel beside the blanket.

"Wait'll I'm in shape again," he warned as he dropped to the blanket. "I'll outswim you then."

She reached into the cooler and took out a can of beer, opening it and handing it to him. "Here's something to revive you."

"I could do with a little pampering. All you've done so far is to show me up as a second-best swimmer."

"I doubt if you've ever accepted second best long, Mike." She opened a can for herself and lay down upon the blanket beside him.

"I'm not sure I wasn't doing that for the eight years I've been away."

"From what you say of your work at Anderson, I don't think so," she said. "You were exploring a new field there and proving you were right about what happened to your ship at the same time. From what you told Yvonne Lang in the interview in the paper this morning, it seems you've made yourself an authority in other fields, too."

"That was something of an accident. They were having a lot of equipment failures at a plant near Anderson and someone got the idea they might be due to human error."

"Why were you chosen for the study?"

"I'd written a few papers on the subject earlier, which made me an expert as far as FSA was concerned. The rocket business puts a special strain on people, whether they're building them at the factory or getting one ready to go on the pad, and once I had studied a few of the people involved, it was pretty easy to come up with the truth that personality problems were to blame for most of the failures."

"Why did you put the burden of the guilt on engineers?"

"For one thing, they occupy most of the important positions at the decision-making level. I'd read about the engineer personality earlier and, when I looked it up again, the whole thing simply fell into place."

"A lot of people aren't going to like you for pointing out their weaknesses."

"Paul Taggar and Dr. McCandless have clobbered me already."

"Paul's a driver like most successful executives. He has a big house on the ocean and with such a big investment in both Spaceport City and Pegasus he'd naturally attack you for intimating that either is less than perfect."

"What about McCandless?"

"He's got troubles enough to keep him disturbed. You saw one of them the other night."

"You're a remarkably good judge of human nature."

"Perhaps because I've had what you might call a crash course in it. Before Bob and I had been married very long, I realized he had chosen me because I resembled his mother."

"That usually doesn't make for a satisfactory marriage."

"It didn't in this case either. But I was so trusting then that I didn't even know there was someone else—until I saw her at the funeral."

"That must have been a shock."

"Not really. Bob and I were already on the point of getting a divorce when his jet flamed out. He finally made an important decision on his own then—not to bail out. But it cost him his life and I've never been sure I wasn't partly to blame for not making him take more responsibility earlier."

"Is that why you haven't married again?"

"I don't want to make the same mistake twice, Mike. It took me quite a while to get over the first one."

"It was the same with me. By the way Shirley came to see me at the motel yesterday morning."

"That means she's still interested in you."

"I don't flatter myself that much. Hal sent her to find out why I came back."

"Did you tell her?"

"Nothing she and Hal didnt' already know, I'm sure. The grapevine has always had an open line between here and Washington. But I've found another reason for staying, since I got here—you."

"Any girl would be flattered to have you interested in her, Mike. But

I think the real reason why you came back is the need to prove something to yourself."

"You seem to know me even better than I know myself," he said wryly. "Before I left California, it had been almost a year since I'd had one of the nightmares—"

"And here you may have a chance to bury the demon once and for all?"

"I hope so—with your help. Is it a deal?"

Her eyes twinkled. "Not if you expect the same sort of fringe benefits every time. Let's get the steaks going, I'm hungry."

It was dark by the time they finished eating; when Mike looked at his watch, he was surprised to see that it was after nine o'clock.

"We'll have to be getting back," said Jan. "I've got to go to Orlando early in the morning with my students."

"What about tomorrow night?"

"I probably won't get back from Orlando before ten o'clock and Tuesday's a school day. If the music competition runs long, I might even stay over there tomorrow night and drive back early Tuesday morning."

"I'll call you Tuesday night then."

It took them only a little while to pack up what they'd brought and deposit it in the car. Just outside the park, where the level of the dunes rose again, hiding the beach and the ocean from the road, a string of cars was parked along the shoulder near a path leading over the dunes.

"Do you suppose the whiting could be running?" Mike asked. "It's been a long time since I've seen anybody seining for them on the beach."

"They might be. Let's go see."

Parking the car on the side of the road at the end of the line, they walked back along the shoulder to the path leading up over the dunes. As he was about to step off the pavement, Mike noticed something that looked like a strip of silver shining on the black hardtop and reached down to pick it up and drop it into the pocket of his shirt.

The moon was just rising over the crest of a ridge of dunes marking the landward edge of the beach, and although they had to dodge clumps of palmetto and an occasional stumpy palm, they had little trouble following the path as it wound back and forth across the piled-up sand. At the top, they found themselves looking down upon a strange and macabre scene; recognizing its significance, Mike quickly drew Jan behind a stunted palm so they wouldn't be seen.

ii.

A fire, such as fishermen often built when dragging their seines at night during the run of whiting, had been built well above the water's edge, but Mike saw no fishermen. Instead, a dozen or so ghost-like figures were weaving crazily about in the light of the fire, while others splashed and shrieked in the surf or lay upon blankets spread upon the sand, locked in close embrace.

Like macabre figures out of Washington Irving, many of those capering about the fire seemed to have two heads. And in the ghostly glow of the rising moon, Mike could almost believe they had stumbled upon some Walpurgisnight celebration, or a festival of witches such as were said to gather still in England and in central Europe—if he hadn't instantly realized the true nature of the scene upon which they had stumbled.

A battery-powered radio was playing a rock and roll tune and some of those about the fire were writhing in rhythm to the music. All were in bathing suits and most of the girls wore the extremely brief bikinis that had become almost a uniform for swimmers in this climate. But, while obviously human, the seeming appearance of the two heads also gave them the aspect of hobgoblins, a strange sight indeed here on the beach more than a month before Halloween.

Farther away from the fire, but not troubling to remove themselves from sight of the main group, others were engaged in a much more easily identifiable activity, their naked bodies locked together. Seeing them, Jan gasped with horror and moved close to Mike in the protection of the stunted palms behind which they were standing.

When a two-headed figure near the fire suddenly pulled off one of its heads and tossed it toward the coals, the globular object exploded in a sudden gush of flames, illuminating the scene momentarily with a bright light and giving it an even stranger character than before. The spurt of flame was gone as quickly as it had come, but others now tossed their second heads upon the fire and the pop of exploding paper bags filled the air.

Mike didn't need to look again at the small object he'd picked up beside the road, as they started across the dunes. He already knew it could only be a tube of the kind of cement used to glue together the parts of plastic models of airplanes, boats, and other objects. In spite of the warning printed on similar tubes—"Contains toluol: do not breathe vapors"—it was still the cheapest and quickest, as well as the most potentially lethal, of the various means used by young people to achieve the state of being "turned on."

"What is it, Mike?" Jan asked in a whisper.

"Glue sniffing." He took the small tube from his pocket so she could see it in the pale light of the moon. "From things like this."

"How awful! Can't we stop them?"

"That stuff drives kids literally out of their minds. In the state they're in now, anything could happen if they should discover us."

While they watched, one of the revelers, a slender girl in a white one-piece bathing suit, noticeable particularly because she was more completely covered than most of the others, many of whom had dispensed with clothing entirely, ran shrieking toward the water. Wobbling about and almost falling more than once, she tumbled into the foam where the shallow waves were breaking upon the shore. A tall boy chasing her pulled her to her feet and they staggered to a blanket, falling upon it together.

"We'd better get out of here," said Mike and Jan made no objection; she stayed close to him as they made their way across the dunes to the car with the shrieks of those on the beach following them like the distant howl of banshees.

They were almost at Jan's convertible, when she stopped beside a sleek and obviously expensive sports car. "I've seen this car, Mike—in Spaceport City," she said.

"Try to remember who it belongs to. We can give the parents a ring when we get to town and tell them what's going on here."

"The name's on the tip of my tongue. I've seen the car around town many times."

"If you were to call the roll down there, on the beach you'd probably find the best names in Spaceport City represented."

She sat close to him in the car, shivering a little, and he put his arm around her as he drove toward town, knowing she was as much disturbed as he was by the scene they had witnessed and most of all by the feeling of being helpless to do anything about it.

"It all reminds me of a story a preacher in the church back home once told in a sermon," said Jan. "A father was walking across the snow —I guess the story stuck in my mind because I'd never seen snow—when he realized he was being followed by his little son. He called back to the boy to be careful, but the child said, 'I can't get lost, Daddy. I'm walking in your steps.' We wonder how kids these days get started on pot and LSD, but after what we saw at Shirley's house the other night, I guess the answer's pretty obvious."

Mike didn't comment. He was wondering what Jan would think if he told her just how near he had been to something even more dangerous than glue sniffing only the night before and admitting to himself that, in not leaving until the effects of the drug had begun to reveal themselves to him, he was perhaps as guilty as those kids on the beach —or the parents whose neglect encouraged such actions.

"Do you mind if I drop you at the motel?" Jan said as he started to turn into the cross street leading to her cottage. "This business has got me pretty upset and I have to get up early anyway to go to Orlando tomorrow."

"Will you be safe going home alone?"

"It's only a few blocks away; I drive it alone all the time after I finish playing at the inn."

"When shall I see you again?" he asked as he kissed her good night in the shadows of the motel parking lot.

"We agreed that you were to give me a ring Tuesday afternoon—but make it late."

"I'd like to take you to dinner Tuesday night."

"On one condition."

"What's that?"

"Let's make it at Howard Johnson's, where we'll be surrounded by nice Midwestern tourists and their families. I need a change from the sophisticated atmosphere of Spaceport City."

iii.

It was nearly eleven-thirty when Jan called Mike on the telephone. "Were you asleep?" she asked.

"I was just finishing the eleven o'clock news."

"So was I. Do you remember the sports car I recognized but couldn't remember who it belonged to?"

"Yes."

"They showed some young people at the beach on the news and I saw that car again. It belongs to Paul Taggar, Mike. His daughter, Ellen, was driving it."

"Are you sure?"

"Absolutely. Do you remember the girl wearing a white one-piece bathing suit, like the blue one I wore this afternoon?"

"Yes."

"Ellen was in a crowd of young people at the beach on the TV news and she was wearing that suit. What can I do, Mike?"

"I'll call the police and report seeing the party," he promised. "If it's still going on, they can send a car to break it up. If you were to call, they would want to know what you were doing on the beach at night."

"What about you?"

"I'll tell them I was with a girl and refuse to give the name. Nobody would expect me to anyway and that way you won't be involved."

"I'm all shook up, Mike. I'd never seen anything like that before."

"It happens pretty regularly; that's one of the things I wrote about in my article on the aerospace syndrome, but Paul Taggar says it doesn't happen in Spaceport City. You go on to bed and don't worry about this, darling. I'll take care of it."

"Thanks, Mike. I feel better already. Good night."

When she hung up, Mike looked up the Spaceport City police and dialed the number.

"Police Department, Sergeant Peters," a man answered.

"Sergeant, this is Dr. Michael Barnes at the Astronaut Inn."

"What can I do for you, Doctor?"

"I was returning from a picnic on the beach front park north of here earlier this evening and saw a number of cars parked beside the road. I thought the whiting might be running and crossed the dunes to the beach but what I ran up on was a bunch of kids having a glue-sniffing party."

"When did you say this was, Doctor?"

"A little after nine o'clock."

"Why didn't you report it earlier?"

"I suppose I should have, Sergeant, but—"

"Wait a minute, Doctor. One of the night prowl cars has just come in from the north end of the beach. I'll ask them if they saw anything."

There was a moment of silence, then the sergeant came back on the phone. "Our men just checked that area, Doctor, and nothing like you described is going on now. Maybe you saw some people swimming on the beach and just thought it was something else." The implication was clear that the police had rather let the matter drop.

"I hardly think so," said Mike. "But if no one's out there now, I won't have to bother you any more."

CHAPTER XI

Mike's sleep was troubled and after an early breakfast he drove to the police station and asked for the chief. He was shown into an office where a heavyset man in a rumpled uniform sat behind a desk smoking a cigar.

"Chief Branigan," he said. "What can I do for you?"

"I'm Dr. Barnes."

"I know. I was a rookie guard for NASA when you were here before."

"Something's going on that I think you ought to know about, Chief."

The policeman lifted his hand wearily. "A lot goes on that we ought to know about, Doctor—and a lot we'd rather not know about. For example, I can tell you practically everything you've done since you arrived here Friday: who you slept with that night—"

"Look here—"

"Spaceport City kind of draws celebrities—people in broadcasting, movies, science, and even in politics. We like to have them here; it helps promote the town. You're sort of a celebrity, too, Dr. Barnes, so we look after your welfare—you know, see that you don't get in any trouble." The chief shook his head sadly. "Sometimes our patience is tried, though—like night before last. The officer following you could have arrested you half a dozen times for driving while drunk—"

"But I—"

"You should thank your stars you're a friend of Colonel Brennan's. When he called and told us you'd just left his place loaded, one of my men followed along to see that you got back safely. From the looks of the report, you must have really tied one on; the man that wrote it said you were lucky to get as far as you did without him having to take you in for your own protection—and everybody else's."

Mike realized it was futile to try to tell the police what had really happened Saturday night, particularly when Branigan probably already knew. It was bad enough that a description of his decidedly random progress from Hal Brennan's house to Yvonne Lang's cottage was already on the record, to say nothing of the fact that Jan Cooper had spent Friday night in his room at the Astronaut Inn.

"Don't bother me unless it's something really important, Dr. Barnes, I've got troubles enough already," the chief continued. "Paul Taggar called me at four o'clock this morning to tell me his daughter didn't come home last night."

"When did Taggar discover she was missing?" Mike asked.

"He came home about midnight and went to bed—"

"Wouldn't you have checked on the girl if she were yours, Chief?"

"Thank God mine are grown and married, but you can't expect an important man like Paul Taggar to remember that today's a school holiday and the kids would be all over the place last night. Taggar's wife got in about one and discovered Ellen was missing. She woke him and he spent the next two hours calling friends she might have stayed with and nursing his wife through an attack of asthma. When he still couldn't find Ellen, he called me."

"Did Taggar and his wife go to separate parties?"

"It's no business of mine who goes to what—as long as they don't get into trouble coming or going, Doctor. But for your information that's the way it's done around here pretty often."

"The TGIF culture."

"What was that?"

"Never mind. Do you have any idea where the girl might be?"

"My guess is that we'll find her shacked up in a motel somewhere with a boy and both of 'em scared to come home. Or she may have decided to go off on her own; all these kids have plenty of money nowadays and their own cars. When she gets ready to let her parents know where she is, she'll do it."

"Maybe she was at a glue party," said Mike.

"What?" He had Branigan's full attention now and he went on to describe the macabre scene he'd witnessed the night before.

"Finding the tubes doesn't prove anything," said the chief. "You can see 'em on the beach any time."

"That stuff can cause permanent brain and liver damage—even death."

"Doc, if kids didn't sniff glue, they'd be smoking pot—a lot of them are doing it anyway. As long as plastic glue and paper bags can be bought in any five-and-ten, how in hell am I going to keep kids from getting high on it."

"In some towns, the stores have volunteered not to sell it except to adults."

"Make the stuff hard to get for kids with the kind of allowances they have in Spaceport City and the first thing you know, we'll have pushers, middlemen, and maybe the Mafia moving in here. A little experimenting with glue looks to me like the lesser of a lot of evils we might have."

"If you'd seen what was going on at the beach last night, you wouldn't shrug it off, Chief," Mike said angrily. "My guess is that some of those kids may have damaged themselves already—to say nothing of how many girls got pregnant."

"You're behind the times, Doctor. A girl can buy a contraceptive foam applicator that looks like a perfume spray or a lipstick in any drugstore nowadays; a lot of them carry those things in their bags when they go out on a date, the ones that aren't on the pill. It isn't considered cool to get pregnant any more and these kids around here are really hep."

"I won't deny that—from what I've seen."

"I've been in this business a long time and it all adds up to the same thing," said the officer wearily. "Everybody's got the right to go to hell in his own way—and usually does. My job is to see that he doesn't take anybody with him who doesn't want to go—like with you Saturday night." The phone rang and the chief picked it up. "Excuse me, please."

Mike was at the door, when he heard Branigan say: "Where did you say they found her?"

He paused while the chief listened briefly, then said, "I'll be there in twenty minutes."

"They found Paul Taggar's daughter," Branigan said as he hung up the phone and reached for his hat.

"Where?"

"Washed ashore on a deserted section of beach at Sebastian Inlet. Some people going fishing found her body this morning."

"Taggar's daughter was on the beach last night," said Mike. "Someone I was with recognized her."

Chief Branigan stopped short at the door and turned back to face Mike. "If I were you I wouldn't repeat what you just said, Doctor."

"Why in hell not?"

"The girl's car was parked in front of Paul Taggar's house when he got home last night; that's why he thought Ellen was already in. Excuse me; I've got to go."

"Mind if I follow you?"

"You come from around here, so you know the way to Sebastian Inlet. But from what the state trooper that just called said, a doctor ain't going to be no help."

It was around sixty miles south of Spaceport City to the narrow inlet that cut through a tongue of land lying between the Indian River and the ocean, forming a connecting passage between it and the Inland Waterway. Traveling at seventy-five miles an hour, Mike was almost halfway there when the chief's car, siren blaring and beacon flashing, passed him. He had only a glimpse of the set, emotion-ravaged face of the man occupying the front seat on his side. But that brief view startled him so much that he almost lost control of his own car.

Paul Taggar had been one of the men at Hal Brennan's Countdown party Saturday night.

ii.

The attendants of a rescue squad ambulance were bringing the body up from the beach when Mike pulled his car to a halt behind half a dozen others parked near the inlet. One look at the girl told him Chief Branigan had been right in saying there wasn't anything a doctor could do for her. Alive she had obviously been pretty, but after some twelve hours in salt water, her skin was shriveled and her hair tangled with kelp. Nor was he surprised to see that she wore a white bathing suit just like the girl he and Jan had seen throw away the glue bag and stagger toward the surf last night.

"The fisherman that found her said she was floating in the shallows," one of the rescue squad men told him. "They pulled her ashore and drained a lot of water from her lungs but couldn't find any heartbeat. She must have drowned hours earlier."

Chief Branigan appeared at Mike's elbow accompanied by a brawny state trooper. "I'll turn in my report to the coroner at Spaceport City," the state officer said to Branigan.

"There'll be an autopsy, won't there?" Mike asked.

"If the coroner orders it," said the trooper.

"The coroner has jurisdiction now," Chief Branigan added pointedly. "We can't do anything more until we get his report."

While the ambulance attendants were putting the body into the vehicle, Mike plucked at the chief's sleeve.

"That girl was among those at the glue party on the beach last night, Chief," he said.

"What makes you think that, Doctor?" The officer's drawl had dropped to an ominous growl.

"We saw only one in a white one-piece suit, the other girls were all wearing bikinis. My friend recognized her car parked on the road with the others, too."

"The moon wasn't very bright, Doctor."

"Bright enough to recognize a Maserati. How many of those are in your town?" He was turning away in disgust, when Chief Branigan caught his sleeve.

"Did you know Ellen Taggar, Doctor?" he asked softly.

"No."

"Are you prepared to swear she was the one you saw?"

"Of course not, but—"

"Would the other witness you mentioned swear to it?"

"I wouldn't ask her to." Mike didn't miss the threat in the officer's tone and with Branigan already knowing Jan had spent Friday night in his room at the motel, he couldn't afford to involve her any further—particularly when nobody could help Ellen Taggar any more.

"Now you're being smart," said the chief.

One other avenue remained, however, by which the truth might be made known and, hopefully, both parents and young people be shocked into realizing what was happening in their supposedly perfect city—the newspaper. When he got back to his motel room, Mike tried to get Yvonne Lang on the phone but she was out on an assignment, so he rang Art McCord's office. The editor, he was told, was back from his fishing trip but was busy in the news plant and not available by phone.

Suspecting a runaround, Mike didn't leave a message but hung up and drove across the tidal stream to where the publishing headquarters of the Spaceport *Call* was located. Art was at his desk when Mike came into the office; the newspaperman gave him a quick glance of appraisal, then got up and closed the door to the outer office where his secretary was working.

"What's eating you, Mike?" he asked.

"The same thing that called you back from your fishing trip—the Taggar girl's death."

"Paul Taggar is the largest stockholder in this newspaper, naturally I came back as soon as I heard Ellen was missing. But I'll never understand why she was fool enough to go swimming alone after dark."

"Is that what they told you?"

Art gave him a searching look. "That's the story we're running in the morning edition. Evidently she decided to go swimming—the Taggars have an ocean front home—and must have been caught in a runout."

"She was caught in a runout all right—her parents."

"What the hell are you talking about, Mike?"

"Has the coroner finished the autopsy?"

"He didn't need one to determine the cause of death; it was drowning."

"But not quite as innocently as you're making it sound, Art."

"Suppose you tell me your version then."

Mike gave a quick running account of what he'd witnessed on the beach last night and his conversation with Chief Branigan.

"Are you absolutely sure about that bathing suit?" the newspaperman asked.

"The other girls—those that wore anything—were mainly in bikinis. Jan saw the car but couldn't remember whose it was, until she saw a film report on the eleven o'clock local news that had been made earlier. It's hard to mistake a Maserati, Art—even in Spaceport City."

"But Branigan says the car was parked in front of the Taggar house when Paul got home."

"Maybe one of the other kids drove it there so nobody would know Ellen was at the party. Or Branigan's men may have found it and driven it home after Paul Taggar called the police."

"Are you sure the kids were sniffing glue?"

Mike took the small flattened tube from his pocket and dropped it on Art McCord's desk blotter. "Call your photographer in; there's the evidence," he said bluntly. "You've got the facts and the girl is dead, so all you have to do is print the real story. If her death helps to keep other kids around here from winding up with liver failure or brain and kidney damage, her life won't have been entirely wasted."

"It's not that simple, Mike."

"Why not?"

"You know as well as I do that kids sniff glue—and do worse everywhere."

"Is that any reason to sweep this particular case under the rug."

"It is when a town's as vulnerable as Spaceport City is. You know what happened at Huntsville and other aerospace centers, when the development work for Apollo ended and the appropriations for FSA were cut back. Scientists and executives who'd been in high income brackets suddenly couldn't get jobs and real estate sales hit bot—"

"What the hell does that have to do with a girl sniffing glue and getting drowned?"

"I'm trying to give you the background," said Art patiently. "After the Manned Spacecraft Center was built in Houston, it was pretty obvious that the space program didn't need all of Merritt Island, but it still took a lot of political finagling before we finally got the government to release some of the land from the Cape Kennedy reservation that wasn't doing anybody any good. When Paul Taggar got the Pegasus contract he moved an assembly factory here and built Spaceport City on the land released from the government reservation—"

"The 'City of Tomorrow—Today'; I've read the advertisements."

"It's a damn good city. The average resident makes over twenty thousand a year, has two cars, a college education, half of a graduate degree—"

"And his children sniff glue weekends while he's blasting off for a trip at Hal Brennan's pad. Or getting drunk with some babe that isn't his wife in a local bar."

"Don't judge us before you've heard all the evidence, Mike."

"Is there more? You've given me a graphic picture of what psychiatrists call the 'aerospace disease'—in a very acute exacerbation. As a doctor, I'd say you've got damn near a fatal epidemic of it right now."

"You're upset, Mike, and I can understand it, but those are the facts of life around any big space complex. So why pick on Spaceport City —unless you're trying to salve your own conscience for what happened to you here eight years ago?"

"That's a hell of a thing to say!"

"I take it back," said Art. "But if you were so disturbed, why didn't you go to the police at once?"

"I didn't want to involve Jan."

"Which makes you guilty of the same sort of neglect you're trying to pin on the parents in our town."

The accusation hurt—mainly because Mike couldn't deny that it was true. "Would the police have done anything?" he asked.

"Of course they would. Branigan's broken up these parties before, without making a *cause célèbre* out of them the way you're trying to do with Ellen Taggar's drowning. Think about that the next time you try to indict a whole city."

"I have thought about it," said Mike soberly. "And I admit my own guilt. But what you've got here is a situation where the innate sickness of other aerospace centers could feed on each other. The volcano's almost ready to erupt, Art; the truth may be that the eruption started last night."

"Just be sure you don't get caught in the lava flow, then. You're standing awfully close to the fires."

"It's too late to go back. Having diagnosed the disease, it's up to me as a doctor to help cure it—if I can."

iii.

Mike took a swim that afternoon and ate a lonely dinner in the motel dining room. Afterward he watched a rerun of "Star Trek" on television, but interplanetary travel by way of the starship *Enterprise* looked too easy. The vessel seemed to possess an almost unlimited supply of fuel and a perpetual atmosphere of its own that required no replenishing, while reality, Mike knew very well from his own experience, was quite different.

In space the lives of men hung on slender threads: the proper functioning of the life environment system; the chance, not too remote, that one of the millions of meteorites flashing through space would smash through the outer skin of a ship, damaging delicate controls at the same moment that the sudden change from the ship's carefully maintained private atmosphere to what was practically a complete vacuum caused the blood of any of the occupants not wearing a pressurized space suit to boil, exploding his body like one of the paper bags of glue vapor tossed upon the fire on the beach that night; the failure of retrorockets to fire and break the speed of orbit to allow safe reentry—all those and a thousand other possible causes of disaster rode with astronauts whenever they ventured into outer space.

He called Jan several times but no one answered, so he assumed that she was either late in getting back from Orlando or had decided to stay overnight. When the phone rang about ten-thirty, he seized it, hoping to hear her voice, but it was Art McCord instead.

"Can you come over to the office, Mike?" the newspaperman asked.

"Sure. But what—"

"My city editor is sick and I'm busy putting the morning edition to bed. Something just came in on the syndicate wires that you ought to see tonight."

Mike dressed hurriedly and drove through Spaceport City to the island containing the newspaper, radio, and television center. When he came into Art's office, the editor handed him a section of teletype sheets from the machine chattering in the corridor outside.

"This is Jake Arrens' latest column, for tomorrow morning's edition," he said. "The part concerning you is at the end in that gossip section Jake calls 'Capers at the Cape.'"

Mike didn't need to be told who Jake Arrens was, or the nature of his column. A skilled mixture of authentic information about the space program, gossip, and sly innuendo titled aptly enough, "The Space Race," it was one of the most popular newspaper columns in the country, and had earned a tremendous following for its author, since the first Sputnik had launched the race to beat the Russians to the moon.

The main part of the sheet Art handed Mike was a column on Pegasus, highly popularized for newspaper readers but still technically correct. The section at the end, however, was something quite different:

A new arrival at the Cape is Dr. Michael Barnes, veteran of the Hermes program and familiar to millions of us old hands for the "Space Chicken" sobriquet pinned on him by Congressman Israel Pond during the days of the Space Committee inquisitions. Sources at the Cape report that the doctor-astronaut, an old friend of FSA herd-riding Senator Lars Todt, has been moving fully as fast on the ground since his arrival as he did while in Hermes orbit. To wit, participation in a late night orgy at the house of a prominent Cape resident and weaving his way to his motel around midnight, followed by a sympathetic police car, to say nothing of the instant romantic conquest of a Cape lovely.

By the way, Dr. Barnes, who was the redheaded thrush seen leaving your motel suite at six o'clock Saturday morning? Were you just bird-watching? Or has Senator Todt sent you down to bird-dog the Flying Horse?

"You're not going to run this?" said Mike.

"I don't have any choice."

"But it's slander."

"Gossip," Art corrected him. "Our contract with the syndicate that supplies Jake Arrens' column says we have to print it exactly as it comes off the teletype. Every subscriber on the Cape reads it at breakfast."

"I can sue—"

"On what grounds? Jake's got a leg man here, so you can bet everything was checked out before it went to Washington for the column."

"But—"

"Could you prove in court that any of it isn't true?"

"No," Mike admitted. "This must be Hal's work."

"Maybe yes, maybe no. But for God's sake, Mike, pack your things and get the hell out of here before they pull you from the surf, too."

"Don't tell me anyone considers me important enough to import a gunsel from Detroit?"

"I'm not joking, Mike."

"Strangely enough, neither am I."

"Then you're going."

"I'm going all right—to Washington to see Jake Arrens."

"You can't fight them, Mike."

"I can damn well try. And I think you just told me how."

"If I did, I take it back—for your sake."

"The party was at Hal's house, remember? In trying to run me off before I find out what this is all about, Hal has overplayed his hand."

"I still say the odds are too great against you."

"I once figured out with a computer the odds against my coming down alive in that bird I flew for Hermes," Mike said grimly. "They came out somewhere near a hundred thousand to one, but I still made it the hard way—swimming."

CHAPTER XII

It was raining in Washington when Mike checked in at the Hilton Hotel, after taking a taxi from National Airport. He had tried to call Jan before leaving Spaceport City but her phone still didn't answer and, judging that she must have stayed in Orlando Monday night, he decided to call her from Washington Tuesday evening.

At the hotel, he washed up, changed clothes, and took a taxi to the Herald Building, where the offices of the syndicate that handled Jake Arrens' column were located. He hadn't taken a chance on asking for an appointment beforehand and being refused, certain that his best course was to barge right in and confront his tormentor.

Arrens' office was a cluttered room on the third floor of the Herald Building. Its occupant was a vast mountain of a man with cigar ashes spattering his shirt front; but the eyes behind big rimmed glasses were alert and intelligent.

"I'm Dr. Michael Barnes," Mike announced.

"The 'Space Chicken'?"

"Get off my back, Arrens. What did I ever do to you?"

"The truth is I've always admired you—as a doctor," said the fat man. "But I still say you had no business risking a first rate scientific mind flying a tub like those Hermes ships around the world. Stick to closed space ecology and aerospace sociology, where you're near the top in my book."

"Why try to lose me the job of consultant on Pegasus then?" Mike found it hard to remain truculent in the face of the other man's tone as well as an obvious knowledge of his work and appreciation for it.

"My bread and meat come from knowing what's going on in space, Doctor, but sometimes my sources at FSA seem to dry up for a while. That happened some time ago, when the Air Force put the heat on for an orbiting space station to take the place of the manned orbiting laboratory they cancelled when the budget started to get tight back in sixty-nine. The best way I know to get back in is to needle the space boys until they choose to loosen up."

"With me as the sacrificial victim?"

Jake Arrens grinned. "I have to use what comes to hand, Doctor. Besides I'm very much interested in that private little empire Paul Taggar and Hal Brennan have built up down there on the Cape, and particularly why somebody's so anxious to set you up for the kill that they fed this gossip item to my source there."

"You mean it was planted?"

"Planted, fertilized, and watered—with details. When she—"

"Yvonne Lang!"

"I'm naming no names. But my representative down there seems to have taken a liking to you, so you must be okay."

"Then why try to destroy me?"

"If we hadn't been given the tip, somebody else would have. What amazes me is how a mild-mannered scientist like you managed to get into so much hot water so quickly after you arrived at the Cape."

"Maybe I carried it with me—although I didn't realize it at the time."

"I figured it might be something like that. What do you know that they're so anxious to keep the rest of the world from finding out?"

"I'm not even sure myself."

"It must be something about that Hermes capsule of yours that went bad," said the columnist. "What really happened there? Did some bird-brain of a technician, who'd probably been drunk the night before, fail to tighten the connections?"

"More likely it was a combined failure of the oxygen reduction valve and a pop-off valve."

"That's another way of saying the same thing," said Arrens. "But I still ask myself why a guy with your ability would want to be a medical nanny to a bunch of space hardware jockeys, taking blood pressures, counting pulses, and stuff like that."

"Maybe I like Florida; after all I grew up down there."

"Those Johns Hopkins and Harvard degrees you have could earn you a lot more money practicing medicine in Brevard County, if you've suddenly developed a yen for sunshine and alligators." Jake Arrens shook his head. "No, there must be another answer, possibly one connected with that paper you wrote on the Lockheed Syndrome. Did Lars Todt send you down there to see why there've been so many minor failures lately?"

"That was one thing."

"The other must be a yen to look at some Taggar-built hardware to see if you can prove what really happened eight years ago."

"You're pretty good at assumptions."

"I'm pretty good at knowing human nature," said Arrens. "Hal Brennan wouldn't want you to find any bugs in his project that might keep it from being lofted on time to jet him into the governor's mansion at Tallahassee."

"You're making quite a case."

"The clincher being the fact that once you're inside, you might be able to prove that Israel Pond and Hal Brennan crucified you before the Space Committee to keep you from finding out just why you almost became our only orbiting corpse—to date. The whole thing adds up now and everything fits in, including the secrecy they're giving what would otherwise be a pretty routine sort of an operation."

"If you know the answer to that," said Mike, "I wish you'd tell me."

"I hope this is the answer." Jake Arrens opened a drawer of his desk and pulled out a folder from which he took a newspaper clipping. "Remember the first Russian rendezvous and docking tests with two ships back in January 1968?"

"Vaguely."

"This will refresh your memory, then; it's part of a UPI dispatch from Moscow. Listen closely:

> 'Tass said the five-day four-man mission had opened the way for the creation of orbital manned stations for scientific and economic purposes. A group of Soviet space scientists enthusiastically look forward to construction of a fixed position station platform twenty-two thousand two hundred and thirty-eight miles above the earth.'"

Jake Arrens looked up from the clipping. "Does that figure mean anything to you?"

"It's the distance required to keep a synchronous satellite in orbit over one spot on the earth's surface."

"Exactly, but listen to this:

> 'As an earlier step, they said in a Pravda article, the Soyuz mission had opened the way to establishing orbital platforms within convenient satellite ferrying distance of the earth.'"

"Are you saying that placing a space station in orbit is important now because it might demonstrate whether men in synchronous satellites could withstand things like the higher Van Allen belt radiation levels they might experience in a synchronous satellite?"

"Go to the head of the class, Doctor. I don't need to remind you that one of those Russian orbiting platforms located over a spot not too far distant from the United States would be just as much of a danger to us as those rockets Jack Kennedy finally turned back from Cuba."

"But the whole thing sounds so fantastic."

"Not as fantastic as something else I'm going to tell you in a moment. Do you see now why getting this first Pegasus off the pad can be extremely important—and why anything that threatens it could also be considered a threat to the people involved?"

"No doubt about it."

"If this first shot goes wrong, a lot of bird-brain congressmen will start shouting that we're spending too much on hardware and not enough on food handouts to the people who vote for them."

The words, Mike realized, were practically the same that Art McCord had used. And both Art and Jake Arrens had one thing in common, besides being newspapermen. Both had an intimate knowledge of America's space program.

"They might be right: if we could trust the Russians to stick to the non-proliferation treaty and the one barring space for atomic weaponry," said Mike.

"True. But do you think a country that would rape one of its own satellites overnight, like Russia did Czechoslovakia a few years ago, is going to worry about the moral side of getting the jump on us in an atomic war?"

"Perhaps not. But—"

"You've heard of the SS-9, haven't you?"

"Yes."

"And a project called SCRAG?"

"I don't remember too much about that one."

"Don't feel badly about it," said the columnist. "The best article on it was in *Barron's* in October '68, but most of the people who read that publication are so busy hunting for profits in the stock market, they ignore anything that doesn't promise them a fast buck."

"What is SCRAG?"

"I can't even pronounce the Russian words that give it the name; the American term is FOBS—Fractional Orbital Bombardment System. While we were busy spending billions to put men on the moon, where they could freeze or cook if anything went wrong with their space suits, the wily Muscovites had already carried out thirteen successful tests of SCRAG. It's now capable of carrying a nuclear payload of over fifteen megatons into fractional orbit, any one of which could hit a target like New York, Washington, and Houston in something like five minutes—instead of the fifteen minutes an ICBM would take—simply by changing its course. Add the MIRV warheads they already have and I ask you what chance we would have even to retaliate, when the effects of heat, blast, and the electro-magnetic disturbances from the first missile had already destroyed half the population and loused up our whole communication system?"

"If what you say about this SCRAG is true, why isn't it a violation of our treaties?"

"According to the high-minded internationalists in the State Department, a fractional orbit doesn't come under that classification. But all the Russians need is just enough of a fraction to get those hydrogen bombs halfway around the world to where they can drop on major U.S. cities and defense centers. They already have a killer satellite that can hunt down ours in space and destroy them."

"So what's the answer?"

"A Manned Orbiting Arsenal—what else? That's what the Russians were talking about in this newspaper dispatch back in 1968 and they gave us an even stronger hint in sixty-nine, when they put up three Soyuz ships practically at the same time. That attempt to link up the three into what amounted to a space station failed, but our Soviet friends don't give up easily and there'll be more. It's a clear warning to us of the future."

"How does the orbiting space station we're trying to put up down at the Cape now figure here?"

"Just let us get one of them circling the earth and we can easily send up enough hydrogen warheads to arm it, if our spy-in-the-sky satellites reveal any suspicious increase in nuclear activity by Russia. You can bet your boots the Soviets would think twice about any funny business then."

Mike was impressed by the fat man's obvious belief in what he was saying—and its logic, particularly in view of the size of the huge rocket he'd seen in the Vehicle Assembly Building at the Cape, a size far greater than any MOL envisioned by air force planners before that project was cancelled.

"So when my representative phoned me the obvious plant from the Cape that you were a hophead, I couldn't help wondering why." Jake Arrens' voice brought Mike out of his thoughts. "Then I remembered that you and Lars Todt were boyhood friends and did a little checking. When I discovered that you'd been in his office last week and then gone directly to Florida, the whole thing became a matter of simple deduction. What I haven't been able to figure out is just why your being down there stirred up the people on the ground so much, unless something is really wrong with Pegasus. Have you seen any signs?"

"As far as I can tell, it seems to be going too smoothly to be true."

"That's it!" Jake Arrens' manner was suddenly brisk and purposeful, as he swung around to the typewriter that stood on a small movable table beside his desk. Reaching for a sheet of paper, he put it into the machine and typed rapidly for several minutes, then pulled out the sheet and handed it to Mike.

Under the headline: "IS PEGASUS FLYING TOO FAST AND TOO HIGH?" the columnist had written:

> FSA officials are concerned, it is reported by a reliable source—

"You're the reliable source," Jake Arrens told him.

> —because progress with the Pegasus program to put a space station in orbit seems to be moving too smoothly. No previous launch preparation has failed to turn up numerous bugs, often slowing down the schedule, but Pegasus is ahead—which makes it unique.

> A piece of machinery as complicated as Pegasus just doesn't operate that smoothly the first time around, according to the FSA source. For example, some two hundred changes had to be made in the first Hermes capsule and similar bugs have developed in all other spacecraft while they were being readied for launching at the Cape.

> Could a bird that's too good be bad news?

"That ought to smoke things out if anything will," Mike said as he handed back the sheet. "When are you going to run it?"

"The syndicate will pick it up this afternoon and put it on the wire, so it'll make the morning papers."

"My guess is there'll be a report of trouble at the Cape in a day or two," said Mike.

"But something that can be remedied without too much difficulty," Jake Arrens agreed. "When are you going back?"

"I don't even know whether I'm going back," said Mike. "First I have to see Lars and perhaps General Green to convince them I'm fit to associate with the people down there."

"Just let me know if there's any talk about giving you the shaft," said the columnist. "A little nudge from this chair has changed many a bureaucrat's mind. I'm curious to see what you're going to discover at the Cape when you really get inside the Flying Horse."

"So am I," said Mike. "But before I team up with you I need to know what you intend to do with any information I might give you. If I do find that Pegasus is really intended to be what you called an orbiting atomic arsenal, what will you do with the information?"

"Sit on it," said Jake Arrens promptly. "I'm first of all an American, friend Mike, but if I find that FSA is overlooking their big chance to protect the country for some damn fool scheme like sending men to Mars, I'm going to build such a fire under them that they'll have to change their ways."

ii.

The Reverend Daniel Sears customarily made his pastoral calls in the morning. Husbands, he had learned from experience, weren't likely to come home unexpectedly before lunch and the children old enough to suspect an ulterior motive in his visits were usually at school. He was whistling softly to himself as he drove over the arching bridge of the causeway from the mainland and turned off on one of the several entry roads to Spaceport City.

A man who enjoyed luxury despite his fulminations against it from the pulpit, he would have chosen to live in this new affluent section if that were possible. But the greater majority of his congregation were not from either the social or the economic levels predominating in the new development that catered to the engineering and management people employed at the Cape, as well as the doctors, dentists, veterinarians, lawyers, and others who derived their income from the needs of such.

From the top of the causeway overpass he noted with approval that many of the women of the community—alone or in small groups—were either swimming or busy acquiring the deep tan that was the hallmark of the recent transplant to Florida, the natives having long since learned that the long time result of such exposure to the sun was a tendency toward skin cancer as well as the sort of leathery epidermis that tended to become more and more irritated with age.

Watching from this distant outpost the bounteous harvest awaiting a skilled reaper, the Reverend Daniel Sears felt his hackles beginning to rise with anticipation. And remembering Sandra Craven's magnificent legs, as she'd sat on the front row directly before his pulpit last Sunday, he felt a warmth considerably greater than that of the mild September morning begin to stir within him, spreading ripple-like throughout his body.

He couldn't really understand how he had failed to notice her before. The eager light of religious fervor in her eyes stirred there by his preaching and the almost charismatic sense of communication he sometimes achieved with feminine parishioners, he knew from long experience, could easily be transmuted into something capable of bringing tremendous satisfaction to himself, as well as, in his considerable experience, causing few if any objections on the part of those in whom it was stirred by his preaching.

Of course there had been an occasional misfire, mainly when he'd been indiscreet enough to make love to an un-married woman, like the blonde in the back row of the choir at his previous church. And particularly when she was the sister-in-law of a deacon, who, he suspected from the practiced cooperation he'd obtained from the girl, must have already staked out his own claim.

There had been quite a row, with the church dividing, as usually happened in such affairs. The younger women generally favored him while the older ones smugly set themselves against him. And the men usually followed the lead of the women in such highly emotional situations, in the interest of preserving household peace, however much they might envy him his conquests.

He had been tempted to stay and make an issue of it that last time, particularly when the controversy had revealed a surprising number of feminine supporters deserving to be rewarded for their ardor in his behalf. But Eunice had put her foot down and threatened a divorce so vehemently that he was convinced she really meant it this time. And besides, although divorced ministers were almost commonplace in many liberal churches, they were distinctly frowned upon by the pentecostal sects.

Fortunately, when the controversy was at its height, the call had come from his present pastorate with a larger church and a considerably increased salary, so the whole problem had been solved effectively, no doubt, he was firmly convinced, by divine providence.

It had been a good move, too, he had discovered quickly. The congregation was a large one composed mainly of native Floridians engaged in the citrus industry and older retired people whose convictions were usually along conservative lines, making them strong supporters of the pentecostal faith.

The population that had swelled the county's census from twenty-five thousand to two hundred and fifty thousand in less than a decade tended to be skilled blue collar or college-trained professional engineers and scientists. And while not so many among the upper levels of this area had gravitated so far to the Reverend Daniel Sears' church, he hoped soon to reach that group which, though just below the strictly professional level, still made good money and carried with them the more fundamental religious impulses of their birth and earlier training.

The rocket men, Daniel Sears had learned very quickly, were hard working, demanding much of themselves and of their families, driven by a need for perfection that made communication inside the family less and less satisfactory, particularly as their economic level increased. Perfectionists themselves, yet obsessed with the knowledge of their own imperfection, they often sought solace in the simple doctrine of confession and expiation preached so effectively from his pulpit. And finding solace for their consciences in the church, they were not unwilling to support it generously.

That their wives, unable or unwilling to measure up to the standards of perfection upon which their husbands insisted for them and their children, often sought help from their pastor, was a fringe benefit, so to speak, for Daniel Sears himself. And being a naturally warmhearted sympathetic man, he had developed considerable skill in quickly achieving a considerably more intimate relationship.

Confident that the Lord had given him this power to ease the minds —and the bodies—of distraught women, he had gone about his work with zest, like Samson about his labors, joying in his strength, much of which—also like Samson—he was convinced lay in his wavy golden blond hair. He'd even started wearing his locks just a little longer than the average man well before the younger male population had discovered its undoubted attractions for the female of the species.

Yes, life was good to Reverend Daniel Sears and, thankful for the strength God had given him, he went about doing good wherever he could, serving distraught souls and filling them with hope that he would come again—which he usually managed to do.

He was whistling softly now as he drove slowly into Spaceport City. When a young housewife in shorts and halter pushing a baby in a stroller along the street came to the corner and paused before crossing, he stopped the car to allow them to pass, while his warm smile enveloped mother and babe alike. When she smiled with an answering warmth, he considered momentarily stopping for a little proselytizing on the spot; after all, who knew but that she might be an Episcopalian and therefore already a heathen according to the rigid theology of Daniel Sears' sect. But he put the thought from him somewhat reluctantly, for the time for such bold sallies—however much the likelihood of success, he knew from experience, might attend them—was not yet opportune.

First he must gain a foothold in this promised land where flowed the milk of feminine kindness. Then after evaluating the situation like a general preparing for a battle, he would move with practiced skill to awaken yearning bodies to the truths of life and love.

Sandra Craven, he'd felt instantly when he looked down from the pulpit last Sunday, would be receptive to his ministrations. The intense look in her eyes; the way they never left his face as he talked; the almost joyous understanding of the truths he was expanding, however little he was able to understand them himself; the tension in her body and particularly the way she'd crossed her legs every now and then, seemingly unconscious of the fact that each movement hiked the short skirt higher—all of these were signs which Daniel Sears had learned to interpret long ago. And feeling that the time was ripe, he had come this Tuesday morning for a pastoral call.

Filled with zeal then, he turned his eyes from the young housewife with the baby and, with only a second admiring glance, drove on to 98 Hibiscus Lane.

iii.

After leaving Jake Arrens, Mike called Lars Todt's office from a telephone outside the Herald Building. Told that the senator was leaving for a committee meeting but would be available that afternoon, he made an appointment to meet Lars in the cocktail lounge of the Hilton Hotel at five-thirty. With nothing to do until he was to meet Lars Todt, and no chance of getting Jan on the telephone at Spaceport City, while she was going from school to school for the music lessons, he decided to go to the Library of Congress and look up a report called "The Changing Strategic Military Balance, USA vs. USSR" Jake Arrens had mentioned to him.

Prepared by a special sub-group of the National Strategic Committee of the American Security Council, and with a truly impressive list of experienced army, navy, and air force figures as its authors, plus several well-known scientists, the report verified everything Jake Arrens had said about the possibilities of the Russian SCRAG missile, as well as other Soviet space efforts, ending with these paragraphs:

"That the Soviet Union would dare to risk the deployment of orbital bombs is at least credible in view of the experience during the Cuban missile crisis. Surprise would be complete, since the United States has no way of determining if an orbital vehicle is bearing a nuclear weapon.

"In the United States we argue variously that space offensive nuclear delivery forces are less efficient, less accurate, and less credible than ICBMs. But if the Soviet Union is dedicated to offensive world objectives, the special effect of space-military offensive forces may appear very useful. Such effects are, for example, prestige, terror, persuasion, coercion, pressure, psychological warfare, and demoralization. The sight and electronic signals coming from Soviet military-orbital forces in the free skies of the world day and night, with Communist satellite TV and propaganda tuned into Western sets around the world, would not be attractive to contemplate in view of the Soviet goals of world-wide Communist domination."

All of which, Mike realized, could make a successful launching of the Pegasus rocket so carefully guarded in the Vehicle Assembly Building at Cape Kennedy the most vital step America had yet taken into space—the first important measure toward placing into orbit what Jake Arrens had called a manned orbiting arsenal, capable of being loaded with hydrogen warheads whenever spy satellites revealed a significant increase in Russian atomic activity and able to destroy quickly any enemy, even after the so-called first strike had been effected. That, and only that, he was beginning to be convinced, could effectively maintain peace in a world which seemed just as effectively bent upon mutual destruction.

CHAPTER XIII

Usually, Sandra Craven's increasingly frequent quarrels with Tom hadn't lasted as long as this one—but then none of the others had been as violent. She'd been filled with zeal and happiness when they'd left the church on Sunday and, after two drinks at the bar of the beach front Space Club, they'd had a delightful dinner. The trouble had come when Tom insisted upon going back to his drawing board in the Taggar Building on the FSA reservation to get down the details of the idea that had come to him during the sermon.

He'd promised to be back in a couple of hours and she'd followed his suggestion that she get some sun by the pool while waiting for him. It had been pleasant to don the bikini she kept in her locker and lie on a comfortable couch in the sun on the poolside patio. She'd even enjoyed several tentative passes made by young officers from the air force base south of Cocoa Beach—not that she'd entertained any idea of encouraging them. When Tom came back, they'd have a few more drinks and then go home for their usual Sunday afternoon diversion. It was too hot for anything else on a muggy September day, but the house was air conditioned, the bar always well stocked, and the bed was king-size.

She'd even dropped off to sleep and dreamed of the time she and Tom had stopped at that country lake on the way home from a pentecostal revival meeting; but when she'd awakened, he still hadn't come back. And, when another hour made it clear that this was going to be a repetition of what was almost a regular occurrence nowadays, she'd dressed and walked home alone.

The afternoon had been hot and she was soaked with perspiration when she got home, so she'd taken a shower, then mixed herself another drink, and gone into the bedroom to read and watch TV. By the time Tom had arrived about nine o'clock, she'd been morose and half hung over, ready for a quarrel and for the pleasure of reconciliation.

Only this time there hadn't been any making up. Tom had been worried about some question of a defective metal partition; she'd never really been able to understand just exactly what it was but the quarrel had escalated as they prepared for bed and they'd finally gone to sleep on the opposite edges of the big bed.

Once during the night, Sandra awakened and, feeling a little cool in her short nightgown, moved closer to Tom, hoping he would awaken and still make up, but he'd only moved away a little. And when a soft snore came from his lips, she had been filled with a surge of resentment against him and had moved back to the other side of the bed.

He'd left Monday morning without even awakening her to get breakfast and his secretary had called later in the day to say he was flying with Paul Taggar to the main plant. Taggar executives always kept a bag packed at the office, never knowing when their hard driving boss might send them off in the private jet he kept at the airport with a pilot always on call.

As the result, Sandra hadn't seen Tom since that quarrel Sunday night, not that it would have been any better, if he'd come home, she told herself resentfully as she poured a second cup of coffee. With Tom away, she hadn't gotten up until nearly eleven and it was now almost noon.

She didn't even feel like calling some of the girls to arrange an afternoon of bridge, for those sessions always turned into gossip fests about who was getting a divorce from whom and which secretary from his office stable of strikingly beautiful young women Paul Taggar had taken with him on his flight last week to Freeport and the gambling tables of the Bahamas.

It was a cruel and lonely world, Sandra decided as she turned on the dishwasher and sat down to look at the kitchen television. But nothing was on except a replay of "I Dream of Jeannie" and the way she felt this morning, the lovely young sprite from the bottle made Sandra feel like an old hag.

On her way back from turning off the TV, she passed the pantry and reached out to shut the open door, but stopped when her eyes fell upon a bottle of Old Crow on the shelf. Obeying an impulse she had hitherto usually resisted—though obeying it more frequently than before they'd come to Spaceport City—she reached in and took the bottle down from the shelf. Carrying it back to the table, she got ice from the ice cube maker in the refrigerator and, pouring a liberal drink, sat sipping it on the rocks, while she thought how much her life had changed since they'd come to Spaceport City and Tom had gotten so involved in solving the problems of Taggar Aircraft and the new rocket called Pegasus.

The whiskey pushed away the borders of the depression that had gripped her that morning. The air in the kitchen was cool but there was still the taint of the breakfast cigarettes in the air, so she went to the thermostat and shut off the central air conditioning, then started through the house opening windows.

The air that came in was fresh, it was true, but it was also hot already with the sticky muggy heat of a Florida September day. So when she finished opening the windows, Sandra went to a dresser drawer and took out the new bathing suit she'd bought the day before Tom had come home with news of his last raise.

Designed for teen-agers, its brevity was certainly not intended for a woman as liberally proportioned as she was. But then she'd never intended wearing it except when she and Tom were swimming in their own pool, hoping it might stimulate him to take more interest in her than he seemed to have been taking lately because of his work.

Stripping off her already sticky clothing, Sandra put on the bikini and stood looking at herself in the mirror. What she saw, plus the whiskey she'd just finished, made her feel a lot better. Maybe she was a bit plump around the tummy, but the legs were superb; she knew that from the compliments she'd had when she danced in the chorus of the Spaceport Follies put on by the Woman's Club earlier that year. And she certainly didn't have to take a back seat to anyone where her bosom was concerned; in fact she was having trouble covering much of it with the decidedly skimpy bra of the new suit.

Picking up a towel and slipping her feet into a pair of rubber-soled clogs, Sandra went through the kitchen on her way to the pool. Momentarily, she considered pouring another drink from the bottle of bourbon, but decided against it and put the bottle back on the shelf instead.

A door led from the kitchen into the garage, where a neck-high partition enclosed a shower, so those going and coming from the pool could leave their wet suits outside the house and not track sand inside. The shower also served a second purpose as a dressing room and, dropping the towel over the partition, she went outside to the pool.

The rising tide of warmth inside her from the bourbon warned her she'd better do something to dampen it so, pulling on her bathing cap, she walked to the side of the pool and dived in, swimming its length briskly several times before turning on her back to lie floating with barely a wiggle of her toes to keep them afloat, as she reveled in the cool embrace of the water in the pool she loved more than anything else about her new home.

She and Tom had moved to Spaceport City from Huntsville, Alabama, when many FSA activities had been concentrated at the Cape

with the Pegasus program. Instinctively distrusting the sleek sophistication and hectic pace of the new town, Sandra had been slow to make
friends here at first. And when the push of rushing the first Pegasus
launching had begun to keep Tom at the plant for longer and longer
hours, she had grown steadily more lonely, turning often to the solace
which so many wives at the Cape used under such circumstances, the
ability of alcohol to wipe away one's troubles—for the time being.

Floating now upon the surface of the pool, suspended halfway between heaven and earth and feeling nothing except the embrace of
the water that gave her a sensation of being without substance, she
knew this feeling must be something like the sensation of weightlessness experienced by the astronauts, which they found so exhilarating,
and allowed herself to imagine she was one of them, rushing through
the sky as master of her own destiny, rather than having to depend
upon Tom and his whims.

Enthralled by the new sensation, she didn't hear footsteps beside
the pool at first. When she did, she turned slowly, thinking it was one
of the neighboring wives who didn't have a pool and sometimes came
to swim and lie in the sun with her on hot days like today. But when
she found herself looking up at the Reverend Daniel Sears, she gasped
with surprise.

"Reverend Sears!" she exclaimed. "I didn't hear you."

"No one answered the bell but I could hear splashing in the pool
and the gate was open, so I came on around," he said. "Hope I'm not
intruding."

"Of course not." Blushing, conscious of the briefness of her swim
suit, Sandra quickly swam to the side of the pool and clung to it.

"I was in the neighborhood and realized I hadn't paid you folks a
visit so I decided to stop by."

"How nice—"

"If it isn't convenient—"

"Oh no. I was just startled."

"Go on with your swim," he said. "I'll sit here and enjoy the shade
and the coolness."

"I was just floating and wondering how it feels not to have weight
like the astronauts when they're in orbit."

"God put men's feet on the earth and instituted the force of gravity
to hold them there," said Daniel Sears.

"I'm sure he did." Sandra didn't know what else to say, flustered by
the way his eyes watched her body in the water—and somewhat excited by it, too.

"I'll come out and get dressed," she said. "Then we can sit in the
house where it's cool and talk."

"That will be fine," he said. "I like to get to know my parishioners as people, not just faces I preach to on Sunday. So when I noticed you and Mr. Craven last Sunday, it reminded me that I had been lax in not paying you folks a call."

"I was in the front row."

"I know." The way he said it, the intensity in his voice, sent a tingling sensation down her spine, a shiver of anticipation which, watching her closely, he did not fail to see.

"You must be cold," he said quickly.

"Oh no. But I *had* better come out."

Quite conscious that his eyes were following her she swam to the shallow end of the pool, where she could step out upon the patio. She heard his sudden sharp intake of breath when she stood up in the brief suit and turned to tell him she'd be only a moment. Instead of going in, however, she found herself gripped by the power of those deep-set eyes that not only sent a warmth surging up through her body but seemed also to deprive her of all volition, like a hypnotist bending her to his will.

"I'll wait for you," he said. "Don't hurry."

Feeling like a character in a play whose dramatic course was already decided, Sandra moved to the door of the garage and stepped inside. In the shower stall, she quickly unhooked the bra of her suit and let it drop to the floor, then reached down to peel the absurdly brief lower half over her thighs and step from it. Still holding the fabric, she was reaching for the towel, when she raised her head and discovered that he had come into the garage from the poolside patio and was standing there watching her.

"Oh!" Instinctively she clutched the handful of fabric she was holding against her body, in a futile attempt to shield what she could of it from his eyes. She could not quell the warm tide sweeping over her at his obvious admiration, however, or the feeling of being fixed by that hypnotic gaze, very much as she had felt when he'd looked down at her last Sunday from the pulpit. Rooted to the spot, she made no attempt to move, nor wanted to, conscious only of the rising beat of her pulse in her ears.

When he spoke softly, the words were strange at first, but only for an instant; then she recognized the measured beat of those lines sung so long ago by a King of Israel to his beloved:

> "Behold, thou art fair, my love;
> Behold, thou art fair . . .
> Thy lips are like a thread of scarlet."

Standing there, fixed by his eyes, she experienced again much the same feeling she'd had in the pool a little while ago, that of floating between heaven and earth and wanting to touch neither, while his voice caressed her:

> "*Thy two breasts are like two young roes*
> > *that are twins . . .*
> *The joints of thy thighs are like a jewel,*
> *The work of the hands of a cunning workman.*
> *Thy navel is like a round goblet,*
> *Which wanteth not liquor:*
> *Thy belly is like an heap of wheat set about*
> > *with lilies . . .*
> *How fair and how pleasant art thou,*
> *O love for delights!*
> *This thy stature is like to a palm tree,*
> *And thy breasts to clusters of grapes.*
> *I said, I will go up to the palm tree,*
> *I will take hold of the boughs thereof."*

Slowly, for her arms seemed no longer to have any weight as he came to her, Sandra dropped the small bit of fabric she was holding. The touch of his hands upon her body was like a benediction or a blessing, and all feeling of nakedness, all shame, was thrust away by the light shining in his eyes.

"We'd better go inside," she said softly. "The neighbors sometimes use the pool."

"Of course." His hand slipped down to rest upon the sweet roundness of her naked hip, as they turned and walked through the door into the house.

ii.

It had been a sobering afternoon and Mike was ready for a drink, when he went to the cocktail lounge of the Hilton. As usual at this time of the day it was crowded but, when he mentioned that he was meeting Senator Lars Todt, he was shown immediately to a table. Ordering bourbon, he sipped it while he watched the ebb and flow of people through the lounge, many of them with faces familiar from newspapers and television.

It was nearly six o'clock when Lars Todt made his way through the crowd toward the table. "Sorry to be late." The tone of his voice told Mike he'd read Jake Arrens' column—or had been told about it.

"I've been pretty busy myself since I got in this morning," said Mike.

"From what I read you've been busy ever since you left Washington."

"Sometimes you only get to read what people want you to read. I seem to remember your saying something like that about FSA last week before I went to Spaceport City."

"Are you implying that what Jake Arrens wrote about you was planted by FSA?"

"By Hal Brennan would be more correct, I think."

"Then it's not true?"

"It's true enough—to a point. I was almost booby trapped into what Jake Arrens called an orgy by Hal, so he could get a club to hold over me."

"Maybe you'd better tell me the whole story. After all I'm responsible for getting you into this mess."

Mike gave him a brief rundown on events since he'd last seen Lars.

"They're after you all right—in full cry," the senator agreed. "How did you learn that Jake Arrens' column was going to mention you? It only appeared in the morning newspapers here today."

"Art McCord edits the Spaceport *Call* and warned me when it came in on the teletype last night. I got an early plane out of Orlando."

"What does Art have to say about all this?"

"He can't afford to commit himself. Paul Taggar owns the paper and Art's afraid of what a slowdown in Pegasus could do to Spaceport City."

"No more than I am about what it would do to the Administration," Lars admitted.

"Art thinks I should quit and go back to Mountain City. What about you, Lars?"

The senator studied the amber liquid in his glass for a moment, then picked it up and drained it in a decisive gesture. "I want to know the truth, Mike, and I think you're on the track of it. Is there any way I can help you?"

"Yes, you can arrange an appointment for both of us with General Green at FSA tomorrow."

"That should be simple enough, with some of his additional appropriation requests coming up soon for a vote in Congress. What else?"

"And you can put in a call to Hal Brennan in Spaceport City, so he'll know you're with me. I'll do the talking."

"We'd better call from your room," said the senator. "But I ought to warn you that I'm still not at all sure I can keep the job of consultant for you after this piece Jake Arrens wrote. Jim Green's no prude but he's tough."

"Hal is going to take care of that for me. Just get him on the phone and let him know you're hearing what I say to him."

Lars Todt called the Cape from Mike's room. "This is Senator Todt, Colonel Brennan," he said when the connection was made.

"It's good to hear from you, Senator." Mike could hear Hal's booming voice in the receiver.

"I'm in Mike Barnes' room at the Hilton Hotel here in Washington. He wants to speak to you."

Lars Todt handed the telephone over but Mike took his arm, keeping him close enough so he could hear the conversation by way of the receiver.

"I thought you were still in Spaceport City, Mike," said Hal.

"Don't give me the innocent bit," Mike said bluntly. "You know perfectly well that I came to Washington this morning; the man Chief Branigan had tailing me would have told you."

"I don't know what you're talking about." Hal's voice was still jovial, but there was an edge to it also. "Why so belligerent? We're still friends, aren't we?"

"That depends on you. Tomorrow, Senator Todt and I are going to see the FSA administrator about my continuing as consultant for Pegasus. When General Green calls you about the appointment tomorrow afternoon, I expect you to give it hearty approval."

There was silence at the other end of the wire for a moment, then Hal Brennan said: "There must be an else—or you wouldn't try to threaten me."

"I spent an hour with Jake Arrens this morning," said Mike. "You can imagine what he would do with the story that the director of the Pegasus program, America's Hermes astronaut hero, has been feeding Speed or LSD or something like it to leading engineers and space people down there so he can keep them under his thumb. You can also imagine what the story will be like when I tell him about a game called Countdown—and how quickly you'll be booted out of your job."

"You win this pot, Mike," Hal said without hesitation. "But next time I'll make sure it's my deal. Good-by."

"I didn't know you could play that rough." There was a note of admiration in Lars Todt's voice when Mike hung up the phone.

"I don't—unless I have to. But I'm not going to let myself be blackmailed just because Hal Brennan wants to be governor of Florida. Will you have your office call me here tomorrow morning about the appointment with General Green?"

"First thing," said Lars Todt. "What are you going to do in the meantime?"

"I spent this afternoon in the Library of Congress studying the American Security Council report for the House Committee on Armed

Services. Jake Arrens thinks it's more important to get the space station in orbit as a countermeasure to the Russian SCRAG and SS-9 programs than as a prelude to exploring Mars."

"He may be right." Lars Todt's voice was sober. "If you think much about the military possibilities of space in the wrong hands, it scares the hell out of you."

"What's the answer?"

"For one thing, all space exploration should be a joint operation—perhaps under the United Nations. With so many people starving in the world it doesn't make sense for the two richest powers to be duplicating each other's efforts in a field where one nation would never be allowed to have full jurisdiction anyway."

"I can think of another angle," said Mike. "Do you remember the Space Science Board report of 1968?"

"Not too well."

"As long ago as sixty-five, some of the most intelligent scientists in America decided that answering questions like how life got started on earth and identifying the processes that have to do with molding the environment around us were a lot more important than which nation got where first."

"We're hoping to accomplish some of those things by sending men to Mars and later to other planets," said Lars Todt.

"You mean that's what the advocates of manned flight tell us," Mike corrected him. "You know as well as I do, Lars, that the real nitty-gritty of space exploration is that whoever gets the upper hand there might also get control of the world. Jake Arrens thinks the Russians may practically have that already with their missile system called SCRAG and that monster called the SS-9 ICBM."

"A lot of congressmen believe the same thing."

"We could have a SCRAG of our own and still explore most of our solar system with unmanned probes for a lot less than Pegasus is costing," said Mike. "Are you familiar with the chemical process called pyrolysis?"

"I'm afraid not."

"By using a gas chromatograph in conjunction with a mass spectrometer, it will be possible for an unmanned probe to make a complete analysis of the atmosphere of Mars without having to go through all the elaborate steps necessary to keep men alive in an atmosphere largely composed of carbon dioxide. By expanding the program a little, we could even identify organic compounds that would give us a real clue to whether life exists there."

"Isn't that a pretty tall order?"

"Not as much as you might think. We already know the Martian atmosphere contains CO_2 in high concentration and, if we find a lot of nitrogen, too, the presumption will be that life has been there—or will be."

"Wouldn't that require almost as much of a payload as putting men on the surface of Mars?"

"The weight ratio is something like forty pounds with an unmanned probe to forty thousand for human support, as a rough guess," said Mike. "NASA managed to hide that fact and FSA hasn't publicized it either."

"Why?"

"Probably because admitting that would also mean admitting we don't need the tremendous empire that's been built up within the government. The presence of water on Mars can be determined with detectors weighing about one pound in the final payload. And with a gas chromatograph weighing only about four pounds, we could determine the presence of hydrogen, helium, nitrogen oxide, carbon monoxide, cyanic acid, ammonia, methane, ethane, and probably a lot of other gases. In fact the whole scientific package weighs only about forty pounds and we had rockets as early as the Hermes program that could toss that kind of a spitball right into the eye of the sun."

"You're pretty convincing," Lars admitted.

"That's because I know what I'm talking about," said Mike. "The real tragedy is that if we weren't spending billions just to stay ahead of the Russians, we could probably feed half the hungry people in the world and even fatten our own pocketbooks by raising their economic level to where they could buy from us."

"A Pegasus vehicle circling up there is going to bring a lot of votes to the Administration," Lars reminded him. "Votes that could help us solve most of the problems here at home."

"It's still a hell of an expensive way to do it."

"Sometimes that's the only way. People who don't give a damn about a sophisticated scientific instrument probe of the Martian atmosphere will get all excited about astronauts floating around in a weightless condition."

"The Air Force did that ten years ago, when we were training for Hermes, by flying a powerful jet on a parabolic course," said Mike. "The sensation I experienced then for a few seconds was exactly like what I felt later when I was in orbit. I knew what to expect but nobody told me what it would be like to fight an oxygen convulsion halfway around the world and down through the atmosphere. If I can make sure that doesn't happen to the next fellow who flies a Hermes space-ship, it will be worth all the trouble."

iii.

Mike started calling Jan as soon as Lars Todt left, but it was after seven before she answered.

"Did you get my telegram?" he asked as soon as she said "Hello."

"It came this morning." Her tone told him that, as he feared, all was far from well between them.

"Believe me I wouldn't have had this happen for the world," he assured her. "Hal Brennan planted that item about the redheaded thrush in Jake Arrens' column, hoping he could drive me away from Spaceport City."

"Maybe it would be better if you just went, Mike. You've had your orgy—"

"Nothing happened at Hal's house, Jan. I went there to talk to him Saturday night and discovered that he was having a party—"

"Playing Countdown?"

"Yes." Concerned as he was, it didn't occur to him to wonder how she knew the name of the game. "I left as soon as I realized what was going on, but Hal had doped the drink he gave me and the police followed—"

"To Yvonne Lang's house."

"Who told you that?"

"It's all over Spaceport City; you know how that sort of news travels. Really, Mike, it would be better for everybody if you didn't come back."

"I can explain about Yvonne—"

"She called this afternoon to assure me you were out cold when you landed on her doorstep."

"Did she tell you why?"

"She gave me a hint."

"Then you know I'm actually innocent."

"I only know that people have been looking sidewise at me all day long and whispering behind my back."

"I can't stop now, Jan. Lars Todt is taking me to see the FSA administrator tomorrow and I may have a chance to prove what actually happened during my flight, besides taking a good hard look at Pegasus, too."

"I don't know." He couldn't be sure but her tone didn't seem quite as cold as before. "You're fighting powerful forces and that means we're both liable to be hurt."

"I promise—"

"You can't control what will happen, Mike. Surely you know that by now. Good night." The phone clicked off abruptly in his ear.

CHAPTER XIV

Lars Todt's secretary called the next morning to tell Mike their appointment with the FSA administrator was set for two o'clock that afternoon. He was in the waiting room of General Green's office when the senator came in and they were ushered in at once. Even so exalted a government official as the head of the vast sprawling empire within an empire that was FSA didn't keep an important senator waiting.

At fifty, Major General James Green was tanned and fit, his manner crisp and direct. An air force officer from the McNamara days, his rise had been meteoric and, when the cumbersome bureaucracy that NASA had become through the years was reorganized as the Federal Space Authority, combining all civilian and defense department activities in that field into a single agency, Green had been a logical choice to head it.

"Before you tell me your impressions of the Cape, Dr. Barnes," Green said after Lars had introduced Mike, "I wish you would bring me up to date on just what happened during your Hermes flight?"

Mike glanced quickly at Lars and saw that the senator was thinking the same thing—undoubtedly Israel Pond had already put in his oar. But it was no more than Mike expected, so he didn't let it disturb him as he quickly described the flight and its dramatic conclusion.

"It must have been a harrowing experience," said Green. "Are you quite sure of the cause?"

"There's no question about it, sir. We duplicated the early symptoms with volunteers in the pressure chamber at Anderson. Of course I couldn't carry the pressure rise to the convulsive stage because of danger to the subjects."

"I take it that you've been briefed on this earlier, General," said Lars Todt.

"Congressman Pond called me just before lunch to say those in charge at the Cape don't trust Dr. Barnes' judgment, when it comes to medical matters. He felt it might be bad for morale to have a—"

"I'm sure I know the term Congressman Pond used," said Mike. "He's never lost the chance to label me a coward since the congressional hearing before the Space Committee."

"Taggar Aircraft have their most important plant in Israel's district and his son owns a large block of stock in the corporation," Lars Todt added pointedly.

"That could be entirely legitimate, you know," said the administrator.

"Not when the son has never made an honest dollar in his life. Israel has him down on the government payroll as an office assistant but all he does is hang around the post office in their home town."

"The Taggar contract for Pegasus was let before I became administrator," said General Green. "It would cost a lot to wind it up now."

"To say nothing of the stink Israel Pond would make," said Lars Todt. "And the expense of getting a new contract started."

"I don't think you should cancel the Pegasus contract, General," said Mike. "All I want to do is to be sure the oxygen system isn't going to get out of whack and kill the crew with convulsions or force the mission to be scrubbed, when it's too late to make whatever changes are necessary."

"Are you sure you aren't being overcautious, Doctor?"

"I don't think so. After all mine wasn't the first time there'd been trouble with oxygen control in a spacecraft. One of the early Mercury launches was delayed two days while a defective oxygen valve was replaced."

"An important valve?"

"Its function was to prevent excessive flow of oxygen inside the cabin, the very thing I'm sure, that happened to me."

The general was obviously impressed. "What changes do you think may have to be made, Doctor?"

"One of several things probably went wrong in my ship," said Mike. "In Hermes—and, I understand, in the Pegasus command ship as well —the main supply of oxygen for breathing purposes during the flight was stored in the supercritical state."

"Mind explaining that, Mike?" Lars Todt asked. "I was never very good at physics."

"The tank used for storage is double-walled for insulation," said Mike. "It is filled with liquid oxygen at atmospheric pressure, but the critical temperature when liquid O_2 begins to boil off in the gaseous form is about minus one hundred and eighty-two degrees Fahrenheit. So when the tank warms up, the pressure rises quickly to about eight hundred and fifty pounds per square inch."

"Atmospheric pressure being about fifteen, as I remember it," said the senator.

"Yes."

"Isn't it dangerous to have the oxygen supply stored at such a pressure?"

"Dangerous—but almost necessary for a long flight," said Mike. "When the gas is in the cryogenic, or low-temperature state, its density is only a little less than that of liquid oxygen, so it requires merely a fraction of the space ordinary oxygen in a tank would occupy."

"Storage space becomes especially important with a space station," General Green added, "particularly where a crew of up to thirty-six men may be on full life support for as long as several weeks, while assembling larger stations in space."

"I'm sure that's why the cryogenic state was adopted for this project," said Mike. "But a complicated and extremely sensitive reduction valve system is necessary to reduce the gas from eight hundred and fifty pounds per square inch in the tank to the level of five pounds per square inch that has proved best for space flight. Besides, when oxygen boils off as a gas from the cryogenic state, its temperature is so low that it must be warmed up, else it would freeze an astronaut's lungs immediately."

"Controls operating at those temperatures have to be pretty rugged," General Green agreed.

"And if they don't function properly, the pressure inside the ship rises," said Mike. "A relief valve to the outside is supposed to pop off when the pressure rises above say five to five and a half pounds per square inch. But, if that fails, too, the amount of oxygen being forced into the blood of those inside the ship begins to go up very rapidly. The trouble is that the crew may not realize what's happening until they're in real trouble from convulsions or from narrowing of the arteries in their eyes and possible damage to the retina."

"The cabin pressure is monitored by telemetry," General Green reminded him. "Wouldn't the telemetry tapes of your flight contain a record of the actual pressure?"

"They should, sir. But when I asked for them at my hearing, I was told they were not available."

"Why?"

"I don't know, sir."

General Green picked up the phone. "Please ask Records to locate the telemetry tapes of Dr. Barnes' flight in Hermes I and the technical report on them," he said. "I want it as soon as you can get it."

"You have a remarkable faculty for explaining complicated scientific principles, Dr. Barnes," said the administrator when he hung up the telephone.

"I guess that's because they're everyday language to me, sir. Since my accident, I've devoted all the time I possibly could to this particular phase of the closed environment in which astronauts must live in space. You'll find a series of papers by me on record in the authority's files."

"I wasn't doubting that you've been busy, or that you're eminently qualified as a consultant to the Pegasus program," said the general. "What does trouble me is the statement that your presence at the Cape might be detrimental to the morale of workers on the Pegasus program, especially since yours was one of the few spacecraft lost during recovery."

"If you call the project director of Pegasus, I believe you'll find that Congressman Pond was mistaken about the feeling at the Cape, sir."

"That's not a bad idea." The administrator reached for the phone.

"You might tell Hal Brennan that I'm in your office when you get him, General, and that Mike is here, too," Lars added casually. "That way there'll be no question in anyone's mind that the cards aren't all spread out on the table."

General Green frowned, as if he realized something was going on of which he was not entirely cognizant, but he completed the call nevertheless.

"Hal," he said. "This is Jim Green in Washington."

"Jim!" The other two could hear Hal Brennan's booming voice in the receiver. "How are things up there?"

"Fine. What about Pegasus?"

"The Winged Horse is about ready to fly, Jim. It's going to be a beautiful sight."

"I called to ask how you felt about Dr. Michael Barnes working as a consultant on the project. He and Senator Todt are in my office now."

"We're glad to have Mike," said Hal Brennan without hesitation. "He's an old friend from the first Hermes days, you know, and an expert in the field."

"Then you have no objections to his checking out the life environment system for us?"

"None at all, Jim; I don't know anyone who could do it better. When are you coming down to see us yourself?"

"It's hard for me to get away from the desk with hearings on next year's appropriations coming up," said the administrator. "But I'll certainly be there for the shot."

"You must come, Jim," said Hal. "That baby is going to look mighty sweet rising into the sky."

General Green hung up the phone and turned back to Mike and Lars. "Want to tell me what's going on here?" he demanded.

"Why do you ask that?" said Lars Todt.

"Yesterday morning Jake Arrens made serious charges against Dr. Barnes in his column and today Arrens says we're concerned that Pegasus may be going too well—the first time I've heard about it, incidentally. Just before noon Congressman Pond tried to prejudice me against the doctor with this story about his being *persona non grata* with the Pegasus people. Yet, when you suggested that I check with Hal Brennan just now, Senator, you obviously knew he would give the doctor the green light. What gives?"

Mike spoke before Lars could answer. "I figured that Israel Pond would use the Arrens column to try to damage me with FSA, sir, so I called Hal earlier from the senator's office and convinced him that I should keep the job."

"That explanation will do, for the time being," said General Green. "But I shall send my own investigator to Spaceport City to make sure everything is as it should be."

"Would you mind letting me know what the telemetry tapes show about the cabin pressure on my ship during the flight, sir?"

"You have every right to know," said the general. "I hope they support your account of what happened."

"If Dr. Barnes finds anything to confirm his suspicions that Pegasus isn't entirely safe, can he report to you directly instead of through channels, General?" Lars Todt asked. "You know how reports sometimes get lost in lower echelons."

"I don't like this sort of thing, Senator," the general said with a frown. "My way is to give a man authority and let him do his job, until he proves he isn't doing it well. Then I break him."

"It will be too late to break anybody after some men have died, as they did in the Apollo disaster," said Mike. "You can be sure I won't abuse the privilege, sir."

"Very well," the administrator said crisply. "Either I'll thank you a few weeks from now, Doctor—or I'll break you as far as FSA is concerned."

ii.

Mike had been too preoccupied by Jan's reaction to read Jake Arrens' column that morning but, after leaving Lars Todt outside the FSA office, he picked up a copy of the morning paper. As always, the column was on the front page of the second section, but the columnist had made sure the item he'd typed out while Mike was in his office the day before wouldn't be missed by placing it at the beginning with the heading: "PEGASUS FLYING TOO HIGH?"

At the hotel, Mike found a message waiting for him to call Jake Arrens.

"Looks like we've hit a tender spot, Doc," the columnist said. "A dispatch came over the teletype about an hour ago from Pegasus headquarters in Spaceport City saying that the discovery of a faulty fuel line in a booster engine may cause a slight delay in the first Pegasus countdown."

"But nothing's wrong with the spacecraft?"

"Hal the Great himself assured newsmen that work on it is so far ahead of schedule men are being shifted to the booster to replace the faulty fuel line. He told them the bird would almost certainly fly on schedule."

"At least that arrow found a mark."

"You don't sound so happy, Doc. Didn't you get the job?"

"I got it—plus General Green's promise to break me, if this all turns out to be a false alarm."

"I see Jim hasn't forgotten his military upbringing." Jake Arrens' chuckle came over the wire. "You'd better produce—or he'll do it."

Mike ate a lonely dinner and afterward sat looking at TV, a fruitless pastime as he very well knew. The earliest flight he'd been able to reserve a seat on departed after lunch the next day for Orlando, where he could pick up his car and head for Spaceport City. With some fourteen hours to kill, he was thinking about having recourse to a Nembutal capsule, when there was a knock on the door. He opened it to find a bellboy outside with a large flat thin package.

"Special delivery for you, Dr. Barnes," the boy said.

The package was postmarked Spaceport City, but had no return address. Inside was a large cardboard folder such as was used for mailing photographs. When he opened that, Mike stared unbelievingly at the picture inside, an enlargement about eighteen by twenty inches in size. In full color, it was of Jan Cooper, completely nude.

Behind her, just visible in the background, was a couch and a naked man, whose features Mike could not recognize but which nevertheless somehow seemed to be familiar.

For a long moment he stood looking at the photograph while a sickness rose inside him. But as he was about to tear it up, something about it struck him as being odd and, taking the picture to the desk, he switched on the light so he could study Jan's eyes.

What he saw confirmed the suspicion that had made him examine the photo more closely. The pinpoint pupils, the masklike look on her face, as if she were walking in her sleep—all fitted one diagnosis. She had undoubtedly been under the influence of a drug when the picture was taken, probably the same one he'd been given during the Countdown party at Hal Brennan's house.

Remembering that night and the TV screen on the library wall, he was able to recognize now the room where the picture had been taken. It was undoubtedly Hal's infrared private studio for closed circuit TV, but this particular photo had been shot with a full flash to reveal so much of the lovely detail he remembered well from that night in the Astronaut Inn.

Slowly he tore the picture into small bits and flushed them down the toilet. But he couldn't flush away the truth that, in the grim game of chess he'd embarked upon that night when Lars Todt had called him in Mountain City, Hal Brennan had gained what looked like an insuperable advantage with an opening gambit.

He could understand now why Jan had been so disturbed, when he called her last night. And why she had said, "You're fighting powerful forces and that means we're both liable to be hurt."

Even more sobering was the realization that he'd fallen in love with a girl who now had every reason to hate him.

iii.

Mike was barely back in his hotel room from breakfast the next morning when General Green's secretary called.

"I have some information on the telemetry tapes made during your orbital flight, Doctor," she said. "Our records show that they were issued out to the chairman of the Space Committee of the House at the time of your hearing."

"Where are they now?"

"We have no record of their ever having been returned."

"Is any explanation of that in your records?"

"No, Doctor. If you remember the circumstances, NASA wasn't asking many questions of the chairman then. Can I be of any further help?"

"No. Please thank the general for me and be sure he gets the same information you've given me."

"The memo is on his desk now," she said.

Israel Pond had lied during the hearing when he'd said the tapes of the flight were not available, Mike decided. Which almost certainly meant that they had shown a failure of the environmental control system of the Hermes spaceship in which Mike had flown and that the congressman's action had been taken to protect Taggar Aircraft. When Mike remembered, too, that Hal had been serving during the flight as Capcom, the ground capsule communicator at Cape Mission Control, whose task it was to remain in voice contact with the astronaut in orbit while he was within range of Cape radio, pieces began to fall into place like a jigsaw puzzle.

Israel Pond's attack upon Mike himself at the time of the hearing had been a smoke screen, designed to cast serious doubt upon anything he might say later about the flight and thus protect Taggar Aircraft from the onus of being responsible for a major space failure. It had worked only too well, for stunned by the "Space Chicken" epithet at a time when he was not sure himself just what had happened, Mike had retreated into the obscurity of a research position at Anderson.

He would have been there still, if the brief spurt of publicity that had followed publication of his article on what, obeying a puckish impulse, he'd designated the "Lockheed Syndrome" hadn't brought him to the attention of Lars Todt again—plus the fact that Taggar Aircraft's being selected as the prime contractor for Pegasus suddenly made him a threat to everyone connected with the project.

The key to the whole thing was undoubtedly the telemetry tapes recorded during his own flight and the one man who probably knew the most about them was the ex-chairman of the committee to which they had been issued. Fortunately, Mike saw when he looked at his watch, he had time to visit Congressman Pond's office before his plane left for Orlando.

The last time Mike had been there Israel Pond's office had resembled an eddy in Grand Central Station, with petitioners waiting hopefully outside while staff assistants came and went amidst a general air of bedlam. Now that the congressman belonged to the minority faction, however, and was no longer chairman of an important committee, the change was startling.

Only two secretaries were typing in the outer office, which had much the same appearance as the county courthouse where Israel had begun his political career many years before.

"I'd like to see Congressman Pond," Mike told the gum-chewing typist who looked up when he came in. We've known each other a long time." He'd hoped she would jump to the conclusion that he was a constituent and she fell for the bait.

"Mr. Pond will be here in a few minutes. Would you give me your name, please?"

"Michael Barnes."

"Just have a seat, Mr. Barnes."

It was hardly ten minutes before Israel Pond came through the door. Among the last of a vanishing breed of Southern politicians, he still wore the uniform that had once distinguished them: the floppy Stetson, the white shirt with a hard collar and string tie, the baggy white suit, and a pair of the antique shoes known as Congress gaiters.

"Mr. Barnes is waiting to see you, sir," said the secretary, adding in a lower voice, "He's a constituent, who wants to say hello."

"Send him in." Israel didn't even give Mike a glance, which suited him very well as he followed the congressman into the office. Hanging his hat on an old-fashioned tree, Pond turned with hand extended but stopped short.

"Don't I know you?" he demanded.

"You should. I'm Dr. Michael Barnes."

"Barnes?" Israel Pond frowned. "You one of the Barneses back in my district?"

"No," said Mike. "I've been living in California."

"The 'Space Chicken'!" Israel's eyes were suddenly wary, the same look, Mike realized, that had been in Hal Brennan's when he'd first seen Hal in the cocktail lounge of the Astronaut Inn at the Cape.

"What do you want?" the Congressman demanded brusquely.

"I'm interested in locating some telemetry tapes of my orbital flight."

"Go to NASA—FSA they call it now. Don't bother me."

"The tapes were issued out to you as chairman of the Space Committee. They were never returned."

"Am I responsible for every clerk I ever hired?" Israel Pond snapped. "If the tapes are gone, somebody mislaid them."

"I think stole would be the better word," said Mike quietly. "I remember asking you about them at the hearing and being told they weren't available."

"Then they must have been lost."

"On the very day of the hearing?"

Israel Pond moved around his desk and dropped into the chair behind it. Pulling a slender stogie from his pocket, he bit off the end savagely, stuck it in his mouth, and lit it with an old-fashioned sulphur match.

"What the hell are you after, Barnes?" he demanded. "We lost a valuable space capsule because you got scared and blew the hatch. Now you turn up at the Cape sticking your nose—"

"Who told you I was at the Cape, Mr. Pond?"

"None of your damn business. I'm the one who asks questions around here."

"Before I get through, you may be the one to answer a few—like why telemetry tapes that might prove Taggar Aircraft built a faulty spacecraft suddenly disappeared from NASA files. I don't think Congress will look very favorably on the suppression of evidence that a contractor was bilking the space program."

"Look here—"

"Especially when the same contractor now controls a far more important—and expensive project. How much did it cost Paul Taggar to buy you, Mr. Pond?"

"You can't prove anything." Israel Pond suddenly looked every one of his almost seventy years, a dried-up string bean of a man who'd lost his power to harass others.

"Without the telemetry tapes, perhaps not. But have you considered what Jake Arrens can make out of what I already know."

Israel Pond straightened his shoulders with a visible effort and managed a ghastly smile, which Mike took to be ingratiating.

"Maybe I was a little hard on you at that hearing, Doctor," he admitted. "But all the information given me indicated that you were to blame for the loss of that capsule."

"Who gave you that information?"

"Hal Brennan swore nothing like what you claimed could possibly have happened. He was connected with the project, wasn't he?"

"He was the Capcom on that particular flight."

"Then wouldn't he know what those tapes you're talking about showed?"

"I'm going to settle that with him as soon as I get back to the Cape," said Mike.

"Let me give you some advice, Doctor," said Israel Pond. "Stay away from down there before something worse happens to you than almost happened with that capsule of yours."

"Is that a threat, Mr. Pond?"

"Just advice, young man, good advice. But you'd better listen to it."

"I'll think it over while I'm flying back to the Cape," said Mike. "Hal Brennan will be very much interested to hear that you're trying to put the blame on him for the raw deal I got eight years ago."

CHAPTER XV

Driving from the airport at Orlando to Spaceport City, after taking the early afternoon plane from Washington, Mike Barnes pulled off the road again at the overpass where he'd stopped the morning of the rocket launch and the start of the swift succession of events that had attended his visit to the Cape after eight years of absence. It was just past four-thirty and, in the bright September sunlight, streams of automobiles and trucks were flowing from the industrial and launch areas.

Spaceport City still looked like an advertising man's dream but, in the short space of less than a week since he'd come there, Mike had learned much about the turbulent currents of emotions surging behind the deceptively pleasant façade with even more force than the tides upon the nearby seashore. None of it was very reassuring either in light of his talk with Jake Arrens about the grim purpose America's newest space venture might well be called upon to fulfill.

At the motel he found a note from the front office under the door with a telephone number penciled upon it. For an instant he dared to hope it was from Jan until he recognized Yvonne Lang's home telephone number. She answered the second ring.

"I called to apologize," she said. "Can I buy you a drink as penance?"

"You did me a favor without knowing it. I'll buy."

"I can meet you in the bar there in ten minutes."

"Make it fifteen. I have to take a shower."

"Maybe I'd better join you. From some movies I've been seeing lately, that could lead to all sorts of fascinating diversions."

"It's an interesting proposition."

"If it's no more than *interesting*, it's not much of a proposition. Take your time; I've got a tip on the dogs for Al anyway."

She was waiting at the bar when he came in; they ordered and chose a table in the corner.

"A few people know I do legwork for Jake Arrens here at the Cape but a lot of others don't," said Yvonne. "Is there any reason why you should spoil my cover?"

"None at all; I found Jake a very interesting fellow. We're both after the same things in a lot of ways, but I still don't understand why you picked on me."

"I *had to*, Mike. Orders from higher up."

"Art McCord?"

"Higher than that."

"Paul Taggar—but why?"

"I could guess, but I want to keep my job so I won't. The package came to me complete, with orders to pass it on to Jake. I hope you know I'd never have put out that business about Jan and Friday night on my own. I've got too much to lose by tattling on my friends."

"Since you're Jake's friend, too, I can tell you we're sort of working together on this thing."

"I saw the release from FSA on the ticker yesterday afternoon about your appointment as consultant. It's time somebody started doing some snooping."

"Any repercussions yet?"

"None that I've heard of."

"How about Pegasus?"

"The same. Tom Craven, Taggar's chief engineer, flew to the main factory Monday afternoon, but I don't know what about. He's back now."

"Has Ellen's funeral been held yet?"

"This morning. The McCandless boy she was going steady with was pretty broken up."

"Abram McCandless' son?"

She nodded. "Jason's a fine boy. He stuck by the mother when the old man moved out and shacked up with that blonde." She got to her feet. "Thanks for the drink. I have to cover an Eastern Star dinner at the Hilton tonight."

"I appreciate your calling Jan."

"She was upset—which means she's pretty well gone on you."

"I hope you're right," he said. "But she's already engaged."

"Don't take that too seriously; Jerry McGrath is a nice boy, but Jan needs a real man and I've got an idea you fill the bill. Give her a few days to get over the snide remarks some people will be making, mainly because they envy her. I know I do."

ii.

Mike knew better than to try to call Jan. Instead, after dinner when the swift September night had finally descended upon the Cape, he drove by her house. A car with Texas license plates was parked in the driveway, however, and disappointed that she had company, he drove around for a while. When he turned into her street once again the Texas car was gone but a lighted window in the living room told him she must be at home. Parking his car, he walked up the curving driveway past a low hedge of scarlet Turk's-caps to knock on the door.

Jan opened it herself. In a frilly white blouse and lemon yellow Capri pants, she was a picture of loveliness—but there was no welcome in her eyes.

"I've got to talk to you," he said quickly.

"Is it any use?" She didn't shut the door in his face, however, so he came inside and closed it behind him. The room was tastefully decorated, the sort of living room he would have expected her to have. When she moved to a wing chair, he took the end of the sofa nearest her.

"I came by earlier, but you had company," he said.

"Jerry flew back from Houston sooner than he expected."

"Because of the column?"

"That, and because Hal has scheduled some tests for tomorrow."

"Did he say what sort of tests?"

"I believe they have a new suit that's lighter and supposed to allow more movement. Tom Craven brought one back with him from the Taggar factory today and Hal wants to test it tomorrow."

"He must be trying to steal a march on me."

"Then you're really going to stay on as consultant?"

"I have to, Jan. In Washington I discovered that the telemetry tapes showing the cabin pressure and oxygen levels in my ship eight years ago are missing from the FSA files. I believe Hal may have them."

"Would they clear you?"

"I hope so. Actually, I think Hal may be holding them as a lever over Paul Taggar and, by staying here for a while, I may be able to get them. But the most important reason for coming back was you."

"Haven't you caused me enough trouble already?" The animation was gone out of her voice again. "Jerry was furious—"

"I thought you had agreed that neither had a hold on the other and each of you could do as you pleased."

"He's a man. His pride was hurt when he learned I'd slept with another man."

"I couldn't blame him. While I was away, I discovered something— I'm in love with you."

"Please—"

"I've got to stay here until after the Pegasus launch, Jan, because that's the job I came from Mountain City to do. But if my presence in Spaceport City is going to embarrass you, I'll leave as soon as it's over.

If McGrath really loves you, he'll get over what was in Jake Arrens' column."

"What about you?"

"I'm certain in my own mind that Israel Pond's charges weren't true and if it's the best I can do, I'll have to live with that. The hardest part would be living without you."

"I was just as responsible as you for what happened Friday night in the motel, Mike. You mustn't let me be your Achilles' heel."

"You're the loveliest heel I've seen in a long time. Did your pupils win at Orlando?"

"Three superiors and a special commendation." Her voice took on animation once more. "More than any other teacher in this part of the state."

"I'm proud of you." At the door he held out his hand. "Are we still friends?"

"Still friends," she said. "Good night, Mike—and be careful."

iii.

The sun was shining brightly, a typical Florida autumn day, when Mike drove to the Kennedy Space Center the following morning about half-past eight. He had no trouble at the gate; his credentials from Anderson were quite sufficient to gain him admission.

The grounds of the old Bioastronautics Facility were familiar and he was even able to park his car in his old slot. The building itself was almost squat compared to the gantry towers and other structures in the area. Like even newer buildings, it was weatherbeaten, too, from the constant attack by the salt spray that battered all structures along the ocean front here and had even been closed up during the Apollo Program. Now, however, there seemed to be activity for several cars were parked in the lot.

Inside, only a secretary was in the outer office.

"Dr. Saltman is over at the centrifuge-simulator," she said. "They're running some tests on a new suit this morning with Major Boggs, one of the pilots scheduled for the next launch. Dr. Saltman said it might take practically all day."

"I'll go over there," said Mike. "I'm curious about this new suit myself."

The centrifuge-simulator building was in two sections. One housed the centrifuge itself, a powerful machine by which men could be whirled in a compartment so closely resembling a spaceship that it was possible to duplicate within it most of the problems that might arise due to the increased G-pressure accompanying ascent and reentry. Like so many structures in the area these days, it bore the Taggar Aircraft stencil on a metal plate beside the door.

The now motionless centrifuge was similar to the navy machine in which Mike had trained at Johnsville, Pennsylvania, prior to his own flight. The test scheduled this morning did not involve the centrifuge, however, but was being carried out in an adjoining room, where a plastic mock-up of a spaceship cabin had been built with walls so transparent that anything happening inside it could be observed.

The cabin was brightly lit, Mike saw when he came into the room, and a space-suited figure was already inside, with the usual hose connecting him to the life environment system of the simulated spaceship. About a half dozen men were grouped around the plastic cabin simulator and two more were seated at an elaborate control panel. Hal Brennan was in the group and, spying Mike when he came in, welcomed him as if nothing had happened between them.

"Gentlemen, this is Dr. Michael Barnes, the consultant FSA has sent us to help get Pegasus safely into orbit," Hal announced to the group.

Mike shook hands with Doctor Saltman, a middle-aged man with the somewhat detached air of a scientist, whose credentials in the field were well known to him. He was also introduced to several engineers, identified as being from the Taggar Aircraft Company, and to Tom Craven, Taggar's chief engineer at the Cape, whom he remembered Jan's mentioning the night before. A tall air force officer, introduced as Major McGrath, nodded coolly, but an older air force colonel, Andrew Zapf, shook hands warmly.

"We're running a test of a new space suit Taggar engineers have developed, Mike," Hal Brennan explained. "As you can see from the way Major Earl Boggs is moving around inside the mock-up, the suit allows considerably more freedom of motion, particularly during the sort of extra-vehicular activity men will be performing with Pegasus."

"What cabin pressure are you using?" Mike asked.

"We started out with an oxygen tension of one hundred and fifty millimeters in the suit and air at atmospheric pressure in the cabin," said Dr. Saltman. "We're trying to determine the lowest oxygen pressure at which a man can work effectively in the sort of vacuum that exists in space."

"When I tried this same experiment at Anderson, a hundred and fifty psia was about the minimum," said Mike. "I began to have considerable air hunger at anywhere below that level."

He saw the chief engineer give him a startled look, but the medical director was busy watching the monitor tube, where the astronaut's respiration and pulse were being recorded by flashing lines of light.

"Can we get on with this, Hal?" Paul Taggar, who had come into the room after Mike spoke brusquely. "I've got other things to do this morning."

"Major Boggs' respiration is about thirty, somewhat faster than it should be," said Dr. Saltman, and turned to the technician at the other panel. "What's the cabin pressure now, Al?"

"Down to five hundred millimeters, sir," the technician answered, indicating that the air pressure inside the cabin was now roughly two-thirds of the normal atmospheric level which it had been at the start of the test. "Shall I step up the amount of O_2 going into the suit?"

"Increase it to two hundred millimeters," Dr. Saltman directed, and the technician reached for a dial, twisting it to increase the flow through the umbilical cord attaching the astronaut to the life environment system.

The needle representing the air pressure inside the plastic cabin had been dropping steadily and Mike saw that it was down to four hundred, roughly twice that of the oxygen in the space suit the astronaut was wearing.

"Pulse and respiration still rising, sir," the second technician announced, and Mike glanced quickly at the flashing pattern of light racing across the cathode ray tube, where the respiration and pulse were being recorded. Breathing nearly forty times a minute now, the astronaut was obviously in some distress, even though the rate of oxygen flow to his suit had been increased.

"I don't understand what's happening," Dr. Saltman said worriedly. "Maybe we should abort the test, Colonel Brennan."

"This suit is very important, Ivan," said Hal Brennan. "We only have a little time to run the necessary tests."

"And Taggar Aircraft has over a million dollars in research invested in that suit," Paul Taggar added pointedly.

"Is it worth killing a man for?" Mike asked curtly.

"Look here—" Hal Brennan's voice was tense with anger but an even more dramatic happening inside the plastic chamber suddenly cut off his words.

The astronaut in the space suit, obviously fighting for air in spite of the pure oxygen he was supposed to be breathing, had seized the bubble-like plastic helmet of the space suit and was desperately trying to twist it off. Before he could succeed, however, he toppled forward, unconscious.

The others seemed stunned by what had happened but, sensing the cause, Mike acted quickly. Seizing the lever that closed the hatch giving access to the plastic-walled simulation of a spacecraft cabin, he pulled it down and, when the hatch opened, almost dived through the open port into the chamber itself as a sudden rush of air through the opening equalized the pressure outside with the partial vacuum which had been obtained by pumping air out of it.

Once inside, Mike's first act was to seize the plastic face helmet attached to the pressure suit by a metal ring and give it a sharp twist. When the threads attaching the suit to the metal collar of the helmet loosened, he was able to lift it off, but Major Boggs' lips and ear lobes were already blue from oxygen lack. He wasn't breathing either, but a sharp slap to the side of his face caused a startled intake of breath, proving, as Mike had surmised, that he had only just slipped over the level of consciousness.

Slipping a finger into the collar of the suit, Mike pulled it forward until the metal ring to which the plastic helmet had been attached was tightened against the back of the astronaut's neck, sending the full flow of the oxygen now pouring upward out of the suit toward his nostrils.

"Breathe deeply," Mike commanded and the still groggy officer obeyed, drinking in great breaths of almost pure oxygen. Within seconds, the blueness of his lips and ear lobes began to change to the normal hue, as his blood absorbed the oxygen he was breathing in.

"Better take it easy," Mike advised when he tried to sit up. "You blacked out."

"But why?"

"I'll explain later." Mike looked up to see a cluster of faces staring through the transparent wall of the plastic chamber; Dr. Saltman's anxious and perplexed, Hal Brennan's angry and disappointed, the chief engineer's puzzled.

"Think you can make it now?" he asked the astronaut, who nodded.

"Can we go on with the test?" Hal Brennan spoke through the open hatch.

"Not unless you want to kill Major Boggs," said Mike.

Hal started to retort angrily but Tom Craven spoke first: "I need to examine this suit again before you run any more tests, Colonel Brennan. If you use it again before I do, Taggar Aircraft cannot be responsible for anything that happens."

"All right," said the project director. "But I want everybody concerned with this in my office in half an hour for a critique. Can Boggs make it?"

"I'm all right, Colonel," the air force officer volunteered. "I just wasn't getting enough air."

"The gentleman who resuscitated you is Dr. Michael Barnes, Earl," said Dr. Saltman, and the air force major grinned sheepishly and held out his hand.

"I guess I owe you my life, Doctor."

"I don't think you were that near asphyxiation, Major, and what happened to you was probably a blessing," Mike said as he gripped the outstretched hand in the glove that was part of the suit. "It wouldn't be quite as easy to resuscitate an asphyxiated astronaut a hundred or so miles in space as it was here in a plastic mock-up, though. We can all be thankful that it happened now instead of after the launch."

CHAPTER XVI

A sober group gathered in Hal Brennan's office a half hour later. A new structure, as was almost everything connected with Pegasus, it was not in the older section of the Cape, where the Bioastronautics Facility was located, but in the newer area near the industrial center for Taggar Aircraft. The office was large, luxuriously furnished and air conditioned; two secretaries outside completed the decorative surroundings Mike would have expected Hal Brennan to provide for himself.

Dr. Saltman was already there with the two astronauts scheduled for the flight, Major Earl Boggs and Major Jerry McGrath, and the backup pilot, Colonel Andrew Zapf, a grizzled veteran of the space program.

Paul Taggar was also there, looking almost as ravaged by grief as when Mike had seen him at Sebastian Inlet early Monday morning; beside him was Tom Craven.

Hal wasted no time on preliminaries but went right to the matter under discussion.

"We all saw Major Boggs suffer a blackout this morning during the pressure test of the new suit Mr. Craven brought back with him from the factory at Houston," he said. "Can you remember anything about what happened, Earl?"

"Only that I was having trouble breathing, like you do at a high altitude when the oxygen is low. The next thing I knew, Dr. Barnes was working over me."

"Could this possibly have been a purely medical condition, Dr. Saltman?" Hal asked, but the physician shook his head.

"I checked Major Boggs with the other pilots on Monday. All of them are in excellent physical condition."

"Major Boggs lost consciousness from anoxia," said Mike. "His lips and ear lobes were quite cyanotic when I got to him; they only cleared up after he'd taken several deep breaths of almost pure oxygen."

"With a tension of two hundred millimeters in his suit, more than the normal tension of oxygen in the atmosphere?" Hal Brennan's voice was sharp. "You may be an authority on closed space ecology, Doctor, but you'll have to do better than that."

"The pressure gauges showed that the suit pressure was rising at the time," Dr. Saltman added.

"For a very good reason," said Mike. "Air was flowing into the suit."

"Impossible," said Paul Taggar harshly. "The whole idea is ridiculous."

"I'll admit that it's ridiculous to look for another answer when the real one is right under your nose," said Mike. "What happened this morning is an almost exact duplication of a near fatal accident that occurred during the Mercury program almost ten years ago."

"There's no record of anything like that," Hal Brennan objected.

"It didn't happen here at the Cape or at any of the test facilities," said Mike. "This was at the factory, while a test pilot was checking out the suits the Mercury astronauts would use. I was there and saw it—which is why I knew exactly what was happening to Major Boggs this morning."

"Perhaps you'd better explain, Dr. Barnes," said Tom Craven.

Hal Brennan started to object, but Colonel Zapf, the oldest of the three astronauts, shut him off curtly.

"Major McGrath, Major Boggs, and perhaps myself are the ones who will have to fly this mission, Colonel Brennan," he said. "Our lives will be in danger, not yours, so I'd like to hear Dr. Barnes' explanation of what he thinks went wrong."

"All right," Hal Brennan said with a shrug. "But it had better be more convincing than what I've heard so far."

"If you remember the conditions under which this test was being conducted, I think you will understand more easily just what caused the trouble," said Mike. "The simulated space cabin was filled with air at the start, while the pilot was wearing a suit into which oxygen was being pumped at a lower pressure than that normally occurring in the atmosphere—or somewhat less than twenty percent. The thing you need to keep in mind, though, is that the air inside the spaceship itself contained twenty percent oxygen and about eighty percent nitrogen."

"Is this lesson in elementary respiratory physiology necessary?" Hal Brennan asked.

"It is." Mike's tone was suddenly caustic. "For the simple reason that during the test those same elementary principles of respiratory physiology were ignored."

"What do you mean, Doctor?" Colonel Zapf asked.

"Just remember that the partial pressure of oxygen inside the space

suit was less at the beginning than that which occurs in the atmosphere and which also existed in the chamber at the start of the test.
It was only raised later, when it became evident that Major Boggs was
beginning to have difficulty in breathing. But that was a matter of too
little and too late."

"With pure oxygen?" Hal Brennan's eyebrows lifted expressively.

"Do you want to know what happened?" Mike kept his voice even.
"Or would you rather wait until the mission has to be aborted because
of a defect in the life environment system?"

"I want to hear the explanation, Doctor," Tom Craven said deci-
sively. "Please go on."

"Theoretically, the suit formed a closed system," Mike continued.
"Outside it was an atmosphere which in the beginning was the same
as that of ordinary air; it was reduced in pressure steadily, however,
as a pump evacuated the plastic chamber used to simulate the cabin of
a spacecraft. Because the fractional pressure of the oxygen inside the
suit represented at all times a considerably lower actual pressure than
that of the oxygen-nitrogen mixture outside it, any defect in the space
suit worn by the astronaut would allow air to flow into his life support
system—air, gentlemen, containing eighty percent nitrogen and only
twenty percent oxygen. It made no difference that he was actually
breathing pure oxygen in the beginning because air from the cabin
outside the suit began to dilute that almost immediately, largely with
nitrogen, which, being inert, was of no value to him. Naturally, the
pressure within the suit rose because air was flowing from an area of
higher pressure into one of lower pressure.

"As Colonel Brennan pointed out," Mike had everyone's full attention now, "only an elementary knowledge of respiratory physiology is
required to see that Major Boggs was breathing a mixture in which
the percentage of nitrogen was steadily increasing while the respective
tension of oxygen steadily decreased, until it reached a point where he
began to suffer from oxygen hunger. At this point his respiratory and
pulse rates began to increase and, even though the amount of oxygen
flowing into his suit was increased from about a hundred and fifty
millimeters of mercury to two hundred, that was still not enough to
overcome the large proportion of nitrogen entering the suit through
a leak. Inevitably, a point was reached when he was not receiving
enough oxygen through his lungs to support life and he blacked out."

"Ingenious," said Colonel Zapf. "A space suit leak that let air in instead of letting oxygen out."

"Mind you," said Mike, "if the pressure inside the simulated cabin
had been reduced below that inside the suit, oxygen would have flowed

from the suit into the cabin. But by that time Major Boggs would undoubtedly have been dead from lack of oxygen."

"We've devoted six months of engineering and production know-how to the manufacture of this suit, Doctor," said Paul Taggar. "Are you saying it's worthless?"

"This particular suit is probably worthless under the present conditions, but that doesn't necessarily mean all similar suits are in the same fix. It simply means that tests will have to be conducted on all of them to make sure they're airtight."

"How?" Tom Craven asked.

"The simplest way would be to have someone submerge, wearing a suit with air being pumped into it—the same principle we used in the old days to locate leaks in an inner tube by putting it in a tub of water."

"Is that what you recommend?" Hal Brennan asked.

"I'll even volunteer to wear the suit myself," said Mike.

"I'll undertake the risk of proving you're right, Doctor," said Colonel Zapf crisply. "You shouldn't be denied the pleasure of watching the bubbles rise when we locate the leak."

ii.

The actual test of the space suit was something of an anti-climax. Colonel Zapf donned the one Major Boggs had been wearing and, connected to an air source by a long hose, climbed down the rungs set into the wall of a steel test tank used to accustom astronauts to some of the phenomena of weightlessness, since the buoyant effect of water on submersion removed almost all the effects of gravity.

No air bubbles appeared until the plastic face helmet was submerged; then a stream rose from the threads where the helmet was attached to the metal collar of the suit. Without question, air from outside leaking into the suit so close to the astronaut's nostrils had diluted his already barely sufficient supply of oxygen, causing the blackout.

An audible sigh went up from the onlookers at this dramatic demonstration and Hal Brennan, who was personally supervising the test, reached over and tapped the helmet Colonel Zapf was wearing, the agreed upon signal for him to climb out of the tank. When the helmet was unscrewed and the cause of the trouble reported to the air force officer, he looked questioningly at Mike.

"What's the answer, Doctor?"

"I'm no engineer," said Mike. "But I did notice that both the collar on the suit and the metal connection at the bottom of the helmet are made of aluminum. My guess would be that the threads didn't hold up because of the softness of the metal."

"That can be changed by using a harder metal," said Paul Taggar.

"Then I'd say this suit is a considerable improvement over the earlier ones."

"I agree," said Colonel Zapf. "It allows much more mobility."

"I'll have the suit flown to the factory this afternoon," said Taggar. "Mr. Craven will take it and Dr. Ordway, our metallurgist here at the Cape, will go with him. We should have another one here by Monday, with threads that will stand up."

"I guess that ends the test, gentlemen," said Hal Brennan. "Just in time for lunch."

iii.

"How about having lunch with me, Dr. Barnes?" Colonel Zapf asked as they were leaving the test laboratory. "I'd like to discuss a few things with you."

"Fine." Mike had been favorably impressed with the senior member of the Pegasus astronaut team.

"There are a couple of cafeterias on the grounds," Zapf said, as they were getting into his car, "but anything you say in one of them is certain to be reported by the guards at the gate before sundown. I've taken a cottage at the beach, so my wife and kids can be here with me until the shot; usually I go home for lunch."

"Are you sure your wife won't mind?"

"I bring a lot of people home to talk shop. Helen's always ready to set some more plates."

The cottage was an A-frame with a private beach in front. Mrs. Zapf was a comfortably upholstered woman in her early forties, plump enough to be pretty but not fat.

"You created a small storm with that interview you gave Yvonne Lang, Dr. Barnes," said Helen Zapf. "The Spaceport City wives are up in arms against you."

"How about you, Mrs. Zapf?"

"Anybody who's lived around space installations as long as we have knows what goes on. If you decide to take up Spaceport City's favorite sport, the very ones who're lambasting you now will probably be your first conquests."

"You can see now why we always live over here on the beach, when we have to be at the Cape," said the astronaut.

"And why he brings his family," said Helen Zapf. "Andy's ashamed to admit that I hold a gun to his head, but I've seen too much of what happens to men who are away from their wives too long."

"Astronauts don't seem to become infected with the aerospace syndrome as a rule," said Mike.

"Perhaps it's because we're a different breed of cat from the engineers and scientists who do the legwork of getting us off the ground," said Zapf as they moved to the table in the corner of the living room overlooking the ocean.

Lunch was a delicious salad of tuna, chopped onion, and celery, with hard-boiled eggs. There was fruit on the side and pots of fragrant tea and rye crackers with a soft spreading margarine.

"We both have to watch the pounds, Mike," said Helen Zapf. "Andy so he won't overload the boosters and me so I won't overload my clothes—to say nothing of our arteries."

"I've been eating too much myself the past several days," Mike admitted. "Washington can be pretty frustrating."

"Do you have any idea why astronauts don't tend to fit into the engineer personality mold, even though a lot of us have engineering degrees?" Andy Zapf asked.

"My guess would be that as a class you possess considerably more self-confidence than the average man who goes into engineering, or even pure science like computer work."

"But why should that be?"

"If you spent much time worrying about whether you were going to get back from a mission, your psychosomatics would soon take over and you'd have some sort of a physical breakdown—like an ulcer or high blood pressure. I went through the early selection routine for astronauts years ago myself and even then psychologic testing was pretty rigorous, so most potential worriers got culled."

"I go back as far as Gemini, which makes me pretty ancient in this business," said Andy Zapf. "But even then, the medical and psychological people making the selections didn't want any devil-may-care flyboys riding spaceships into orbit."

Something in the air force officer's voice told Mike this was probably why he had been invited to lunch. Helen, too, was looking at her husband with a somewhat troubled expression.

"I can remember only one of the earlier astronauts who'd fit that description," Mike said deliberately.

"Hal Brennan," said Zapf.

"Is that what you wanted to talk to me about?"

"Part of it."

"Did something happen this morning that troubled you, Andy?" Helen Zapf asked.

"Earl Boggs was testing the new suit. If Dr. Barnes hadn't been there, he might have been in real trouble."

"Major Boggs is a pretty rugged young man," said Mike. "I think he could have stood a considerably longer period of anoxia with no serious effects."

"The point is that Earl shouldn't have been subjected to it at all," said the air force officer. "Making those connections of soft aluminum, instead of something that would stand up under repeated use and still be airtight, is an example of the sort of shoddy design and fabrication the Taggar people are capable of."

"Have there been other deficiencies?" Mike asked quickly.

"Only minor ones yet, thank God—things like brackets breaking under half the strain they should be able to bear. Or a LOX valve sticking and ruining the static test of a booster."

"I remember we had to make a dozen or so changes after the first Hermes I capsule was shipped from the main Taggar factory to the Cape for final assembling," said Mike.

"That's par for the course. And, naturally, it's comforting to know the designers have tried to duplicate practically every system of importance so if one factor fails, a second can take over. But redundancy still shouldn't be an excuse for anything less than attempted perfection."

"I agree," said Mike. "If one operation can fail, there's no law that says the redundant one designed to take over can't fail, too."

"Tremendous trifles," said Helen Zapf.

"What?" her husband asked, startled.

"It's the title of a nursery poem I was reading to Sally just a day or two ago. Let me see, how does it go:

'For want of a nail, the shoe was lost;
For want of the shoe, the horse was lost;
For want of the horse, the rider was lost;
For want of the rider, the battle was lost;
For want of the battle, the kingdom was lost;
And all from the want of a horseshoe nail.' "

Mike saw her grope suddenly for her husband's hand. "Andy, I'm afraid."

"Having Dr. Barnes here is the best thing that could happen to the program, Helen. The way he picked up that collar failure this morning could only come from knowing this business inside out."

"I've worked both sides of the street," Mike agreed. "As an astronaut and as a scientist studying the life environment system."

"Thank God for that!" said Andy Zapf.

"A rumor was going around Spaceport City over the weekend that FSA was going to drop you as a consultant, Doctor," said Helen.

"Because of Jake Arrens' column?"

"I imagine so."

"I straightened all that out in Washington. Hal Brennan himself assured General Green by telephone in my presence that he welcomed my being here."

"How did you manage that?" Andy Zapf looked startled. "Blackmail?"

"I can play rough, too—when the chips are down. Now tell me why you think something's wrong with Pegasus."

"It isn't anything you can put your finger on, more a case of things being pushed too fast."

"Faster even than Apollo?"

"The pressure is fully as great. And it was just by the grace of God that we didn't have a greater catastrophe than we did, when we were rushing to get to the moon ahead of the Russians."

"Three men dead—and a record of mistakes that could justify saying they were murdered by inefficiency?" said Mike. "I'd say that was quite a catastrophe."

"At least those failures happened on the ground. I'm talking about things like men circling the moon in a lunar command module forever. Or landing there and not being able to get off. What really troubles me though, is that one day a bunch of small errors might suddenly add up to a big one—like those tremendous trifles Helen was talking about."

"Do you believe Hal's rushing the first Pegasus flight dangerously fast?"

"I don't know," the flyer admitted. "But there's no question that a spectacular success with Pegasus will help everybody concerned—the Administration in the coming elections, Hal's chances of becoming the governor of Florida, the next FSA appropriation, even the price of Taggar Aircraft stock. From what I hear, Paul has had heavy losses lately at the Freeport casinos."

"What do the other astronauts think about all this?" Mike asked.

"McGrath isn't married and Boggs isn't the worrying kind. This is their first flight, too, so they're naturally eager and inclined to take some chances."

"I was that way eight years ago," said Mike.

"So was I, and maybe I'm just getting the willies, but I can't help thinking about what would have happened if one of us was outside the ship during extra-vehicular activity and oxygen started leaking out of that new suit. I'd hate to be the command pilot, too, with an unconscious man dangling outside at the end of an umbilical tether, to say nothing of having to drag him into the ship when my own suit was leaking and I was close to blacking out."

CHAPTER XVII

For more than a month since the big push had begun to get the first Pegasus rocket off the pad, Sandra Craven had been resentful of the fact that Tom had spent practically his entire waking time working on it and was so tired when he got home that he fell into bed, with hardly any notice of her. But after Daniel Sears' second visit in less than a week to 98 Hibiscus Lane, she was her old self again.

That Sears' visits had not gone entirely unnoticed, Sandra learned when she and Yvonne Lang happened to meet in the Ladies Lounge of the club one day after a bridge luncheon.

"What's this I hear about your having a gentleman visitor these mornings, Sandra?" Yvonne was reapplying her lipstick. "A gentleman of the cloth, no less."

"You know how people talk, darling." Sandra hoped her tone was airy but wasn't sure.

"A neighbor of yours tells me that handsome pentecostal preacher over on the mainland—"

"Oh, you must mean my pastor."

"I didn't know you were a member of Dan Sears' flock." Yvonne's eyebrows lifted. "Usually he appeals to a more earthy level—but maybe I've overlooked something."

"I belonged to a Church of Prophecy in South Carolina before Tom and I were married," Sandra explained hurriedly. "We've been going to Dan's—to Reverend Sears'—church occasionally since we moved here. Naturally he pays a pastoral call upon us every now and then."

"The way I hear it, he always manages to arrive when husbands are at work," said Yvonne. "Maybe you can tell me something I always wanted to know. Does he really go into the stretch reciting the Song of Solomon?"

ii.

When Mike got back from lunch with the Zapfs, he found a note in the Bioastronautics Facility asking him to come to Hal Brennan's office at two o'clock. Driving through the FSA reservation, from the old, so to speak, to the new, he was struck again by the difference in even the atmosphere between the two sections.

In the older area, now serving largely as a museum of former space efforts for the thousands of tourists who thronged through it every day, he could have shut his eyes and almost believed he was still in the quiet peaceful world of Merritt Island before the coming of the rockets and the rocket men who were their slaves. But once over the line into the newer section devoted to Pegasus, there was a hectic pace, almost a sense of panic, that was disturbing to someone who knew what that pace could generate.

He found Hal in his office—and friendly.

"Thought we might have a little talk before knocking-off time," said the project director. "I've got to run up to Daytona to speak to a club, but before I leave, I wanted you to know how grateful I am for saving us from a pretty serious mistake this morning. I hope you'll accept my apology for being rude during the test but this whole thing is pretty important to me and I made the mistake of assuming that you were only trying to throw a monkey wrench into the works."

"You should know better, Hal."

"Times change, Mike, and so do people. I guess you've been lucky to be relatively isolated these past several years out there at Anderson and not involved in so much of the sort of thing that goes on down here."

"Like Countdown parties?"

"Eight years is a long time and I'd forgotten that you always were a bit of a puritan." Hal seemed to be sincere. "Things move at a pretty fast pace around here and I assumed that, being single again, you might enjoy a little romp in the hay without any responsibilities. As soon as I discovered you'd left, I called Branigan's office and made sure one of the boys saw that you got home safely."

"I made it," said Mike rather grimly. "Just."

"So I heard. Yvonne's quite a girl. Maybe you did even better there than you'd have done at my place."

Nothing was to be gained by protesting his innocence, Mike decided. It would only make Hal Brennan believe him even more of what he had labeled him—a puritan.

"We could have lost an astronaut during that test this morning," Hal continued. "I want you to know I'm grateful and how glad I am that we're going to have your knowhow going for us."

Mike was waiting for some mention of the photograph and some intimation of the kind of gimmick he could expect next from Hal Brennan. To his surprise, there didn't seem to be one; he deferred mentioning the photo.

"I know you feel badly toward me for testifying against you at the hearing," Hal added. "But I'd flown one mission without trouble in a Hermes spacecraft and I was honestly convinced that nothing could have gone wrong with the life environment control system in yours. Besides, you admitted blowing the hatch—"

"As Capcom you were in touch with me all during those last ten minutes or so. Didn't I sound as if I were in trouble?"

"I thought you had panicked when the heat of reentry started consuming the edges of that heat shield and you saw part of it go flying past the window. It scared the hell out of me the first time I saw it."

"What about cabin pressure telemetry?" Mike asked casually.

"I didn't see it; you know the Capcom is busy staying in voice communication with the pilot."

"But did you see the tapes later?"

"No. I assumed that the hatch cover had blown itself, the same way it did with Virgil Grissom's flight earlier—until you admitted at the congressional hearing that you'd set it off yourself. Later, after you went to Anderson and started publishing articles about oxygen poisoning, I began to doubt—"

"Then why did you fight my coming here?"

"I'm a flyer, Mike, while you're a scientist who had been publicly critical of manned space flights, so there would naturally be a certain amount of distrust between us. At first glance it looked to me like you might be using your pull with Senator Todt to cramp me at a time when I could least afford to be cramped. I even thought you might have been sent here to replace me as head of Pegasus."

"That's the last thing I want," Mike protested. "I'm a doctor, not an engineer, an administrator, or a flyer."

"This morning showed me how valuable your scientific knowledge can be to us," Hal agreed. "I want you to work here as chief consultant in closed space ecology, Mike. We're going to have problems with Pegasus later; they're shaping up already."

"Like what?"

"The heart of the space station is the second stage of the assembly, but it also has to function as a rocket during launch. The booster exhausts itself quickly getting the entire rocket off the pad, then drops away. After that, the second stage goes into action and lofts itself, along with the Hermes II spacecraft on top of it that forms the command module, into the particular orbit we want, somewhere about two hundred miles above the earth."

"That sounds simple enough with the sort of power plant you've got."

"It is, compared say to Apollo. But in order to get Pegasus into the orbit we want, so we can study things like the Van Allen belt radiation, as well as the effects of prolonged weightlessness, infrared radiation, and the like, we've got to fire the second stage motor several times, and that's where we might have trouble. Then once we've got the bird into the parking orbit we want, the men will have to toss a lot of stuff out of the second stage to make room for housekeeping there. It's a complicated piece of business; I don't need to tell you that."

"You're not planning to stop with one station are you?"

"The original Air Force MOL plan never got any farther than that, but later on, we'll send up a duplicate of this first Pegasus and lock it on, doubling the size of the whole satellite—which is what it will actually be by then."

"And so ad infinitum?"

"Theoretically, yes. But we think two joined into one should give us in about a year all the information we'll need before launching an actual space exploration of Mars."

Hal had made no mention of the other use for an orbiting Pegasus —as an arsenal of hydrogen warheads—and Mike decided it was too early to bring up such a sensitive subject. He could learn more by keeping his eyes and ears open, once he was on the inside of the project.

"Our greatest problem is going to be maintaining a satisfactory life environment system in the main orbiting laboratory," Hal continued, "with an airlock device so men can come and go, while performing extra-vehicular activity, without having to depressurize the whole setup every time somebody goes outside."

"That's a tall order."

"What happened this morning showed me that the people we've got working on that part of the project haven't really got the elasticity of mind we need so badly. I'd like for you to supervise the life environment end of the whole project."

"What if I have a run in with Paul Taggar? He doesn't have much use for me."

"Paul's had a lot of trouble lately; his wife's a lush and you know about the girl. But a failure here at the start would be as bad for Taggar Aircraft as it would be for me, so I'll have no trouble convincing Paul that we need you badly. Is it a deal?"

"On one condition," said Mike.

"What's that?"

"I discovered in Washington the other day that the telemetry tapes recording cabin pressure readings during my own flight are missing from the files. They were issued out to Israel Pond's committee and were never returned."

"Does Israel—"

"I checked with him and he claims to be innocent but whether or not he's lying, I can't tell. You have a lot of inside knowledge about FSA, Hal. Is there any chance that you might be able to find them?"

"If I find the tapes, I'll turn them over to you," Hal promised. And with that Mike had to be content, whatever his doubts might be that Hal was telling him the truth.

iii.

Tom Craven had expected Sandra to explode when he finally remembered she had said something about a bridge luncheon at the Space Club and called her there a few minutes before the Taggar jet was scheduled to take off for the main factory.

"I've been trying to get you at home since twelve o'clock, hon," he said.

"Is anything wrong?" Sandra knew a moment of panic that whoever had told Yvonne Lang about Daniel Sears' visits might have spoken to Tom, too.

"We tested the space suit I brought back from the factory with me and that new doctor, who's been sent down as a consultant, found a defect. I'm taking off in a few minutes to show the factory people what needs to be done and Dr. Ordway is going with me."

"When will you be back?" To his surprise she didn't seem very much upset, but what he couldn't know was that she was so filled with relief she had to lean against the wall by the telephone.

"Not before Monday evening at the earliest," he said. "We're going to put extra men working on the suit over the weekend so I probably won't get any sleep, but I hope to wrap it up in time to fly back Monday afternoon."

"Is this bad, darling?" she asked. "I mean about the suit."

"It would have been, if this doctor hadn't spotted the trouble. We should be able to correct that now without holding up the shot."

"I'm glad."

"What will you do?"

"Oh, I don't know: probably go to church Sunday morning."

"If you do, thank the preacher for giving me the idea about Ezekiel's wheels. Paul is going with me to Houston and I can talk to him about it on the flight. Maybe as soon as the shot is over he'll let us use the jet to fly to Freeport. We'll have ourselves a ball."

Sandra was humming as she hung up the telephone. Daniel would be happy to hear that Tom had been inspired by his sermon. Of course, she couldn't really explain it to him in the few minutes while they shook hands after the sermon, but maybe he could stop by the house again on Monday morning. . . .

iv.

He was the most fortunate of men, Asa Childs told himself as he turned into the entrance drive of the apartment house and found his parking slot. He was whistling as he climbed the steps to the entryway and put his key into the lock and, in his happiness, didn't notice a car parked several slots away with some kind of lettering on the side of the door. Albert had gone to Orlando because of some family emergency but he had promised to be home Saturday so they could have the weekend together. Asa had even bought a couple of bottles of champagne to celebrate his return and the thought of coming home to a comfortable apartment with Albert there to meet him once again filled Asa with a warm glow, a sense of belonging he'd never experienced before.

Gone was the overpowering need to visit bar after bar hunting for partners, the likelihood—it happened quite often—that some thug would pretend to be gay, too, then roll him for his wallet when they were alone. Asa had lost a lot of money that way and once, in Houston, had almost been killed when he'd been sapped with a blackjack.

As Asa was pushing the door open after unlocking it, a man who had been standing a few yards away on the landing that gave access to the upper floors of the garden style apartments moved toward him.

"Are you Asa Childs?" he asked.

Asa stopped with the door half open; the voice of authority was something you came to recognize in his world and, in the long run, it was always better to stop and not panic. Besides, he hadn't done anything that hundreds like him didn't do and the law usually took a broad view of two consenting adults establishing the sort of relationship that existed between him and Albert.

"I'm Childs," he said.

"My name is Fenner; we'd better go inside."

"What's the trouble, Mr. Fenner?" Asa put down the bag of groceries he was carrying and shut the door behind the other man.

Fenner took a small leather folder from his pocket and opened it, showing his picture on one side and some sort of an official seal that Asa didn't recognize on the other.

"I'm a special investigator for the health department," he said. "Do you know an Albert Ragor?"

"He rooms here." Asa's voice was suddenly taut. "Has there been an accident, officer?"

"Ragor has been arrested, but he's all right." An old hand at his job, Fenner recognized the anxiety in Asa's voice as genuine and couldn't help feeling sorry for him.

"Arrested?" The color drained out of Asa's face. "Where?"

"In Orlando—for male prostitution. He and a Pierre Carvin."

"Pierre!" With a cry of anguish, Asa Childs dropped into the chair and buried his face in his hands. Pierre and Albert had been lovers before Asa had persuaded Albert to live with him and Albert's taking up with Pierre again—the obvious reason for the visit to Orlando—was a cut to the heart. But then Albert couldn't have been to blame, Asa assured himself quickly. He was so soft and feminine, so pliant to a stronger will, that a louse like Pierre could easily have led him astray.

"It's Pierre you should arrest," he said. "He got Albert into trouble."

"I rather think you're right, Mr. Childs," said Fenner. "But I'm not an arresting officer; I'm from the health department. Both Pierre Carvin and Albert Ragor have primary syphilitic lesions. We're tracing all contacts."

"Contacts?"

"Ragor named you—among others. All we ask of you is to have an examination and a blood test. If it shows up positive, you can go to a rapid treatment center and be cured in a short time, not more than a few weeks at most."

"What about Albert?"

"I'm afraid that's not in my hands—or yours. He and Carvin are under treatment now. When that's over, they'll come up for trial."

"But they won't—"

"I doubt that your friend will get more than a normal jail sentence; it might even be suspended, since he cooperated with the health authorities. If we locked up all the fag—all the people in similar circumstances—the jails would be so full there'd be no room for real criminals."

"Then I'm not under arrest?"

"Not if you agree to be examined. All the others have."

Asa Childs took a deep breath. "How many?"

"We have a record of twenty contacts so far—the ones they had names for."

Asa Childs straightened his shoulders. There was no use putting off what had to be done and, besides, it really wasn't Albert's fault. He had known all along that Albert was weak; anybody so desirable usually was in the gay world. If he went ahead and took treatment,

he'd be well by the time they let Albert out. And Albert would be needing him then—not that bastard Pierre.

"How about Monday afternoon, after I get off work?" Asa asked, for
an even better plan than taking the treatment at all was taking form
in his mind, one he'd used several years before under somewhat similar
circumstances.

"The clinic's open until six, but you couldn't get the test before
Monday anyway," said Fenner. "The lab technicians don't work weekends and they like to knock off early on Friday."

From his pocket, the health investigator took a pad of appointment
slips and filled one out, tearing it off and handing it to Asa. "Just give
that to the lab, the address is on the slip."

v.

"Sometimes this job gets to you," Jack Fenner told his wife as he was
broiling steaks in the back yard of his house in a small mango grove
overlooking the Indian River.

"Who is it this time?"

"A fellow that has an apartment in what they call Swinger Lane.
I checked on his job with FSA and he's a damned important cog in this
Pegasus project; makes over fifteen thousand a year."

"What does he do?"

"Metallurgical technician is his job category. He runs a laboratory
testing metal strength and things like that."

"Even though they know he's a fag?"

"What difference does that make? You have your hair done in a
beauty parlor and a lot of those fellows are fags. Did you know the
Indians had a whole clan of homos?"

"You're kidding. The noble redskin prided himself on being a mighty
warrior."

"There were plenty of gay ones among the Indians just the same.
The Creeks in Alabama and Georgia even let 'em grow their hair long
like women and do women's work. One special job was to take care of
the wounded after a battle." He grinned. "I'd sure hate to be unconscious and have one of 'em working over me."

"I still don't understand how they do it—you know what I mean?"

"If I told you some of the ways you wouldn't believe it," he said. "But
when you come down to it, they've actually got a lot more on the ball
in many fields than the rest of us have. This guy's apartment was beautifully decorated and he was a lot more concerned about this Albert than
he was about himself. When I told him a guy named Pierre Carvin
was with Albert, it practically broke his heart."

"So what happens to him now?"

"If his test is positive, he gets treated."

"What about his spreading it around?"

"To another fag, maybe, but the doctors at the health department tell me he's no more of a menace to other people than some guy going around with a flu bug coughing it out in the air."

"I'll never believe you can't get it in bathrooms."

"Oh, you can get it there all right, but the floor's awfully cold and hard," said Fenner with a grin. "Would you believe that in this list of twenty-odd contacts the two fags put the finger on, there's a lawyer —prominent, too—and a couple of bankers? One of 'em I had to investigate before for the same thing."

CHAPTER XVIII

Knowing Jerry McGrath was in town and that Jan would no doubt be occupied with him, Mike was resigned to spending a lonely weekend. He was surprised, shortly after he came in from the swim he loved to take in the warm surf before going to dinner, to receive a telephone call from Shirley.

"Hal's gone to Daytona to make a speech to some club," she said. "I know Jan has to play in the lounge Friday evenings, and Jerry McGrath's in town, so she'll be seeing him afterward. How about our having dinner together—for old times?"

"Do you think that's wise?"

"This is the twentieth century, Mike, not Salem, Massachusetts, in the days of Cotton Mather."

After Hal's referring to him as a puritan that afternoon, her words stung just enough to make him agree. "Where shall we go?"

"The gentleman names the place."

"How about the Spaceport Hilton?"

"How about Grand Central Station?"

"It's a little late for a reservation. And a little far, even for TGIF."

"Forgive me, Mike; I'm a little edgy these days. I know you don't want to take me to the Astronaut Inn, where Jan will be playing, and the food's lousy there anyway. I'll go wherever you want to go."

"I was about to suggest the Sea View." It was the ocean front restaurant where Mike had eaten dinner the first night he was in Spaceport City.

"We had some wonderful times there," she said, and he wondered whether he had made a mistake. "I'll stop by about seven, if that suits you."

"I'll call and have them hold a table facing the ocean," he said, and was waiting in front of the inn when she drove up about seven-fifteen, which, as he remembered it, was early for her. She was driving an Eldorado and, for a wonder, appeared to be sober.

"This is quite a car," he said, getting in.

"Jake Stein left me well fixed and I haven't buried my money like that fellow in the Biblical parable. Anybody's a fool to bet against the Mafia, like Paul Taggar does in Las Vegas and the Bahamas, but a smart woman can do very well in the stock market."

"Too bad I didn't have anything for you to work with."

"Things might have been different if you had. I pay my servants more now than you were making back then."

They pulled up in front of the sea front restaurant and she gave the car to the doorman to park. Inside there were only a few diners as yet and they were shown to a table overlooking the ocean. Shirley refused a drink and they ordered the stone crabs for which the restaurant was famous.

"I needed someone to talk to tonight, Mike," she said over coffee and key lime pie, as they were finishing a leisurely meal.

"Are you sure my advice is that important?"

"You're the only really honest person I know, even if you are a bit of a prude. Did you know we both had Number Five at Hal's Saturday night?"

"I discovered the disk in my pocket the next day."

"It wasn't very polite of you to go rushing out like you did. I ended up in a sandwich."

"I apologize, Shirley." He could well imagine what that phrase meant in the kind of party that had been in progress that night.

"Are you sorry?" She looked at him intently across the table and he didn't try to kid himself that some of the old lure wasn't still there. You couldn't have been married to a woman like Shirley for five years and not remember a few things that could still stir a sense of warmth within you.

"I don't like being on TV," he countered, and Shirley laughed.

"You get over being camera shy after a while. And you ought to see some of the pictures Hal takes. He's got an expensive camera with a strobe flash rigged up in that guest house. It's so fast, most people don't know they've been on candid camera."

He considered briefly asking her to help him find the negative of Jan and discarded the idea. Letting somebody else know about it would mean betraying Jan; and besides, he thought he could get the negative himself, now that Hal had admitted needing him with Pegasus.

"Are you going to marry Jan Cooper?" Shirley's question startled him; it was almost as if she'd been reading his thoughts.

"If she'll have me."

"She will. Any woman would be a fool not to."

"Is that expert testimony?"

"It is—now. You've matured a lot since we broke up, Mike—become a real man instead of an idealistic boy."

"There's still Jerry McGrath."

"He doesn't stand a chance with you on the scene. You and Jan will make an average American couple with a split level somewhere, a station wagon to haul the kids to choir practice and Boy Scout meetings, seats at the symphony—the whole bit." Her voice cracked for a moment. "But don't stay in Spaceport City, Mike. The air here is polluted with sophistication and sex—the wrong kind."

"Is anything wrong with you, Shirley?" he asked.

"Nothing you can do anything about. Would it surprise you if I told you Hal suggested our having dinner tonight?"

"No."

"He seems to think he's conned you into believing he needs you."

"He does need me. I saved him from an expensive mistake this morning in a space suit test and, with the launch less than two weeks off, he's already beginning to sweat."

"Is Pegasus likely to fail, Mike?"

"No more than the others, from what I've heard; actually it's a far less complicated operation than Apollo was. Of course, you always find a lot of little bugs at the last minute but most of the time they get ironed out. Starting Monday I'm going to go over that spacecraft with a fine-toothed comb. It's quite similar to the Hermes I flew."

"I recognized that when I saw one on a truck as I drove to Pegasus headquarters the other day to take Hal to the airport to fly to Boca Raton for that meeting."

"The industrialists? I remember reading something about it in the paper in Washington."

"The meeting was a front. Hal's campaign is being handled by a public relations firm in Palm Beach and he went down there for a strategy session."

"It looks like he's pretty confident that Pegasus will take off on schedule."

"They've got the campaign programmed into a computer with the launch time. When that rocket fires, they'll start the computer and by the time the bird is in orbit, the whole thing will be under way, fueled partly by a half million from me."

"That's a lot of money."

"It *was* to buy a wedding in the governor's mansion at Tallahassee during the inauguration. We were going to save on the reception by having it there."

The way she'd said *"was"* told Mike they had come to the real reason why she had asked him to have dinner with her, but he waited for her to go on.

"That was before another woman came on the scene. Her father owns the biggest corned beef plant in the world; you and I probably lived off some of it when we were trying to make both ends meet on your salary a long time ago."

"Where is she now?"

"For the time being Hal's keeping her under wraps in places like Palm Beach, Orlando, Jupiter Island, and Nassau—until he's ready to trot her to the post for the bettors to take a look at her. You can imagine how an old mare like me will stack up beside a young filly."

"I'd think any politician would hesitate to turn down a half million dollars as a campaign contribution."

"The girl's father would probably put up a million, maybe more, to see his daughter the wife of a governor of Florida. But with my track record in the marriage derby, I can't afford to invest more than a half million."

"You're being very realistic about this."

"Jake Stein didn't just leave me rich; he taught me a lot, too."

"If you're afraid Hal plans to take your contribution and leave you in the lurch, why hang on to him?"

"I made the mistake of falling in love with the bastard, for one thing. For another, with me managing his career, Hal could go a long way after Tallahassee—to the Senate for certain, maybe even to the White House."

"Do you think he's only pulling the strings to make me jump by pretending to want me here in the Pegasus setup?" Mike asked.

"From what you say about the accident this morning, I think he needs you. But my advice to you would be to take Jan and get out of Spaceport City."

"I can't do that."

"Why not?"

He told her about the telemetry tapes and Hal's promise to help him get them.

"Will you help me, Shirley?" he asked at the end of the account.

"Not as long as Hal thinks he needs to control those tapes because of his campaign—and I've got a possible shot at the governor's mansion."

"What connection could they possibly have with politics?"

"Paul Taggar is bankrolling Hal's campaign pretty heavily, too. If those tapes prove that a Taggar spacecraft failed, they could be a club Hal is holding over Paul." She put her hand over his on the table. "All *you* need to do is prove something that anybody who knows you well would be sure of anyway, Mike—that when you say something, it is true. To me, Hal is the key to a big white house in Tallahassee and maybe one in Washington later on, so I've got to look after my own interests first."

Asa Childs wasted no time after the health department inspector left. With the expense facing him of having to pay a lawyer to get Albert off after he finished treatment at the Rapid Treatment Center—using as grounds the fact that Pierre had led Albert into trouble—Asa couldn't afford to lose the time from work that would follow the discovery of a positive blood test, when he visited the public health syphilis clinic Monday afternoon. There was a quicker way to ensure that the test would be negative, a way most people in his position already knew, and fortunately Irv Sacks, a Daytona Beach pharmacist who was also a homosexual, owed him a favor; Asa always kept a detailed mental record of those who were indebted to him, against a future time of need like this.

Going downstairs, he got into his car, drove westward to I-95, and headed north. At the South Daytona exit about an hour later, he took the ramp eastward and shortly parked his car outside the drugstore where Irv worked.

Sacks was serving a customer in the back of the store; when she left, Asa went back.

"Hi, Irv," he said. "How've you been?"

"Fine, Asa. What can I do for you?"

"I need a lot of penicillin—in a hurry."

Irv Sacks didn't ask why; he'd had other requests under similar circumstances.

"Got a prescription?"

"No time. I've only got 'til Monday afternoon for a blood test. If it's positive when they run it Tuesday in the public health lab, I'll be laid off and might even lose my job."

"That's cutting it close." The pharmacist frowned. "You may not get a negative test by that time, Asa."

"I've got to chance it. What's the biggest dose you have?"

"Five million units."

"Give me a half dozen."

"Can you give it to yourself?"

"I'll make it. Just get the stuff for me."

Irv Sacks went into the pharmacist's cubicle at the rear of the store and came out shortly with a package in a paper bag.

"I'm letting you have this wholesale," he said, "but it's still thirty bucks."

While Asa was counting out the money, Sacks reached across the counter and took a small bottle from the shelf and a little package of sterile absorbent cotton. "Use this isopropyl alcohol, to sterilize the skin," he advised. "And be sure you don't touch the needle after you take off the plastic guard."

Asa paid the money and left the store. At a motel and service station complex where I-95 crossed the road to the beach on an overpass, he drove into the station and gave instructions to fill the tank.

Getting the key to the men's room, he unlocked it and went inside, being careful to lock the door. Then, after washing his hands thoroughly, he opened one of the six packages of penicillin and carefully took out the ampule of white fluid with the needle attached.

Soaking a pad of cotton with the alcohol Irv Sacks had given him, he scrubbed a place on the skin of his right buttock as far back as he could reach comfortably. Picking up the syringe, he slipped the plastic guard off the needle itself and jabbed the point home, wincing as it went through the skin and deep into the muscle.

Maintaining an even pressure on the plunger of the syringe, he injected the potent drug into the tissues of his buttock until the plunger would go no farther and pulled out the needle. Carefully gathering up everything he had brought in with him, he carried it out in the paper bag Irv Sacks had given him at the drugstore and, hanging the key inside the station, signed the charge slip. Then he put his credit card back in his wallet, and drove back toward I-95.

Another shot at bedtime, two more tomorrow, and two Sunday should make certain, he was sure, that his blood would be negative when it was taken late Monday afternoon. Just in case, though, he'd get a test somewhere else in a month or two and, if that was positive, arrange for another series of injections with a doctor he knew on the mainland.

iii.

Sandra Craven was early for the Sunday morning service, which suited her fine. That way she was assured of a seat in the front pew, where the Reverend Daniel Sears could not fail to see her when he began the service.

The reverend himself had been busy working on a sermon, the inspiration for which had come to him in Sandra's own bedroom a few days earlier. He was preaching from the Book of Revelation, a favorite with pentecostal exhorters because one could find in it support for almost any position one chose to take—as well as damnation for the opposition.

Daniel Sears didn't miss Sandra's presence, or the fact that she was alone and wearing a shorter dress than usual—an unconscious act of resentment against Tom, who sometimes objected to the height of her skirts. He didn't miss the glow of worship that began to burn in her eyes at the sight of him either, but this troubled him somewhat for he could see that Eunice, from her position in the front row of the choir, was studying the younger woman thoughtfully, no doubt noting that taking this seat was coming to be a habit with her.

The next time he saw Sandra, he'd have to warn her against adoring him so openly, Daniel Sears decided—while not discouraging her from doing so privately, of course. The eagerness and enthusiasm she brought to the king size bed at 98 Hibiscus Lane was not something to be dismissed until circumstances made such a renunciation inevitable —and that time, the handsome preacher assured himself, was not yet. But he also had to be careful to avoid arousing Eunice's easily stirred suspicions at a time when he was preparing to take the step that would make him an internationally known figure practically overnight.

Wearing his white robe with the golden embroidery at the cuffs and collar, and with his blond locks carefully waved and sprayed surreptitiously with Eunice's hair set, lest the breeze from the air conditioner duct behind the chancel spoil their glossy perfection, Daniel Sears strode across to the pulpit to read the Scriptures. As he stepped up into the elevated space, a shaft of sunlight breaking through the window at his back enveloped his blond curls, turning them to gold and causing a sigh of admiration to rise from the feminine members of the congregation.

Opening the Bible, he paused and looked out over the flock that packed the church to the last pew, savoring the worship in the eyes of so many of those uplifted to him.

"Beloved." He rolled the word like a sweet morsel upon his tongue, sending a shiver of pure bliss through Sandra, as well as some others, who also knew very well what it meant when uttered under somewhat more intimate circumstances.

"Beloved, I read to you today from the Book of Revelation of St. John the Divine, written in his own words:

> 'To show unto his servants things which must shortly come to pass . . . Blessed is he that readeth, and they that hear the words of this prophecy, and keep those things which are written therein: for the time is at hand.'"

He looked up from the page and found Sandra's eyes shining so brightly with a warm light of adoration that he had trouble concentrating on other things.

Looking down again, he turned the page and said, "Continuing from the Eighth Chapter and the Eighth Verse, we read:

'The second angel sounded, and as it were a great mountain burning with fire was cast into the sea: and the third part of the sea became blood. And the third part of the creatures which were in the sea, and had life, died; and the third part of the ships were destroyed. And the third angel sounded and there fell a great star from heaven burning as it were a lamp. . . .'"

Turning another page, he continued:

"'The fourth angel sounded and the third part of the sun was smitten, and the third part of the moon, and the third part of the stars; so as the third part of them was darkened, and the day shone not for a third part of it, and the night likewise. And I beheld, and heard an angel flying through the midst of heaven, saying with a loud voice, woe, woe, woe, to the inhabiters of the earth by reason of the other voices of the trumpet of the three angels, which are yet to sound!

And the fifth angel sounded, and I saw a star fall from heaven unto the earth: and to him was given the key of the bottomless pit. And he opened the bottomless pit; and there arose a smoke out of the pit, as the smoke of a great furnace; and the sun and the air were darkened by reason of the smoke of the pit. And there came out of the smoke locusts upon the earth; and unto them was given power, as the scorpions of the earth have power. And it was commanded them that they should not hurt the grass of the earth, neither any green thing, neither any tree; but only those men which have not the seal of God in their foreheads. . . .

And in those days shall men seek death, and shall not find it, and shall desire to die, and death shall flee from them.'"

Daniel Sears closed the big Bible and stood looking down at his congregation with the sunlight wreathing his head in a golden halo.

"Beloved, I say to you that the words of prophecy which I have read to you are much more than just the words of the Disciple John, revealed to him by God but spoken with his voice nearly two thousand years ago. Yes, these are the very words of God Himself, speaking to us all in this time and this place, warning of a great calamity unless we, to whom have been revealed the words of prophecy, stir ourselves to carry out the will of God.

"And what is that will? Listen again to the words of the Prophet Ezekiel:

'And I looked, and, behold, a whirlwind came out of the north, a great cloud, and a fire infolding itself, and a brightness was about it, and out of the midst thereof as the color of amber, out of the midst of the fire.'

"How many times have you looked to the north when you heard the voice from the whirlwind and, seeing the great cloud and the fire, fallen on your knees to ask for God's mercy? That mercy has been granted us until now but no longer can we hope for it, if we allow those who would mock the very words of God Himself to flaunt themselves and launch their fiery darts into the very face of God.

"Beloved, God was not mocked when men dared to set foot upon the moon, for that, they tell us, was once part of the earth. But now they dare to take the first steps into God's own firmament, perhaps even to the gates of heaven itself, and do not think this act of blasphemy will not bring down the wrath of God upon us all. For has He not warned us through the mouth of the Apostle John himself:

'And lo there was a great earthquake; and the sun became black and as sackcloth of hair, and the moon became as blood; and the stars of heaven fell into the earth, even as a fig tree casts its untimely figs, when she is shaken of a mighty wind. And the heaven departed as a scroll when it is rolled together; and every mountain and island were moved out of their places. And the kings of the earth, and the great men, and the rich men, and the chief captains, and the mighty men, and every bondman and every freeman, hid themselves in the dens and in the rocks of the mountains; and said to the mountains and rocks, Fall on us and hide us from the face of him that sitteth on the throne and from the wrath of the lamb: for the great day of his wrath hath come and who shall be able to stand?'

"Beloved, the time has come to stand against those who mock God Himself. To us alone, here in this place, the voice of prophecy has spoken the thunderous tones of God Himself, so all may hear. Mere man may not aspire to sit upon the very throne of God, lest the wrath of the Almighty come upon him, and he be destroyed, even as you have heard from God's own Revelation. The whole world looks to us, who have received the voice of prophecy in our souls; it cries out for us to stop these godless men before they cause the trumpets of the angels of doom to be sounded."

Sitting enthralled at his feet, Sandra Craven felt his voice flow around her and caress her, as it had that first day when he'd spoken the beautiful words of the Song of Love. She could still feel the touch of his hands upon her breasts, her flesh, her very soul. And, sensing that touch to the very core of her being, she felt herself flooded again by the same warmth of ecstasy that seized her when she was in his arms.

Fighting to restrain the impulse to leap from the pew and throw herself at his feet, crying out that she, too, was seized by the spirit of the Lord, she raised her eyes again. But this time they met those of the sallow woman in the choir, who was his wife, and the chill in those eyes was like a cold dash of water upon her, enabling her to control herself and sit back in the pew.

CHAPTER XIX

Asa Childs' tail was sore but he was content as he drove to work Monday morning. He'd injected the final dose of penicillin last night and, unless this particular bug happened to be penicillin-resistant, he was pretty sure his blood test would show up negative when the health department ran it. He didn't feel so hot, though, but that was probably to be expected, he thought, considering the shots he'd given himself since Friday night.

When he saw Dave Landers on his way to the main metalworking shop, he deviated so his path would cross that of the welder.

"Where you been keeping yourself, Dave?" he greeted the other man.

"My tail's been in a vise," said Landers. "The way that guy Craven's after us, you'd think he's going to push that damn rocket up single-handed."

"He's been on us in metallurgy, too," said Asa. "Running tolerance tests on all the cables and stuff like they hadn't been run already at the factory."

"Yeah. I'll be glad when this one gets off the pad."

"Me, too," said Asa. "Any chance of lending me a fin 'til payday?"

"Well, I'm pretty short myself." Dave had been expecting the touch, but made a routine demurrer anyway.

"After that strike you made at Daytona? Don't kid me, boy; you're loaded."

Resignedly Dave Landers pulled out his wallet and, extracting a ten dollar bill, handed it to Asa. He knew he'd never see that ten bucks again, but it was a cheap price for the assurance of being able to get a shot that packed a real wallop whenever you came to work hung over.

"Thanks, Dave." Asa stopped at the walkway leading to the metallurgy laboratory. "Be seeing you."

"Sure, Asa. So long."

In the laboratory, Asa hung up his coat, and taking a clean pair of coveralls from his locker, stepped into them, wincing at the pain that shot down his leg when he moved his hip joint. Must've got one of the penicillin injections too close to a nerve, he decided; finding a place for the last two shots had been tough.

He couldn't even get much pleasure out of having taken Landers for the ten bucks; his tail was too sore. Besides, his head ached and the inside of his mouth felt like it did with a hangover, though he hadn't taken a drop over the weekend. He remembered reading someplace that penicillin killed so many of one kind of germs that people sometimes got into trouble from the ones it didn't kill. But all he asked was for it to kill those little squilly ones—spirochetes was the name he remembered —that made the blood test positive.

Which reminded him, he mustn't forget to go by the health department laboratory, when he got off that afternoon, and let them take a blood sample.

ii.

Mike Barnes moved into an office in the old Bioastronautic Facility when he came to work Monday morning. He spent an hour with Dr. Ivan Saltman, medical chief for the project, going over reports of routine tests of the life environment system of the Hermes spacecraft that would ride the giant Pegasus rocket into the sky as the command module, but everything seemed in good order.

"Coastal Airlines has the housekeeping contract here and maintains a medical dispensary for anyone who gets ill on the job or has an accident that can be treated here," said Dr. Saltman, as they were winding up the conference about eleven o'clock. "Dr. Snyder from their staff was scheduled for duty today but he came down this morning with a case of the Green Death. I covered for him earlier but I've got to fly to Houston this afternoon for a final briefing in preparation for the launch and I wonder if you could help out the rest of the day and tomorrow with the dispensary?"

"Of course," said Mike.

"Coastal's nurse has had a lot of experience with routine things like dressings and minor injuries. All you'll have to do is backstop her in case she needs a little more expert help; anything really serious, we send on to the hospital."

Only two patients that day required Mike's services. One was a woman with a piece of metal filing in her eye, a rather frequent accident when people working with metal became careless about wearing protective goggles. A drop of butacaine gave the necessary local anesthesia and, since the speck of metal was not imbedded, he was able to remove it easily with a small magnet kept in the dispensary for that purpose.

The second case seemed more serious—at first glance.

Mike was called to Dr. Abram McCandless' office in the FSA administrative building shortly before quitting time. He found the astrophysicist lying on a couch; he was pale and sweating, breathing with deep
sighing respirations, and his pulse under Mike's fingers had a hurried
beat. In the stethoscope, however, his heart sounded normal, except for
the rate, and Mike decided that what McCandless was experiencing had
all the earmarks of an anxiety attack, an emotional reaction rather
than an actual physical one.

"Are you having any pain?" he asked.

"I'm all right, Doctor; it's just that I've been upset a little lately. My
secretary is making a mountain out of a molehill."

Remembering the blonde McCandless had been with at Shirley's
TGIF party, as well as some other things he'd heard, Mike wasn't surprised that the older man seemed to be having an anxiety reaction.

"An attack like this can be a warning of something serious," he said.
"At the very least you should have an electrocardiogram."

"Had that a month ago—at Harry Metzger's office. It was perfectly
normal."

"Let me take you home then. You're not in any condition to drive a
car."

"I'll drive your car to the apartment after I get off, Dr. McCandless,"
the secretary offered. "I'm riding in a car pool today, so I didn't bring
mine."

The scientist started to protest, but the effort made him breathless
and he lay back on the couch. "I'll take you up on the offer of a lift,
Doctor," he agreed.

McCandless lived in one of the new apartment houses in Spaceport
City fronting on Banana River, a less desirable area than the ocean
front itself but still very attractive. The quarters were surprisingly small,
though, only two bedrooms, obviously rented furnished from the looks
of the furniture. By the time Mike helped him into the apartment, he
appeared to be much better.

"Thank you for bringing me home, Dr. Barnes," he said. "I'll be all
right now."

"Are you sure I can't do anything else for you? Call your regular
physician or something?"

"I'll call Dr. Metzger if I have any more trouble. Thank you again."

As Mike was driving back to the dispensary, he passed a neat office-
bungalow just off the causeway with the name "Harry Metzger, M.D."
on the sign outside and beneath it the designation "Internal Medicine."
Remembering that McCandless had mentioned Dr. Metzger and still
worried about leaving the older man with no one to look after him,

he pulled into the parking space in front of Metzger's office and went inside.

A sign on the door leading from the waiting room to the inner office said, "Please ring and be seated," so he pushed the bell beneath it and took a seat in the otherwise empty room.

Various framed diplomas on the wall indicated that Dr. Harry Metzger was a certified specialist in internal medicine, had served honorably for two years as an officer in the United States Army Medical Corps, was a graduate of Yale University School of Medicine, and had served residencies in internal medicine.

"I'm Dr. Michael Barnes," he said when a gray-haired woman in a white uniform opened the door to the inner office. "I'd like to see Dr. Metzger."

"As a patient, Doctor?" A faint change in her manner told him she had read Jake Arrens' column and recognized the name.

"It's about one of Dr. Metzger's patients—Dr. McCandless."

"Come right into the office; the doctor will be with you in a moment."

The internist was a slender dark-haired man in his late thirties with a warm easy manner.

"Glad to meet you, Dr. Barnes," he said. "After I read Yvonne Lang's piece in last Sunday's paper I gave you a ring at the inn Tuesday—but you were out."

"I had to go to Washington to straighten out a few things. Did you disagree with what I told Yvonne?"

"I agree wholly," said the internist. "We're just starting a small mental health clinic here in Spaceport City and I've been helping out one afternoon a week there. I took a psychiatric residency before I decided internal medicine was a more fertile field for my taste, and down here the combination works very well indeed. What can I do for you?"

"I was covering the dispensary Coastal Airlines maintains at the base for FSA this afternoon and was called to see Dr. McCandless in his office. He appeared to be having an acute anxiety attack."

"When was this?"

"Around four o'clock; I just took him home. Dr. McCandless promised to call you if he had any more trouble, but I thought I'd better drop by and tell you what it looked like when I saw him."

"Poor McCandless has been having his difficulties," said Metzger. "I never could understand why so many fifty-year-old men think the only way they can prove their manliness is by trying to satisfy the sexual ardor of a twenty-year-old girl. It's like trying to run a high speed engine on kerosene."

"I never heard it put that way but I guess you're right," said Mike. "Isn't he liable to kill himself with a heart attack?"

"That sort of activity rarely causes exitus, else the death rate would be a lot higher than it is," said the internist. "You put your finger on the heart of the matter when you said he was having an attack of acute anxiety; it isn't the first."

"Surely not over a girl who could be his daughter."

"No. Those things take care of themselves when the testosterone level starts to fall. When Abram first joined the space program, he was intellectually busy and probably didn't even realize time was passing, until his mind ran out of puzzles to solve."

"He could always quit and go back to university work."

"Maybe not as easily as you think—judging from some of the things he told me. While McCandless was helping prepare for manned exploration of the moon, his contemporaries in the universities were concentrating on unmanned probes far beyond anything we can reach with manned flight for perhaps the next twenty-five or thirty years at least. Then Apollo finally takes men to the moon and McCandless discovers he's been left behind before he's sixty. In a panic he tackles the symptoms instead of the cure by going after young women, but that rarely helps for long."

"Are he and his wife divorced?"

"Only separated; Irene still loves him and doesn't want to make the break, but meanwhile the girl has been taking him to the cleaners."

"I guess he's lucky not to have something worse than what he had today," said Mike.

"The spells of anxiety are getting more frequent, so things must be working up to some sort of a crisis," said Metzger. "The trouble is nobody can really help him but himself and he's unwilling to take the necessary steps to face reality."

"Any chance of his going into a fugue state?"

"Thousands of people with less problems than Abram McCandless do wind up with an amnesia," Metzger conceded. "But I've an idea he has too good a mind to kid himself that walking away from his problems is ever going to solve them. Besides, he's too prominent a man just to escape into oblivion the way most amnesia victims do."

"So what choice does that leave him?"

"Nothing, except more attacks like today, I suppose, until he goes into a real anxiety state and maybe cracks up. Involutional melancholia isn't limited to menopausal women, as you very well know; I see a lot of men with it, too. If McCandless should get depressed enough, the end could be suicide."

"This mental health clinic you spoke of," said Mike as he was leaving. "One of the things I'm supposed to look into here at the Cape is the effect emotional tension may be having on operations and your clinic could be a good place to do it."

"You'll find this one of the most interesting communities you've ever studied," Metzger assured him. "Sometimes I think it's unique in the world, but I suspect from reading your article on the Lockheed Syndrome that things are not so different around other space installations."

"Spaceport City seems to have certain special conditions but I haven't finished identifying them yet," said Mike. "I want to talk a little more to Yvonne Lang and also to Art McCord."

"Take a look at the seamier side of the community, too," said Metzger. "Chief Branigan could fill you in there."

"I'm afraid he has orders not to help me."

Mike hesitated only a moment, then decided to tell the internist about the scene he and Jan had witnessed that first Sunday night. Long before he finished, the other man's face was grave.

"Are you sure Ellen Taggar was at that beach party?" he asked.

"Her car was there; a friend who was with me recognized it. And one of the girls we saw on the beach was wearing the same sort of white bathing suit Ellen was when they found her. It all adds up."

"Except one thing. When Sally Taggar got home and found that Ellen hadn't come in, she went into a severe asthmatic attack—she stays only one jump ahead of *status asthmaticus* most of the time anyway—and Paul called me before he telephoned Chief Branigan. When I got there to take care of Sally, a Maserati was parked in front of the house; I saw it there myself."

"One of the kids could have driven her home and she was so high from glue that she wandered into the ocean."

"That could be it," Metzger agreed. "Ellen was going steady with McCandless' son, Jason. He's a freshman at the new university near Orlando but I'd see him around town almost every weekend—usually driving that Maserati with Ellen."

"Maybe Dr. McCandless discovered his son was sniffing that night, too. That would be enough to throw a normal father into an anxiety attack."

"It would me," Metzger agreed soberly. "I'm even afraid to ask my son if he's ever smoked pot for fear he'll tell me he's doing it now."

iii.

Mike was checking the last of the test reports on the Pegasus life environment system the next morning, when his telephone rang.

"Dr. Barnes?" a man asked.

"Yes."

"This is Tom Craven."

"The chief engineer for Taggar?"

"Yes—and possessor of one of those one-track minds you were telling Yvonne Lang about."

"No offense meant. I was talking about a class."

"I'm probably as guilty as the rest; my wife says I'm more married to a rocket than I am to her. Doctor, I need some advice."

"Personal?"

"No, technical."

"I'm not an engineer."

"But you know a lot about what's troubling me. I'm working on plans for a modification of the second stage of Pegasus for future shots, and I need some help with the oxygen system."

"Where are you?"

"At the new Taggar assembly plant. I'd come over there but my drawings are still on a board here and it's hard to move them."

"I'll be there in ten minutes."

Mike found himself liking Craven from the moment they shook hands. The engineer was stocky with a freckled face, reddish hair, and an engaging grin.

"You don't waste time," he said. "I clocked you at eight minutes."

"I once circled the globe in less than an hour and a half."

"What a dope I am. I'd even forgotten you were an astronaut."

"An ex-astronaut. I was shot down and in this business they don't brag about the casualties. Do I detect a Boston *a* in your accent?"

"Roxbury. How did you know?"

"Took my pre-med at Harvard."

"I'm MIT—in systems," Craven explained as they entered the plant. "Worked one summer at the Savannah River center of the Atomic Energy Commission and married a South Carolina girl. That ended my career as a Yankee."

The chief engineer's office was large and sunlit. The desk was in the corner, with a drawing table occupying the most prominent place in the room.

"I got this idea for modifying the second stage of Pegasus while listening to a preacher last Sunday," he said.

"The Lord moves in a mysterious way."

"You'd think so, if you ever heard this guy spout. Sandra's bugs on this pentecostal business; it's part of her South Carolina upbringing, so I humor her by going to a Church of Prophecy over on the mainland. A couple of Sundays ago the preacher was sounding off on Ezekiel— you know that business about a wheel in the sky?"

"A wheel in a wheel?"

"That's it. Anyway it gave me this idea." Craven moved over to the drawing board. "I've made only a rough drawing so far, but you can see what it's all about."

Tom Craven's creative flair was obvious in the geometric pattern of lines delineating the shape of the huge metallic cylinder portrayed in the drawing. Actually, there were two drawings—one of the second stage in flight; the other with fuel tanks already expelled from inside the outer shell but still tethered to it.

"What's your next step?" Mike had seen at once the possibilities in Tom Craven's device for almost exactly doubling the capacity of a Pegasus rocket's second stage.

"Pull them in and attach them to the outer shell," said Craven.

"How?"

"I haven't figured that out yet—but it shouldn't be too much of a problem. There are several possibilities. Why do you ask?"

"I'd like to see the whole picture," said Mike, which was the truth, for what he was seeing was what Jake Arrens had described that morning in the cluttered Washington office of the columnist—an orbiting arsenal with the capacity to control the world, if that were necessary finally to ensure peace for everyone on it.

"What do you think of it?" Craven asked.

"It's nothing less than inspired," said Mike. "Are you sure you aren't Ezekiel himself in another incarnation?"

Tom Craven grinned, but Mike could see that he was highly pleased.

"Working out the life environment system for this baby is going to be pretty tricky," said the engineer. "I was hoping you could give me some hints."

"I'll do better than that. If you'll let me, I'd like to work with you on the project, from that angle, of course."

"You're a full partner as of now." Craven held out his hand. "Tell you what—I promised Sandra to pick her up at the Space Club for a swim when I leave this afternoon. Why don't you come along? I'll have them issue you a temporary guest membership, if you don't already have one. We can have dinner there afterward to cement the partnership."

"My swim trunks are at the Astronaut Inn and that's a pretty good distance away."

"The club has a surf shop where you can pick up anything you need. Shall I see you there around five-thirty?"

"Five-thirty it is," said Mike, glad of a chance to avoid the loneliness of his room at the Astronaut Inn, and the certainty that Jan would be with Jerry McGrath.

CHAPTER XX

It was five-twenty when Mike got to the Space Club, to find a telephone message at the desk from Tom Craven, saying he'd be a bit late, and leaving a guest card there.

"Mrs. Craven is at the pool, Dr. Barnes," said the desk clerk. "The locker room is downstairs at the pool level."

In the locker room, Mike undressed and put on new swim trunks. It was warm and sunny when he came outside to the patio surrounding the pool, so he plunged in and swam its length and back before climbing the ladder to the terrace.

An attractive dark-haired young woman with a well-rounded body got up from the beach chair where she'd been sitting and came over to meet him.

"I'm Sandra Craven; recognized you from your picture in the Sunday paper," she said. "Tom called about noon and said he'd invited you to meet us here for a drink and a swim."

"He left a message at the desk for me just now saying he'd be late," Mike told her.

"The story of my life." Sandra Craven made a wry face and for an instant there was a sharpness in her voice and a note of exasperation Mike had heard from many rocket men's wives, when he'd been studying the aerospace syndrome. "Tom's really got two wives—me and that Flying Horse. Sometimes I wonder who's number one."

"I'd bet on you. Can I order you a drink?"

"A Gibson—double," she said, and added on a confidential note, "Tom doesn't like for me to drink them."

Mike considered briefly whether Craven might be incensed if he arrived and found her drinking the potent Gibson, balancing that against the fact that she obviously needed an outlet for her irritation against her husband—and decided not to argue. He gave her order—and his for a double bourbon—to the waiter.

Sandra Craven was a Southern chatterbox type of girl, he quickly discovered, capable of talking endlessly without really saying anything. But she was attractive and, as long as he didn't ask any particular intellectual depth of her conversation, he found himself enjoying being with her. Halfway through his drink—Sandra had finished hers—he looked up to find Jan Cooper standing about a yard away, with Major Jerry McGrath. Both were in bathing suits.

Jan's eyebrows lifted when she saw him with Sandra Craven but McGrath stopped to shake hands.

"I didn't get a chance to thank you for saving Earl Boggs' life the other morning, Dr. Barnes," he said.

"Dr. Saltman is too experienced at this business to let Boggs really get in trouble," Mike assured him. "Do you know Mrs. Craven? Major McGrath and Mrs. Cooper."

"I know Jan." Sandra's voice was faintly slurred from alcohol. "How do you do, Major McGrath?"

"Hello, Sandra." Jan turned to watch some children playing in the adjoining pool and smiled when one toddler threw water on another. For a moment Mike pictured her with a brood of her own—and his— a very exciting thought. But when she turned back to face him, the warmth went out of her face and she began abruptly to pull on her bathing cap.

"Come on, Jerry," she said. "I have a musical rehearsal at the high school at eight o'clock. Nice to see you again, Sandra."

"Did you two have a tiff?" Sandra asked, as Jan dived in.

"Why do you ask?"

"From Jake Arrens' column—"

"You can't believe everything you read in gossip columns," he said somewhat pointedly. "Care for a swim?"

"You go in if you want to; I'll just sit here and get quietly loaded while we wait for Tom. It serves him right for not stopping work at four-thirty like everybody else does at Taggar Aircraft."

"Does this happen fairly often?"

"How would you like to get bathed and dressed every night, fix a hot dinner, and then have your husband call half the time and say he's got to work?" she demanded indignantly.

"I'm sure I wouldn't like it."

"Besides, how do I know he isn't shacked up with some secretary, like they say Dr. McCandless has been doing?"

Mike would have preferred to be almost anywhere except where he was, but he had ordered the drink for Sandra, which made him somewhat responsible.

"Tom got another promotion when he was at the factory and tonight was to be sort of a celebration," Sandra confided. "But what good is it when I never see him?"

"Isn't he free weekends?"

"Not since they put the rush order on Pegasus. Anytime something goes wrong, it's Tom they call first."

"At least that shows Taggar Aircraft has confidence in him."

"What good does that do me—when I'm home crying?"

"Look," he said. "Why don't we have a cup of coffee out here while we wait for Tom."

"And spoil the nicest buzz I've had in years?" Sandra Craven giggled. "I just thought of something, Dr. Barnes—Mike. With the reputation that newspaper column gave you, it would serve Tom right if people started talking about you and me. Maybe we should give them some reason to talk."

"Tom wouldn't like that." Mike voiced the thought that was most prominent in his mind at the moment but could think of nothing to do about it. He was saved by a waiter who approached just then.

"Mr. Craven just called, Mrs. Craven," said the waiter. "He says he's going to be tied up at the office for another hour or more and for you and Dr. Barnes to go on in to dinner."

When he saw Sandra Craven's eyes suddenly fill with tears, Mike was sure she could go on a crying jag at any moment, probably right in the club dining room. Fortunately, she solved that problem for him.

"Do you mind if I go home, Mike?" she asked.

"Not at all," he said. "We'll both get dressed and I'll drive you home."

"That'll give 'em something to talk about here at the club." She giggled again. "And serve Tom right, too. But maybe I ought to have another drink before I go."

"I think not," he said firmly.

"I can drive myself home," she said with maudlin indignation. "You don't have to wait here with me."

"I don't want your husband gunning for me." He kept his tone light. "Shall we get dressed?"

"All right." She stood up but swayed and would have toppled into the pool, if he hadn't caught her by the arm.

"How many drinks did you have before I got here?" he asked.

"Only two." She giggled again and leaned against him. "Tom rations me to two so, when I'm going to meet him here, I always have Vodka and tonic first. That way nobody knows I've had it."

Until somebody is fool enough to order you a double and winds up with a drunk woman on his hands, Mike thought, resignedly.

"I'm going to dress now, Sandra." It was Jan. "If you're going in, too, we could talk about the symphony plans for next season."

Mike had no chance to thank Jan, for Sandra came out of the locker room alone—and swaying slightly. They left the club in his car and just beyond the bridge across Banana River, he spied the garish yellow sign of a drive-in hamburger stand and pulled into it, choosing the parking slot farthest away from the stand itself where they would be less likely to be noticed.

"How about hamburgers and coffee?" he asked.

"I don't want anything," she said petulantly.

"Just some coffee then?"

"All right—if you're going to be sticky about it."

They drank the coffee in silence and drove to the Craven home. It was only a few blocks off the causeway in a section of Spaceport City which, though not in the luxury area where Shirley's and Hal Brennan's homes were located, was still obviously at least upper middle class. Parking in front, he walked up the drive with her and unlocked the door with the key she gave him.

"Won't you come in?" she asked, but he shook his head.

"I think not."

"I won't seduce you," she flared, "if that's what you're afraid of."

"It's you I'm thinking of. After all you did mention my reputation at the club."

"I'm sorry about that, Mike. I guess you're pretty mad at me aren't you?"

"Of course not. But don't be too hard on Tom. He's dedicated to his job and that's better than a lot of things he could be dedicated to."

"Good-by, Mike. Thank you for bringing me home."

At a telephone booth outside a drugstore, he rang the Taggar plant and asked for Tom Craven. It was perhaps a minute before the engineer answered.

"I just took Sandra home," Mike told him. "My advice to you is to drop whatever you're doing and go home, too."

"Is she drunk again?" Craven's voice was resigned.

"Not unless she's had another since I left her."

"Sandra never could hold liquor."

"She doesn't *want* to hold it now," Mike said bluntly. "If you don't want her to become an alcoholic, you'd better start thinking more of her and less of whatever you're doing over there."

"Look here—"

"Don't waste time getting mad with me. Use it being angry at yourself before you wreck your marriage."

There was a moment of silence, then Tom Craven said: "Guess I owe you an apology. I'm glad it was you that brought her home, Mike."

ii.

Depressed by his experience with Sandra and Tom Craven, Mike had an early snack in the motel coffee shop and went up to his room. But when the television news was over, he found himself still restless and, recalling that Jan had said she had a rehearsal at the high school at eight o'clock, he drove over there about eight-thirty and parked outside the school.

Jan came out shortly after nine o'clock. He waited until she said goodby to a group of students, then walked over to the white convertible.

"I was hoping you'd have time for a snack with me," he said.

"Why?"

"I need somebody to talk to, somebody normal."

"There's a LUM's on the Astronaut Trail not far away," she said. "It's very nice."

"I'll follow you there."

They found a quiet corner in the restaurant with its attractive gaslight era decor and ordered the roast beef sandwiches with tall glasses of imported beer for which it was famous.

"Thanks for taking Sandra Craven to the dressing room this afternoon at the club," he said when the waitress had taken their order.

"I gave her a bromo, too. Do you always try to get your women drunk so early in the evening?"

"Sandra had a head start, but I didn't know it and ordered the double Gibson she asked for. We were waiting for Tom; they were going to celebrate his promotion but he got stuck on the job and couldn't leave."

"There's a rumor out that she's fallen for a curly haired wolf of a preacher over on the mainland whose specialty weekdays is pastoral calls on young housewives."

"Do you suppose Tom suspects?"

"The husband—or wife—is always the last to know."

"This could be serious. Tom Craven is a very important cog in the Pegasus machinery."

"Are you going to tell him?"

"No. After I left her I called him and told him he should go home and take care of her—but I don't think I got anywhere."

"Maybe you should set up shop as a marriage counselor."

"Not with my record. Divorced once and now thrown over by you makes my batting average zero. By the way, I like Jerry McGrath, even if you *are* engaged to him."

"I told you it was only an understanding—maybe less than that now."

"Would it be prodding to ask why?"

"I suppose not, since you're the cause. After the piece Jake Arrens wrote in his column, a lot of people seem to have changed their attitude toward me."

"I'm really sorry about that column. Jake says you're one of the nicest people he met when he was here at the Cape."

"He often came down for the launches and stopped at the inn. We chatted together a few times."

"Jake was trying to find out something about Pegasus. Things have been pretty secretive out there and he was just fishing for information."

"I'm even beginning to enjoy being considered a loose woman," she said with a smile. "A member of the school board called me up the other night and wanted a date. The position of music supervisor for the city will be vacant on January 1, and he thought I might like to be considered for it. My life was quiet and uneventful until you came along; now men are propositioning me at every turn."

"They wouldn't—if you weren't so desirable."

"Have you found any of the answers at Pegasus to what you came here for?"

"No answers yet, but a lot of clues. The whole program has me worried."

"Why?"

"It's not any one thing in particular, just a succession of little happenings. That accident Earl Boggs had in the test chamber would never have happened, if everybody concerned had been on the ball. Then there's what you just told me about Sandra Craven, plus an anxiety attack Dr. McCandless suffered. Harry Metzger says he's been seeing more and more of that sort of thing among workers at Pegasus and their families."

"But these are all separate occurrences."

"Which may not add up to anything definite at all," he admitted. "But somehow I get the impression that a pattern is here somewhere, almost as if a curse was on Pegasus."

"Your feeling that way could be a natural result of your own experience, you know."

"I tell myself that, but somehow I'm not very convincing," he said. "How does McGrath feel about the project?"

"He's all excited. I guess the first prerequisite for being an astronaut is to have a sublime confidence that everything is going to be all right."

"I had it years ago—but disaster still struck."

"Aren't there more safeguards now than you had then?"

"More safeguards—and more dangers. The boosters we used then were mere work horses, offspring of the rockets the Germans devised to bombard England. Now you've got liquid oxygen and hydrogen adding to the possibilities of trouble, to say nothing of one of the most complicated pieces of apparatus ever devised by the mind of man."

"We live with it all the time here, so I guess we don't realize the dangers," she said. "But now that Apollo has been phased out, won't there be less manned shots than before?"

"I hope so. But there's talk that the Russians will beat us to Mars and the whole thing could heat up all over again—particularly with an election coming up."

"It's like a bad dream." She shivered.

"But with a silver lining for me—because I found you. Now that the Jake Arrens business has blown over, can't we start from the beginning again, Jan?"

She looked away and when she spoke, her eyes were still upon the traffic passing outside the restaurant, easily visible through the sliding glass that made up most of its walls.

"I wonder if anybody ever can really start over?"

"We can try. One night when this first Pegasus shot is over, I'll come into the dining room and request a song. Afterward I'll thank you for playing it and we'll make a date to have supper somewhere after you get off—just like any other two people falling in love."

"Please, Mike. There are reasons why you shouldn't."

"We'd be starting over, Jan. Nothing in the past will have anything to do with us."

"It isn't that easy." Her voice was so low he could hardly hear it over the Muzak and the chatter of people at nearby tables. Sure now of what was troubling her, he dared to mention something he hadn't spoken to her about before.

"Is it that picture you're worried about?"

He saw her body stiffen with the shock of the question and the color drain from her cheeks.

"What picture are you talking about?" she asked almost in a whisper.

"The one of you taken in that infrared studio of Hal Brennan's."

"How did you know about that?"

"I called Hal from Washington and told him I would give the whole story of his Countdown parties to Jake Arrens, if he tried to keep me from staying on at the Cape. When General Green called Hal the next day to check the appointment with him, Hal approved it. But that night I received a color print by special delivery at the hotel."

"I've never seen it."

"You were very lovely—and obviously drugged."

"Where is it now?"

"I tore it in pieces and flushed it down the drain."

"Couldn't you have saved the print—as evidence, if I ever need it?"

"I suppose I should have," he admitted. "But there was a man in the pic—"

"Who?" she asked quickly.

"He seemed familiar, but I couldn't recognize him; he was in the background and not in focus. Tearing the print up was a normal male reaction. Besides," he added on a softer note, "I prefer to remember you as a lovely dryad in the moonlight of a motel room, after I'd had the nightmare."

For a moment she didn't speak, but he could see that she was touched by his affirmation. Then she said: "I still don't see why he sent you the print."

"Hal seems to have known I was in love with you before I did. The picture was meant to be a threat to hold me in line, but if he ever tries to make trouble for you—or me either for that matter—I'll give Jake Arrens the whole story of how Hal gets rocket people high on a drug —probably the form of methamphetamine the kids call 'Speed'—and photographs them when they don't know what they're doing."

She shivered. "It's all like a dream—or a nightmare."

"A drug-induced nightmare. If the truth about those parties is ever revealed publicly, Hal's career would be ended both in FSA and politics, so he knows he's got a lot more to lose from it than you or I. I don't think you need to worry but just in case, one day I'm going to make him give me the negative."

She stood up suddenly. "Order me another beer please, Mike, I'll be back in a minute."

When she came back from the washroom, he saw that she had bathed her face and eyes and put on fresh make-up. "I want to tell you about the picture," she said.

"You don't have to. I came close enough to the same thing to know what it's like."

"I still want you to know how it happened," she insisted. "When Bob died in the crash, I couldn't help feeling that maybe I had nagged him too much about his indecisiveness—and other things. It was a pretty rough time for me, and I guess I over-reacted."

"A lot of people do after an experience like you'd been through."

"The night that picture was taken, I didn't realize the party was any different from the ordinary TGIF affairs they have at Hal's home until—"

"The first inning?"

"I think they called it that. By that time I was so high on—what did you call it?"

" 'Speed' is the popular name, I guess because it hits you like a jolt of lightning. One minute I was enjoying a stinger and the next minute it struck. By the time I got out of Hal's house and started down the drive, I could have sworn the palm trees were dancing a hula."

"I remember that, but not much more. I didn't even know the picture had been taken until later."

"It's all over now. You don't have to worry about it a minute longer."

She glanced at her watch. "We'd better be going. I have some private classes in the morning."

"When shall I see you again?"

"I have another rehearsal tomorrow night, but it will be finished around ten."

"I promised Dr. Metzger to cover the Teen-age Hot Line at the mental health center from nine o'clock until about two," he told her. "Would you like to sit in on it? They tell me it's sometimes quite a while between calls, but they do provide coffee and sandwiches."

"I know where the center is," she said. "I'll come as soon as I finish the rehearsal."

Outside the restaurant in the parking lot, he leaned across the door of her convertible to kiss her. She didn't draw back, but there was time for only a brief touch of their lips before a car pulling into the lot threatened to catch them in the beam of its lights. He drew away and stood watching as she drove out into the traffic.

When she waved good-by from the convertible just before turning into a cross street, he started whistling as he got into his own car. Nor was he surprised that the tune turned out to be "Stardust."

CHAPTER XXI

"I guess I owe you an apology." Tom Craven came into Mike's office just before the afternoon siren blew at four-thirty. "But I've been too busy before."

"Working on that expendable fuel tank idea?"

"No. Paul decided we should run some X-ray tests on the material we used for the bulkhead between the kerosene and LOX tanks of the booster."

"You didn't tear out the bulkhead, did you?" Mike asked quickly.

"We're too far along for that. But we had some extra material and we can check that out."

"Any particular reason?"

"Two would be my guess," said Craven. "First, your coming has sort of put everybody here on edge. And second, back in 'sixty-three with the Centaur, they discovered that at cryogenic temperatures, very small holes, less than one ten-thousandth of an inch, can open up and let the fuels mix before ignition. Paul wants to make absolutely sure this material doesn't have any imperfections like that."

"That's going the second mile, but I'm glad to see it," said Mike. "How's Sandra?"

"Never saw her happier."

"She wasn't very happy last night when I took her home from the club."

"Women put a lot of store on little things—like going out to dinner on special occasions. I had promised Sandra we'd celebrate my promotion and she was naturally upset, but a string of pearls cured that."

"I guess this makes you top man on the manufacturing side of Pegasus, doesn't it?"

"Under Paul. He always keeps a tight rein on everything."

"What sort of a person is Taggar?"

"A brilliant engineer, tough and very demanding. I guess one reason I've been able to get along so well with him is because I'm somewhat like he is—at least that's what Sandra says. Paul has guts, too; even

Ellen's drowning hasn't stopped him from wielding the bullwhip where Taggar industries is concerned."

"Does he wield it over his family, too?"

"They pretty much jump when he speaks. Of course, Sally has been a semi-alcoholic for years—"

"Perhaps he made her that way."

Tom Craven flushed. "Are you insinuating that I'm making Sandra into a lush the same way?"

"No," said Mike. "I learned long ago not to put in my oar where a man and woman are concerned, whether they're married or not."

"I learned the same thing about religion," said Craven. "Sandra was raised up in a small South Carolina town that's a stronghold for one of the pentecostal sects. She drags me over to the mainland every Sunday I can get off to hear a stemwinder shout about the prophecies in the Bible. He says we're all going to suffer for pushing our noses into the rest of the universe and I wouldn't be surprised if he doesn't think we might accidentally land a spaceship on heaven one day."

Mike smiled. "Has he located it?"

"Apparently not. Most of what he says sounds like gibberish to me but the guy looks like a movie actor and the women really go for that sort of preaching."

"What does this fellow say is actually going to happen at the Cape?" Mike didn't even consider telling Tom Craven about the rumor that Sandra was going for the preacher even more than his preaching.

"He's always shouting about fire and brimstone and the wrath of God—you know the kind of hogwash these people hand out. But Sandra laps that sort of stuff up and is even talking about joining the women of the church movement over there, so maybe it's a good thing for her. Until we get the second bird off the pad, I'm going to have even less time off than I had before, so it's just as well that she has something to keep her mind occupied, especially with me in the sweat I've been in lately."

"Is anything wrong with the rocket?" Mike asked quickly.

"Not that I can see, but Paul got disturbed and had us replace both the cabin pressure valve for the spacecraft itself—"

"The one we used to call the 'pop-off'?"

"Yes. And the main valve controlling the flow of oxygen from the cryogenic state into the life support system, too. I had to put one of our best metal men on the job for a whole day of overtime last Saturday to get it done."

"I'd like to take a look at both those valves," said Mike.

"Sure. Come by tomor—" Tom Craven broke off in the middle of the word. "Come to think of it, didn't you have trouble with that same system in a Taggar ship a long time ago?"

"The 'pop-off' froze on me while I was in orbit. The Capcom neglected to tell me if it was showing up on the telemetry tapes though, and I didn't even know it until oxygen pressure had risen enough to almost cause a convulsion and I had to bring the ship down fast and blow the hatch. We lost the ship by sinking."

"If those telemetry tapes showed the oxygen pressure readings, it might help us get the bugs out of that valve."

"Is there trouble again?" Mike asked quickly.

"Twice in the last month during tests, the O_2 pressure rose too high in the ship but those were static dry runs with nobody inside. If they'd been manned flights, something like what you experienced could very easily have happened. I sure would like to see those tapes."

"So would a lot of other people—particularly me. Unfortunately, they seem to have disappeared."

"Seem to?"

"Nobody can find them or will admit he knows where they are. But I've got an idea that somebody does."

"Who was Capcom during that flight of yours?"

"Hal Brennan—but he swears he doesn't know anything about the tapes being misplaced."

Tom Craven nodded thoughtfully. "You arrive here on a Friday afternoon and Saturday morning early the order comes down to replace both the oxygen control and cabin pressure valves on Hermes II. Are you implying that there could be a connection?"

"Draw your own conclusions," said Mike. "But first I'd like to see another test of those valves."

"We'll run them Thursday morning at ten o'clock if that suits you?"

"I'll be there."

ii.

The new mental health clinic for Spaceport City was located just off the causeway in a small building Taggar Development Corporation had used as an office in the earlier days of the town's beginning. The rapid growth of the city had already used up practically all the land released by FSA from the original portion of Merritt Island preempted for Cape Kennedy, however, and, with not much more to sell, the sales office had been moved to the Taggar Building on the beach.

Only a secretary was in the clinic when Mike entered shortly before nine o'clock that evening. She was obviously in a hurry to get away, presumably for a date with the young man he'd seen waiting in a car parked outside.

"We have two phone lines coming in here, Dr. Barnes," she explained. "And two tape recorders."

"Then all conversations are taped?"

"That's automatic; you don't even have to turn on the recorders. There's a direct line to the telephone company, too, so you can locate where any call is coming from, in case help needs to be sent—like an emergency or suicide."

"How do I do that?"

"Just dial O and tell the operator to call Locator Service; they'll give you the address in a few moments. We aren't supposed to be an emergency service for ambulance or fire calls but it works out that way quite a bit of the time, so there's a list of numbers to be called for emergencies beside the telephone. Mostly, though, your job is to let people talk their troubles out and try to advise them."

"What percentage of these calls are really important?"

"Not very many—except over weekends; a lot of kids still call up as a joke. But we've thwarted several suicides and gotten medical help to a number of people who didn't have a doctor. I come on about three o'clock in the afternoon and take care of the filing, so just leave the tapes on the recorder. All the old records are in the cabinets over there." She nodded toward the corner of the room. "And, oh yes, push the door shut and make sure it's locked before you leave. Good night, Doctor."

For a half hour nothing happened, except one call with a lot of child-ish giggling on the line, obviously of no significance. Jan came in shortly after ten, looking lovely in a pale green dress with a green ribbon holding back her hair.

"Any action?" she asked.

"None so far. Everybody in Spaceport City must be on their good behavior tonight."

"I doubt that," she said. "I was in this place when they opened it a few months ago and I seem to remember a kitchen. We could have some coffee."

"There are supposed to be sandwiches, too, but the secretary was in such a hurry to leave on a date she forgot to say where they were."

"I used to be a Girl Scout. I'll find them."

She came back in a little while with a pot of coffee and a tray of sand-wiches. The phone rang once while they were eating but it was only Dr. Harry Metzger, checking to see how Mike was making out. At the assurance that things were very light, he said good night and hung up.

"If tonight's a fair sample of how much the 'Hot Line' is being used,"

Jan said shortly after eleven, "it's certainly not living up to its publicity."

"Both the secretary and Dr. Metzger told me the main use is over weekends, when there's a lot more act—" Mike broke off suddenly and stood up.

"What's wrong?" Jan asked.

"The secretary said tapes of previous 'Hot Line' calls are stored in those cabinets. I'm wondering whether anything came in the night we saw that glue party on the beach." He moved over to one of the cabinets. "I'll take this one and you take the one next to it."

"I'm almost afraid it might be here," Jan said as she began to look through the tapes stored there according to the dates upon which they had been recorded.

"This section ends with Saturday night of that weekend," Mike said after a brief search. "If any record is here, it will be in your filing cabinet. That was a Sunday night—"

"And there wasn't any school because of the teachers' meeting on Monday." Jan reached into the stack containing reels of magnetic tape and pulled one out. "Here's the one for that date; we can play it through on the spare recorder."

It took only a few minutes to adjust the tape and start it rolling. Since a record was only made when the telephone "Hot Line" was actually in use, they were able to scan the time period for that evening fairly rapidly. The first several calls were obviously cranks; one a youthful voice shouting obscenities. Only toward the end of the tape did they find anything that seemed remotely applicable and that was difficult to hear very well.

It was a girl's voice with some sound in the background that made the words difficult to distinguish. Besides, they seemed to be slurred, as if the speaker were crying.

"I didn't know it would be like that," was the first intelligible sentence in the anguished childish voice; then came a hurried jumble of words from which they were only able to distinguish: "Daddy . . . Mother . . . Where are you?"

More sobbing followed, then: "Don't hate me—Mother . . . I . . ." and for a long moment there was nothing more on the tape except the same background noise, a peculiarly rhythmic rushing sound that Mike couldn't identify.

"It's the ocean!" Jan cried. "She must have been calling from somewhere close by."

"Maybe a cabana?"

"That could be it."

"Daddy. . . . Don't hate me." The childish sobbing was renewed.

"The others dared me. . . . I didn't know it would be like that. . . . Good-by."

There were no more words, only the rushing sound of breakers on the shore and finally a click, as the telephone in the health center had been hung up.

"Mike." Jan's voice was taut. "Do you suppose that could have been Ellen Taggar?"

"Did you recognize her voice?"

"I didn't know her to speak to; I don't work at that school and only saw her with other kids—or driving that Maserati. But where could she have been calling from?"

"Somewhere near the ocean, that's certain."

Jan shook her head hopelessly, "Down here that covers a lot of territory—I'm afraid we're licked Mike."

iii.

Asa Childs rarely drank very much but, when he got to the laboratory this morning, he seriously considered taking a shot of ninety-five percent alcohol. His head ached worse today than it had yesterday and even filling his lungs with air required an effort now.

His body ached, too, as if he had been given a beating, and red splotches had appeared on his torso, some looking very much like the hives he used to get as a child when he was emotionally upset. Moreover, although the laboratory was air-conditioned, sweat was pouring off his body and he seemed to have trouble focusing his eyes.

He was under no illusion as to the reason for his discomfort; it could only be caused by the massive doses of penicillin he'd injected into his body over the weekend. The problem was how to keep going until knock-off time when he could visit the doctor on the mainland who had treated him once before, after he'd been unlucky enough to pick up syphilis from another man.

Every practicing homosexual knew the danger of V.D. of course. But so great was the drive that sent many of them out seeking contacts almost nightly that they willingly took the undue risks which made the venereal disease rate among the gay set so high. The only salve for Asa's misery at the moment was that by the time he got Albert out of jail in Orlando, the boy was sure to have learned his lesson. As for Pierre Carvin, he could rot.

Asa came out of the X-ray dark room after checking the temperature of the developing solutions to find Carlos Arundel in the office outside. Carlos had an engineering degree from the University of Havana and worked as an assistant to the chief engineer for Taggar Aircraft. He was carrying a sheet of metal some two feet square.

"The boss wants X rays of this sheet, Asa," said the Cuban. "He's looking for cracks or little holes that might be in it."

"Doesn't he know Dr. Ordway's at the factory working on a new collar for the space suit Dr. Barnes found the leak in?" Asa demanded aggrievedly. "Who's going to read the films?"

"Craven said to tell you he'd look at them later. What's the matter, Asa? You sick?"

"Or something."

"Maybe worrying about Albert getting himself locked up in Orlando?"

"Where did you hear that?"

"A twinkie from here was caught in the same raid. Pierre had rented two rooms in this motel and was packing 'em in at five dollars a head, when the owner decided he hadn't been paid enough for the rooms and tipped off the fuzz. They let the twinkie go because he was under age and they were afraid to put him in the juvenile detention shelter."

Oddly enough, the news cheered Asa. Twinkies were juvenile homosexuals and the courts were pretty sticky about anyone caught debauching—the word the courts used—them, although usually they were already old hands at the game. If Pierre was convicted of using an underage boy for purposes of prostitution, he might be shut up for a long time, which was no more than he deserved as far as Asa was concerned.

"What are you going to do with this?" Carlos held out the sheet of metal.

"Put it under the high voltage tube and get a picture."

"You got one of the real high power generators?"

"Not so high—only a couple of million electron volts."

"Mind if I watch?"

"Not as long as you stay where I tell you to."

Asa could read the other man's mind like a book; you developed that sense pretty quickly in the gay world. The darkness of the developing room, or even a closet that could be shut for a few moments, was a lot better than the public toilets where so many homosexuals carried out their hurried, furtive encounters, haunted always by the fear that the police were watching. But Carlos was barking up the wrong tree this time; Asa had enough troubles already with his own body rebelling against the penicillin, plus his worries about Albert, to start anything with a lug like the Cuban.

Asa had first met the refugee engineer almost a year ago in one of the gay bars along US 1 right after Carlos had just come to the Cape. They'd gone to Asa's apartment for sex, so he knew what Carlos was after and wanted none of it. More than anything in his relationship with others, Asa enjoyed the feeling that his partner was dependent upon him and a loudmouthed Cuban like Carlos, with no consideration for any need except his own, was the last person he could expect to give that kind of affection.

"Bring the metal in here." Asa opened the door of the X-ray laboratory.

In the middle of the room stood the massive machine that generated the high voltages necessary to produce rays which could penetrate through metal and show its inner structure. Ensconced in a metal protective housing, it was taller than Asa himself; inside the outer case was the X-ray tube itself, containing the small target by which the powerful rays were deflected downward in a beam with a fine focal spot, affording the best possible definition to the final picture.

"How do you handle something as big as that?" Carlos asked curiously.

"With a bridge crane and yoke mounting we can move it into almost any position and angle we want, in spite of its weight," Asa explained.

"What's the advantage of using such high voltages?"

"Mainly to penetrate through large castings." Asa was wondering what sort of a degree Carlos had really got from the University of Havana. "You need a lot of penetration to study heavy weldments, like the ones used in boilers, or fuel tanks for rockets. What did you say Mr. Craven's looking for here?"

"This is the same material that forms the bulkhead partition between the kerosene and LOX in the big booster. Craven said there was a leak in one of the earlier rockets a long time ago and it damn near blew up, so Mr. Taggar wants to make sure this one is solid."

"He didn't take this out of the booster, did he?"

"Christ, no—not with the bird set to fly Thursday a week. This is the same material that's in the bulkhead and they want to make sure there aren't any little cracks."

Asa had turned on the machine and its humming filled the room. With the help of Carlos Arundel, but moving warily so the Cuban didn't get close to him, Asa attached a cardboard film holder snugly to the metal sheet, pressing it very closely, for the two had to be in exact contact at every point in order to secure a good film image.

"This film is heavier than I would have expected," Carlos observed.

"That's because of the lead screens."

"You mean there's lead in front of the film?"

"Yes."

"Why doesn't it shut out the X rays?"

"It does shut out some, the secondary electrons from the specimen and the film holder and sources like that. In a picture taken without screens you get so many extra rays from side sources that there's a mottling effect and the image is poor. Besides, the screens intensify the effect of the X rays."

Asa carefully positioned the film holder and the specimen of metal beneath the tube, with its center just over the mark that showed the focal point of the rays.

"Didn't they teach you anything about this is that engineering school in Havana?" he asked.

"I only went into engineering because my father wanted to put me in charge of a sugar mill out in the country," said Carlos with a grin. "The peasants don't understand gay people; you're a lot better off in a big university, especially in Latin countries where women don't take to education the way they do here and mostly men go to college. I had myself a ball."

With the sheet of metal to be X-rayed in place and the tube-to-specimen distance set at three feet, Asa sent Carlos out and went into the small control cubicle adjoining the room where the monster stood. It was hot in there and sweat was pouring down across his eyes, making vision even more difficult than it already was. And when he looked at the exposure chart, the rows of figures along its bottom edge and up the side swam hazily, as did the darker graph lines angling upward across it.

"2.0MV, O.25ma. Type A Film. D=1.5. TRANSMITTED BEAM —STEEL HALF-VALUE=0.83 inches," he read off the chart with considerable difficulty, straining his eyes to see the smaller figures indicating the thickness of aluminum, lead, or steel being tested and, ascending along the side of the chart, the column that gave the exposure time for each thickness.

Twice he shook his head to clear his vision and knew, with a moment of panic, that it wasn't simply the sweat that was making it hard for him to read the figures. The force inside him that had restricted his breathing and caused his skin to break out in great weals was also affecting his eyes.

He could have called Carlos in to read the chart for him but that would have meant admitting his difficulty and having it broadcast all over the Cape. So, wiping the sweat from his eyes again with his sleeve, he concentrated on the upward slanting graph line across the chart where the exposure times for various thicknesses of metal were indicated. But the lines swam again and finally he poked his head out of the cubicle so he could see Carlos, who was standing in the door of the small room, studying the generator.

"What did Mr. Craven say about the equivalent steel thickness of this specimen?" he asked.

"Oh, I forgot," said the Cuban. "You're supposed to multiply by four over seven and eight-tenths to get the equivalent for this alloy. You having trouble?"

"Just wanted to get it right," Asa said shortly. "I'm going to expose the film in a second or two. Better get out of there if you don't want to get radiated; it might keep you from ever fathering any children."

Carlos departed, guffawing his appreciation of the joke, and Asa turned back to the exposure table. The figures still swam but when one of them momentarily came into focus long enough for him to recognize it, he reached over and turned the timer to that setting. Then, throwing the control switch that sent the powerful X rays, driven by the force of two million electron volts, surging down through the specimen of alloy to register on the sensitive film beneath it, he waited until the tube was shut off automatically by the timer, then went to take both specimen and film from beneath the powerful machine.

Carlos was looking into the open door of the dark room used for developing films when Asa came into the laboratory office carrying the cardboard holder.

"You going to develop that now?" he asked with studied casualness.

"The film has to cool down a while," Asa lied, pretty sure that the other man didn't possess enough knowledge in the highly specialized field of metallurgy to know he wasn't telling the truth. Right now the last thing he wanted was to get in that dark room with Carlos Arundel.

"When can Craven see the film?" the engineer asked.

"Give me an hour to develop it. Any time after that."

While the film was developing, Asa poured himself a jolt of alcohol, mixed it with Coke, and drank it down. If Tom Craven found him shaking, sweating, and barely able to see, he'd be in trouble sure enough; it was better to risk Craven's detecting the smell of alcohol on his breath.

Even with his eyes troubling him, Asa could see when the film came out of the developer that it wasn't as good as it should be. He'd probably flubbed the exposure time when he'd read it off the chart, he decided, but his vision was getting worse, if anything, and he didn't want to go through the agony of taking another film. With Dr. Ordway out of the city, he doubted that Craven would be familiar enough with high voltage X-ray films to know whether it was right or not anyway and, as far as Asa could see, the film didn't show any defects that might cause them to pull out a whole bulkhead this close to launch time and probably delay it a week or two.

God, would this day never end? he thought, as he felt the alcohol begin to take hold inside his body. Fortunately, with the sick certificate the doctor on the mainland would give him, if he could only last that long, he could stay home tomorrow, or until he got over this terrible feeling.

In the dark room he took the film out of the fixing solution and put it into the tank to wash. A wave of dizziness went over him as he bent over the tank and he had to hold on to keep from sliding to the floor.

Like most dark rooms, this one was painted black inside and the entrance was built in the form of a maze to shut out light from outside. Half blind now and gasping for breath in the confined space, Asa bumped into the partitions of the maze as he groped his way out toward the office. Once there, he started for the desk, but managed to get only halfway across the room before he crashed to the floor.

Seized now with the fear of death, he tried to cry out but no one else was in the laboratory and his groans went unheard. Summoning all of his strength, he did manage to drag himself across the laboratory to the desk where the telephone rested. He couldn't raise himself to the level of the desk but, when his groping hand closed on the cord leading to the wall, he managed to pull the phone off the desk, sending it crashing to the floor.

Almost blind now from the powerful forces of the anaphylactic reaction that was trying to destroy his life, he managed to reach the dial and thrust his finger into the opening at the bottom, spinning the dial around and connecting himself with the operator.

When she answered, he tried to call into the phone but all his strength was needed now merely to suck air into straining lungs through respiratory passages whose walls were swelling rapidly from the allergic reaction and only a faint croak came out. Though he could hear the telephone operator's voice, he was not able to ask her to summon help and that final effort of attempted speech was too much.

A wave of blackness poured over him, blotting out all consciousness.

iv.

Mike was considering going to lunch, when the telephone rang in his office. "This is Tom Craven, Doctor. The Coastal Airlines nurse wants you in the dispensary pronto."

It took Mike only a few minutes to reach the dispensary; one glance at the mottled bluish color of the man lying on the table in the small surgery told him the emergency was grave indeed. Tom Craven was helping the nurse; they were trying to give the victim artificial respiration with a positive pressure respirator, apparently without any success, for the main valve of the machine was stuttering rapidly, indicating a blocked respiratory passage.

"What happened here?" Mike asked as he pulled a stethoscope from the medical bag standing on a small table in the dispensary and moved up beside the table.

"I came into the metallurgy laboratory about ten minutes ago to read some films Childs had taken earlier and found him unconscious," said Craven. "He's our head technician in Dr. Ordway's lab."

"He was in acute respiratory distress when they brought him here, Doctor," said the nurse. "We've been trying to give him oxygen but can't seem to get it into his lungs."

"Does he breathe at all?"

"Every now and then, but only by straining very hard."

Mike listened briefly to the front of the patient's chest. The heart sounds were fairly good, though hurried, indicating that the trouble was respiratory, as the nurse had stated.

"Get me a laryngeal mirror," he directed, and reached for a head mirror from the top of the instrument cabinet in the corner. A not infrequent cause of sudden respiratory obstruction was the lodging of meat or other food against the opening of the larynx, blocking the airway. If this were the case here, he should be able to see it and grasp it with a forceps or flip it out with the small mirror on the end of a metal rod some six or eight inches long.

Adjusting the head mirror with its center hole, Mike seized Asa Childs' tongue with a gauze square, pulling it forward. The tongue itself was swollen and oddly blackened in color, more it seemed than the bluish hue of cyanosis in the mucous membranes of the rest of the mouth would seem to justify. Somewhere inside Mike's mind a faint warning bell rang at this observation but it didn't give him the answer to what had caused the condition in which Tom Craven had found the metallurgical technician. And there was no time at the moment for any action not designed to save life.

Reflecting the light from the bulb of the stand lamp the nurse had moved up beside the table so the beam was thrown down into the patient's throat, he observed that the lining membranes were badly swollen, almost turgid. And when he thrust the small mirror on the end of the metal handle into the back of the pharynx to visualize the opening of the larynx, he saw that no foreign body was causing the obstruction. Instead, the vocal cords and the tissues around them were so badly swollen that the normal opening through which air passed in and out of the lungs appeared to be closed.

"We're dealing with acute laryngeal edema," he told the nurse. "Do you have a tracheostomy tube sterile?"

"There's one in the reserve cabinet. We've never had to use it before."

"We're going to use it now. I'll need a scalpel, too—sterile if possible."

The nurse was already opening a sterile tray on a metal stand beside the table where the patient lay. It contained a scalpel, a pair of thumb forceps, a needle holder, and several hemostatic clamps. While Mike pulled on a pair of sterile gloves, she rummaged in another cabinet and came out with a small package, which she opened to drop a curved, double tracheostomy tube on the sterile tray beside the scalpel.

Mike had already placed a square of gauze between the jaws of a pair of hemostatic forceps and was swabbing the front of Asa Childs' neck between his Adam's apple and the notch at the top of his breastbone with a scarlet antiseptic solution.

"You'll have to hold his head steady for me," he told Tom Craven. "I've got to get a tube into his windpipe and the nurse will be needed to hand me things."

The engineer nodded and took the dying man's head between his hands, pressing against the temples to hold it still. Craven was sweating and a little pale, but Mike was pretty sure he would come through all right.

Placing a sterile towel across the patient's neck at its base and another at the level of the Adam's apple, Mike reached for the scalpel. There was no time now for elaborate draping and, being unconscious, the patient needed no anesthetic. Feeling with his gloved finger downward along the neck from the Adam's apple, he identified the narrow swelling of the isthmus connecting the two lobes of the thyroid gland in front of the semi-rigid trachea, or windpipe. Thyroid tissue was highly vascular—blood-filled—and to cut through the isthmus would mean flooding the wound with blood, hindering him in making the opening into the trachea.

Below the thyroid, his finger felt the bands of cartilage, or gristle, that encircled the windpipe, giving it a semi-rigid state and preventing its collapse, an event which could have caused immediate death.

Tensing the skin over the area by spreading his left thumb and index finger apart, he made an incision across the neck nearly two inches long in a single stroke, cutting through to the trachea beneath. Blood spurted from small vessels and he heard Tom Craven gulp but he paid no attention to that, realizing from the almost black color of the blood that the patient was approaching, if indeed he had not already reached, a fatal state of anoxia, oxygen lack, from obstruction to the passageway leading to the lungs.

Separating the edges of the incision by spreading his thumb and fore-
finger still farther, Mike turned the blade of the scalpel to cut downward and set it against the semi-rigid wall of the trachea. The cartilage
of the wall resisted the blade considerably more than had the skin and
he was forced to press much harder before it suddenly cut through the
tough gristle with a faint grating sound, opening the trachea itself to
the outside.

Air whistled into the straining lungs of the sick man through the
opening but Mike didn't immediately remove the blade, which had now
penetrated into the respiratory passage itself. Moving the sharp edge
downward, he cut through another of the cartilage rings, then quickly
lifted the knife from the wound, reversing it, and slipped the end of
the flat handle into the wound to hold it open while he reached for
the curving tracheostomy tube lying upon the instrument table.

Actually the device consisted of two tubes, one inside the other, each
with a ring or collar at the outer end to keep it from slipping into the
trachea through the wound in the skin and the windpipe. In that way,
the inner tube could be removed for cleaning from time to time without
disturbing the outer tube.

With the curved end pointed downward toward the lungs, Mike
slipped the tube through the opening he had made in the windpipe and
set it snugly into the respiratory passage. He could see now that the
lining of the trachea was as severely swollen as the passages in the back
of the throat had been. But since the trachea itself was much larger in
diameter than the relatively narrow aperture of the larynx there was no
real obstruction to breathing, once an opening was made below the
larynx and vocal cords.

Even as he slid the tube into place, allowing air to rush in and out
of the patient's lungs with a rhythmic whistling sound, Mike was able
to diagnose what had happened, though not yet the cause. Mucous
membrane swelling to this degree was practically always the result of a
severe allergic reaction from some outside source, often a drug. But with
the patient still unconscious, there was no way of discovering the culprit
at the moment. Besides it was far more important, now that the immediate danger of suffocation had been removed by Mike's dramatic sur-
gical intervention, to take measures combating the serious effects of a
severe anaphylactic reaction upon other organs—notably the brain.

The steady flow of air in and out of the patient's lungs through the
tracheostomy tube told Mike the airway was now clear. Holding the
tube in place with his left hand, he picked up a gauze sponge from
the small table and pressed it against the edge of the wound on either
side of the metal collar around the outer opening of the tracheostomy

tube. As he had hoped, there was only a little bleeding when he took the gauze away.

"I'll need a few black silk sutures, fairly heavy, for the skin," he told the nurse.

She went immediately to the wall supply cabinet and removed a small sterile package, which she opened, dropping its contents on the tray beside the scalpel he had used to open the skin and the trachea. Wrapped about the square of gauze inside the package were several silk sutures, attached to curved sharp pointed needles.

It took only a few moments to place four stitches through the wound in the skin and subcutaneous tissues. When Mike tied them, the small amount of bleeding stopped but he left the ends of two of the sutures long, cutting the other two. Then, carefully placing a strip of gauze sponge over the skin wound on either side of the metal tube, around which the skin was now tightly closed, he threaded the ends of the sutures through small openings on either side of the metal collar of the larger and outer of the two tracheostomy tubes and tied them securely, holding the collar snugly to the neck and to the dressing.

"We can use the respirator now," he said. "You all right, Tom?"

The engineer nodded. "I thought I'd drop once, when the blood spurted, but after that I was too busy watching what you were doing with the tube to pass out."

Removing the face mask of the respirator, Mike connected the nozzle on the hose from its oxygen tank directly to the open end of the tracheostomy tube and set the control to allow a free interchange of pure oxygen. As the small breathing bag filled and emptied rhythmically now with near normal respiration, speeding vital oxygen into the lungs and thence into the blood stream, the bluish tint of Asa Childs' ear lobes and lips began to clear up rapidly.

"You'd better send for an ambulance," he told the nurse. "We'll have to get him to the hospital on the mainland."

"You mean he'll have to have something else done?" Tom Craven asked.

"We've only taken care of the symptoms. Now we have to find the cause of this reaction and treat it."

"What could the cause be?"

"Some sort of an allergic reaction would be my guess. Give him a half cc. of one-to-one-thousand epinephrine intramuscularly, please, Mrs. Gans."

"The ambulance is waiting outside, Dr. Barnes," said the nurse as she prepared the hypodermic. "I ordered it when Mr. Craven brought him in. Shall I give him the epinephrine anyway?"

"Yes. I'll go with him to the hospital. As soon as we leave, see if you can find Dr. Harry Metzger and ask him to meet me there."

"Are you sure you've told me everything you remember about Childs?" Mike asked Tom Craven as the attendants were taking Asa, still connected to the respirator, out to the ambulance on a stretcher.

"He appeared to be trying to get to the phone, but didn't make it, except to jerk it off the desk," said the engineer. "The scuttlebutt around the office is that he's a homo but that's probably not important here."

"Was he working with anything special today, something he might have been allergic to?"

"Nothing that I know of. He takes X rays all the time and develops them, so the solutions shouldn't bother him."

"Maybe we'll find out when he becomes conscious," said Mike.

"Skilled metallurgical technicians are hard to find," said Craven. "Taggar Aircraft owes you a vote of thanks for saving Childs."

"Be sure and tell Paul Taggar that," said Mike. "Maybe he'll come to like me."

CHAPTER XXII

Dr. Harry Metzger was at the hospital when the ambulance arrived. By then Asa Childs was breathing considerably easier from the action of the epinephrine in shrinking the repiratory system linings, but he had not regained consciousness. He was taken immediately to a cubicle in the Intensive Care Section, where the hospital oxygen supply was connected to the tracheostomy tube in place of that from the respirator.

"Looks like your diagnosis of a severe allergic reaction is the answer," the internist said when Mike finished a quick rundown on what had happened. "I'll start an intravenous drip of norepinephrine while we're looking for a cause, but with something as severe as this we ought be be able to pin a particular item down, once he's conscious."

"I did notice one thing, though its meaning escapes my memory," said Mike. "His tongue seems blacker than the other tissues."

Metzger took a tongue depressor and a flashlight from his own medical bag and, pressing down Asa Childs' lower jaw, centered the light on the tongue. As Mike had already noted, it was still black, although with an adequate supply of oxygen flowing into the sick man's lungs and out to the body tissues by way of the circulation, the surrounding tissues had now almost regained their normal pink color.

"A black tongue like this is almost pathognomonic of penicillin allergy," said Metzger. "Not all cases have it but when it does occur, you can usually get a history of having been given a shot by the family doctor a few days before, or taking some of the penicillin tablets found on almost every medicine shelf these days."

"So all that remains is to find out what he's taking penicillin for—and how much he's had."

"We'll start by checking his backside," said Metzger crisply.

When they turned Asa Childs over, the evidence was there, six needle marks in the skin of the buttocks. Beneath the skin around each they could easily feel the hardness called induration that often resulted from the injection of a drug directly into the muscle.

"Six doses!" Metzger exclaimed. "Even if they were the usual six hundred thousand units each, the fellow's still lucky to be alive, with the kind of reaction penicillin causes in his body."

"Notice anything peculiar about the location of those injection marks?" Mike asked.

Metzger studied the pattern for a moment, then nodded. "If a doctor had been giving that much—and God knows he shouldn't without having the patient under observation for the possibility of just what happened to this one—he would have spaced his injection locations in quadrants each separated as far as possible from the others. These are located helter skelter."

"Not only that; they're peripheral, about where a man could reach, if he were making the injections into himself."

"You're right," Metzger exclaimed. "Well at least we can be sure no doctor was damn fool enough to do it that way."

"One other thing, Tom Craven told me it's pretty common knowledge around the Cape that Childs is a homo."

"That would explain it," said Metzger. "The incidence of syphilis among the gay set is far higher than in the general population because they have so many more contacts than the average promiscuous girl— or even a prostitute. I'll check with the health department as soon as I get this intravenous started; knowing what we know now, I'm going to add some penicillinase and hydrocortisone to that intravenous."

"Anything else I can do?" Mike asked.

"No. I take it that your session with the 'Hot Line' wasn't very exciting the other night."

"On the contrary. I'm almost certain now that I know exactly why Ellen Taggar died." He gave the other doctor a quick resumé of what he and Jan had learned from the "Hot Line" tapes the night before. "All I need to find out now is where she was calling from and we'll know just where she walked into the ocean."

"There's an extension phone in the cabana on the beach in front of Paul Taggar's house," said Metzger. "Paul has called me once or twice from there when Sally was having an asthma attack and I remember hearing the ocean."

"That's the answer then."

"Mike." Metzger's face was grave. "Is it quite fair to exhume a dead girl just because you don't like her father."

The question brought Mike up short. "I don't hate Taggar," he protested. "But I hate what he did to his daughter and if it's necessary to expose that, I won't hesitate. Why should that trouble you, Harry?"

"I have a son almost as old as Ellen was—"

"Your son has done nothing wrong."

"I wish I could be as sure of that as I am that it never occurred to Paul Taggar his daughter would ever sniff glue."

ii.

Mike met Tom Craven at his office the next morning and they were driven to the VAB where the rocket called Pegasus was being given its final checkouts before being moved to the launch pad. The usual queue of tourists was already waiting to be ushered into the great building, where a lecturer would acquaint them with details about Pegasus, subtly influencing them in favor of FSA and the space program with a brain washing hardly less thorough than that used by the enemy in the Korean War.

As on the previous occasion when he'd been a tourist himself, Mike was struck by the size of the giant projectile, particularly the second stage, which must serve both as a container for fuel to help push it and the command ship riding atop it into orbit and as a workshop for the two astronauts who would ride the winged horse into space. In addition, if all went well, it would form part of a future large laboratory complex where studies could be carried out to determine whether men could safely embark upon the months-long voyage to Mars.

"My old Hermes ship looked like a firecracker compared to this," Mike said as an elevator lifted them to the top of the giant projectile, where the spacecraft was perched.

"The original plan was for a station about half this large," said the engineer. "But right after we got the contract to design this baby, they asked us to double the size of the second stage."

"Why the change?" Mike was instantly alert.

"Nobody gave us a satisfactory explanation and we didn't ask because the money was doubled, too."

"Are you sure nobody ever gave you a reason for the increased size of the second stage?"

"Like I said, we didn't ask," said Craven. "Do you know something I don't?"

Mike decided to confide in the engineer, whom he'd come to like.

"Jake Arrens thinks the extra size may be intended to allow an orbiting station to be armed with hydrogen warheads," he said, "in case we discover that the Russians are planning a nuclear attack."

"Does anybody doubt that they would do just that—if they're ever able to get the jump on us?"

"A lot of misguided idealists are muddled enough to think so," said Mike. "But, judging from the size of this thing, it's a comfort to know somebody seems to be convinced that the Russians are going to keep on acting the way they've always acted. Personally I'd like to see us go a step farther and send up an extra propulsive stage that could be attached to this station. Then, if the international scene got sticky, the whole thing could be put into a synchronous orbit and hang over any point on the surface of the earth where we wanted to put it."

"That should be feasible." Craven's eyes had begun to glow with creative inspiration. "But why not go a step farther and use those two fuel tanks we're going to push out of the second stage shell of a future Pegasus as storage containers for hydrogen warheads?"

"It makes sense," said Mike. "We'll work on it after this one gets off the ground."

"But in secret," said Craven.

"Of course, the official administration line is still to push for disarmament and more nuclear control treaties."

"Treaties didn't keep the Communists from pouring missiles into Cuba —until we clamped down," said Tom Craven. "And they got away with it in Vietnam, using smaller weapons."

"The beautiful thing about a space station in a synchronous orbit," Mike reminded him, "would be that the Russians could never be sure whether we had the thing armed or not. That way they'd hesitate to start anything with the fractional orbital bombardment system called SCRAG, or with their SS-9s, knowing that even if they were to eliminate our entire second strike capability on the ground, a U.S. arsenal-in-orbit with a crew of astronauts could still destroy their cities and industrial centers."

"Give me until next week, when we've got this baby off the pad, and I'll ask Paul to let me work full time on old Ezekiel's wheel-in-a-wheel with you."

"It's going to be a challenge, but I think we can lick it."

"The escape tower for Hermes II is a lot larger than the sixteen foot one you had on Hermes I, because of the extra size of the capsule." Tom Craven pointed to the rocket attached to the top of the tripod tower. "Those three jets you see up there have a thrust of about seventy-five thousand pounds, enough to hurl the entire spacecraft a half mile into the air and allow the parachutes to lower it to earth. So far we've never had to use one of those towers and some people suggested leaving them off when we planned this rocket, but I fought against it."

"It's a tremendous comfort to know that rocket is up there, when you feel the first surge of power under you as the booster ignites," said Mike. "I'd vote to leave escape towers on."

The space inside Hermes II was still cramped and enough like Mike's own vehicle had been to bring back rather unpleasant memories, but he set his jaw against their power to disturb him and the moment of tension passed. They spent perhaps twenty minutes inside, so he could become familiar with the details of the craft, then Craven pulled himself out through the open hatch and Mike followed, breathing deeply of the air outside.

"We'll pressurize the cabin with oxygen for the test," said Craven. "That way we can check the control valve on the supply tank and also see whether the cabin exhaust valve operates properly."

"Was anything wrong with the ones you took out?"

"Nothing we could see. Like I said the other day, the new ones were put in as an added precaution—mainly, I suspect because of your arrival."

On the ground floor of the massive VAB, they entered a control room where a battery of panels enabled the engineers to watch every action of the rocket. High above them, workmen had already closed the hatches of Hermes II and started the oxygen flow.

"The oxygen system is working fine," Tom Craven reported as he looked over the shoulder of an engineer sitting at one of the panels before an array of dials and controls. "The cabin is almost pressurized already."

When he pointed to a dial among the bank on the panel Mike saw that the needle was moving steadily, measuring the pressure inside the spacecraft several hundred feet above them. At just over one-fifth of an atmosphere, the needle suddenly halted and went no further, but vibrated back and forth almost as if it had struck a block.

"The needle vibrates because the valve is letting excess oxygen escape to the outside," the engineer at the control panel explained.

"Satisfied?" Tom Craven asked Mike.

"We ran the same test before my own flight—yet both valves stuck and I had to make an emergency reentry."

"We'll check it again before launch," Craven promised. "It takes a pretty stable valve to handle liquid oxygen."

"Especially when the boiling point is two hundred and ninety-seven degrees below zero Fahrenheit," Mike agreed. "The day before MA-6 was supposed to fly in the Mercury program, a faulty oxygen regulator was discovered and had to be replaced."

"You never give up, do you?" said Tom Craven. "But thank God for people like you, just the same. We can design and supervise the manufacture but, when it comes to putting the pieces together, we're still at the mercy of a mechanic who's more interested in whether his union representative can get a few extra bucks for him to spend on the dogs than he is in whether a rocket costing billions is going to get safely off the pad."

"We had an example of that with one of the earlier model space suits when the wrist pressure seal kept giving us trouble," said Mike. "It finally had to be removed, and we discovered that the seal had been installed backward at the factory."

"I remembered that when you discovered the leaking collar the other day," said Craven. "Incidentally, Dr. Ordway called from the factory last night. He's pretty sure we've licked that problem."

"Any trouble with that bulkhead metal you had X-rayed?"

"The films look all right to me. I examined them after Asa Childs was taken to the hospital."

"Wasn't it rather late in the day for such examinations?"

"That was Paul's idea, too, like the valves; he's pretty edgy these days. I'd forgotten all about the ruptured aluminum membrane that caused so much trouble, when they were getting Mercury-Atlas VI ready for John Glenn's flight."

"I hadn't," said Mike. "We were just starting the Hermes program about that time."

"At least it's a comfort to know there'll be no leaking of LOX into the kerosene with this one. I can guarantee that much."

"By the way," said Mike, "who did the calculations to determine the launch window for this shot?"

"McCandless I imagine; he's head of that department. Why?"

"He's been under quite a strain."

Craven grinned. "I've seen the girl and he's certainly a lot more confident of his staying power than I would be."

"My guess would be that McCandless has gone off the deep end psychologically and doesn't know how to get back."

"I'm sure FSA must have checked him on those calculations with the computer."

"But suppose the information he fed into the computer was wrong in the beginning? If Pegasus misses the launch window, several million dollars will go up in a path that might give it a perigee so low it would reenter the atmosphere and be consumed by the heat."

"The command pilot in the spacecraft could always separate the components in flight and make an emergency reentry."

"But could he get his angle of reentry readjusted in time to keep from skipping in and out of the atmosphere like we used to scoot shells on the surface of the Indian River?"

"You've been an astronaut, what do you think?"

"It would depend on a lot of things, any one of which could easily go wrong."

"Aren't you the optimistic one this morning?" Craven observed.

"I'm a scientist. We don't believe in leaving anything to chance."

"So what do you do? Walk up to McCandless and ask him whether he's been so busy humping his broad that maybe he's made a mistake in his calculations?"

"That's Hal Brennan's job."

"Hal's been pretty busy, too, with his campaign and that chick from Argentina. From what I hear, she makes McCandless' girl friend look like a boy."

CHAPTER XXIII

Mike was working in his room at the Astronaut Inn, examining some reports Tom Craven had sent him of further tests made on the life environment system of the Hermes II capsule, when there was a knock on the door. He opened it, to find Dr. Harry Metzger outside.

"I'm on my way home from the hospital and thought you might be interested to know Dr. McCandless was admitted tonight," said the internist.

"Anything severe?"

"The first electrocardiograms aren't too conclusive. I think he has a mild coronary thrombosis, but he doesn't seem to have any anxiety at all now; in fact I'm not sure he isn't relieved."

"That sort of profound conclusion needs discussion over a stein of premium lager," said Mike. "Any objections?"

"No, I'd like to talk to you about this anyway."

Mike put on his jacket and they went down to the bar; it was almost empty.

"I've been worried that McCandless' preoccupation with other matters might have led him to a possible error in calculating the parameters for next week's orbit," Mike admitted while Al was bringing them their beer. "Do you suppose he could have been troubled about the same thing and found an error that hit him so hard he had a coronary?"

"That's a possibility but several studies have shown that, contrary to what we used to think, it isn't the tensed-up executive who comes down most frequently with a coronary at all. Instead, it's men from the blue collar group."

"I've read those reports but I'm not really qualified to judge," said Mike.

"Neither am I," the internist admitted. "Most of my patients come from what is possibly the most highly competitive sociological unit in America today."

"The aerospace centers are certainly that, but even here, we may be dealing with another psychophysiological process," said Mike. "After all, more men have coronary heart attacks after they reach a plateau in life, like finishing a highly competitive job, than during actual combat —if you can call the fight to survive combat."

"For my money it's the most vicious form there is," Metzger said gravely. "You sound like you have a theory."

"It's probably no more than that," Mike admitted, "but ten years ago, McCandless was one of the most respected minds in Cambridge. From what I hear, he's been marking time since he finished calculating the parameters for Pegasus though, and now he finds himself in an impossible situation. He's lost status in the eyes of fellow members of the intellectual community, and he has taken on something his body just isn't able to stand up to—I use the phrase advisedly—any longer."

"Plus finding a mistake in calculating those parameters?"

"That could have happened, too. Maybe now that he's off the hook, he'll tell us."

"That's an interesting phrase 'off the hook.' Are you implying that this mild coronary McCandless has now may be a way out of the mess he's gotten himself into."

"With a history of having had a coronary, won't he have to go easy on vigorous sexual exercise?"

"That will certainly be my advice."

"Then this attack may have served much the same purpose for him that amnesia, for example, does for a less intelligent person. It gets him out of an intolerable situation, at least for the time being."

"And the future?"

"I'd have to talk to him some more before I'd even hazard a guess, but I doubt if he'd ever want to see me again."

"That's where you're wrong," said Metzger. "He asked me to stop by and tell you he would like to see you."

"I wonder why."

"Didn't you tell me you knew him when you were both at Harvard?"

"Yes. But he was a professor and I was only a student."

"Maybe you've come to symbolize the intellectual community to him —the one he forsook for the filthy lure of FSA."

"That's a pretty wild assumption," Mike said with a grin. "I'll try to drop by the hospital in a few days. They're moving Pegasus to the launch area with the big crawler units tomorrow morning. That's something I want to see."

ii.

The winged horse called Pegasus was an awesome sight as it moved slowly out of the bay in the eight-acre Vehicle Assembly Building where its many intricate parts had been fashioned into a cognate whole during the past several months. Towering skyward on the mobile launcher, itself resting upon four double-tracked crawler units driven by sixteen traction motors, it moved at a snail's pace. Yet its very movement was all the more impressive because of the mechanical miracle that enabled such a structure to be transported at all.

Watching from the main gate of the Pegasus complex, Mike was startled by the sheer beauty of the giant rocket as the morning sun was reflected in a blinding glare from its shining sides. Ordinarily, he knew, the rocket would have been moved to the pad from which it would begin its flight at least a month before the actual launch date. But the relative secrecy which had surrounded Pegasus from the beginning was still the order of the day and the hordes of tourists who usually swarmed into the center had been forced to forego their visit to the Vehicle Assembly Building this morning. Ostensibly the precaution had been taken to guarantee the visitors' safety while the crawlers were shifting the rocket, but actually, Mike suspected, lest its purpose as something more than simply a research laboratory be suspect from its size. Once Pegasus reached the launch area, it would be some three miles from the tourist route and its size much less apparent because of the distance.

"I almost wish I were going along," a familiar voice said, and Mike turned to see Colonel Andy Zapf and Helen standing nearby.

"I didn't worry when Andy made his Gemini and even his Apollo flights." Helen showed no signs of sharing her husband's enthusiasm for the rocket. "But that monster there gives me the shakes."

"Everything checks out fine, Helen," said Mike.

"Did it have to be so big?"

Mike gave Andy Zapf a quick glance to see whether or not he noticed the question, but the air force colonel was studying the crawlers with their massive caterpillar-type tracks, each lug of which measured seven and a half feet across and weighed a ton.

"With a couple of those second stages locked together, there'll be plenty of room for men to work without getting into each other's hair," Mike explained to Helen. "By putting a really big one up there at the beginning, we can get a head start on studying a lot of things."

"With the doors of the bay that bird just came out of still open, we should get a real view of the terrain from the top of the elevator shaft," said Andy Zapf. "Let's see whether we can get the operator to take us up before the doors are closed again."

Both Colonel Zapf and Mike were well known to the workers by now and they had no trouble persuading one of the elevator men to lift them several hundred feet skyward. The view spread out before them was magnificent, with the sprawl of the northern part of Merritt Island lying between the VAB and the distant launch site, toward which the crawlers were moving now at their usual mile-an-hour pace over the broad roadway connecting the two.

The ocean was a sparkling blue in the morning sunlight with a line of whitecaps showing where the long rollers swept in from the east to break upon the bar not far from the shore itself. Less than a half mile from the new launch site for Pegasus an arrow-straight drainage canal cut across the palmetto- and saw-grass covered terrain, its flatness broken here and there by the silhouette of a cabbage palm against the morning sky.

Dug when the new section had been opened in order to turn what had formerly been largely mud flats into usable land, the canal served also as a fire barrier between the launch site and the new industrial complex spawned by the decision to go on with the Pegasus program after Apollo was phased out.

Only the Pegasus launch area and the new forward central block-house, itself almost buried in the sandy terrain, lay between the drain-age canal and the ocean. On either side of the canal, sand and shell taken from what had once been ocean bottom eons ago formed bul-warks that shut away any view of the channel itself from ground level, but viewed from the elevation close to the top of the VAB, the straight line of the canal could be seen easily for its full length.

Besides the broad highway of crushed stone along which the crawlers were moving, several other paved roads cut across the intervening area, leading from the Taggar assembly plant and other centers to the launch pad area itself where, for the next week, an army of men would be working day and night in the final preparations for the flight.

"When I was a boy, the highest place we could get to around here was the top of an oak tree, except when we were lucky enough to be taken to the lighthouse—which wasn't very often." Mike pointed to the old lighthouse with its stripes fading from the continual battering of the salt-laden wind. "I was six years old the first time I went up in that lighthouse and as far as I was concerned it was the top of the world. Now it looks like a pygmy beside even the first gantry towers."

"When we came down here the first time, Merritt Island was covered with orange and mango groves," said Helen Zapf wistfully. "To me it was the loveliest spot on earth, but now look what men have done to God's handiwork."

"Better watch out or you'll become a follower of that preacher over on the mainland who claims all this is blasphemy," said Mike.

"Why?" Andy Zapf asked.

"Apparently he thinks we're going to fire one of these rockets right through the Pearly Gates some day—and the end of the world will begin."

"When you look at that thing there, you can almost believe it could make it," said Helen.

"When do you have time to go to church, Mike?" Andy Zapf asked.

"I haven't had any yet. Sandra Craven drags Tom there sometimes and he told me about it."

"Isn't that Tom over there—in the jeep with Paul Taggar?" Helen asked.

Mike looked in the direction she was pointing and saw a tall man in a hard hat driving a jeep with the shorter figure of the chief engineer beside him. They were following the crawler, as if shepherding it and its precious towering burden to the new location.

"I discovered that Ellen Taggar made a 'Hot Line' call from the Taggar cabana the night she was drowned," Mike told the Zapfs and Helen gave a quick cry of anguish and sympathy.

"Was anyone else there?" she asked.

"Both parents were out—at different places."

"As usual." Helen shivered and moved closer to her husband. "Let's get away from here, darling—right away."

"I can't leave until after the shot next Thursday," Andy told her. "But we'll be going back to Houston right afterwards."

"Houston's almost as bad. Promise me you'll ask for some quiet post, like maybe Langley. Even Bolling would be better than this."

"I wouldn't take what that preacher says too seriously, Helen," said Mike. "The rumor is that he spends his weekdays entertaining dissatisfied wives."

"I'm sure he keeps very busy then," she said. "And from some things I've been hearing lately, pretty close to Pegasus itself."

iii.

Abram McCandless was propped up in bed when Mike visited him at the hospital early Friday afternoon. The oxygen tube was still connected to the control valve and the bottle of water through which the gas bubbled when in use hung from a rack on the wall. But the valve was closed and the nasal catheter through which a patient was able to receive oxygen without the use of an unwieldy and often quite uncomfortable, oxygen tent, now hung upon the corner of the bed, though still ready for instant use if it became necessary.

"Thank you for coming, Dr. Barnes," said the scientist cordially. "I'm afraid I was rather short with you the other day when you were kind enough to take me home from the office."

"You were under a strain," said Mike. "I understood."

"But not the reason. I'd discovered that I'd made a stupid mistake during some calculations and it upset me."

"Not with the parameters for the flight next Thursday," Mike said quickly.

"No. I've checked them since and they're correct."

Mike drew a deep breath of relief. "Thank God for that."

"The mere fact that I had doubted my own calculations enough to feel it necessary to redo them entirely made me realize just how far I've drifted from the path I set for myself back in Cambridge," said the astrophysicist.

"Not many of us reach the goals we set that early."

"This heart attack gave me a chance to look at myself," said McCandless. "The all-seeing eye up there took care of that." He pointed to the lens of a closed circuit TV camera located above the door, by which the nurse at the intensive care nursing station was able to watch patients in the unit at all times. "It searches your soul while it watches your body, and makes you face up to reality."

"It's a new way of self-analysis all right—and a hard one, I imagine."

"The soul you see is pretty shriveled—at least it was in my case—but I do hope to make amends. When I leave here, I shall go home and tender my resignation to FSA."

"Is that necessary, sir? Your calculations of the parameters were correct so you haven't failed as far as FSA is concerned."

"Nevertheless I failed in my own eyes—and those of the scientific intellectual community where I first met you—but fortunately, I've been given a chance to regain that standing with a professorship at the Florida Technological University at Orlando, heading their department of astrophysics and computers."

"They couldn't have made a better choice."

"Dr. Metzger was telling me this morning about your interesting theory that this heart attack may have been a means of escape for me from the mess I'd gotten myself into. I'm inclined to believe you're right, Doctor, and you can be sure I won't need that means any more."

"Don't push your luck with the coronary," Mike advised. "I'd better go before you tire yourself out."

Outside the room, a technician who had been waiting in the corridor, said: "Dr. Metzger would like to see you in the lab, Dr. Barnes."

Mike hadn't known Metzger was in the hospital but followed the technician to the laboratory at the end of the corridor. The internist was bending over a colorimeter and looked up as Mike came in.

"I thought you might be interested in a patient I just sent over from my office for admission, Mike," he said, and moved back to make room before the colorimeter. "Take a look at that."

"Looks like a heavy concentration of bile in the blood serum," said Mike, after studying the specimen in the instrument for a moment. "Jaundice?"

"Of a sort. That specimen came from young Jason McCandless."

"That's tough luck. They've already got enough problems without the boy having infectious—" He stopped, as something Jan had said the night he came back from Washington suddenly came into his mind. "Wasn't he going steady with—"

"Ellen Taggar," said Metzger. "I don't think a virus caused that jaundice, Mike. It's more likely to be toluol."

"Good God!"

"I felt the same way. Did the person you were with that Sunday night at the beach recognize Jason McCandless?"

"No. She wasn't even sure Ellen was there, except from the Maserati and the bathing suit. The boy could tell us though."

"I hate to ask him," said Metzger. "Do you remember my telling you that when I got to the Taggar house to see Sally about the asthma attack, the Maserati was parked in front of it?"

"Yes. He probably drove her home. They might have gone swimming."

"That could mean he left after she disappeared in the water."

"He could have left before. We'll still have to ask him."

Jason McCandless was enough like his father that Mike would have recognized him almost anywhere. He appeared to be about nineteen —and intelligent. Seeing the fear in his eyes, Mike knew he already suspected they had learned at least a part of the truth.

"This is Dr. Barnes, Jason," said Metzger. "I asked him to see you with me."

"Glad to know you, Dr. Barnes," said the youth. "Do you know what's wrong yet?"

"You have a severe case of jaundice, Jason," said Dr. Metzger.

"Several students at the college had it last spring." There was a note of relief in the young man's voice. "Some of that's always going around, isn't it?"

"Jaundice can also come from poisons," said Metzger.

"Poisons? Then that's out—"

"Toluol is a poison; it's the solvent agent in the glue used to join plastic pieces together to form models."

The stricken look in the boy's eyes, before he buried his face in his hands, was a more eloquent confession of truth than words could have been.

"I saw that party on the beach the other Sunday night, so I already know something of what happened," Mike said gently. "Do you want to tell us about it?"

"Could I have a glass of water first?"

"Certainly." Dr. Metzger poured a glass from the thermos flask on the bedside table and gave it to him. The boy drank it gratefully, then straightened his shoulders.

"I had tried sniffing a few times at college; you can get turned on pretty fast with it," he said. "Ellen had a row with her old man that night; her mother's pretty much of a lush and she blamed Mr. Taggar. I imagine you've heard those stories about the secretaries he takes to Freeport—well they're true. I worked there a while this summer and saw them."

"Was Ellen trying to get back at her father?" Mike asked.

The boy nodded. "I couldn't blame her, either. I felt right much the same way about— Well, when some of the others started sniffing, Ellen did too, and I—I guess I didn't do much to discourage her."

"Who drove her car back to the house?" asked Metzger.

"I did after—well we'd gone pretty far and I thought she ought to get back home to, you know, take some precautions."

"How did you know she hadn't."

"Most of the girls carry those little things that make foam, but Ellen said she never had. We drove to her house and left the car. She said she was going into the house and I was pretty groggy so I started walking home."

"You didn't hear her use the telephone?"

"What telephone?"

"There's one in the cabana."

"Ellen didn't go near the cabana while I was there, Doctor. I left her at the side door of the house, where you come in from the beach. She said she was going to leave her bathing suit in the dressing room there. What do you mean about a telephone?"

"A girl called the 'Hot Line' that night. She seemed very disturbed and the surf could be heard in the background breaking on the shore."

"You mean she—? Oh my God!"

"What's happened is done and over with, Jason," said Metzger. "The important thing now is to get some support for your damaged liver. The admission diagnosis will be infectious hepatitis, and what you've told us here tonight doesn't have to go any farther than this office. Do you agree, Dr. Barnes?"

"In view of the fact that Ellen is dead, yes," said Mike. "We can't help her now and with Jason under treatment, the case might as well be closed."

"But don't you see how wrong it is to hush up the whole thing?" Jason McCandless cried. "Kids nowadays take everything their parents forbid them to do as a challenge; Ellen would never have gone that far, if she hadn't been angry at Mr. Taggar. I—I can't help her now but I can help myself—and others—by telling the truth. Kids will listen to me, too, because I rebelled and they can see what it got me."

"You don't have to do it," Mike warned him. "Nobody knows better than I how rough things can get when you challenge the status quo."

"Young people today claim they're challenging the status quo by sniffing, smoking pot, taking LSD, and the like, Dr. Barnes. If I don't tell them what the consequences are, I can never look myself in the mirror again and feel I have any respect for who I'm seeing."

"We both know how you feel and we respect you for it, Jason," said Dr. Metzger. "Please think about this tonight and don't make any hasty decisions."

"Whatever happens to me will be no more than I deserve," said the youth. "But I'd hate to think Ellen and I could both be dead and our deaths not be a lesson to others."

"I know it's an imposition, Mike," Dr. Metzger said outside the room, "but could you possibly go by the McCandless house and tell Irene what has happened? I've got another possible cardiac to see."

"It's not an imposition; it's my duty," Mike said soberly. "You see if I had called the police as soon as I got back to the motel that night, the party might not have gone far enough to put that boy's life in danger— or Ellen's."

The McCandless home was in the older section of the Cape outside Spaceport City itself, a cottage set in the midst of a grove of orange and mango trees. Irene McCandless, a tall, serene-looking woman, with intelligence and breeding written in her face, greeted him courteously. She stiffened a little when he told her of the damage to her son's liver but she didn't break down.

"Dr. Metzger thinks Jason is going to be all right," Mike assured her. "He's a fine young man and you can be proud of him."

"We are, Doctor."

"If there's anything I can do at any time—"

"We shall certainly call on you, Dr. Barnes, if there is."

Driving back to the Astronaut Inn, Mike found himself remembering a few phrases from a poem—he couldn't remember the source—that seemed to fit women like Jason's mother:

> "*A perfect woman, nobly planned;*
> *To warm, to comfort and command.*"

Jan Cooper was made of much the same sort of stuff, he suspected, which was one reason why he had been attracted to her so strongly. Yet he had realized almost from the first time he saw her that—like so many people in Spaceport City—she was deeply troubled.

Most disturbing of all was the fact that, even though he loved her deeply, he had not yet found a way to help her—probably, he suspected, because he was still at a loss to know where the real trouble lay.

CHAPTER XXIV

Irene McCandless' assurance that they wouldn't need Mike's help was ill founded; the telephone in his motel room rang not much more than an hour after he left the McCandless home.

"I'm calling on one of the house telephones here at the inn, Dr. Barnes," Irene said. "Could I talk to you privately for a moment or two?"

"Would you like to have coffee with me in the coffee shop? It's early and people will hardly be going in for dinner yet."

"That would be fine. I'll meet you there."

She was sitting in a booth when he came in.

"I came from the hospital; Jason told me all about Sunday night," she said after the waitress had brought coffee. "My son and I have always been able to communicate—as well as parents can ever communicate with their children nowadays. With his father it's different."

"Dr. McCandless belongs to a special personality type—"

"My husband is a genius, Doctor. Geniuses are hard to live with, especially for the young."

"I must say you seem to take a very tolerant view of things."

"When a man passes fifty, and feels his sexual powers waning, Dr. Barnes, he often experiences something of a panic lest they leave him altogether. With women, the same decrease is a protective mechanism to save them the danger of childbearing at an age when it could put a considerable strain on their bodies. If women have had a good life and been loved, they mellow into old age, but unfortunately many men fall into it rather suddenly, if you will forgive me for being symbolic."

"You're giving me a far more concentrated lesson in psychology and hormonology—if it can be called that—than I ever had in medical school."

"Abram had to come to admit, shall we say, an inevitable weakness, plus adjusting to changes in his professional status. It has been a difficult time but I think we're safely through that valley, Doctor. It's Jason I'm concerned about now."

"Both Dr. Metzger and I think he will be all right, though his liver will certainly be scarred and he'll have to be careful."

"We trust your medical judgment, but Jason still feels he must tell others what happened to him before they are worse scarred than he."

"Do you agree?"

"Our son was a leader in high school, Dr. Barnes, a top scholar, a letter man in three sports, voted most popular and most likely to succeed. He feels that a public revelation of what happened to him will help keep other young people from taking the same sort of chances he took. I agree."

"People looking for excuses to justify their own failings will undoubtedly try to make things unpleasant for him," Mike warned. "I know something of what that can be."

"We still think it should be done."

"What do you want me to do?"

"Miss Lang wrote the article about you when you first came here. Could you arrange for her to talk to Jason?"

"I'm willing to try."

"Jason would like to get it over with as soon as possible. Dr. Metzger has not restricted his visitors."

"I'll call Yvonne Lang right away," Mike promised. "And may I tell you how much I admire you and your son for your courage."

Irene McCandless stood up and picked up her handbag. "We come from a rather hardy New England strain, Dr. Barnes. My mother carried a banner in the suffrage parades and I campaigned for Roosevelt at Wellesley. It runs in our blood."

ii.

Mike reached Yvonne Lang by telephone in the city room of the Spaceport *Call.*

"I was beginning to think you'd forgotten where I live," she said. "You don't have to be loaded to pay me a visit, you know."

"I'll remedy that oversight as soon as I get a chance to light," he told her.

"You *have* been busy. By the way, my fat boss in Washington thinks you're quite a guy."

"This is something he can use, too."

"My pencil is sharp, go ahead."

"Do you know Jason McCandless?"

"Of course. He's one of the finest young men this area has ever produced."

"Metzger has just admitted him to the hospital—with jaundice."

"Worse luck. A friend of mine had it—"

"This came from glue—Jason was with the group I told you about on the beach that Sunday night. He wants to tell the whole story so other kids will realize how dangerous it is."

There was a brief pause, then Yvonne asked, "Jason wasn't alone, was he?"

"He and Ellen Taggar were together—with a crowd of kids. In fact, he drove her home."

"You didn't persuade him to do this, did you, Mike?"

"On the contrary. I argued against it but both he and his mother insisted that I call you."

"What about Dr. McCandless?"

"I gather from what she said that they felt he would approve and they may even have talked to him about it. Can you go over to the hospital and see Jason?"

"I don't think so, Mike."

"Why not?"

"Maybe Art had better tell you. After all he's my immediate boss."

"Can you put him on?"

"I'll get the operator to transfer the call."

The transfer was made after some minutes of delay. Art McCord's first words told Mike that Yvonne had managed to warn the editor during the period while the connection was being switched.

"What the hell are you up to now, Mike?" the newspaperman demanded.

"I told Yvonne I had no part in this, Art. Mrs. McCandless asked me to call her, so she could talk to Jason. He wants other kids to know what happened to him could easily happen to them."

"A story like that would blow this town wide open."

"Did it ever occur to you that maybe it needs to be blown open?"

"A lot of people would be hurt."

"Maybe they're going to be hurt worse, if things go on like they are. Spaceport City gives every evidence of being a fool's paradise, but you can't live in a fool's paradise forever."

"Be reasonable, Mike." Art was pleading now. "Everybody knows Jason McCandless and Ellen Taggar were practically going steady and Yvonne says they were shown together on a TV news program the night she died."

"I know; that's how Jan identified the Maserati we saw parked on the shoulder back of the dunes that night. I don't think Jason has in mind mentioning Ellen, though."

"He doesn't have to. Anybody who can add two and two will know what happened."

"You got any children, Art?"

"Thank God mine are married and have children of their own."

"That's the argument Chief Branigan gave when I told him about the glue party, but it's a damn poor reason for not trying to save some younger ones. Jason McCandless thinks they'll listen to what he says, when they wouldn't pay any attention to what an adult told them."

"We can't do it, Mike. Paul Taggar practically owns this newspaper—"

"From what Jason tells me he drove Ellen to suicide, too, so maybe it would be a good thing for him to know that."

"I'm certainly not going to be the one to tell him—and neither is this newspaper. Plead with Mrs. McCandless to talk Jason out of this, Mike—for his own good."

"I already tried but got nowhere, Art. And I don't think I'll get anywhere the second time either. Good-by."

Irene McCandless didn't argue when Mike called to tell her of his talk with Yvonne Lang and Art McCord. "Thank you for trying, Doctor," she said.

"What are you going to do?"

"I don't know yet. I'm going back to the hospital and we'll talk it over. Good-by."

iii.

The ringing of the telephone in his motel room woke Mike Barnes Sunday morning. When he rolled over and reached for the phone, he saw by the bedside clock that it wasn't nine o'clock yet.

"Hello," he said sleepily.

"Thanks for the double cross, chum." It was Yvonne Lang. "With you for a friend, who needs enemies?"

"What are you talking about?"

"The Orlando Sentinel—and Jake Arrens. He woke me at eight o'clock to give me hell for not tipping him off on the Jason McCandless story."

"Where did he get it?"

"Off the AP ticker."

"You mean there's a story about Jason in the Sentinel?"

"Is there a story! It names names, even to the stationery store where the kids buy the glue—owned by one of Spaceport's leading citizens."

"I don't know anything about it, Yvonne. After Art refused to publish Jason's story, I called Irene McCandless and told her of his decision. But she didn't say they were going to carry it any farther."

"Then you really didn't have anything to do with giving the story to the *Sentinel?*"

"I just told you I didn't."

"Wait a minute till I look at it again; I was so mad when Jake called and chewed me out, I didn't even read it closely." She came back on the line a moment later. "This story is under the byline of their best feature writer, Val Cindor. Jason is on the staff of the college newspaper over there; he must have had his mother call Val."

"Tell Art that, will you? I'm going to get some breakfast and read the story. Will it help any if I call Jake in Washington and tell him you're innocent?"

"Probably not," said Yvonne. "I'm supposed to be a newspaperwoman, but here I let the biggest story of the year go by because the owner of the paper would be mad as hell if we printed it. Now he'll probably give us hell because it got to somebody else. If you meet Paul Taggar in the next few days—dodge. He's got a foul temper and Chief Branigan is bound to have told him about your seeing the glue party, so he'll jump to the conclusion that you spilled this story to Orlando. Sorry I woke you up with bad news."

Outside the motel restaurant, Mike slid a coin into the slot of a vending rack and took out a bulky copy of the Sunday Orlando *Sentinel.* He didn't have any trouble finding the story; a red line of type across the front page told where it would be—on the front page of the second section.

It was an expert job, even an eloquent one, with Jason's concern and guilt coming through in every line, plus a picture of him in the hospital bed with intravenous tubes attached, taken, Mike surmised, with a Minox and rice grain flash bulb. The reporter had even gone into the stationery store and purchased a half dozen tubes of plastic cement, along with a package of paper bags—also photographed—with no questions asked.

Altogether it was about as damning an indictment as could have been made of the callousness of merchants in selling the glue. The end of the article also hinted that other revelations might come later and Mike didn't doubt that Jason McCandless knew enough about the extracurricular activities of Spaceport City's high school and college population to make a startling news exposé.

After breakfast, he drove to the hospital and went up to Jason's room but, to his surprise, found one of Chief Branigan's men sitting in a chair outside the door. When he started to go into the room, the policeman rose to bar his way.

"Nobody can see the prisoner," he said woodenly.

"Prisoner?"

"Jason McCandless was placed under arrest this morning."

"On what charge?"

"Inducing minors to use narcotic drugs. He'll be moved to the city jail as soon as the city physician certifies that he's well enough."

"Who ordered his arrest?"

"A warrant was issued this morning by the district justice of the peace." The policeman obviously wasn't too happy with his job.

"Do you know on whose complaint?"

"The chief asked for it."

"Thanks, Officer. Can you tell me where I'll find Chief Branigan?"

"Sundays, he usually goes fishing. Got a dock back of his house."

Mike looked up the address in the telephone book and drove through the less expensive section of Spaceport City to a cottage on one of the canals that served to connect the area with the Inland Waterway and also furnished drainage for much of the low-lying section of sand and palmetto scrub which had been turned into the location of the Pegasus project.

He found Chief Branigan in dungarees and a T-shirt, fishing off the dock. Several sheepshead and croakers on a string hanging down into the water attested to his skill.

"Morning, Chief," said Mike. "I haven't caught a sheepshead in twenty years. Do you still have to jerk just before they bite?"

"That's how it's done, Doctor. Too bad we can't catch people that way."

Mike sat on the sawed off top of a piling that served to moor a small outboard runabout beside the dock. "I went by to see Jason McCandless just now but was told he's under arrest."

"Yuh."

"On your order, the guard said."

"On a warrant issued by a justice of the peace, Doctor. It's all legal."

"I'm sure it is; Paul Taggar is very thorough."

The chief pulled up his line, saw that the bait had been eaten off the hook, rebaited it, and threw it back—without answering.

"How long do you figure to keep up this farce, Chief? Long enough to scare the boy into not telling any more about what goes on here in Spaceport City?"

"He admitted breaking the law, Doctor; you can look it up in the statute books. Furnishing a narcotic drug to minors is a felony."

"Since when has glue been a narcotic drug, Chief?"

"I ain't no lawyer, Doctor."

"The active agent that turns on kids who sniff glue is toluene. I looked it up right after a little incident I mentioned to you not long ago and the dictionary says toluene is a liquid hydrocarbon derived from coal tar and used commercially as a solvent. I don't think the city attorney could make a very good case for its being a narcotic and even if he did, you'd have to arrest the owner of that stationery store mentioned in the article in the Orlando *Sentinel*."

"You threatening me, Doctor?"

"Not at all, Chief; in fact, I think you're a pretty decent guy who's working for some unprincipled people. But I'd still hate to see Jake Arrens start working you over for the rest of the country to see in that 'Capers at the Cape' column of his."

"You a good friend of Arrens?"

"You might say that. He's very much interested in what's going on down here these days and I'm sure he'd like to know about a girl who called the 'Hot Line' one night, when she couldn't find either of her parents to talk to, and wound up on the shore of Sebastian Inlet the next morning, dead. If I were you, Chief, I'd pass that information on to whoever you report to."

The burly officer looked up from the bobbing float of his fishing line. "Did it ever occur to you that you're looking for a lot of trouble, Doctor?"

"Not when I've got the strong arm of the law to protect me, Chief. You swore to uphold it when you took your job—or had you forgotten?"

iv.

When Mike went back to the hospital that afternoon, he wasn't surprised to see that the guard was no longer outside Jason McCandless' door. The boy's jaundice was as deep as ever, however, and a glance at the laboratory report on the chart confirmed the assumption that he had not yet suffered the full aftereffects of the highly volatile toluene he'd inhaled on the night of the beach party.

The ultimate result, and Jason's fate, Mike knew, would depend upon how many of the delicate and extremely vital liver cells had been damaged or killed when they tried to perform their very important function of neutralizing poisons entering the body from any source. Fortunately for Jason, the condition had been recognized and he was receiving intensive treatment, massive doses of glucose to protect the liver, along with vitamins. But even then, a long period of recovery would be necessary, while new cells were regenerating to replace the old. And during that period Jason would be extremely vulnerable to any of the wide spectrum of noxious agents that were always being taken into the body in a day when the fruits and vegetables one ate had been sprayed several times with poisons before being harvested and the air was tainted with hundreds of dangerous pollutants.

"How's it going?" Mike asked.

"Not so hot," said the youth. "I guess I was worse off than I realized. Did you see the article in the *Sentinel?*"

"At breakfast this morning. It's a fine job and ought to help a lot."

"Val Cindor teaches classes in journalism and advises us with the college paper. When Mother told me you'd tried to get Miss Lang to do the story and she wouldn't—"

"That wasn't her decision, Jason. She's a first-rate newspaperwoman."

"I know Mr. Taggar nixed the story, but he didn't have to worry, I didn't mention Ellen's name in it. Even Val doesn't know there was a connection."

Mike could see no point in reminding Jason that practically the whole of Spaceport City knew he and Ellen Taggar had been going steady and had, no doubt, put two and two together immediately. The boy had troubles enough already—with his body and his conscience.

In the hospital parking lot, Mike caught up with Yvonne Lang, who was leaving, too.

"My how you do get about, Doctor," she said. "What mischief are you up to now?"

"I'm innocent of anything except the desire to buy you a beer."

"I take it that Jerry McGrath's in town."

"For the launch. He's the command pilot, you know."

"And a nice guy," said Yvonne Lang. "Well since you're fair prey this afternoon, just follow me to the bar of the Spaceport Hilton."

She drove skillfully, as she did everything else, and he parked his car beside her Maverick in the parking lot before the towering ocean front hotel. The tavern was about half filled, as Yvonne led the way to the curving bar and two seats toward the end.

"I like to be able to see who's with who," she explained. "Get some of my best stories that way. By the way, Jake said to tell you he'll be down for the launch. Hasn't missed one since they built the first pad down here."

"Jake's quite a character."

"Speaking of characters I hear that another one, whose name I could mention if pressed, had a little talk with Chief Branigan this morning and not long afterward the guards were taken off Jason McCandless. Any connection between the two events."

"Nothing except cause and effect."

"What gives?"

"The Spaceport *Call* wouldn't publish it if I told you."

"Touché. But then I've got better sense than to go twisting the lion's tail, no matter how much I'd like to hear him roar. The question is, do you?"

"Probably not. I don't like to see a kid like Jason McCandless pushed around."

"Could they have made the narcotic charge stick?"

"Probably not, once the case got beyond a fixed court. But by that time Jason's record would have been so tarnished he'd have had trouble getting back into college, especially in a state where Paul Taggar is one of the biggest employers and Hal is running for governor."

"It's a real can of worms, all right. Did you know Spaceport City almost got named an all-American city last year?"

"No."

"We would have made it, too, if a jealous Orlando paper hadn't come out with some statistics about divorce, juvenile delinquency, alcoholism, and drug addiction. The joke is that those things really make us an all-American city but nobody around here has the guts to admit it." She put down her glass. "I've got to run, Mike. Got a date with the dogs over in Orlando."

"I didn't know they raced on Sunday night."

"They don't, which makes it the best night of the week to study them and do the handicapping. That's my friend's job."

"Give me some good tips and I'll go to the races myself, once we get this bird to fly."

"Lew—my friend—says there's only one sure sign of a winner. Always pick the dog that lifts his leg on the way to the starting boxes—he'll be running light. Thanks for the drink, chum."

Mike paid for the drinks, got his car, and drove slowly to the Astronaut Inn. He didn't relish the idea of another night of Sunday night television, which he was beginning to think the poorest of the week, but there didn't seem to be anything else to do.

It was still quite light and he stood by the pool for a while, watching the young people splash and romp there. When he opened the door to his motel room, he saw two messages on the floor inside the sill. One headed "FROM THE DESK OF HAL BRENNAN" was on a familiar memorandum slip such as Hal used to send messages inside the administrative organization of Pegasus. The message itself was typed but initialed at the bottom.

Mike,
    The mechanics have been doing some repairs on the gondola of the centrifuge-simulator and I want to schedule some final tests

with it in the morning. If you have time Sunday evening, would you check it out and make sure it's O.K.? I've been caught by some politicians, or I'd do it myself.

Thanks,
Hal.

The other message was to call Colonel Andy Zapf. Mike rang the number of the veteran astronaut's beach front cottage and Helen answered.

"Andy's gone out to get some beer," she said. "We were hoping you could come over for a swim and some barbecued ribs."

"Hal wants me to check out the centrifuge-simulator so it will be ready for some tests in the morning," Mike told her. "I'm going over there now, but it shouldn't take very long."

"Come by when you've finished; we won't be eating until it gets dark. Andy's got one of those new lamps that electrocutes bugs and we can sit around and give vent to our aggressive impulses by watching it fry mosquitoes. We'll save you some ribs and a couple of cans of beer."

"I can hardly wait. Can I bring Jan, if she's free?"

"Of course—and Mike—"

"Yes."

"Andy's worried about the shot. He doesn't say anything about it to me but I can tell."

"I'm a bit worried myself, though I can't tell exactly why either."

"If you prod Andy a little, he might talk to you and maybe together you can come up with something concrete."

On the chance that Jan might not be with Jerry McGrath, Mike dialed her number and, to his delight, she answered.

"Are you alone?" he asked.

"Yes. Jerry left a while ago; we—had an argument."

"The Zapfs have invited us over later for beer and barbecued ribs. Can you go?"

"That would be nice. When?"

"Hal sent a memo to the motel asking me to check the gondola of the centrifuge-simulator for some tests he's ordered tomorrow. It shouldn't take more than an hour. I'll pick you up at home when I finish."

"I'll be ready," she promised.

v.

Only on Sundays were visitors allowed to drive private cars through the government reservation at Cape Kennedy and inspect the launch areas directly, except where prevented by road barriers guarding work in progress—such as the upcoming Pegasus launch. The gates were still open to visitors when Mike drove in but only a few visiting cars were inside the reservation.

The road to the new centrifuge-simulator, built since FSA had taken over America's space activities to decentralize some of the functions formerly belonging to the Manned Spacecraft Center at Houston, crossed the drainage canal that cut across the Pegasus area, dividing it almost in half. A hundred feet or so down the canal, the elongated object lying exposed on a sand slide from the palmetto-bordered artificial dune created beside the waterway, where sand and shell had been excavated in its construction, could be either the trunk of a cabbage palm, its top cut off by the last hurricane, or an alligator sleeping in the warm September sun.

The canal itself cut straight across the wide expanse of the wildlife sanctuary that included much of the Cape, what had not been cut off already through the influence of Israel Pond and his cronies in Congress and practically given to Paul Taggar as the site for Spaceport City. A mile or so to the west, Mike knew from studying the chart of the area, the canal drained into one of the tributaries of Indian River.

He had been so busy with other activities during the short period since he had returned to the Cape that he had found no opportunity to give the new centrifuge laboratory more than a cursory inspection. Dr. Ivan Saltman had taken him on a quick tour of the medical facilities, when he'd taken up his duties as a consultant, and he had watched the test of the space suit in an adjoining room to that housing the massive centrifuge. But even that brief inspection had been enough for him to see that the new Cape installation was almost a duplicate of the first such major project at the U. S. Naval Air Development Center at Johnsville, Pennsylvania, just outside Philadelphia, where much of Mike's training for his own flight had been conducted years ago.

Almost circular in shape, the new laboratory was built of reinforced concrete. More than a hundred feet in diameter, it was the highest structure on the reservation, except for the giant Vehicle Assembly Building and the gantry cranes of the several launch pads in active use. Designed to house the fifty foot centrifuge arm and the one hundred and eighty ton, four thousand horsepower motor that drove it, the building also contained the controls and the computer connected to the powerful machine itself.

By means of the centrifuge, men and equipment could be whirled at various speeds, achieving an acceleration as high as forty times the force of gravity itself, far more than would occur with even the most powerful rocket the United States was liable to build in the forseeable future.

Inside the building, Mike switched on the lights and stood beneath the massive arm, a framework of steel some forty feet long and strongly trussed to withstand the tremendous forces of acceleration and deceleration of which the powerful motor was capable.

The gondola at the far end of the arm was a huge bulbous knob about ten feet in diameter. Entered by way of a port in its upper cap, with both caps removable from the main body of the gondola so the various couches, supports, and other material being tested could be placed inside the gondola, it was constructed to house the entire heart of a spacecraft under test, reproducing even the instrument panels and major controls.

From the ceiling of the building, a glass-fronted blister, or suspended cubicle, allowed constant inspection of the entire machine while in operation. Auxiliary technical controls which could stop and start the centrifuge were placed there for use in the event of an emergency, such as the blackout of a subject being tested for his ability to withstand the forces of acceleration upon his body reproduced by the centrifugal force of the massive rotating arm.

Both the technician watching from the blister during a regular test and those controlling the entire operation from the main control panel in a room outside the area, where the arm was rotating, were able to see the person inside the gondola at all times by means of a closed circuit television system. In actual use, however, control of the entire system was usually vested in a computer that stood beside the main control panel, allowing any previously programmed operation to be carried out automatically.

The major function of the centrifuge-simulator was to test the capability of pilots in training to respond to the problems created by certain situations. For this purpose, the controls of any type of spacecraft or airplane could be reproduced inside the gondola and, through a closed loop system, the pilot could actually operate it. Since the gondola was also suspended upon gimbals, the angles of the pilot's body to the accelerative force being applied to it could also be changed by the controllers outside the gondola, forcing him to respond to hypothetical problems that might arise in actual flight.

So faithfully did the gondola reproduce the actual spacecraft or aircraft cabin that it was also possible to vary the atmosphere within it. Thus, the pressure of air or oxygen being breathed by the pilot under test could be reduced to whatever level desired, usually the partial pressure of five pounds per square inch used in spacecraft cabins during actual flight.

All in all, the centrifuge-simulator was a marvelous instrument for accustoming astronauts and pilots of high speed aircraft, like the faster-than-sound jets used in modern day warfare, to the forces generated by acceleration, as well as by the sharp turns which often made the difference between life and death to a pilot during combat. Situations could also be created artificially which, in actual flying, would require a decision in fractions of a second under forces that could strongly affect the circulation of the brain, as well as that of the arms, hands, and eyes.

The entire building was empty this Sunday afternoon, however, and, climbing to the control blister, Mike examined the panel of dials and switches there. He saw nothing wrong—nor any sign of the work Hal Brennan had said in his memorandum had been recently done on the gondola—so he descended to a platform that extended from the wall of the circular building out to the gondola and the ports by which it could be entered and climbed into the gondola itself through the opening in the upper cap. The interior of a Hermes II spacecraft had been faithfully re-created inside it, he saw, simulating for the astronauts the surroundings they would be in during actual flight.

Intrigued by the changes—and improvements—over the relatively primitive cabin of Hermes I, in which he had flown, Mike began a careful inspection of the interior and the controls. He was examining the contoured couches upon which the two astronauts would lie, when the sound of metal creaking against metal caused him to look up.

To his amazement, he saw the port through which he had entered the gondola closing slowly—apparently of its own accord.

CHAPTER XXV

Startled by the uncanny, even chilling, movement of the hatch, Mike failed to react for an instant. The hatch was half closed when he stepped on one of the astronaut's couches and reached up to catch the edge, thinking it must have been jarred loose by his passage through the port. But as his hand touched the inside of the metal disk it was slammed shut from above and locked—obviously not of its own accord—cracking his knuckles and causing him to give a yelp of pain.

His cry bounced back from the walls of the gondola and, suddenly apprehensive now, he pounded his fist against the closed hatch. Unable to budge it, however, he dropped to one of the contoured couches, where the subjects lay during simulation of the blast-off G-forces, and seized the oxygen mask hanging from a hook beside the couch. Pressing the switch on the microphone, he shouted again and again into it, but could not tell whether his voice was being heard outside.

Convinced now that something other than a chance vibration from his presence inside the gondola had caused the hatch to close, he forced himself to be calm while he tried to puzzle out what might have happened, but found no answer—until a sudden movement of the gondola, as the centrifuge started rotating, slammed him against the metal wall, half stunning him. And in an instant of spine-chilling clarity, he knew now that the odd memorandum he had received almost an hour before could mean only one thing—Hal Brennan had lured him into the centrifuge gondola to kill him by subjecting him to the enormous pressures of acceleration developed by the machine if allowed to run unchecked.

The plan was diabolically simple; in fact, all that had been necessary was to program in advance the computer controlling the automatic operation of the centrifuge so the giant arm would start rotating soon after the port in the gondola cap was closed, locking Mike inside. What was more, Hal had even been able to provide time to leave the building for, once programmed, the rest of the sequence was automatic and the computer would cut itself off later, stopping the gondola.

By the time the centrifuge stopped rotating, however, Mike would long since have been killed by the sheer force of the column of blood inside his arteries and veins and the weight of the organs within his body, as they responded to the inexorable accelerative power generated by the swinging arm.

Even as he sought desperately for a way out of this fatal dilemma, Mike couldn't help appreciating the fiendish ingenuity of what was almost certainly the most novel way ever devised to kill a man. For, once the machine had completed its programmed run and come to a halt, no one could tell from the machine itself that it had been run at all, since the memory pattern implanted into the micro-circuits of the control computer for the run would erase itself.

The relatively slow gain in speed of the gondola told Mike his enemy had not set the computer to achieve the maximum G-force in the shortest period of time—forty times the force of gravity in seven seconds would have been too merciful a death for anyone who hated him enough to want to kill him. But the pressure upon his body did tell him that the G-force of acceleration was increasing steadily, so he knew any chance he might have of remaining alive for even a part of the programmed run of the centrifuge depended upon his protecting himself quickly in the only way open to him, by assuming the position in which his body could withstand the greatest force upon it for the longest period of time.

From his own training and the supervision of thousands of tests on the smaller centrifuge at Anderson, Mike knew that the so-called "eyeballs in" position, with the force of acceleration directed from back to front perpendicular to the spine, was his only hope. A quick glance around the interior of the gondola told him the couches were already oriented for this position—no doubt because the astronauts who would fly the Pegasus on Thursday were being accustomed to the initial forces of the blast-off—so he moved into place and adjusted his body to the couch nearest to him.

The pressure inside his chest was already making breathing difficult and a steadily increasing pain in his abdomen told him the vital organs of his torso, too, were being influenced by the increase in force generated by the rising speed of the centrifuge arm and the gondola at its farther end. Once, while positioning himself upon the couch, he moved his head too quickly and a wave of blackness warned him that any sudden motion could bring on unconsciousness, removing all chance of his taking even the few precautions available to him in the brief period before the steeply rising pressure gradient passed the limits of tolerance for his brain as its blood supply was sharply curtailed, and he lost consciousness entirely.

During normal operation, the closed loop system of controls between the person being tested inside the gondola and the computer controlling the centrifuge-simulator allowed changes in the position of the gondola itself through moving it upon the gimbals by which it was suspended. Remembering this, Mike reached for the control stick at his side, so placed because earlier experiments had demonstrated that limitation of arm and leg action during high-G acceleration made the handling of controls extremely difficult in the normal "center stick" position.

His arms and hands felt like lead, however, and all his strength and concentration were required even to reach the controls before the force necessary for movement exceeded his strength. Even after he had theoretically switched off the current to the giant motor driving the centrifuge arm, however, the speed of the gondola failed to slow, telling him the closed loop between him and the computer had been broken, removing any control he might exert over the whirling centrifuge arm by means of the instruments inside the gondola itself.

Refusing to yield to panic, even though he was at the mercy of the computer whose mind, however humanlike, was still inhuman, Mike forced his brain to review what was happening inside him, hoping for a possible clue that might give him the strength he needed to survive the swiftly increasing acceleration and the effect upon so many vulnerable systems of his body.

The haziness of vision that made it difficult already for him to see clearly, except at the central point of whatever he looked at, was produced by the forcing of blood downward into his chest from the brain and the consequent sharp limitation of the arterial supply to the light-sensitive retinas of his eyes. The sluggishness of his arms and legs came from the same cause, plus their additional weight because of the centrifugal force exerted by the whirling arm.

At the same time, the massive pooling of blood into the heart and vessels of the chest and abdomen, as it was driven out of the blood vessels of the head and the extremities, created a steadily increasing back pressure inside his heart, obstructing the return flow through the veins and causing an increasing degree of congestion proportional to the distance from the center of the trunk. Breathing, too, was difficult and the hurried pounding of the pulse in his ears told him his heart was seeking to cope with the difficulties under which it was being forced to operate in the only way available to it, by increasing the rate of its beat.

Although the closed loop of communication between the occupant of the gondola and the computer controlling it had been left open by whoever had programmed the operation for murder, the bank of dials inside the gondola indicating the speed of the whirling arm and the G-pressure being generated by it was still illuminated. Watching both indicators rise inexorably, while his vision slowly approached near blindness, Mike felt the old terror grip him. This time it was no nightmare, however, and seizing the microphone he had dropped on the couch on which he lay, he tried to shout for help in those last moments, but only managed to croak hoarsely until, tired out by the efforts of merely trying to speak, he slumped down in the seat.

Mercifully, the sudden change in position added to the forces already being exerted upon his body was enough to bring on complete unconsciousness and he knew no more.

ii.

Mike awakened to see Andy Zapf looking down at him anxiously. At first he thought he must be having a hallucination and that he was still in the gondola of the centrifuge. Hallucinations among jet pilots under the increased G-force of acceleration were frequent, and had even caused fatal accidents. Besides, he had been talking to Helen Zapf just before he left the motel to test the centrifuge-simulator and had expected to see Andy later, so such an aberration was not without logic. When Andy spoke, however, Mike realized that he was, miraculously, still alive and that the antiseptically white walls were those of a hospital room.

"Of all the damn fool stunts," the veteran astronaut exclaimed. "To program a centrifuge run and then shut yourself up in the gondola with nobody at the controls."

Mike took a deep breath and, feeling none of the heaviness and pain he'd experienced while breathing during those last moments before he blacked out, was reasonably sure he had not been seriously harmed by the experience.

"Was the run completed?" he asked.

"Completed?" Andy Zapf exploded. "If I hadn't cut the power you'd be in the morgue instead of alive and kicking."

"How did you get there?"

"Helen told me you said on the telephone you were going to check out the centrifuge because of some tests on the astronauts scheduled for tomorrow. I knew no more tests were planned, so I came over to the centrifuge, and there it was, running like mad with you slumped down unconscious inside the gondola."

"How did you know that?"

"The closed circuit TV was working beautifully. When I threw the main switch and cut the power, you were barely breathing, so I dragged you out of the gondola, and put in an emergency call for medical help to the Bioastronautic Facility. Fortunately, Dr. Saltman was on call."

"What time is it?" Mike asked.

"Around eight o'clock. You were out about an hour."

"I don't remember what time the centrifuge started."

"It started when you set it to start!" Andy Zapf was still angry. "Don't you remember?"

Mike shook his head and felt a wave of nausea sweep over him at the motion, saving him from having to answer his friend's question. Until he could look into the affair and confront Hal Brennan with the truth, it was simpler to let Andy Zapf go on believing he had programmed the centrifuge run himself.

"I guess I owe my life to you, Andy."

"You won't have it much longer if you keep on doing stunts like that."

"Never again, I promise." Mike managed to smile. "How were the beer and ribs?"

"I missed them, too."

"Better get home then. I'll be all right now."

"Saltman isn't too sure. He's going to keep you in overnight."

"I won't argue with that decision. Do me a favor, please, and don't say anything about this."

The astronaut gave him a probing look. "Why?"

"Would you want everybody to know you'd made a fool of yourself?"

"It will get out—especially with you involved. But I won't be the one who leaks it."

"Thanks. Tell Helen I'm sorry I missed the ribs."

"We'll have them next Thursday night to celebrate the shot—providing you don't knock yourself off before then."

As Andy was leaving, Mike remembered that he had failed to pick up Jan and take her to the Zapfs.

"Call Jan Cooper and explain what happened, Andy," he said. "She'll be wondering why I didn't go by to get her."

"Sure. I'll invite her to help us celebrate the shot Thursday night."

After Andy Zapf left, Dr. Saltman examined Mike thoroughly, particularly his eye grounds. "I was afraid you might have had some internal hemorrhages, particularly in the retina," he said when he'd finished. "But everything seems to check out O.K."

"Can I get out tomorrow?"

"I'll check you over again before breakfast and see whether we need any additional fasting tests."

"Do you have any idea how much longer I could have lasted if Andy Zapf hadn't found me?"

"A few minutes at most; the computer was programmed to increase the G-force pretty rapidly. Who in hell gave you the idea you were superman anyway?"

"Guess I didn't know my own strength," said Mike. "Is there any way to keep this quiet?"

"You had a near fatal accident and you're in the hospital," the physician said severely. "We keep records, too, you know."

"Could you hold off the reports until tomorrow afternoon then? I have a good reason for the request, but I can't tell you yet."

The other doctor nodded. "When Andy Zapf told me what the computer was programmed for, I wondered how anybody could have been stupid enough to make that kind of mistake—most of all you. I'll keep your secret as long as I can, which means no later than tomorrow."

"By the way, what was it programmed for?"

"Forty Gs, full power, for fifteen minutes—sure death in any language."

iii.

About an hour after Andy Zapf left Mike was debating whether to ask the nurse for a sleeping pill, when there was a knock on the door. He called "Come in" and Jan entered. She came over to stand beside the bed and, when he reached for her hand, didn't draw it back.

"Andy Zapf called to tell me there'd been an accident with the centrifuge," she said.

"Whatever happened, it was worth all the trouble to know you were worried enough to come."

"You said 'whatever happened.' Then it really wasn't an accident?"

"Someone lured me into the centrifuge gondola on the pretext that it needed to be inspected for some tests tomorrow," he explained. "He had programmed it for a full run, so once I was inside and he'd closed the hatch, all he had to do was throw the switch activating the computer and leave."

"That means whoever tried to kill you was familiar with the controls of the centrifuge."

"No question about it. He even set the computer to start long enough after he shut me up in the gondola for him to get safely out of the building."

She took a deep breath. "Do you have any idea who it was?"

"It had to be Hal Brennan."

"How can you be so sure?"

"Just before I called you about going over to the Zapfs for supper, I had a memo from Hal, asking me to inspect the gondola."

"Are you sure it was from Hal?"

"His initials were on it; my brain took a beating in the short time the centrifuge was running, but I remember that much."

"You didn't see Hal?" The odd intensity was once again in her voice.

"No. I was pretty busy trying to get the hatch open and right afterward, the centrifuge started to move. I'm sure of one thing, though— Hal wanted me to live long enough to realize what was happening."

She shivered. "How do you know that?"

"The centrifuge is capable of reaching forty Gs in seven seconds. If he'd wanted to, he could have killed me from the acceleration in less than a minute."

"I don't see Hal leaving such a wide trail of evidence pointing to him."

"That troubled me for a while, but I believe I have the answer. Running at top speed, the centrifuge uses a maximum armature voltage of six hundred volts and can draw as high as twenty thousand amperes. The main power station is always notified before the centrifuge is to be used at full speed, so Hal probably didn't program the computer for the full G-force at once for fear that some engineer in the main power control station might notice the power draw down. Knowing the centrifuge wasn't scheduled to operate and thinking it had been accidentally started by a short circuit in the controls, he would have cut the power on the main lines coming into it to protect the instruments and the machine might have been stopped while I was still alive."

"It scares me just to hear you tell it."

"With the computer programmed for gradual increase, the power change would hardly have been noticed in the main station for a while—at least long enough to be sure I was dead. Then once the engineer shut off the power, part of the whole Pegasus project would have been shut down and Hal would have been notified first. He could easily have been there when they took what was left of me out of the gondola and that way he could have removed the memo from my jacket and with it, all evidence leading to him."

"You may be right." But he could see that she wasn't convinced.

"It's all pretty technical, I know," he said. "And I may not have done too good a job of explaining."

"I'd better go and let you get some sleep," she said. "When are you going to face Hal?"

"As soon as I can get out of here—probably tomorrow morning. I want to see his face when I put that memo on his desk and he realizes the jig is up."

"Please be careful, Mike." She leaned down quickly to kiss him. "Don't take anything for granted."

He was still puzzling out her last statement, when he dropped off to sleep from sheer exhaustion.

iv.

Mike was finishing breakfast in his room, after Dr. Saltman had checked him over and written an order for his discharge, when the nurse on duty brought him a message that Hal Brennan wanted to see him in the administration building immediately.

"Colonel Brennan himself called," she said. "He sounded mad."

"How did word of my being here get out so quickly?"

"The same way everything else does—the grapevine. A guard at the gate told me about it when I came to work this morning."

"I suppose it's already in Washington then. Well I'd better get over to the ad building."

"Good-by, Dr. Barnes," said the nurse, and added pointedly, "It's been nice knowing you."

"I'll take you right in, Dr. Barnes," Hal Brennan's secretary said when Mike came into the outer office. "The colonel's waiting for you."

The secretary closed the door behind Mike, leaving him facing the desk and the project director's anger. Hal didn't speak but handed Mike a sheet of paper marked C O P Y at the top and addressed to FSA Administrator General James Green in Washington. On it were typed the curt words:

> Transfer of Dr. Michael Barnes to another installation immediately is requested for the good of operations here. Subject is a menace not only to himself but to others.

"That's your copy," Hal Brennan said in a tone of controlled fury. "We're putting the original on the teletype to Washington right away." The message was initialed by Hal—as the one yesterday afternoon had been.

"I wouldn't do it if I were you," Mike said quietly.

"Why the hell not?"

"I received another message from you about six o'clock yesterday afternoon." From his jacket pocket Mike took the memo that had been shoved under the door of the motel room and placed it on Hal Brennan's desk blotter.

"Naturally I went immediately to inspect the gondola—as you re-quested," Mike added. "If Andy Zapf hadn't gotten suspicious because he knew no tests were scheduled for the simulator Monday and come to see what was going on, you wouldn't have had to ask Washington to get rid of me. I'd be dead, just the way you planned."

Mike had never expected to see Hal Brennan stunned by anything, but he was seeing it now. The normal ruddy color had drained out of the ex-astronaut's face, leaving it almost gray.

"Don't you think you'd better cancel that teletype before it's sent?" Mike asked, and Hal picked up the phone.

"Don't send the teletype about Dr. Barnes, Maggie." His voice was hoarse. "Destroy it." Then he put down the phone and swung back to face Mike. "Maybe you'd better tell me about this."

"Why should I—when it was your idea?"

"You've got the copy of the message I was going to send to Wash-ington this morning with my initials on it." Hal Brennan picked up the memorandum Mike had received at the motel and shoved it across the desk. "See how they compare with those on the memo I'm supposed to have sent you yesterday."

No expertise in handwriting was required to see that the scrawled initials were entirely different. Whoever had written the memo Mike had received, sending him to what was intended to be his death, it certainly hadn't been Hal Brennan.

"It looks like you're in the clear," Mike admitted. "But who could be that anxious to kill me?"

"That's what I want to find out. Let's start at the beginning."

"It had to be someone familiar with everything about the centri-fuge," Mike said, as he finished a quick description of what had hap-pened before he'd lost consciousness. "Whoever it was knew how to program the computer, too, so the centrifuge arm wouldn't start mov-ing until he was safely out of the building, leaving the computer to administer the *coup de grâce*."

"Death by computer—programmed in advance; it was a diabolically clever plan." Hal Brennan leaned back in his chair and rubbed his eyes, as if they were paining him. "What can I do to persuade you to leave here before you're killed, Mike?" he said at last.

"I'm going to stay and find out why someone has it in for me."

"Whoever thought of using the centrifuge is clever enough to think of something else that might work. If I were in your shoes, I would get out of here—fast."

"I don't give up that easy. You should know that."

"I've already admitted making some mistakes where you're concerned, Mike, and apologized for them. What do I have to do to convince you that I'm on your side?"

Looked at in retrospect, Mike had to admit, as Jan had said last night, that the whole attempt on his life was too directly pointed toward convicting Hal Brennan of murder to be convincing, unless there had really been two purposes behind it—one to destroy him, another to get rid of Hal at the same time by ensuring that he would be named the murderer.

"You can do *one* thing for me?" said Mike.

"What?"

"Remember the color print you sent me in Washington the night after I made you recommend me as consultant to General Green?"

"I remember being mad as hell because you put the screws on me—but nothing about any color print."

"Don't deny it or I might not believe your other claim of innocence."

"I don't know what you're talking about, Mike. What print was it?"

"Of Jan Cooper—taken in that infrared studio of yours."

Again Mike was startled to see Hal Brennan disconcerted—and obviously afraid, though of what, he had no inkling.

"That was a long time ago, Mike," he said. "I give you my word that Jan hasn't been in that studio for at least four years."

"All I want is the negative. You have a file of them, don't you?"

"I kept some—as a gag. I'll look if you wish, but I doubt that the negative is still there."

"Why?"

"Obviously somebody stole it and used it to try to scare you away from staying here at the Cape—most likely the same person who tried to kill you with the centrifuge."

"But who could that be?"

"If you want me to, I'll request that someone from the FBI be sent here to investigate. This happened on a federal reservation, so it's in their bailiwick."

"The first thing the FBI would do is to request FSA to transfer me from the Cape."

"That would be sensible, for your own protection."

"And the end of the investigation. No, I've got to stay here so whoever tried to kill me, will try again."

"Anyone smart enough to use the centrifuge-simulator as a murder weapon would know how to use all sorts of potentially lethal devices that exist around here. You might not be so lucky next time."

"I'll take my chances. What do you want me to do now?"

"Tom Craven says you and he have been working out a plan to utilize the fuel tanks from a second stage as auxiliary space for the next Pegasus. Why don't you stick to that?"

"I'd like that," said Mike. "And thanks for the advice."

"I may be a louse—in your eyes—but I'm not a killer, Mike. The real murderer is bound to know you'll try to run him down, so he almost has to strike again. Be careful, for God's sake—and mine. I don't want to be accused of trying to murder you another time."

v.

Sandra Craven was sunning beside the pool, lying face down on a couch with the straps of her bra untied, when the sound of the gate clicking caused her to turn and sit up, holding the bra in place with her right hand.

"Daniel," she said warmly, when she saw him standing there. "I didn't expect you. Let's go in—"

"Can I see your boat first?"

"Sure, it's tied right there at the dock. But it's only a little outboard Tom uses for fishing; we haven't bought a bigger one because he stays so busy with his work, we'd never have a chance to use it."

On the small dock, Daniel Sears looked down at the outboard runabout tied there. It was really only an aluminum fishing skiff, as she had said, with an outboard motor attached to the stern and a snap-on plastic cover protecting both the motor and the inside of the hull from rain, but it exactly fitted the use he had in mind for it.

"Why are you interested in our boat?" For the first time, Sandra noticed that he was carrying a rolled up cardboard tube under his arm, such as maps and charts were mailed in. "And what's that under your arm?"

"A chart. Could we take a ride?"

"If you want to. Why?"

"I'm thinking of getting a boat of my own and thought I'd look over some of the waterways." He reached down to unsnap the cover of the skiff and removed it, putting it on the dock.

"Maybe you'd better steer," he said as he stepped down into the boat and reached up to help her down from the landing. "I want to study the chart."

The motor was one of the new battery-started silent types; when Sandra pressed the starter button, it caught and purred softly. While she backed away from the dock and headed the bow down the canal that ran behind the houses on her street, Daniel Sears studied the charts he had taken from the cardboard tube and spread out on his knees.

"Which way?" Sandra asked a little crossly, when the canal they were following debouched into a somewhat larger waterway.

"Toward the government reservation."

"There's nothing in that direction, except the mouth of the drainage canal that cuts across the Pegasus section. And that's closed with a fence."

"I'd like to take a look at it anyway." Realizing that she was a little miffed at his not choosing to go into the house with her immediately, he reached back to place his hand on the inside of her thigh. "Please?"

"Careful." She was smiling now and the flush of beginning excitement stained her cheeks. "You'll make me run the boat into the bank."

She turned up the throttle and the skiff surged forward, the bow rising from the force of the motor. Sandra closed her thighs together on his hand, but so intent was he on his purpose at the moment that he didn't even notice.

At the outskirts of Spaceport City, the row of houses that backed up on the canal ended and a tall, chain mesh fence took its place, indicating that they were now opposite the section of the government reservation which had not been released for building houses. Perhaps a mile farther on, they reached the mouth of the drainage canal that had been cut across the area of salt marsh and palmetto-covered wasteland forming the special domain of Pegasus.

"This is as far as I need to go," said Daniel Sears.

Because of the high banks of sand and shell on either side of the canal, he was forced to stand up in the small boat and hold to the fence where it crossed the waterway leading straight into the heart of the Pegasus area and the launch pad built for the winged horse. From that vantage point, he was able to see the top of the giant rocket resting upon the carrier that had brought it from the Vehicular Assembly Building.

"What are you looking for?" Sandra asked.

"I wanted to see the rocket close up."

"You could take one of the tours."

"This is better—and besides, it's off limits to tourists."

"Tom could get you a pass."

"It's better this way." He didn't elaborate, for he was studying the fence.

Although no daily rise and fall of the tide occurred in this area, because no major outlet to the sea existed for almost fifty miles in either direction, a seasonal rise and fall did occur and he noted with satisfaction that the fence had been built to take that into consideration, just as he had been hoping. Perhaps two feet separated the level of water flowing out of the canal from the bottom of the chain mesh fence, a space quite high enough for them to ease the boat through into the canal, by holding to the fence itself. He didn't suggest that they do it now, however, afraid she might suspect his purpose and accidentally reveal it to her husband.

"Why are you so interested in this spot?" Sandra asked.

"Just curious."

"If you ask me this whole thing is curious," she said petulantly, thinking how lovely it would be back at the house with the air conditioner purring and them on the big bed with the satin sheet that always made her feel like a wanton.

"We can go back now," he told her. "I've seen all I need to see."

Sandra gunned the motor and headed the boat back up the canal. Being light, it was amazingly fast even with the low powered motor; they skimmed along the waterway, sending the V-wave of the wake washing up on the sides and disturbing the graceful white egrets stalking there in search of unwary fish. Only about ten minutes were required to reach Tom Craven's dock and tie up the boat.

"I'll put the top back on later," said Sandra. "Right now I'm dying for a drink; you'll have some lemonade won't you?"

"If you insist." Daniel Sears was not one to waste opportunity, even though he had come this morning for another purpose.

"Come on inside where it's cool then."

Driving away nearly an hour later, Daniel Sears thought with regret that it was too bad women couldn't enjoy what a man like him could bring them without getting possessive.

After Thursday, he'd definitely have to break off the affair before Eunice started getting suspicious again. But then, after Thursday he'd be famous and ready for a far wider world than Spaceport City, one in which conceivably he might not even need Eunice and the trust fund of blue chips set up for her by her father.

vi.

Mike had just gotten back to his office after the session with Hal Brennan, when the telephone rang. To his surprise, it was Jan.

"Have you seen Hal yet?" Even over the phone he could detect the same tension in her voice that had been there last night, when she had visited him at the Bioastronautics Facility.

"I just got back from his office. Hal didn't write that memo, Jan; the initials aren't his." He suddenly remembered her parting words last night. "But you were sure of that already, weren't you?"

"Mike, I've got to see you." The words tumbled out in such a rush that they were almost incoherent.

"Of course, darling. Where are you now?"

"At home. I didn't go to work this morning."

"Are you sick?"

"No. I just needed to do some thinking."

"I can come right away."

"I'll fix us some lunch."

"You don't need to—"

"It will give me something to do."

She was more composed when she opened the door to him. The air conditioner was running and the house was pleasantly cool. "Are you sure you're all right?" she asked.

"Ivan Saltman gave me the all-clear this morning, and now that I know you love me enough to be troubled about me, I don't have any more worries." He took her hands and drew her to him. But when he sought to kiss her lips, she moved her head and, seizing him tightly with her arms, clung to him with her cheek pressed against his. Even before he felt the warm dampness of her tears, he knew she was crying.

"What's the trouble, darling?" he asked.

She only shook her head, and clung to him even more tightly, however, so he held her gently until she stopped crying, then took her face between his hands and kissed the tears away from her eyes.

"When are you going to marry me?" he asked. "You must know by now that you can't put me off much longer."

"Let's go now, Mike!" Her eyes brightened suddenly and the color came back to her cheeks. "We can be married just across the Georgia line and keep on going—to California or wherever you want to be."

"Except Spaceport City?"

"I don't want to see this place again—ever. Let's go, Mike! I can be packed in half an hour."

He took her chin between his fingers and kissed her gently, tasting the salty tears still upon her lips. "It wouldn't work, Jan."

"But if you love me—"

"I've loved you ever since that night in the motel—no, it really began in that service station. But I can't marry you just to get away from here and whatever it is you're afraid of."

"It's you I'm afraid for!"

"Then why can't you tell me who you think is trying to kill me?"

"It's no use, Mike, no use at all." She turned away, and seeing the droop of defeat in her shoulders, he was tempted to take her in his arms again and tell her they would leave as she had wished. But the moment of capitulation had passed.

"If you would only—" he said but she cut him off.

"The day before Bob crashed that plane, I told him I was divorcing him—"

"But you said he was unfaithful."

"A woman can forgive unfaithfulness in a man she respects. Bob could have saved his life by ejecting when his plane flamed out, but he tried to earn my respect by staying with it and saving the lives of others. In Mountain City, you and I could be safe. But here—"

"Darling, if you would only tell me—"

"Please go, Mike. If you loved me as much as you say you do, you would understand."

"But it's because I do love you that I can't let you give me this way out," he protested. "I could have stayed eight years ago to face Israel Pond and all he could do to me, but I chose the easy way out and haven't been able to face myself in the mirror since without feeling ashamed. If I marry you now and leave before I find out what is really happening here, I'll be running away again. I love you too much to let you sacrifice yourself, because you think it would save me—and then realize you no longer respect me."

"Please go, Mike. We don't even seem to be speaking the same language any more."

" 'I love you' is the same in any language."

"Good-by, Mike."

"Are you going to stay in Spaceport City?"

"I can't leave now," she said. "Not when I have work to do."

He was back in his office when he remembered the note of resignation in her voice as she spoke those last words. And remembering them now, he was even more troubled than when he had left her.

CHAPTER XXVI

With barely three days remaining until launch time for the first Pegasus unit, the whole Cape area had begun to swarm with newsmen, the crews of technicians required to keep television watch on the giant rocket, dignitaries from Washington—and the simply curious. These last always flocked to such affairs, drawn unconsciously by the same urge that had sent Romans streaming into the gladiatorial games— the possibility of actually witnessing the taking of human lives by one of the most violent agents yet created by man, the explosive charges of a powerful rocket.

General Jim Green—with his retinue, Lars Todt and several other members of Congress—arrived Tuesday morning and immediately ordered a full dress pre-launch review for that afternoon. It was one minute after three when the general came into the conference room in the main administration building. All there rose at once, but he waved them to their seats.

"No formalities, please, gentlemen," he said. "Is everybody here?"

"Everybody, Jim," said Hal Brennan.

As project director, Hal was seated at Green's right, with Paul Taggar next to him, then the two pilots, Majors Jerry McGrath and Earl Boggs. Lars Todt was at the general's left, with Mike next to him, then Andy Zapf, Tom Craven, the station meteorologist, Dr. Saltman, head of the medical side of the unit, and a number of others concerned with the launch.

"What's the status of Pegasus, Hal?" the general asked.

"Everything is go for Thursday morning, sir."

"No last minute difficulties?"

"We always discover a few minor bugs during the countdown, but we'll lick them without having to stop the clock," Hal said confidently.

"How about the weather?" Green asked the meteorologist.

"Perfect, sir. A few high cumulus clouds. The TV pictures should be excellent."

"Good," said the FSA administrator. "Since Major McGrath and

Major Boggs won't be coming down for some time, we don't have to worry about conditions in the landing area right now. What about the likelihood of sunspot activity?"

"None of any importance is expected sir," said the meteorologist. "Our satellites are monitoring the Van Allen belt levels and also the occurrence of solar flares. With the window this one's going through, the danger of radiation should be minimal."

"Has that window been checked finally?" Green asked Hal.

"Dr. McCandless refigured everything just to make sure."

The administrator turned to Mike, and with him every eye in the room. "What do you say, Dr. Barnes?"

"I'm not happy about seeing a launch Thursday," said Mike. "I would advise postponement."

General Green frowned. "Everybody else seems to feel that the time is perfect, Doctor. What have you got against it?"

"All I have is what you could call an educated guess," Mike admitted, and a snort of indignation came from Paul Taggar.

"Dr. Barnes doesn't like to see anyone else make a successful flight in a Hermes craft, since he managed to sink the final one in the old series," said the aircraft manufacturer.

"No personal grievances from the past, please, gentlemen." The general's voice was stern. "I would like to hear your reasoning, Dr. Barnes."

"I'm afraid it's more of a hunch, General. An accumulation of many small events adding up to a conviction that this isn't the right time for a launch of anything so important as Pegasus."

"Can you be specific?"

"For one thing it has been pretty obvious since I came here that someone thinks I'm a menace to the project."

"A menace, Doctor? That's hard to believe."

"Not when at least one serious attempt has been made on my life," Mike said quietly.

"Did you know of this, Hal?" the administrator demanded.

"Someone lured Dr. Barnes into the gondola of the simulator last Sunday and started the centrifuge." Hal was sweating, although the room was air-conditioned. "If Colonel Zapf hadn't happened by—"

"I didn't just happen by," Andy Zapf interrupted. "When I learned that Dr. Barnes had gone to the centrifuge to check it out because of some alleged tests, I suspected something was wrong and went there myself."

"Just in time to save me from being subjected to forty Gs," Mike added, and a murmur of surprise ran around the table.

"We're investigating the occurrence but nothing has turned up yet."

Hal Brennan still looked uncomfortable. "Whoever was responsible forged a memo from me asking Mike to check out the gondola. While he was inside, the centrifuge started turning on a gradual full power program."

"Why would anyone want to kill you, Doctor?" General Green asked.

"I testified at the hearing before Congressman Pond's committee that I thought two valves had probably stuck on my spacecraft, letting the oxygen level build up to a dangerous degree, sir. Naturally, after that experience, I would be suspicious of any Taggar-built capsule."

"If Dr. Barnes is insinuating that I tried to kill him, that's hogwash," Paul Taggar snapped. "Frankly, he's too small for me to bother with."

"But you did have the two valves in question changed on this ship and the new ones doubly checked," Mike reminded him.

"Nothing was wrong with either the ones we took out or the new ones we put in," said Taggar.

"Then why put them in?" The general's voice was frosty.

"Because I anticipated that Dr. Barnes would try to damage any Taggar Aircraft project, if he got a chance. It's well known that he was sent here to spy on us."

"Perhaps because you needed spying on, Mr. Taggar," said Lars Todt.

"Nobody ever proved that the spacecraft Dr. Barnes let sink, because he got claustrophobia and blew the hatch after it landed safely, was defective." For a moment, Mike thought Taggar was going to attack Lars Todt, but the senator showed no sign of being afraid of the much larger man.

"Mr. Taggar neglects to mention that the reason we have no such proof is that the telemetry tapes which would have shown the pressure changes in the cabin of Dr. Barnes' ship were filched from the files of NASA," said Lars Todt. "Perhaps he would like to comment on that, since he and Congressman Pond are so close."

"I ordered an investigation as soon as I found that the tapes were missing," General Green said before Paul Taggar could speak. "We traced them to Congressman Pond's office and he is quite sure a clerk destroyed them without realizing what they were."

"Since Senator Todt admits that Dr. Barnes was sent here as a spy," said Paul Taggar, "I don't think we need to consider the doctor's opinion as far as Pegasus being ready for the shot."

"Does anyone else here share Dr. Barnes' feeling?" General Green asked.

"I do," said Andy Zapf. "If someone was so afraid Dr. Barnes would find a defect in the rocket that he tried to kill him, it stands to reason there must be a defect. I say postpone the shot until we can check it out and find it."

"I just finished telling you we *have* checked the rocket," said Paul Taggar. "Mr. Craven assures me that he finds nothing wrong."

"That is true," said Tom Craven.

"Our own technical people have the same opinion," Hal Brennan added. "If we doubted for a moment that Pegasus is ready, we would postpone the shot, of course."

"What about the pilots?" General Green asked.

"I'm ready," said Jerry McGrath confidently.

"So am I," said Major Boggs.

"Senator?" The FSA administrator looked at Lars Todt.

"This is your decision, General," said Lars Todt. "I have neither the technical knowledge nor the authority to advise you."

"The countdown will continue then," General Green said crisply. "No change will be made in launch time, unless something else develops. I believe that is all, gentlemen."

Lars Todt caught up with Mike as he was leaving the administration building for his car, which was parked at the curb some distance away.

"I suppose you think I let you down in there just now, Mike," said the senator.

"You certainly didn't give me much support."

"As I told you in Washington, this launch has considerable political importance—"

"A failure could be even more important in the other direction."

"If you could find even one flaw in the rocket, Mike, I'd be the first to insist that it be delayed."

"What worries me most is the evidence of strain in the people who work on the project—from Hal Brennan down," Mike admitted. "This community has so much tension bottled up inside it that it's ready to explode of its own accord."

"Why—after all the launches these people have handled?"

"For a lot of reasons, some of them not necessarily peculiar to Spaceport City. Mainly, I think Pegasus has generated a feeling of uncertainty because it doesn't have a definite goal."

"I'm not sure I understand."

"Obviously we need an orbiting laboratory to study the effects of prolonged life in space on the men who will be living there, but that's not a tangible goal, like putting men on the moon was, or defending the country against destruction by Russia."

"You and I know that what we need most right now is an orbiting arsenal of hydrogen warheads," Lars agreed. "But if we came right out and advocated that as the next goal in a crash phase of the space program, all the doves in the country would start screaming and we'd have a rebellion in Congress—to say nothing of the country."

"Then what we're really doing with Pegasus," said Mike, "is only creating a stop gap designed to give the Russians second thoughts about a first strike with SCRAG and their SS-9s, plus maybe those manned space stations they've been talking about?"

"That about sums it up."

"It isn't enough, Lars. We've got to have something in orbit with real teeth, capable of the only kind of force the Russians respect, complete destruction. If we don't let them know the real potentialities of Pegasus, they might consider it simply another purely scientific venture and jump the gun."

"Pegasus could be that."

"But only if that's its main purpose. Otherwise the technical people here have got sense enough to know that, if the Administration has a little setback somewhere and is forced to start retrenching, one of the first things to go will probably be any future development of Pegasus. And with it will go both their jobs and the safety of their families."

"Enough of us know the enormous potentialities of Pegasus to fight for the project, Mike."

"That's not much reassurance for people who are afraid of losing their jobs and homes. Just look at what happened here in Brevard County even before the moon landings. As soon as the development phase of Apollo ended, the bottom dropped out of both construction and real estate and a lot of skilled people began moving into more promising regions. It's hard for people to do good work when they're worried about whether they'll have a job three months or six months from now—or even be alive. That's why I say what really worries me most about this shot on Thursday is the human factor."

ii.

When Mike came out of the surf after his before-dinner swim, he found Jake Arrens sprawled in a beach chair under a palm tree. Beside him was a small ice cooler, with several cans of beer sticking out of the pile of crushed ice.

"Sit down and have a beer, Doc," said the columnist. "From what I hear, you need a friend."

"Word does get around." Mike dropped into a chair and opened a can of beer. "Who was your stooge at the briefing?"

"Privileged communication," said Arrens with a grin. "How's your romance going?"

"I seem to have struck out there, too. She's still seeing Jerry McGrath."

"If the launch Thursday is successful, McGrath will be traveling for a couple of months and you can make hay while he's in orbit. If it fails, he'll be gone permanently, so either way, you stand to win."

"That's a gruesome thought, but somehow she seems to think I'm a worse risk than he is."

"That could be—after last Sunday. From what I hear, if that centrifuge had gone a few minutes longer, they would have had to scrape you out of the gondola with a basting spoon."

"Since you know so much about it, why didn't you use it in your column?"

"I'm playing for the jackpot."

"Come again."

"Jim Green has clamped the lid tight on everything connected with that adventure of yours. If I publish the story of how somebody tried to kill you, I not only get in Dutch with FSA but I might even scare your enemy off. Leaving you as bait gives me a chance to get a real scoop, when the next attempt is made, by telling what went before."

"I only hope I'm here to read about it."

"You're news, Doc, whichever way things go. If you catch the guy, it will be the story of the year. If he gets you, the lid will be blown off and I can reveal the other attempts and maybe help the police catch him." Jake Arrens pulled the tab from another can of beer. "See what a friend I am?"

"I suppose you'll get more column inches out of it if he gets me first."

"Undoubtedly. But I like you, so I'm betting on you."

"That's comforting."

"I just hope the Russians don't get nervous, now that they've had a chance to see the size of that bird out there on the launcher, and decide to create a little diversion nearer to us—like maybe a revolution or two in South America. If a few more oil companies are expropriated down there, big business is going to start pushing the Administration to act. I'd hate to see your son, or mine, risking his life standing guard over oil wells on foreign soil, just so some Texas millionaire can get another depletion allowance."

iii.

After opposing the launch at General Green's conference, Mike was hardly surprised to find himself half ostracized during the final hours of the countdown. Even Andy Zapf was busy, checking out details of launch procedure with the two astronauts who would be inside the cabin when Pegasus took flight at dawn on Thursday.

Wednesday afternoon, Mike left the government reservation with the flow of cars at quitting time for the day shift and drove to the hospital on the mainland where Abram and Jason McCandless were patients. The day's laboratory reports on the medical chart showed that Jason's jaundice had not deepened, an indication that the supportive measures for his damaged liver, which Dr. Metzger had taken as soon as he was admitted, appeared to have stopped any further destruction of liver cells.

When he came into Jason's room, he found Irene McCandless with her son; both greeted him warmly.

"I hope Dr. McCandless is doing as well as our young friend here is," said Mike.

"My husband is fine, Dr. Barnes. The dean of the university was here from Orlando this morning. They have great plans for the new expanded department."

"Then everything is working out well?"

"Except in one area. Val Cindor isn't going on with the series we had planned on the use of dope and alcohol among high school and college students in this area."

"I'm not surprised," said Mike. "Newspapers are pretty vulnerable to threats to their advertising revenue."

"It isn't the newspaper this time," said Jason. "Val's family has been threatened in anonymous telephone calls."

"Do you think there's any danger, Dr. Barnes?" Irene McCandless asked. "These calls are often made by cranks."

"I'm sure it's very real, Mrs. McCandless. My advice would be to go slow at the moment."

"But isn't there anything I can do to make young people—and parents too—realize what's going on?" Jason asked.

"I'm afraid people would rather shut their eyes to such things than become involved," said Mike. "It takes a major tragedy to bring the danger home. Do you think Ellen would want that, if she were alive?"

"I suppose not," Jason admitted. "She'd been protected all her life, and I guess she had never really had a chance to come into contact with reality. But then neither had I, or I would have known—"

"You had the courage to take the first step," said Mike.

"But only after I realized how near I had come to losing my own life for a cheap thrill. The worst part is knowing I didn't even have the courage to go for the Big High."

"Would that be marijuana—pot?"

"Pot's tame. The Big High is LSD—or heroin. It's sort of ironical, isn't it, that I darn near killed myself sniffing glue—a kid's trick?"

"A dangerous kid's trick," Mike corrected him. "More dangerous than LSD or even heroin, as far as your body is concerned."

"Why do you say that?" Irene McCandless asked.

"Narcotics can kill your mind but toluene strikes at the most vulnerable parts of the body, the organs mainly concerned with keeping men from being poisoned by their own wastes."

"That's all the more reason why Jason feels he must still make an effort to make the truth known, Doctor," said Irene McCandless. "Even though Mr. Cindor has refused to go any farther."

"What do you have in mind, Jason?" Mike asked.

"When I'm well enough to leave the hospital, I'm going to write the story of what happened to me."

"Naming names?"

"Of course. It's the only way to do what I want to do."

"Have you spoken to anyone else about this except me?" Mike asked quickly.

"No, but—"

"Don't—until you're safely away from Spaceport City. I don't know where I'll be, but if you write me at the Anderson Research Center in Mountain City, California, I'll get the letter. Senator Lars Todt is a good friend and I'm sure he'll help us at the right time, perhaps by arranging for you to testify before the Congressional committee."

"That's kind of you, Doctor," said Irene McCandless.

"But remember—no word of this until Dr. Metzger discharges Jason from the hospital and he's out of Spaceport City."

As he was waiting for an elevator to take him down to the hospital lobby, Mike heard his name called and turned to see Harry Metzger coming down the corridor. When the elevator came, he held the door, and the two entered it together.

"I just finished making before-dinner rounds," said Metzger. "What brings you here?"

"I came by to see Jason McCandless. He tells me the man who wrote the *Sentinel* feature isn't going on with the series they had discussed."

"It may be just as well," said the internist. "There are people in Spaceport City who would try to crucify Jason—and probably succeed—if they thought he was going to reveal the names of some of those concerned with that sort of traffic."

"It's been tried already," said Mike. "You heard about the arrest incident, didn't you?"

"The hospital called me when Branigan's men arrested Jason," said Metzger. "I refused to let them take him to the county jail and got on the phone to the city physician. When I told him I'd get a court order at a higher level than Spaceport City, if he tried to certify that Jason could be moved, he saw the light. How did you manage to get the charges against the boy quashed?"

"Branigan's no fool. I reminded him that he was going to have to bring the owner of the store where Val Cindor bought the glue into court."

"I'd think it would take more persuasion than that."

"Well, I did mention that I was a friend of Jake Arrens. By the way, how's the man I did the tracheostomy on the other day?"

"He's over the hump, too. The damn fool had given himself six injections of penicillin, five million units each, over the weekend, trying to make sure his Wasserman would be negative."

"Why?"

"It seems that his boy friend was picked up in Orlando for prostitution and the authorities there found an open lesion. Homos usually cooperate with the law whenever they can; judges don't like to have them in court and things usually go easier for them that way, so Childs' friend talked plenty, naming him a contact, along with several prominent citizens. A health department inspector had ordered Childs to have a blood test Monday so over the weekend he tried to make sure it would be negative by injecting the penicillin. It's an old trick."

"What about the other homo?"

"That's the touching part of the whole thing. Childs is a lot more worried that his partner may get out of jail and into trouble again before he's able to look after him, than he is about himself. It's a hell of a commentary on marriage in Spaceport City when a homo is more concerned about his partner than a lot of married couples are about each other."

iv.

As Mike was driving back from the hospital, he passed a popular tavern-restaurant not far from the causeway. Busy thinking about what Harry Metzger had told him, he wasn't paying much attention to anything except the road, until the shape of a car parked in the parking lot before the restaurant suddenly caught his eye. Bringing his own car almost to a halt, he turned in at the far side of the parking lot, parked and got out. Walking back to the car that had attracted his attention, he studied it for a moment, but there was no doubting the evidence of his eyes.

It was the Maserati he and Jan had seen parked on the shoulder of the road the night of the glue sniffing party on the beach.

Thinking that Sally Taggar might be inside the tavern and hoping she would be drunk enough to reveal something that would give him at least a temporary advantage over her husband, Mike opened the side door allowing people to enter the tavern section without passing through the main part of the restaurant. With the door only half open, he saw Paul Taggar sitting with a woman in the far corner of the tavern; nor did he need a second look to recognize her.

It was Jan.

The two were talking earnestly and didn't look up, so Mike backed out quickly, allowing the door to close before they saw him. But his heart was heavy as he walked back to his own car, for a whole pattern of seemingly unrelated events had suddenly begun to fall into place, like a jigsaw puzzle.

Back at the motel, he put in a call for Lars Todt at the Spaceport Hilton and, told that the senator was at dinner, asked the operator to have him paged in the restaurant.

"What the hell is this, Mike?" Lars' harsh voice sounded in his ear after a few moments.

"Are you going to be in the forward Pegasus launch control blockhouse Thursday morning, Lars?"

"Yes."

"I want to be there, too."

"I don't know, Mike. After Tuesday afternoon—"

"I still say that shot may fail, Lars—"

"Are you holding something out on me?"

"No, but there are too many loose ends about this project to suit me. If I'm in that blockhouse, I may be able to spot anything that starts to go wrong before it's too late and prevent a disaster."

"Well—"

"You can do it, Lars. General Green doesn't dare refuse you, with his appropriation request for the next step in Pegasus coming up in Congress."

"All right, Mike. I'm having dinner with him and some of the others now. Where are you?"

"At the Astronaut Inn."

"You'll be notified there."

"Thanks, Lars."

"If you cause any trouble in that blockhouse, Mike, anything that might queer the shot, I'll take it out of your hide myself."

"I'll let you use my knife," Mike promised. "See you early in the morning."

The call came from Dr. Ivan Saltman about an hour later. "Hal Brennan wants you to take my place in the blockhouse tomorrow morning, Mike," said the medical director. "I'm only there to administer first aid anyway, in case somebody can't stand the suspense."

"Thanks, Ivan."

"I should thank you," said the other doctor. "When something that big goes off, I'm just as happy being as far away from it as I can get."

CHAPTER XXVII

It was after four Thursday morning, when Sandra and Daniel Sears eased the fishing skiff beneath a bridge where a narrow road leading from the Taggar Aircraft assembly factory several miles away to the pad where Pegasus waited for today's launch crossed the drainage canal. Resentfully, Sandra watched Sears climb the sandbank wall of the canal that had hidden their presence from the workmen on the pad who were completing the final preparations for the morning launch.

Knowing they had no business this near anything with such a potential for destruction as the great rocket, Sandra was afraid. Besides, she was beginning to think Daniel Sears had been using her because she had a boat that would enable them to steal into the reservation undetected where the outer fence crossed the canal and reach this spot only a few hundred yards at most from the launch pad itself.

The rocket, poised for its journey and wreathed in the white vapors of escaping LOX like incense being burned upon an altar to the pagan god of metal and plastic, had no lure for her either. Not only had it taken her husband away from her most of the time with its siren call but now it had taken her lover, too, leaving her forlorn and cold in the night breeze from the nearby ocean.

Brooding over the injustice fate had dealt her, Sandra was startled by a stream of sand cascading down into the water at the end of the bridge. Daniel Sears followed it, panting as he crouched beneath the timbers; but when Sandra started to speak, he put his fingers, gritty with sand, across her mouth.

She was almost tempted to bite him until she heard the jeep approach. Moments later it roared across the short bridge just over their heads.

"Sorry," he whispered, taking his hand from her mouth. "I saw them coming and had to slide down so their lights wouldn't pick me up."

"Let's go home, Daniel," she wailed. "We can watch the launch on TV."

"You're doing the Lord's work, my dear. God has revealed to me in a dream that I must stop this rocket from being launched into His firmament."

"He didn't reveal it to me. You're just using me—"

"You are God's handmaiden, selected through me for His purpose."

"I'm cold—and scared," Sandra insisted. "Let's turn the boat around and leave while we can."

"I shall not turn back," Daniel Sears declaimed, as if he were standing in his pulpit. But down here, crouched over in the small boat under the bridge, with sand filtering down between the timbers upon them every time one of the vehicles leaving the rocket area passed, Sandra felt none of the elation that normally seized her in his presence.

"Help me turn the boat around, anyway," she said. "Then if somebody sees us, we can get away in a hurry."

"All right—if it will make you feel better."

The space beneath the supporting timbers of the narrow bridge was just wide enough for them to turn the boat around until the bow pointed down the drainage canal in the direction they had come. There was very little current so they had no trouble securing the boat to the bridge framework, where it was completely hidden from anyone crossing above them—unless they were to look down between the planks. And, fortunately, the cracks between them were not wide enough for that.

"Daniel." Sandra was close to tears. "Hold me, I'm cold."

Moving to the thwart seat, he put his arm around her, but was careful not to caress her and stir her easily aroused passion. She was too scared and cold for that, however, and, nestled against him, she slept after a while like a tired child. It was a very uncomfortable position for him but better than having her awake and complaining, so he didn't awaken her until his watch showed that it was after five o'clock, barely an hour before the launch would occur.

They ate some sandwiches she had brought and drank coffee from a thermos, huddled together in the boat while the dawn wind rustled in the saw grass and palmettos along the bank of the canal. Somewhere not far away a dove sounded its mournful cry and, startlingly, a "whippoorwill" appeared to answer.

From their position beneath the bridge on this little used road, they could see nothing of what was going on at the launch pad, however, so Daniel switched on the small transistor radio he had brought, keeping the sound low. The calm voice of Cape Launch Control, rebroadcast through the local station that always carried the final stages of a rocket flight, assured them everything was proceeding according to schedule. The two astronauts who were to ride Pegasus into the sky were already sealed in their cabin, he said, and the service tower had been moved away.

When several more vehicles rattled across the bridge over their heads, leaving the rocket area, they could be sure the final minutes of the countdown were approaching. Daniel Sears started to climb out of the boat but Sandra seized him and tried to hold him back.

"Don't do this, Daniel," she begged.

"I am God's messenger—"

"Hiding under a bridge like a thief?"

"You don't understand."

"I understand that you want the satisfaction of stopping this rocket for yourself. You're not at all concerned about God's will."

"That's absurd!"

"You just took up with me because you knew Tom worked on Pegasus and you could con me into letting you use this boat." She was crying now, sobs of disappointment and anger that would surely be heard by anyone crossing the bridge and ruin his whole elaborate plan.

"Be quiet!" he said and, when she continued sobbing, leaned over and slapped her face hard, causing her to gasp with pain and shock.

"Fifteen minutes and counting . . ." said the calm voice from the transistor set and Daniel Sears reached under the thwart for the paper-wrapped package he had carefully placed there before they had left the landing behind Sandra's home.

"The time has come," he announced. "I must be about the Lord's work."

"What about me?" she wailed. "They'll put me in jail for bringing you here."

He paid no attention to her but tucked the package under his arm and, swinging himself around the end of the bridge, seized the supporting framework and began to climb the bank of the canal toward the end of the bridge. Stepping out upon the bridge itself in the early light of dawn he knelt over the package and tore away the paper wrappings to unfold the white robe with the golden embroidery at collar and sleeves.

Pulling the robe over his head, he stood erect and let its folds fall about his tall form. Then, as the rays of the rising sun enveloped him, he started marching toward the shining complex of metal cylinders towering into the morning sky a few hundred yards away.

"Stop in the name of the Living God!" he shouted as he marched, arms upraised like Elijah of old on Mount Carmel calling down the fires of heaven upon the priests of Baal. And when a sense of exultation and power seized his every fiber, he knew it could be only the spirit of God Himself, telling him he could not fail.

"In the name of God cease this blasphemy!" He shouted again his defiance of the rocket, as well as the men who had created it.

With the rays of the sun turning his blond mane into gold and surrounding him with an aureole of golden light, Daniel Sears did indeed seem to have suddenly appeared by some heavenly miracle. Sandra Craven saw none of this, however, for overcome by the fear that had been gnawing at her ever since they had left the boat landing back of her home, she had loosened the rope holding the boat against the timbers of the bridge and reached for the starter button while he was still climbing the bank to the road above.

She pressed it hard and, when the motor caught at the first turnover, jammed the throttle full open. The boat fairly leaped from the water and raced down the canal but, fighting to control the light boat in the light of early dawn, Sandra had no time, nor desire, to look back.

Nor would she have seen much except the upper stages of the rocket and the launch escape system above the spacecraft itself, for the base where the flames of ignition would first emerge, was shut away from her view by the piled-up wall of the canal, which also hid Daniel Sears from her eyes during his moment of highest glory.

The transistor radio was still operating, however, and above the whine of the motor, she could hear the voice of Launch Control repeating the familiar words of the countdown's final seconds:

"Pegasus is on internal power now. The tower has been moved away and the rocket stands alone, a thing of shining beauty, carrying with it man's hope for a new era of space exploration—"

Suddenly the counting broke off and the voice of the announcer was loud and shrill with shock and amazement:

"A man has appeared near the pad!"

ii.

Mike had joined the group inside the forward blockhouse about an hour before dawn. The reinforced concrete walls of the dome-shaped building were designed to stand far more than the concussion ordinarily attending a launch, but those inside were allowed to watch the actual ignition and blast-off only by means of closed circuit television, with a camera atop the building maintaining a close observance on the launch site.

No duties had been assigned to Mike, beyond standing by with first aid equipment in case of an accident involving the occupants of the forward launch station. He had nothing to do therefore, except watch the screen and the consoles where Hal Brennan, Tom Craven, and others from both Taggar Aircraft and FSA were monitoring the launch.

A CBS-TV cameraman on a tower some two miles away was the first to detect on the small screen at the back of the camera the tiny figure moving toward the rocket in those final moments of splendid isolation before actual ignition. Except for the two astronauts sealed inside the Hermes II spacecraft atop the giant projectile, Daniel Sears was alone in the blast-off area and, by the time he was detected, was actually closer to the base of the rocket than were the astronauts perched high above it.

Automatically, the cameraman twirled the lens mount of his camera bringing his most powerful telescope to bear on the man who was defying the shining cylinder of steel and the cloud of icy oxygen vapor that hung around it like a mantle. Millions of watchers thus saw in full color the spectacle of Daniel Sears marching to his death, saw him so plainly that they could detect the glow of pentecostal conviction upon his face, transformed, it seemed, into the very likeness of God Himself by the rays of the just risen sun.

No human ear was close enough to hear the words Daniel Sears shouted, but so powerful was the magnification of the telescopic lenses, now bearing upon him from a dozen cameras, that viewers could read his lips as he shouted defiance of those who dared to probe the mysteries of heaven itself and ordered them to cease their blasphemy.

As soon as the closed circuit system by which those in the concrete-walled blockhouse watched the launch revealed Daniel Sears' presence, Tom Craven, who was at the main control console, threw the switch to halt the countdown and prevent ignition of the great booster. But when Mike Barnes turned his eyes from the TV screen, where the absorbing drama was approaching its denouement, to the one console in the half buried control room that could prevent the rocket from igniting upon the pad, he needed only the look of horror on Tom Craven's face to realize that the controls were not functioning.

"Override!" Mike shouted, and, startled from his momentary paralysis by the word, Tom Craven threw the second switch, designed to take over if the first failed, activating the principle of control redundancy built into all circuits concerned with igniting the highly explosive material that gave rockets their power.

Deep in the bowels of the giant booster, the sudden surge of extra power found a metallic pathway never designed to be in that place, an ordinary pair of needle-nose pliers used by electricians the world over. Racing through the metal, it shorted the main circuit instantly, making a shambles of the entire control system of the booster itself and locking the countdown in the automatic ignition sequence so it could not be countermanded from outside the rocket itself.

In their concern for the multi-staged rocket and the two men in the spacecraft, those in the blockhouse had forgotten the man still marching toward the rocket. Then the FSA cameraman controlling the lenses there switched to a higher power, and Daniel Sears' face suddenly loomed as large on the blockhouse screen as it already was upon millions of TV sets throughout the country and the world, sped there by the miracle of communications satellites spotted in strategic places around the globe. Thus, in the seconds that preceded ignition, they were able to watch, horror-seized, as Daniel Sears marched on, the halo-like aureole around his head suddenly dimmed when he came within the shadow of the great rocket standing upon the pad.

"God help him!" somebody inside the blockhouse exclaimed in those dramatic final seconds while the locked-in and now uncontrollable countdown ticked away.

Watching and waiting helplessly for the sudden gush of flame at the base of the booster, Tom Craven recognized the tiny figure defying it and knew he should have foreseen that something like this might happen when he'd first heard Daniel Sears thunder his denunciation from the pulpit of those who dared to intrude into the territory reserved by God for His use alone. But he had been so intrigued that Sunday by the "wheel within a wheel" idea the preacher had given him from the Book of Ezekiel and the possibilities for using that principle when the next Pegasus rocket was prepared for launch, that he'd dismissed the shouting of the man in the pulpit as mere oratory.

And now it was too late.

iii.

Paul Taggar had been one of the last to leave Pad 29. As builder of Pegasus, he could have joined the engineers and others inside the control blockhouse to watch the actual launch on closed circuit TV there. But confined spaces always gave him a feeling of being shut in and he preferred to watch from the open air the launch of the great machine his company had built.

Since it was hard to see details of the launch area from the place where he had parked his jeep inside the main gate closing off the Pegasus area to visitors, Paul Taggar had brought a small-screen battery-operated color TV set so he could take advantage of the long-range lenses used by the commercial broadcasters.

On the screen, Taggar saw Danied Sears suddenly appear, as if by magic, even before those in the blockhouse realized the intruder was there. And impelled by a surge of blind rage at the man who would dare try to stop the great rocket upon whose success so much of the future of Taggar Aircraft depended, he started the motor of his jeep.

Before the guard lounging inside the gate to keep the crowd outside realized what Taggar was doing, he had gunned the jeep and was racing along the road leading to the launch pad, his fingers tight upon the wheel of the jeep as he guided it along the narrow blacktop road across the wasteland of palmettos, stunted palms, and salt marsh separating the launch area from the Taggar plant. Just so, he fully intended, would those same fingers grip the throat of the damned fool who dared to interfere in the project whose success could make him the most important man in the entire aerospace field, once that shining pillar of metal was launched into flight.

Straining to hold the speeding jeep on the road while keeping his eyes fixed on the rocket and the puny figure marching toward it at the same time, Paul Taggar had no time to turn on the radio. The bucking of the jeep made reception with the small color TV very poor, too, so he didn't hear the announcer from Launch Control, speaking to a world whose attention was centered upon the white-robed figure shouting defiance of the rocket and the men who had built it, confess that those same men no longer had any control over the machine.

The first gush of orange-tinted flame, as the five engines of the booster ignited the potent mixture of kerosene and liquid oxygen, enveloped Daniel Sears, killing him instantly while millions watched in horror. With the rocket still anchored by clamps to the launch pad while the engines built up thrust, the flaming inferno at its base was a remarkable sight upon color screens of the world. But no one could see the openings in the metal partition separating the kerosene from the highly volatile LOX near the center of the booster, or know that minuscule though they were, they spelled doom for the giant machine of which they were a vital part.

Those same openings would have been apparent in the X ray Tom Craven had ordered of a section of metal like that used for the partition, had the kilovoltage of the X-ray tube been set to cause just the right degree of penetration of the metal to register a true picture of its internal structure upon the film. But when he had set the machine Asa Childs had been half blind from the beginning of a severe penicillin reaction, so the films had not been as sharp as they should have been and the tiny openings had gone undetected.

Only when the tanks within the huge booster were pressurized, some two minutes before actual ignition, had the volatile fuels begun to mix within the body of the booster, instead of only at the base. And seconds later, the needle-nose pliers Ted Chandler, the electrician, had dropped into the bowels of the booster—managing to escape reporting their loss

at the tool check-in and thus ensuring that their presence would go undetected—had shorted the main control line, making ignition, and
everything that followed, inevitable.

At the moment nothing still seemed lost, however, except the man
who had been foolish enough to steal into the reservation and pit his
will against the rocket. The great engines burned, building up power
and the clamps still held, rooting the booster to the pad until enough
thrust was obtained to ensure normal lift-off, but deep within its vitals,
a second ignition was already occurring as the area of the leak burst
into flame.

The shock wave of concussion, as the giant booster started to dis-
integrate under the explosive pressure building up within it, knocked
watchers to the ground two miles from the launch site. Paul Taggar's
jeep was lifted as if by a giant hand and hurled through the air to crash
among the palmettos.

The surge of flame accompanying the second, and unprogrammed
ignition was like the fireball of an atomic explosion, except that instead
of spouting into the sky, it rolled out across the wasteland purposely
left between the launch pad and other structures in the area, destroying
everything in its path including the jeep and its occupant and scorching
the earth itself.

iv.

The piled up sand on either side of the drainage canal shielded
Sandra Craven, already over half a mile from the exploding rocket,
against much of the concussion. Half stunned, she fought to control
the plunging boat and was tossed out of it into the drainage canal when
the bow struck the fence where she and Daniel Sears had entered the
Pegasus section of the government reservation shortly before four
o'clock that morning.

Drowned for the moment when the boat flipped over from the impact
with the fence, the motor stopped running and Sandra instinctively
crawled beneath the hull, now canted up against the sandy bank of the
canal. Lying with her body almost beneath the surface, while she
breathed in shuddering gasps of pure relief, she was fairly well protected from the holocaust accompanying the explosion and from the
racing wall of flame that swept the area.

Half conscious, she clung to the upturned boat until its hull became
too hot to hold, then managed to seize a post of the fence where it went
down beneath the water at the edge of the canal and hold herself almost
entirely submerged except for an occasional gulp of air that was itself
almost like a flame.

v.

In the forward blockhouse, Mike Barnes was the first to note the central part of the great booster start to bulge, as the force of the explosion inside it sought to escape from the confinement of the great metal tube. Perhaps because he had been half expecting a catastrophe, he was also the first one to see the rocket itself start to topple and realize what was happening.

"Abort the ship," Mike shouted to Hal Brennan who was acting as range safety officer for the launch, charged with the task of putting the escape mechanism into action and freeing the astronauts, if anything went wrong. But Brennan was staring at the screen, where his hopes for so many things were being destroyed in a brief instant of time, seemingly hypnotized by what he saw.

Lunging across the distance of some six feet that separated him from the console where Hal was sitting, Mike pushed the switch designed to fire the escape rocket attached to the tower above the spacecraft. He couldn't tell whether the circuit to the escape rocket was still in operation for, while his fingers were still on the control, the main blast wave of the booster explosion struck the blockhouse itself, melting the closed circuit television camera on its roof and its connections, by which those inside the blockhouse had been watching the launch, causing the screen inside the blockhouse suddenly to go blank.

The concrete walls of the blockhouse were cracked in a half dozen places, by the sheer force of the explosion, but the commercial television cameras located miles away continued to operate throughout the disaster, reporting everything in detail, and in full color, with their telephoto lenses. Thus the world saw the rocket attached to the escape tower fire, seemingly at the very moment of the booster explosion, and jerk the spacecraft with its human occupants from the top of the now doomed body of Pegasus.

Because the entire Pegasus assembly had already started toppling slowly, when the escape rocket fired, the spacecraft followed an arcing trajectory, but the force of the small rocket was still sufficient to send it a half mile into the air, safely away from the sea of flames surrounding what was left of the doomed Pegasus. There its brightly colored main parachutes opened and it began to descend slowly to a rather ignominious, but soft, landing upon a mud flat in the middle of Banana River miles from the launch area.

The succeeding major explosion, as the second stage dropped into the midst of the fireball representing all that remained of the first, was not nearly so great as that which destroyed the booster. Those inside the concrete-walled forward control blockhouse felt it only as an anti-climax, for the first concussion had already knocked almost everyone inside it to the floor.

Hal Brennan, as well as several of the technicians watching the consoles, which should have allowed control of the great projectile but had failed because a single pair of pliers were where no such metal bridge should be, was knocked unconscious by the force of the exploding booster. Mike Barnes himself was thrown across the console where an instant earlier Tom Craven had been desperately trying to stop the surge of current through the vitals of the rocket.

A little shaken from the blast and from watching the inferno on the screen, Mike got to his feet and went to where Hal lay upon the floor unconscious, bleeding from a cut in his scalp over the temple. As he was bending over the project director, a sudden roar of steam—audible through cracks in the concrete walls, told Mike the entire launch pad was being flooded with water in the automatic routine procedure following a launch. But the blockhouse itself was too far away to benefit much from the dousing of the pad and the temperature inside it was rising rapidly as flames raced through the entire launch area.

General Jim Green was leaning against one of the consoles, shaking his head to clear it. When Mike went to help him, he waved him off, however, so Mike moved to the Capcom console, where Andy Zapf was slumped with his head between his hands. When Mike shook Andy's shoulder gently, however, he looked up and nodded that he was all right. None of them knew yet, of course, whether Mike's quick action in firing the escape rocket had saved the two astronauts or not.

Lars Todt had been stunned by the blast and was bleeding from a cut on his temple but was conscious. Handing Lars a handkerchief to hold against the cut, Mike ascertained that Hal Brennan appeared to have sustained at the very least a fairly severe concussion and quickly bandaged the wound on his head with a dressing from the first aid kit in the blockhouse, to stop the bleeding until the wound could be taken care of later. By the time Mike finished the dressing, Lars was able to stagger to a chair and sit down while he bandaged a dressing into place to control the wound in the senator's scalp.

The surge of flame and the concussion of the two explosions had destroyed all direct communication with the outside so those in the blockhouse had no way of knowing what was going on except by way of the emergency Capcom radio circuit, which should be intact, if the escape rocket had fired in time. Andy Zapf was trying the Capcom controls now, his voice hoarse as he called: "Hermes II. Hermes II.

This is Pegasus Advanced Launch Control; Capcom calling. Do you read me?"

There was a crackle of static, then Jerry McGrath's voice sounded loud in the room. "This is Hermes II. That you, Andy?"

"Roger. Are you two all right?"

"Roger. Main chute has deployed and it looks like we'll land on a mudbank. Is anybody alive in the pillbox besides you? From here it looks like the whole world is on fire down there."

"We're all O.K. except Hal," said Andy Zapf. "Try to raise Cape Launch Control. Tell them it's getting hot as hell in here, and we need an ambulance pronto for Hal."

"Roger," said McGrath. "What really happened?"

Andy Zapf glanced at Mike. "For want of a shoe," he said softly.

"What's that?" Jerry McGrath asked.

"Nothing. Safe landing."

"Pegasus Advanced Launch Control." A new voice broke in. "This is Patrick."

Patrick Air Force Base, from which the jets flew to photograph rocket launches and where rescue helicopters were held ready in case a mission had to be aborted, was about twenty-five miles to the south.

"Roger, Patrick," said Andy Zapf. "This is Pegasus."

"We have Hermes II in sight on main chute. It should land in a few minutes and the copters are out. Are you O.K. up there? We felt the shock all the way down here."

"We're sweating but still alive," said Andy Zapf. "If you've got any flying water tanks, we could use a few dumped right on top of us."

"Roger. If we see any, we'll send them your way."

General Green was still groggy but when Mike broke a small ammonia ampule beneath his nose, it seemed to revive him.

"What happened?" he asked.

"The booster exploded on the pad and the second stage followed," said Tom Craven, who had recovered rapidly.

"Are McGrath and Boggs all right?"

"Helicopters from Patrick are waiting to pick them up," said Andy Zapf.

"Thank God for that." The general turned to Mike. "You were right, Doctor; we should have listened to you. God, but it's hot in here."

"We may all still wind up being roasted alive," said Mike soberly.

"Pegasus Advanced Launch Control." A new voice sounded.

"This is Pegasus Capcom," said Andy Zapf.

"This is the fire marshal. We're sending several foam trucks through trying to reach you. Any casualties?"

"Colonel Brennan is unconscious; we'll need an ambulance. And hell couldn't be much hotter than it's getting to be in here."

"We'll be there as soon as we can."

"Roger." Andy Zapf pushed his headphones forward until they rested just in front of his ears, where he could hear anything by radio through bone conduction, but could also hear those inside the control block-house. "One reason why it seems so hot I guess," he confessed, "is because I'm too scared to sweat."

"Thank God Jerry McGrath pushed the panic button in time," said General Green.

Andy Zapf looked at Mike and, when he didn't speak, turned to the FSA administrator.

"It wasn't McGrath," he said.

"Then Hal—"

"Hal froze at the console when he saw the booster start to bulge. Mike here hit the abort switch."

"I guess we owe you two apologies then, Dr. Barnes," said the general.

It was about a half hour later when the first of a group of fire trucks, laying down a wide border of foam on either side of the road to smother the flames, reached the blockhouse. By that time everyone inside was panting from the heat in the closed space, but no one had suffered any serious damage, other than a few bruises, a cut or two, and Hal Brennan's apparently severe concussion.

The scene that met their eyes when they emerged from the block-house was unbelievable. In spite of the thousands of gallons of water which had been doused automatically upon the pad, pockets of fire still raged there, some of them unnaturally bright as magnesium and other highly combustible metals from the rocket assembly still burned. Even the steel of the service and gantry towers had melted and rivulets of molten metal had coursed away from the slightly higher elevation of the launch pad, looking for all the world like the lava flow from a miniature volcano.

In the immediate area of the pad, the sand itself had been melted into crude glass by the terrible heat, but two things had prevented the area of destruction from being even larger than it was. One was the proximity of the ocean, whose waves washed upon the beach a few hundred yards from the launch site itself, preventing any spread of flames in that direction. The other was the canal cut through the sec-tion of Merritt Island where the new Pegasus center had been built in order to drain marshy areas and create enough spoil to fill in and level some places that had been below the water level. It had acted as a partial barrier, slowing the spread of flame until the fire could burn itself out in many areas.

Perched on top of a fire truck as they moved away from the disaster area through the lane created by the layer of foam laid down by the incoming trucks, Mike saw that palmettos, saw grass, and sea grape had been seared level with the earth itself, along with anything living there at the time. Fortunately one concrete bridge across the canal remained relatively undamaged, though in some places the flames had leaped the water barrier. Groups of men were already busy fighting those to keep the destruction from spreading to other parts of the reservation and, except for the pad itself, the fires were already under control.

"I flew over Hiroshima soon after the atomic bomb was dropped," said General Green in a tone of awe. "This looks like some of the outskirts of the city did then."

"This accident makes it even more important than ever that we get to work immediately on the next Pegasus launch, General," said Mike quietly, and the FSA administrator gave him a searching look. "Mr. Craven and I have some ideas about increasing the available storage space for a manned station on the next shot."

General Green nodded. "I'll want to hear them tomorrow—after we've had a chance to recover a bit from this disaster and analyze its causes."

"I recognized the man who tried to stop the launch; he was a pentecostal preacher over on the mainland," said Tom Craven. "I got the idea for the device Dr. Barnes and I have been working on while listening to him preach about the Prophet Ezekiel and a wheel in the sky."

"'A wheel in a wheel.'" The general smiled. "I remember hearing the Tuskegee Institute choir sing that spiritual when I was at Maxwell Field a long time ago."

"Sears—that was his name—also predicted a disaster with Pegasus, because we're trying to send rockets into what he called 'God's heaven,'" said Tom Craven. "It's sort of ironical in a way, isn't it, that he should be destroyed with it."

At the main gate to the Pegasus section of the reservation, they found Dr. Ivan Saltman waiting with two ambulances. Hal Brennan, not yet conscious, was transferred to one and Senator Todt went along at Mike's insistence so some stitches could be placed in the small cut upon his temple.

"I want a full dress debriefing on this whole affair tomorrow morning at ten o'clock in the main conference room," General Green announced as he got into his own jeep. "Good day, gentlemen, I've got a press conference waiting."

"He's a cool one," said Andy Zapf as they watched the jeep depart. "But I know one who's cooler—name of Mike Barnes. I'm going home and hold Helen's hand for a while over a good stiff drink. You and Tom both look like you could use one; why not come along?"

"I guess there's nobody I need to notify that I'm alive," said Mike. "Hadn't you better call Sandra, Tom?"

"I'll call from Andy's house," said the engineer. "She probably saw the whole thing on TV so she already knows I'm safe. We'll have to go over and see Sally Taggar, though. I've always known Paul had a terrible temper but it's hard to believe he would have been such a fool as to start for the rocket during the last minutes before ignition."

"Everybody was counting on a human factor," said Mike.

"Like what?" Andy Zapf asked.

"Sears undoubtedly figured that as soon as he appeared the countdown would be stopped. Paul Taggar probably made the same assumption but he was so mad that he wanted to get to Sears first."

"Sears was a loser either way," Tom Craven agreed. "Even if he had stopped the countdown, Paul would have throttled him."

"This time the human factor was predicable but the machine wasn't," said Mike. "Somewhere inside it one circuit must have jammed and from then on nothing could have prevented ignition and disaster —except another circuit failure."

"I could almost show you the one if anything was left," said Tom Craven. "It had to be in the very guts of that booster."

"I think we'd better all get a drink," said Andy Zapf. "If either Jerry McGrath or Boggs had gotten a virus at the last minute, I'd have been in that ship this morning. The very thought gives me the willies."

At Andy Zapf's beach front house, they found Helen hunched before the TV screen. On it, Jerry McGrath was stepping out of the helicopter that had plucked the two astronauts from the mudbank minutes after the spacecraft landed and brought them to Patrick Air Force Base to be interviewed by TV reporters. Jerry was a handsome and boyish figure in his silver-colored space suit and Mike couldn't repress a twinge of envy.

"Jerry's just explaining how it felt when the escape tower rocket fired," said Helen.

"Aren't you even going to say you're glad I'm alive?" Andy Zapf asked.

"Of course I'm glad you're alive." Helen didn't take her eyes from the screen. "Here I was worried to death because I knew you were in that blockhouse and it was all covered with flame. Then the next thing, I see you, big as life, riding a fire engine like you were the chief or something."

Zapf grinned. "Women have the damnedest ways of telling you they love you. Let's get that drink, Mike."

"Pour one for me," said Helen. "I'm still shaking inside."

"Do you think we'll ever know exactly what happened today, Mike?" Andy Zapf asked, while Tom Craven was phoning Sandra.

"I doubt it. With my ship, everything sank to the bottom of the ocean and with this one, everything except the spacecraft was consumed by fire. Even the metal wouldn't be identifiable, if it wasn't consumed or melted."

Helen switched off the TV and took the glass Andy handed her. "Did you call Jan?" she asked Mike.

"No."

"Why not?"

"We had a sort of argument after that accident in the centrifuge. I guess when you've lost one husband in a flying accident, you don't want another in a high risk job like this one has turned out to be. Besides, there are other things."

"What about you?" she asked.

"I'm going to stay with Pegasus, if the general will let me."

"That means whoever has been trying to kill you will get another chance."

"Maybe—but that's a risk I'll have to take. Tom Craven and I have figured out a way to double the cargo capacity of the next Pegasus—if the general gives us the goahead."

"Why the hurry?" she asked.

"Someday another Khrushchev in the Kremlin will get the idea he can put a gun to our heads with a few SCRAGs, SS-9s, or a space arsenal. When that happens, it's going to be very important to have something orbiting up there that's already armed with a few hydrogen warheads or can be armed quickly and kicked into a synchronous orbit near the industrial part of the Soviet Union so they'll have second thoughts about starting anything."

"Will there never be peace?" Helen Zapf said with a shiver.

"The only way peace can be kept at the moment is for someone to be strong enough to keep it," said Andy. "The rest of the world has got to decide pretty soon whether it wants peace and personal freedom guaranteed by the United States, or peace with slavery under the Soviet Union."

vi.

Scrambling in the mud of the canal bottom, Sandra Craven had managed to right the boat and slide it beneath the lower edge of the fence around the Pegasus reservation where it crossed the canal. The air was still almost unbearably hot but where she was the fire itself had been stopped by the canal and the mud and water soaking her blouse and slacks had also given her considerable protection from the heat.

Miraculously, the motor caught after a few times and she sent the boat roaring up the canal toward home. Tying up the boat, she staggered into the garage where she washed the mud from her body under the shower and stuffed the suit she'd been wearing into the garbage can. She'd just dressed and was pouring herself a drink, when the phone rang. It was Tom.

"Just wanted you to know I'm all right, darling," he said. "Did you see what happened?"

"I—I was afraid to look. And then I was so worried."

"That damn fool preacher of yours tried to stop the launch; then a short circuit blew up the booster and the second stage. You must have felt the shock of the explosion."

"I did. It scared me. . . ."

"Me, too. Paul Taggar was killed along with Sears, so I'll have to take charge here until the company can send someone from the main factory to handle the business. We ought to go see Sally tonight; I'll be home in a little while."

"Are—are you sure you're all right, Tom?"

"Just singed a little. It was pretty hot in that blockhouse."

"Hurry home, darling."

"I'll make it as soon as I can. General Green has ordered a full dress debriefing tomorrow morning, so we've got to give that spacecraft a going over. I want to send some men in to examine the pad area, too, as soon as the ground is cool enough to look for evidence of what really went wrong. Good-by."

vii.

It was late afternoon before Mike reached Jan by telephone at her cottage. "I tried to get you earlier," he said, "but nobody was home."

"I had an afternoon rehearsal for the high school operetta. Will you be going away, now that the explosion proved your case?"

"No. Tom Craven and I are developing a modification of Pegasus for the next shot."

"The radio said the Reverend Sears and Paul Taggar were the only ones killed."

"Miraculously yes; the drainage canal stopped most of the fire or the whole Cape would have gone up in smoke."

"Was anybody else hurt?"

"After Ivan Saltman got Hal Brennan to the hospital, he discovered some signs that looked like a beginning extradural hemorrhage, so an ambulance plane from Patrick flew him to Walter Reed this afternoon. When will I be able to see you?"

"Do you want to—after all this?"

"Of course."

"Then I'll call you. Good night, Mike."

"Good night, darling." He hung up the phone, but it rang again immediately.

"Mrs. Stein is in the lobby and wants to speak to you, Dr. Barnes," said the clerk downstairs.

"I'll be right down."

Shirley was sitting on a sofa in the lobby. She was dressed for traveling—and cold sober.

"I'm on my way to the airport to catch a plane for Washington," she said. "Hal asked them to call me; a neurosurgeon is going to operate right away."

"He should be all right," Mike assured her. "They have topnotch men at Walter Reed."

"Hal never really needed me before but this time he sent for me." A note of pride was in her voice. "I want to be there when he wakes up but I had to be sure before I left you knew it wasn't Hal who tried to kill you last Sunday afternoon."

"I know that; it was Paul Taggar."

"When did you find out?"

"I began to suspect it Monday morning, when I saw that the initials on the memorandum I got weren't Hal's; then something else happened later that made me certain. Actually, the evidence was there all the time, if I hadn't been so busy suspecting Hal. Taggar Aircraft built the centrifuge-simulator, so Paul knew how to operate it."

"Do you know why he wanted you out of the way?"

"When I appeared on the scene Paul naturally thought I was here to wreck his prospects by proving he had built a defective spacecraft for my own flight, so his natural instinct was to get rid of me."

"Then you don't—" She broke off whatever she had been about to say. "That must have been it," she said instead. "Well, good-by, Mike."

"Can I drive you to the airport?"

"My maid is going with me to bring the car back."

"See you in Tallahassee then."

"Or Washington."

CHAPTER XXVIII

General Green's news conference on the Pegasus disaster, announced as a no-holds-barred critique, began promptly at ten Friday morning. When the administrator came in, followed by a retinue of lesser FSA officials, the conference room in the administration building was crowded with Pegasus personnel, newsmen, and TV cameras.

Mike and Andy Zapf had seats in the front row at the general's request, as did Tom Craven. Beside Tom was a gray-haired man, whom he introduced to Mike and Andy as Mr. Tarnov, a vice-president of Taggar Aircraft, who had flown from the main factory the night before to take charge of Taggar activities at the Cape for the time being. The other man with the chief engineer was Dr. Ordway, the Taggar Aircraft metallurgist; he carried a paper-wrapped flat package in his hand and Mike noted that an X-ray view box had been set up in one corner of the room. A portable television tape projector was also set up, with a large screen.

"Gentlemen," said the general. "We're going to start the conference by playing back a tape of the attempted launch yesterday. Lights, please."

As the lights were turned off, motor-driven blackout curtains covered the windows and the projector began to throw upon the screen a picture of yesterday's events during the final minutes of the countdown. Pegasus was a beautiful sight in color as the sun, just rising above the dunes to the east, joined its brilliance with the floodlights to bathe the great rocket and add a touch of gold to the silvery hue of the metal cylinder.

An involuntary "Ahh!" went up from the audience when the tiny figure of the man first appeared on the road between the canal and the launch site, marching with upthrust arms toward the rocket itself.

"Mr. Sears evidently managed to reach the launch area by means of a boat on the canal sometime before dawn," said General Green. "It seems obvious now that he was hiding beneath the bridge where the road you see him on crossed the canal. The boat he used has not been found, so we can only assume that someone brought him there during the night and left him to wait under the bridge. That also accounts for the fact that no one saw him before the TV camera did."

On the screen, events moved with stunning speed now to their inevitable conclusion: the first ignition with flames rolling out from beneath the giant booster was right on schedule, and the watching audience could see the rocket straining at the metal leashes that held it fixed to earth, while the thrust of the five great engines built toward maximum power.

A second "Ahh!" came from the watchers as the smaller rocket attached to the launch escape tower fired, sending the spacecraft itself hurtling upward just after the explosion on the ground caused the entire midsection of the booster to erupt into flames with a force that sent pieces of metal flying in all directions, while an orange tide enveloped the mobile launcher at its base and rolled away like the beginning of an atomic mushroom cloud.

"The explosion had to occur at the point where the kerosene and LOX compartments of the booster were contiguous," said General Green, as the second stage, like a child's toy crumpling when struck from the bottom, began to fall into the pool of flame that now enveloped the pad. The explosion of the second stage, when the hypergolic fuel inside it was set off by the intense heat, piled another mushroom atop the first one.

"I think that is all we need to see this morning," General Green said briskly. "I ordered the scene replayed so all of you could refresh your minds as far as the sequence of events connected with this disaster is concerned. I contacted the President last night and asked him to appoint a commission of eminent scientists in various categories of the space effort to study this entire accident and report upon it to Congress. Our meeting here this morning is for the purpose of discussing what happened, while the memory of it is still fresh in our minds, and trying to profit from what we discover. The details of this meeting are being recorded, of course, and will be presented to the investigating committee when they convene later.

"You will all be happy to know," he added, "that Colonel Brennan was operated upon last night at Walter Reed for a brain hemorrhage resulting from the force of the explosion inside the blockhouse and the doctors there assure me they expect full recovery. He had already indicated to me by letter his intention to resign as project director following the first Pegasus launch in order to begin activity in another field, so I have accepted his resignation as of this date.

"I might add that representatives of the press here today are at my

278 COUNTDOWN

own invitation, so there shall be no question that anything in connection with this disaster is being hushed up. Nor is the empty chair at the end of the table to be considered a witness box. It is merely placed there so those whom I shall ask to speak in connection with the disaster can be photographed as part of the record."

"Colonel Zapf?" he said, and Andy Zapf took the empty chair, looking solidly capable in his air force colonel's uniform with the rows of decorations on the left breast of the tunic.

"At the pre-launch conference on Tuesday, you suggested postponing the shot, Colonel, and, as it turned out, you were something of a prophet," said the FSA administrator. "Can you tell us on what ground you based your decision to oppose the launch?"

"I'm afraid it wasn't anything I could put my finger on, sir. Just a lot of little things."

"Like what, Colonel?"

"The space suit test, when Major Boggs became unconscious, for one thing. For another, we were always finding circuits out of order in the electrical and life environment systems of the spacecraft."

"You've had considerable experience with the space effort haven't you, Colonel?"

"I came in right after the Hermes series, sir."

"In your opinion, were more things wrong with Pegasus than with the others?"

"I got that impression, but it could be because Pegasus events are more recent in my memory," said Andy Zapf. "I'm sure we have all been more conscious of what can happen during a rocket launch since the Apollo disaster."

"Was there any other reason why you thought Pegasus might fail?"

"Only one, sir."

"What is that?"

"I have a great deal of respect for Dr. Barnes, General. When I saw how concerned he was about Pegasus, I felt that my own reservations were justified."

"Anything else, Colonel?"

"No, sir."

"Thank you," said the administrator. "Dr. Barnes?"

As Mike took the seat Andy Zapf vacated, he saw Jake Arrens sitting among the newsmen in the section of the conference room reserved for the press. Then the red light of a television camera facing him winked on and he gave the general his entire attention.

"Would you tell us why you opposed the launch yesterday, Doctor?" Green asked.

"I felt that the entire Pegasus community was approaching a dangerous state of tension, as far as the people involved with the rocket itself were concerned, General."

"On what did you base your conclusions, Doctor?"

"Largely on studies I have made of other aerospace installations. For instance, the day I arrived, I was told in a service station on the causeway that Pegasus was having its troubles."

"Couldn't that have prejudiced you in advance?"

"I think not, sir."

"What kind of troubles did you discover?"

"They were mainly minor failures, as Colonel Zapf has said, but I felt that most of them were caused by undue haste in getting the launch under way and by personal tensions among Pegasus personnel."

"Can you be more specific, Doctor?"

"It is my conviction that yesterday morning, what might be called a constellation of small errors during the preparation for the final stage of the rocket launch came together in a close enough sequence to destroy it."

A murmur of interest ran over the room and the general waited for it to subside.

"That is an interesting theory," he said. "Can you support it?"

"I'm afraid not, sir. The evidence that might prove my theory was destroyed yesterday in the fire."

"Not all of it, General." Tom Craven spoke from the front row where he and the metallurgist were sitting.

"Why do you say that, Mr. Craven?"

"Just an hour ago, a diver I sent to explore the ocean floor in the area of the beach opposite the launch pad found this." He held up the flat package Dr. Ordway had brought into the room.

"What is it, Mr. Craven?"

"Part of the metal bulkhead that separated kerosene from LOX in the booster, sir. Our metallurgist, Dr. Ordway, has examined it—"

"I will excuse you, Dr. Barnes," said the general. "Please come forward, Mr. Craven and also Dr. Ordway."

Tom Craven and the metallurgist moved to the place Mike vacated. When Craven unwrapped the package, the audience could see that it contained a sheet of metal, burnished from the flame, but apparently intact.

"Dr. Ordway is far more competent to explain to you the significance of this finding, General," he said.

"Please do, Doctor," said the general, and the metallurgist moved to the X-ray view box and switched it on.

"This is a film of a section of metal exactly like that used for the bulkhead separating the two fuels in the booster," he said, pointing to the outlines of the metal sheet visible upon the X-ray film. "It was taken at Mr. Taggar's request last week, in order to make sure that no possible leak between the fuel tanks could occur in the booster. However, a very exact technique is required to demonstrate openings of the size we need to consider here by X ray and the exposure time for this film appears not to have been sufficiently long."

"Would that tend to keep defects from showing up, Doctor?"

"Yes, sir. But let me remind you that this metal had been approved by FSA metallurgists. Mr. Taggar only ordered it X-rayed so he could be absolutely certain that it was impervious."

"You made your point, Doctor," said the general dryly. "Please go on."

"We now turn to the piece of metal found this morning, which we feel quite certain was part of the partition or bulkhead between the kerosene and the LOX tanks of the booster that exploded. You all saw pieces of metal flying in every direction just now in the film, and we feel certain that this one was blown into the sea by the first explosion. I made an X-ray film of this specimen just before coming here."

Taking the first film from the view box, Dr. Ordway substituted another and stood back so the audience could see.

"I believe you can detect the difference in technique here," he said. "The second film has a much sharper look than the first and there is excellent delineation of the internal structure of the metal, where the first one was hazy.

"If you look closely with a magnifier," he continued, "you can see very fine cracks, almost microscopic, running through this piece of metal. Some of these may possibly have been due to either the tremendous pressures to which the partition was subjected at the time of the explosion, the heat that caused the burnishing we see on the surface of the metal, or its immersion while very hot in salt water, when it fell into the sea. But most of them, I believe, were there before the launch."

"In your opinion, Doctor, would the first X ray have shown these same cracks, if the technique had been the same that you used in taking the second one?"

"I cannot be sure, sir—but the presumption can certainly be made."

"Do you know why a different technique was used in the first film?"

"It was taken by our metallurgical technician, a very capable man, during my absence at the factory working on the collar of a space suit which had been found to need revising. However, at the time this film was taken, Mr. Childs was ill and required hospitalization that same day. I would remind you again that FSA inspectors had approved the metal before it was used at the factory, after it was fabricated into the fuel tanks, and again here at the Cape. In fact, we wouldn't have known anything before the accident about the metal used in the tank, if Mr. Taggar had not wished to be doubly sure of it and had it filmed."

"Do you have any idea why Mr. Taggar suspected the metal in the tanks?" General Green asked, but Ordway shook his head.

"I think my being here may have been responsible for that, General," said Mike quietly. "You will remember that this matter came up at the pre-launch conference in connection with oxygen control valves of the life environment system."

"I do remember. Thank you, Doctor."

"I think I can add something, sir," said Tom Craven, "though it doesn't affect this disaster."

"Please go on, Mr. Craven."

"I ordered our engineers to examine the spacecraft carefully, sir, as part of our over-all evaluation program in connection with this disaster. The valves Dr. Barnes spoke of were intact but the installation of the new one into the wall of the spacecraft cabin was faulty. If this ship had actually been launched, I doubt that it could have survived the heat of reentry without failure of the valve."

The general looked startled, but recovered quickly.

"You are very honest, Mr. Craven. Do you have anything else to tell us?"

"Only that Taggar Aircraft is checking all other spacecraft under construction."

"Then I think we can sum up the facts as we know them now," said the administrator. "Considering the tremendous heat and destruction involved, the causes of this unfortunate accident would appear to be much clearer than we could expect—for which we can be thankful, since they may help us to prevent similar happenings in the future. First, it appears that the partition between the kerosene and the LOX was not impervious, as we believed, although again I must remind you that dozens of rockets having exactly similar construction have been fired without accident. That, in this case, the two fuels did mix other than in the engines seems certain, as well as the fact that a short circuit—which we can only presume, since everything in that section of the booster was destroyed by the fire—ignited the mixture resulting in the explosion.

"Second, it seems inescapable that an unauthorized person did enter the area for the purpose of creating a demonstration against the launching of the rocket. And that, in attempting to shut down the automatic sequence and keep the booster from firing, additional current may have been added which could have ignited the LOX-kerosene mixture at the leakage point."

General Green paused, while the newsmen scribbled furiously, making notes for the story which would shortly appear in headlines from coast to coast.

"Except for imperfections in the metal then," he continued, "all of the factors contributing to the disaster can be attributed to human error, including the faulty seating of the valve Mr. Craven has reported to us. In the case of the metal partition the defect might have been discovered, if our inspection procedures had been more thorough. It is my conviction therefore, that all must share the blame and all must resolve to do a more thorough job in the future. I should like to see Dr. Barnes, Colonel Zapf, and Mr. Craven after we finish here. Now you gentlemen of the press may fire when ready."

ii.

It was nearly seven when Mike came into the dining room of the Astronaut Inn, the session with General Green after the debriefing and press conference having lasted through the afternoon. He'd only gotten away from the government reservation after six, but he'd been wondering all afternoon whether he'd find Jan playing there, and his heart took a leap when he saw her at the piano in the alcove between the cocktail lounge and the dining room.

She was wearing the same dress she'd worn the first night he'd seen her there, and it hardly seemed possible that several weeks had elapsed. While the waitress went to bring him his usual half-bottle of sparkling burgundy, he picked up the pad of request slips marked "FOR JAN COOPER."

In the space for the title of the song he wrote: "Love Walked In," and beneath it added, "If you play it, I'll be waiting for you at ten-thirty."

She did not acknowledge his presence in any way and even the stimulation of the wine was beginning to wear off from food and disappointment by the time he'd finished his meal. Then, just as the waitress was bringing him his check, the piano rippled suddenly into the lovely melody and she began to sing the words. He didn't stop by the piano on the way to the desk to sign the check, but had been waiting outside in her white convertible for over half an hour when she came out and got beneath the wheel.

Taking the ignition key from her handbag, she unlocked the glove compartment silently and handed him a small package.

"What's this?" he asked.

"The telemetry tapes you wanted."

He took them but didn't open the package, his heart suddenly like lead at realizing what her having the tapes implied.

"Aren't you going to ask me how I got them?" she said.

"No."

"Why?"

"The Maserati was parked in the lot of a tavern on the mainland Wednesday afternoon. When I saw it, I thought Sally Taggar might be inside and I could talk to her and find out whether she knew anything about the tapes. But when I saw you sitting with Paul, I didn't go inside."

"Don't you want to know what I had to do to get the tapes?"

"I only want you, Jan—on whatever terms you make, no matter what has happened before."

"It was a long time ago, about a year after Bob was killed. Paul Taggar was a very vital man, the sort who could easily sweep a girl who was no longer sure of anything off her feet."

"I didn't ask for any confession—"

"I know, and that's all the more reason why you're entitled to one. It was a brief affair, but only that. One night we went to Hal's house and they were playing Countdown; you know the rest of what happened there. I refused to see Paul after that and was never alone with him again until Wednesday afternoon, when I called him and asked him to meet me at the tavern."

"Why?"

"He had tried many times since that night at Hal's to get me to go away with him; Paul didn't give up easily. Wednesday afternoon I offered to do so."

"With the provision that he would make no more attempts to kill me?"

"Yes—but he laughed at me. After the Tuesday conference with General Green he was convinced you were powerless to harm him."

"He was right."

"When he boasted that you would have no choice now except to slink back to Mountain City, I left him at the tavern. The last time I saw him, he was picking up a blonde who'd been sitting in the next booth."

"But the tapes . . ."

"They came this morning, along with the negative of that print you saw in Washington. Sally Taggar found them in Paul's safe, when she opened it in the presence of the company's vice-president, who was named executor in Paul's will. She recognized me in the negative and sent both the film and the tapes to me."

"Can I have the negative?" he asked.

"Of course." She took it from her handbag and gave it to him. "But why—"

He pushed the cigarette lighter on the dashboard in and waited until it popped out, glowing. Then holding the film by the corner outside the car, he touched the hot wires to it. The negative caught fire at once and he dropped it to the concrete of the parking lot where it was consumed. When he felt her hand creep into his, he knew she understood that by his action everything from the past had been swept away.

"Paul felt that he had to destroy you because you represented defeats for him, in areas where he'd never admitted defeat before," she said. "You had proved that he was a failure as a father. You were a threat to the success of Taggar Aircraft as prime contractor for Pegasus. And he realized that once I had met you, I could never belong to anyone else."

"I hope you know what you're saying," he said as he drew her close, even though the car was parked under one of the floodlights illuminating the lot.

"I've known since that night in the motel."

"Can you stand living in Spaceport City for a while longer?"

"With you I could live at the North Pole. Why?"

"General Green is turning over the direction of Pegasus for the time being to a triumverate—Andy Zapf, Tom Craven, and myself. I may not be home as often as we'd both like."

"I'll get a job as a lady welder with Pegasus. Then at least I can see you as you pass by."

He was kissing her, and enjoying it immensely, when he heard voices and looked up to see two women, who had come out to get their car, standing by the convertible, looking down at them with shocked amazement and shaking their heads in disapproval.

"I'm beginning to think what we hear about this place is true, Mabel," one of them said in a typical Midwestern accent. "Imagine two grown people necking brazenly right here in the open. What will they do next?"

"You're way ahead of us, madam," Mike said gravely. "But thanks for the suggestion, anyway."